Oscar Fingal O'Flahertie Wills Wilde (16 October 1854 – 30 November 1900) was an Irish poet and playwright. After writing in different forms throughout the 1880s, he became one of London's most popular playwrights in the early 1890s. He is best remembered for his epigrams and plays, his novel The Picture of Dorian Gray, and the circumstances of his criminal conviction for homosexuality, imprisonment, and early death at age 46. Wilde's parents were successful Anglo-Irish intellectuals in Dublin. Their son became fluent in French and German early in life. At university, Wilde read Greats; he proved himself to be an outstanding classicist, first at Trinity College Dublin, then at Oxford. He became known for his involvement in the rising philosophy of aestheticism, led by two of his tutors, Walter Pater and John Ruskin. After university, Wilde moved to London into fashionable cultural and social circles. (Source: Wikipedia)

Literary works:
Ravenna (1878)
Poems (1881)
The Happy Prince and Other Stories (1888)
Lord Arthur Savile's Crime and Other Stories (1891)
A House of Pomegranates (1891)
Intentions (1891)
The Picture of Dorian Gray (1890)
The Soul of Man under Socialism (1891)
Lady Windermere's Fan (1892)
A Woman of No Importance (1893)
An Ideal Husband (1898)
The Importance of Being Earnest (1898)
De Profundis (1905)
The Ballad of Reading Gaol (1898)
The Portrait of Mr. W. H. (1889)

MISCELLANEOUS APHORISMS
THE SOUL OF MAN,
MISCELLANIES
&
POEMS,
WITH THE BALLAD OF
READING GAOL

OSCAR WILDE

PRINCE CLASSICS

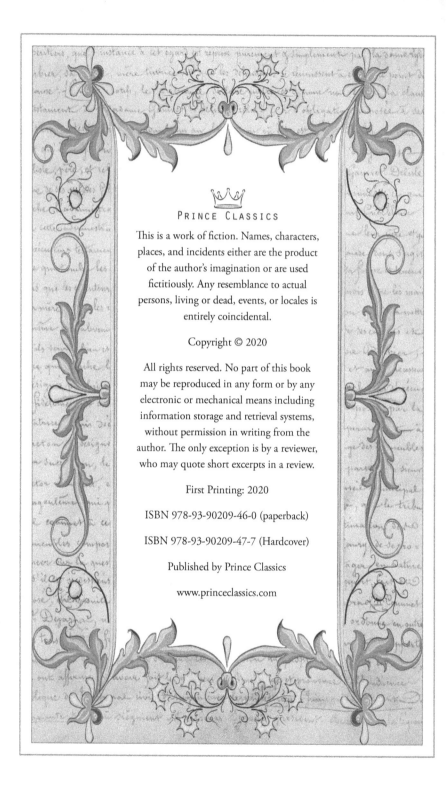

First Printing: 2020

ISBN 978-93-90209-46-0 (paperback)

ISBN 978-93-90209-47-7 (Hardcover)

Published by Prince Classics

www.princeclassics.com

Contents

MISCELLANEOUS APHORISMS
THE SOUL OF MAN,
MISCELLANIES
&
POEMS,
WITH THE BALLAD OF
READING GAOL

MISCELLANEOUS APHORISMS: THE SOUL OF MAN

SEBASTIAN MELMOTH

(OSCAR WILDE)

The mystery of love is greater than the mystery of death.

Women are made to be loved, not to be understood.

It is absurd to have a hard and fast rule about what one should read and what one shouldn't. Moren than half of modern culture depends on what one shouldn't read.

Women, as someone says, love with their ears, just as men love with their eyes, if they ever love at all.

It is better to be beautiful than to be good, but it is better to be good than to be ugly.

Nothing looks so like innocence as an indiscretion.

Misfortunes one can endure, they come from outside, they are accidents. But to suffer for one's faults—ah! there is the sting of life.

Beauty is the only thing that time cannot harm. Philosophies fall away like sand, creeds follow one another, but what is beautiful is a joy for all seasons, a possession for all eternity.

Questions are never indiscreet; answers sometimes are.

Twenty years of romance make a woman look like a ruin; but twenty years of marriage make her something like a public building.

The only thing that one really knows about human nature is that it changes.

Anyone can sympathise with the sufferings of a friend, but it requires a very fine nature to sympathise with a friend's success.

Selfishness is not living as one wishes to live, it is asking others to live as one wishes to live: and unselfishness is letting other people's lives alone, not interfering with them.

A man who does not think for himself does not think at all.

Nowadays people seem to look on life as a speculation. It is not a speculation. It is a sacrament. Its ideal is love. Its purification is sacrifice.

In old days nobody pretended to be a bit better than his neighbour. In fact, to be a bit better than one's neighbour was considered excessively vulgar and middle class. Nowadays, with our modern mania for morality, everyone has to pose as a paragon of purity, incorruptibility, and all the other seven deadly virtues. And what is the result? You all go over like ninepins—one after the other.

All sympathy is fine, but sympathy with suffering is the least fine mode.

If you pretend to be good the world takes you very seriously. If you pretend to be bad it doesn't. Such is the astounding stupidity of optimism.

It is most dangerous nowadays for a husband to pay any attention to his wife in public. It always makes people think that he beats her when they're alone. The world has grown so suspicious of anything that looks like a happy married life.

Actors are so fortunate. They can choose whether they will appear in tragedy or in comedy, whether they will suffer or make merry, laugh or shed tears. But in real life it is different. Most men and women are forced to perform parts for which they have no qualifications. The world is a stage, but the play is badly cast.

Men know life too early; women know life too late-that is the difference between men and women.

He who stands most remote from his age is he who mirrors it best.

There is only one thing in the world worse than being talked about, and that is not being talked about.

Life is not governed by will or intention. Life is a question of nerves and fibres and slowly built-up cells, in which thought hides itself and passion has its dreams.

Man is a being with myriad lives and myriad sensations, a complex, multiform creature that bears within itself strange legacies of thought and passion, and whose very flesh is tainted with the monstrous maladies of the dead.

As long as a woman can look ten years younger than her own daughter she is perfectly satisfied.

There is always something infinitely mean about other people's tragedies.

Public and private life are different things. They have different laws and move on different lines.

When one is placed in the position of guardian one has to adopt a very high moral tone on all subjects. It's one's duty to do so.

I have always been of opinion that a man who desires to get married should know either everything or nothing.

An engagement should come on a young girl as a surprise, pleasant or unpleasant, as the case may be. It is hardly a matter that she could be allowed to arrange for herself.

If the lower classes don't set us a good example what on earth is the use of them? They seem, as a class, to have absolutely no sense of moral responsibility.

If a woman cannot make her mistakes charming she is only a female.

The world was made for men and not for women.

It is always with the best intentions that the worst work is done.

If you wish to understand others you must intensify your own individualism.

Why do you talk so trivially about life? Because I think that life is far too important a thing ever to talk seriously about it.

What a pity that in life we only get our lessons when they are of no use to us.

It is better to have a permanent income than to be fascinating.

Relations are simply a tedious pack of people who haven't got the remotest knowledge of how to live nor the smallest instinct about when to die.

Charity creates a multitude of sins.

My experience is that as soon as people are old enough to know better they don't know anything at all.

Truth is a very complex thing and politics is a very complex business. There are wheels within wheels. One may be under certain obligations to people that one must pay. Sooner or later in political life one has to compromise. Everyone does.

Men can love what is beneath them—things unworthy, stained, dishonoured. We women worship when we love; and when we lose our worship we lose everything.

The proper basis for marriage is a mutual misunderstanding.

The one advantage of playing with fire is that one never gets even singed. It is the people who don't know how to play with it who get burned up.

There are moments when one has to choose between living one's own life fully, entirely, completely, or dragging out some false, shallow, degrading existence that the world in its hypocrisy demands.

When one is in town one amuses oneself. When one is in the country one amuses other people. It is excessively boring.

Romance is the privilege of the rich, not the profession of the unemployed. The poor should be practical and prosaic.

An acquaintance that begins with a compliment is sure to develop into a real friendship. It starts in the right manner.

The truths of metaphysics are the truths of masks.

Science can never grapple with the irrational. That is why it has no future before it in this world.

The happy people of the world have their value, but only the negative value of foils. They throw up and emphasise the beauty and the fascination of the unhappy.

In this world there are only two tragedies. One is not getting what one wants, and the other is getting it. The last is much the worst—the last is a real tragedy.

Disobedience in the eyes of anyone who has read history is man's original virtue. It is through disobedience that progress has been made—through disobedience and rebellion.

It is not wise to find symbols in everything that one sees. It makes life too full of terrors.

Comfort is the only thing our civilisation can give us.

Politics are my only pleasure. You see nowadays it is not fashionable to flirt till one is forty or to be romantic till one is forty-five, so we poor women who are under thirty, or say we are, have nothing open to us but politics or philanthropy. And philanthropy seems to me to have become simply the refuge of people who wish to annoy their fellow-creatures. I prefer politics. I think they are more ... becoming.

One's past is what one is. It is the only way by which people should be judged.

In a very ugly and sensible age the arts borrow, not from life, but from each other.

It is always a silly thing to give advice, but to give good advice is fatal.

Secrets from other people's wives are a necessary luxury in modern life.

So, at least, I am told at the club by people who are bald enough to know better. But no man should have a secret from his own wife. She invariably finds it out. Women have a wonderful instinct about things. They discover everything except the obvious.

Life holds the mirror up to art, and either reproduces some strange type imagined by painter or sculptor or realises in fact what has been dreamed in fiction.

I feel sure that if I lived in the country for six months I should become so unsophisticated that no one would take the slightest notice of me.

To recommend thrift to the poor is both grotesque and insulting. It is like advising a man who is starving to eat less.

A thing is not necessarily true because a man dies for it.

I am always saying what I shouldn't say; in fact, I usually say what I really think—a great mistake nowadays. It makes one so liable to be misunderstood.

Experience is the name everyone gives to their mistakes.

The true perfection of man lies, not in what man has, but in what man is.

The basis of every scandal is an absolute immoral certainty.

People talk so much about the beauty of confidence. They seem to entirely ignore the much more subtle beauty of doubt. To believe is very dull. To doubt is intensely engrossing. To be on the alert is to live, to be lulled into security is to die.

Every effect that one produces gives one an enemy. To be popular one must be a mediocrity.

It is a sad truth, but we have lost the faculty of giving lovely names to things. Names are everything. I never quarrel with actions, my one quarrel is with words. That is the reason I hate vulgar realism in literature. The man who could call a spade a spade should be compelled to use one. It is the only thing he is fit for.

A high moral tone can hardly be said to conduce very much to either one's health or one's happiness.

There are terrible temptations that it requires strength—strength and courage—to yield to. To stake all one's life on one throw—whether the stake be power or pleasure I care not—there is no weakness in that. There is a horrible, a terrible, courage.

Nowadays it is only the unreadable that occurs.

All charming people are spoiled. It is the secret of their attraction.

There is more to be said for stupidity than people imagine. Personally, I have a great admiration for stupidity. It is a sort of fellow-feeling, I suppose.

All men are monsters. The only thing to do is to feed the wretches well. A good cook does wonders.

There is no such thing as an omen.

Destiny does not send us heralds. She is too wise or too cruel for that.

Crying is the refuge of plain women but the ruin of pretty ones.

Love art for its own sake and then all things that you need will be added to you. This devotion to beauty and to the creation of beautiful things is the test of all great civilisations; it is what makes the life of each citizen a sacrament and not a speculation.

It is always worth while asking a question, though it is not always answering one.

It takes a thoroughly good woman to do a thoroughly stupid thing.

With a proper background women can do anything.

Chiromancy is a most dangerous science, and one that ought not to be encouraged, except in a 'tête-à-tête.'

One should never take sides in anything. Taking sides is the beginning of sincerity, and earnestness follows shortly afterwards, and the human being becomes a bore.

The work of art is beautiful by being what art never has been; and to measure it by the standard of the past is to measure it by a standard on the reflection of which its real perfection depends.

There are three kinds of despots. There is the despot who tyrannises over the body. There is the despot who tyrannises over the soul. There is the despot who tyrannises over soul and body alike. The first is called the prince. The second is called the pope. The third is called the people.

Costume is a growth, an evolution, and a most important, perhaps the most important, sign of the manners, customs, and mode of life of each century.

I really don't see anything romantic in proposing. It is very romantic to be in love, but there is nothing romantic about a definite proposal. Why, one may be accepted. One usually is, I believe. Then the excitement is all over. The very essence of romance is uncertainty.

What consoles one nowadays is not repentance but pleasure. Repentance is quite out of date.

Ideals are dangerous things. Realities are better. They wound, but they are better.

Unless one is wealthy there is no use in being a charming fellow.

Shallow sorrows and shallow loves live on. The loves and sorrows that are great are destroyed by their own plenitude.

An eternal smile is much more wearisome than a perpetual frown. The one sweeps away all possibilities, the other suggests a thousand.

To disagree with three-fourths of England on all points is one of the first elements of vanity, which is a deep source of consolation in all moments of spiritual doubt.

Women live by their emotions and for them, they have no philosophy of life.

As long as war is regarded as wicked it will always have a fascination. When it is looked upon as vulgar it will cease to be popular.

There is only one thing worse than injustice, and that is justice without her sword in her hand. When right is not might it is evil.

We spend our days, each one of us, in looking for the secret of life. Well, the secret of life is in art.

The truth isn't quite the sort of thing that one tells to a nice, sweet, refined girl.

If one plays good music people don't listen, and if one plays bad music people don't talk.

How fond women are of doing dangerous things. It is one of the qualities in them that I admire most. A woman will flirt with anybody in the world as long as other people are looking on.

Englishwomen conceal their feelings till after they are married. They show them then.

Moderation is a fatal thing. Nothing succeeds like excess.

Actions are the first tragedy in life, words are the second. Words are perhaps the worst. Words are merciless.

Life is terrible. It rules us, we do not rule it.

In art there is no such thing as a universal truth. A truth in art is that whose contradictory is also true.

One's days are too brief to take the burden of another's sorrows on one's shoulders. Each man lives his own life, and pays his own price for living it. The only pity is that one has to pay so often for a single fault. One has to pay over and over again, indeed. In her dealings with man Destiny never closes her accounts.

Pleasure is Nature's test, her sign of approval. When we are happy we are always good, but when we are good we are not always happy.

25

The people who love only once in their lives are really the shallow people. What they call their loyalty and their fidelity I call either the lethargy of custom or their lack of imagination.

Better to take pleasure in a rose than to put its root under a microscope.

Of Shakespeare it may be said that he was the first to see the dramatic value of doublets and that a climax may depend on a crinoline.

Plain women are always jealous of their husbands; beautiful women never are! They never have time. They are always so occupied in being jealous of other people's husbands.

What between the duties expected of one during one's lifetime and the duties exacted from one after one's death land has ceased to be either a profit or a pleasure. It gives one position and prevents one from keeping it up.

A man who moralises is usually a hypocrite, and a woman who moralises is invariably plain. There is nothing in the whole world so unbecoming to a woman as a nonconformist conscience. And most women know it, I am glad to say.

It was a fatal day when the public discovered that the pen is mightier than the paving-stone and can be made as offensive as a brickbat.

A map of the world that does not include Utopia is not worth even glancing at, for it leaves out the one country at which Humanity is always landing. And when Humanity lands there it looks out, and, seeing a better country, sets sail. Progress is the realisation of Utopias.

What is the difference between scandal and gossip? Oh! gossip is charming! History is merely gossip, but scandal is gossip made tedious by morality.

All beautiful things belong to the same age.

It is personalities, not principles, that move the age.

Modern pictures are, no doubt, delightful to look at. At least, some of them are. But they are quite impossible to live with; they are too clever, too assertive, too intellectual. Their meaning is too obvious and their method too clearly defined. One exhausts what they have to say in a very short time, and then they become as tedious as one's relations.

To know nothing about our great men is one of the necessary elements of English education.

The truth is rarely pure and never simple. Modern life would be very tedious if it were either and modern literature a complete impossibility.

You may laugh, but it is a great thing to come across a woman who thoroughly understands one.

The majority of people spoil their lives by an unhealthy and exaggerated altruism.

The number of women in London who flirt with their own husbands is perfectly scandalous. It looks so bad. It is simply washing one's clean linen in public.

The chief thing that makes life a failure from the artistic point of view is the thing that lends to life its sordid security—the fact that one can never repeat exactly the same emotion.

We teach people how to remember, we never teach them how to grow.

Vulgar habit that is people have nowadays of asking one, after one has given them an idea, whether one is serious or not. Nothing is serious except passion. The intellect is not a serious thing and never has been. It is an instrument on which one plays, that is all. The only serious form of intellect I know is the British intellect, and on the British intellect the illiterate always plays the drum.

It is absurd to divide people into good and bad. People are either charming or tedious.

It is only the modern that ever become old-fashioned.

It is only the Philistine who seeks to estimate a personality by the vulgar test of production.

Musical people are so absurdly unreasonable. They always want one to be perfectly dumb at the very moment when one is longing to be absolutely deaf.

Nothing is so dangerous as being too modern. One is apt to grow old-fashioned quite suddenly.

The fact of a man being a poisoner is nothing against his prose. The domestic virtues are not the true basis of art.

To the philosopher women represent the triumph of matter over mind, just as men represent the triumph of mind over morals.

The only way a woman can ever reform a man is by boring him so completely that he loses all possible interest in life.

The only horrible thing in the world is 'ennui.' That is the one sin for which there is no forgiveness.

French songs I cannot possibly allow. People always seem to think that they are improper, and either look shocked, which is vulgar, or laugh, which is worse.

It has often been made a subject of reproach against artists and men of letters that they are lacking in wholeness and completeness of nature. As a rule this must necessarily be so. That very concentration of vision and inversity of purpose which is the characteristic of the artistic temperament is in itself a mode of limitation. To those who are preoccupied with the beauty of form nothing else seems of so much importance.

The work of art is to dominate the spectator. The spectator is not to dominate the work of art.

One should sympathise with the joy, the beauty, the colour of life. The less said about life's sores the better.

You can't make people good by act of Parliament—that is something.

Art creates an incomparable and unique effect, and having done so passes on to other things. Nature, on the other hand, forgetting that imitation can

28

be made the sincerest form of insult, keeps on repeating the effect until we all become absolutely wearied of it.

It is perfectly monstrous the way people go about nowadays saying things against one behind one's back that are absolutely and entirely true.

A true artist takes no notice whatever of the public. The public are to him non-existent.

One should never trust a woman who tells one her real age. A woman who would tell one that would tell one anything.

Nothing is so aggravating as calmness. There is something positively brutal about the good temper of most modern men. I wonder we women stand it as well as we do.

The truth is a thing I get rid of as soon as possible. Bad habit, by the way, makes one very unpopular at the club ... with the older members. They call it being conceited. Perhaps it is.

My own business always bores me to death. I prefer other people's.

Don't be led astray into the paths of virtue—that is the worst of women. They always want one to be good. And if we are good, when they meet us they don't love us at all. They like to find us quite irretrievably bad and to leave us quite unattractively good.

Men are such cowards. They outrage every law in the world and are afraid of the world's tongue.

Wicked women bother one. Good women bore one. That is the only difference between them.

To know the principles of the highest art is to know the principles of all the arts.

I don't believe in the existence of Puritan women. I don't think there is a woman in the world who would not be a little flattered if one made love to her. It is that which makes women so irresistibly adorable.

When I am in trouble eating is the only thing that consoles me. Indeed, when I am in really great trouble, as anyone who knows me intimately will tell you, I refuse everything except food and drink.

When one is going to lead an entirely new life one requires regular and wholesome meals.

The soul is born old, but grows young. That is the comedy of life. The body is born young, and grows old. That is life's tragedy.

One can survive everything nowadays except death, and live down anything except a good reputation.

The past is of no importance. The present is of no importance. It is with the future that we have to deal. For the past is what men should not have been. The present is what men ought not to be. The future is what artists are.

Men become old, but they never become good.

By persistently remaining single a man converts himself into a permanent public temptation. Men should be more careful; this very celibacy leads weaker vessels astray.

I think that in practical life there is something about success, actual success, that is a little unscrupulous, something about ambition that is scrupulous always.

Every man of ambition has to fight his century with its own weapons. What this century worships is wealth. The god of this century is wealth. To succeed one must have wealth. At all costs one must have wealth.

I love scandals about other people, but scandals about myself don't interest me. They have not got the charm of novelty.

Moderation is a fatal thing. Enough is as bad as a meal. More than enough is as good as a feast.

The English can't stand a man who is always saying he is in the right, but they are very fond of a man who admits he has been in the wrong. It is one of the best things in them.

Life is simply a 'mauvais quart d'heure' made up of exquisite moments.

There is the same world for all of us, and good and evil, sin and innocence, go through it hand in hand. To shut one's eyes to half of life that one may live securely is as though one blinded oneself that one might walk with more safety in a land of pit and precipice.

Married men are horribly tedious when they are good husbands and abominably conceited when they are not.

Between men and women there is no friendship possible. There is passion, enmity, worship, love, but no friendship.

Everybody is clever nowadays. You can't go anywhere without meeting clever people. This has become an absolute public nuisance.

I don't think man has much capacity for development. He has got as far as he can, and that is not far, is it?

I am not quite sure that I quite know what pessimism really means. All I do know is that life cannot be understood without much charity, cannot be lived without much charity. It is love, and not German philosophy, that is the explanation of this world, whatever may be the explanation of the next.

I do not approve of anything that that tampers with natural arrogance. Ignorance is like a delicate exotic fruit: touch it, and the blossom is gone.

The whole theory of modern education is radically unsound. Fortunately, in England, at any rate, education produces no effect whatsoever. If it did it would prove a serious danger to the upper classes, and probably lead to acts of violence in Grosvenor Square.

No woman should ever be quite accurate about her age. It looks so calculating.

Emotion for the sake of emotion is the aim of art, and emotion for the sake of emotion is the aim of life and of that practical organisation of life that we call society.

Men of the noblest possible moral character are extremely susceptible to the influence of the physical charms of others. Modern, no less than ancient,

31

history supplies us with many most painful examples of what I refer to. If it were not so, indeed, history would be quite unreadable.

I am not in favour of long engagements. They give people the opportunity of finding out each other's character before marriage, which I think is never advisable.

It is a terrible thing for a man to find out suddenly that all his life he has been speaking nothing but the truth.

The two weak points in our age are its want of principle and its want of profile.

Thirty-five is a very attractive age. London society is full of women who have of their own free choice remained thirty-five for years.

Never speak disrespectfully of society. Only people who can't get into it do that.

It is always painful to part with people whom one has known for a very brief space of time. The absence of old friends one can endure with equanimity. But even a momentary separation from anyone to whom one has just been introduced is almost unbearable.

To be natural is to be obvious, and to be obvious is to be inartistic.

One is tempted to define man as a rational animal who always loses his temper when he is called upon to act in accordance with the dictates of reason.

The essence of thought, as the essence of life, is growth.

What people call insincerity is simply a method by which we can multiply our personalities.

In a temple everyone should be serious except the thing that is worshipped.

We are never more true to ourselves than when we are inconsistent.

There is always something ridiculous about the emotions of people whom one has ceased to love.

Intellectual generalities are always interesting, but generalities in morals mean absolutely nothing.

To be in society is merely a bore, but to be out of it simply a tragedy.

We live in an age when unnecessary things are our only necessities.

One should never make one's début with a scandal. One should reserve that to give an interest to one's old age.

What man has sought for is, indeed, neither pain nor pleasure, but simply life. Man has sought to live intensely, fully, perfectly. When he can do so without exercising restraint on others, or suffering it ever, and his activities are all pleasurable to him, he will be saner, healthier, more civilised, more himself. Pleasure is nature's test, her sign of approval. When man is happy he is in harmony with himself and his environment.

Society often forgives the criminal, it never forgives the dreamer.

It is so easy for people to have sympathy with suffering. It is so difficult for them to have sympathy with thought.

Conversation should touch on everything, but should concentrate itself on nothing.

There is a luxury in self-reproach. When we blame ourselves we feel that no one else has a right to blame us. It is the confession, not the priest, that gives us absolution.

There are only two kinds of people who are really fascinating—people who know absolutely everything and people who know absolutely nothing.

The public is wonderfully tolerant; it forgives everything except genius.

Life makes us pay too high a price for its wares, and we purchase the meanest of its secrets at a cost that is monstrous and infinite.

This horrid House of Commons quite ruins our husbands for us. I think the Lower House by far the greatest blow to a happy married life that there

33

has been since that terrible thing they called the Higher Education of Women was invented.

Once a man begins to neglect his domestic duties he becomes painfully effeminate, does he not? And I don't like that. It makes men so very attractive.

Experience is a question of instinct about life.

What is true about art is true about life.

One can always be kind to people about whom one cares nothing.

I like men who have a future and women who have a past.

Women, as some witty Frenchman put it, inspire us with the desire to do masterpieces and always prevent us from carrying them out.

In matters of grave importance style, not sincerity, is the vital thing.

The only way to behave to a woman, is to make love to her if she is pretty and to someone else if she is plain.

Women give to men the very gold of their lives. Possibly; but they invariably want it back in such very small change.

Define women as a sex? Sphinxes without secrets.

What do you call a bad man? The sort of man who admires innocence.

What do you call a bad woman? Oh! the sort of woman a man never gets tired of.

One can resist everything except temptation.

Don't let us go to life for our fulfilment or our experience. It is a thing narrowed by circumstances, incoherent in its utterance, and without that fine correspondence or form and spirit which is the only thing that can satisfy the artistic and critical temperament.

It is a dangerous thing to reform anyone.

One can always know at once whether a man has home claims upon his life or not. I have noticed a very, very sad expression in the eyes of so many married men.

A mother who doesn't part with a daughter every season has no real affection.

To be good is to be in harmony with oneself. Discord is to be forced to be in harmony with others.

A really grand passion is comparatively rare nowadays. It is the privilege of people who have nothing to do. That is the one use of the idle classes in a country.

There is no secret of life. Life's aim, if it has one, is simply to be always looking for temptations. There are not nearly enough of them; I sometimes pass a whole day without coming across a single one. It is quite dreadful. It makes one so nervous about the future.

All thought is immoral. Its very essence is destruction. If you think of anything you kill it; nothing survives being thought of.

What is truth? In matters of religion it is simply the opinion that has survived. In matters of science it is the ultimate sensation. In matters of art it is one's last mood.

It is so easy to convert others. It is so difficult to convert oneself.

A little sincerity is a dangerous thing, and a great deal of it is absolutely fatal.

Life cheats us with shadows, like a puppet-master. We ask it for pleasure. It gives it to us, with bitterness and disappointment in its train. We come across some noble grief that we think will lend the purple dignity of tragedy to our days, but it passes away from us, and things less noble take its place, and on some grey, windy dawn, or odorous eve of silence and of silver, we find ourselves looking with callous wonder, or dull heart of stone, at the tress of gold-flecked hair that we had once so wildly worshipped and so madly kissed.

There are two ways of disliking art One is to dislike it and the other to like it rationally.

There is nothing sane about the worship of beauty. It is too splendid to be sane. Those of whose lives it forms the dominant note will always seem to the world to be mere visionaries.

I am afraid that good people do a great deal of harm in this world. Certainly the greatest harm they do is that they make badness of such extraordinary importance.

A sentimentalist is a man who sees an absurd value in everything and doesn't know the marked price of any single thing.

Punctuality is the thief of time.

Self-culture is the true ideal for man.

There's nothing in the world like the devotion of a married woman. It's a thing no married man knows anything about.

No woman should have a memory. Memory in a woman is the beginning of dowdiness. One can always tell from a woman's bonnet whether she has got a memory or not.

There are things that are right to say but that may be said at the wrong time and to the wrong people.

The meaning of any beautiful created thing is, at least, as much in the soul of him who looks at it as it was in his soul who wrought it. Nay, it is rather the beholder who lends to the beautiful thing its myriad meanings, and makes it marvellous for us, and sets it in some new relation to the age, so that it becomes a vital portion of our lives and a symbol of what we pray for, or perhaps of what, having prayed for, we fear that we may receive.

The Renaissance was great because it sought to solve no social problem, and busied itself not about such things, but suffered the individual to develop freely, beautifully, and naturally, and so had great and individual artists and great and individual men.

In England people actually try to be brilliant at breakfast. That is so dreadful of them! Only dull people are brilliant at breakfast.

When one is in love one begins by deceiving oneself, and one ends by deceiving others. That is what the world calls a romance.

The secret of life is never to have an emotion that is unbecoming.

No artist is ever morbid. The artist can express everything.

The development of the race depends on the development of the individual, and where self-culture has ceased to be the ideal the intellectual standard is instantly lowered and often ultimately lost.

An idea that is not dangerous is unworthy of being called an idea at all.

To elope is cowardly; it is running away from danger, and danger has become so rare in modern life.

When a man is old enough to do wrong he should be old enough to do right also.

The Book of Life begins with a man and a woman in a garden. It ends with Revelations.

In married life three is company and two is none.

Out of ourselves we can never pass, nor can there be in creation what in the creator was not.

Don't tell me that you have exhausted life. When a man says that one knows that life has exhausted him.

When a woman marries again it is because she detested her first husband. When a man marries again it is because he adored his first wife. Women try their luck; men risk theirs.

The highest criticism really is the record of one's own soul. It is more fascinating than history, as it is concerned simply with oneself. It is more delightful than philosophy, as its subject is concrete and not abstract, real and not vague. It is the only civilised form of autobiography, as it deals, not with the events, but with the thoughts of one's life, not with life's physical accidents of deed or circumstance, but with the spiritual moods and imaginative passions of the mind.

To know anything about oneself one must know all about others.

Duty is what one expects from others, it is not what one does oneself.

After a good dinner one can forgive anybody, even one's own relations.

Talk to every woman as if you loved her and to every man as if he bored you, and at the end of your first season you will have the reputation of possessing the most perfect social tact.

Man—poor, awkward, reliable, necessary man—belongs to a sex that has been rational for millions and millions of years. He can't help himself; it is in his race. The history of women is very different. They have always been picturesque protests against the mere existence of common-sense; they saw its dangers from the first.

More marriages are ruined nowadays by the common-sense of the husband than by anything else. How can a woman be expected to be happy with a man who insists on treating her as if she were a perfectly rational being.

It is very vulgar to talk about one's business. Only people like stock-brokers do that, and then merely at dinner-parties.

It is awfully hard work doing nothing. However, I don't mind hard work when there is no definite object of any kind.

To do nothing at all is the most difficult thing in the world, the most difficult and the most intellectual. To Plato, with his passion for wisdom, this was the noblest form of energy.

To Aristotle, with his passion for knowledge, this was the noblest form of energy also. It was to this that the passion for holiness led the saint and the mystic of mediæval days.

Youth! There is nothing like it. It is absurd to talk of the ignorance of youth. The only people to whose opinions I listen now with any respect are persons much younger than myself. They seem in front of me. Life has revealed to them her latest wonder.

Romance lives by repetition, and repetition converts an appetite into an art.

I adore simple pleasures. They are the last refuge of the complex.

There is nothing like youth. The middle-aged are mortgaged to life. The old are in life's lumber-room. But youth is the lord of life. Youth has a kingdom waiting for it. Everyone is born a king, and most people die in exile—like most kings.

All crime is vulgar, just as all vulgarity is crime.

Society, civilised society at least, is never very ready to believe anything to the detriment of those who are both rich and fascinating. It instinctively feels that manners are of more importance than morals, and in its opinion the highest respectability is of much less value than the possession of a good chef. And, after all, it is a very poor consolation to be told that the man who has given one a bad dinner or poor wine is irreproachable in his private life. Even the cardinal virtues cannot atone for half-cold entrees.

While, in the opinion of society, contemplation is the gravest thing of which any citizen can be guilty, in the opinion of the highest culture it is the proper occupation of man.

Life is terribly deficient in form. Its catastrophes happen in the wrong way and to the wrong people. There is a grotesque horror about its comedies, and its tragedies seem to culminate in farce. One is always wounded when one approaches it. Things last either too long or not long enough.

If a woman wants to hold a man she has merely to appeal to what is worst in him.

We are all in the gutter, but some of us are looking at the stars.

Beauty has as many meanings as man has moods. It is the symbol of symbols. It reveals everything, because it expresses nothing. When it shows us itself it shows us the whole fiery-coloured world.

Men always want to be a woman's first love. That is their clumsy vanity. Women have a more subtle instinct about things. What they like is to be a man's last romance.

Anything approaching to the free play of the mind is practically unknown amongst us. People cry out against the sinner, yet it is not the sinful but the stupid who are our shame. There is no sin except stupidity.

One regrets the loss even of one's worst habits. Perhaps one regrets them the most. They are such an essential part of one's personality.

It is through art, and through art only, that we can realise our perfection; through art and through art only, that we can shield ourselves from the sordid perils of actual existence.

A man who can dominate a London dinner-table can dominate the world. The future belongs to the dandy. It is the exquisites who are going to rule.

It often happens that the real tragedies of life occur in such an inartistic manner that they hurt us by their crude violence, their absolute incoherence, their absurd want of meaning, their entire lack of style. They affect us just as vulgarity affects us. They give us an impression of sheer brute force, and we revolt against that. Sometimes, however, a tragedy that possesses artistic elements of beauty crosses our lives. If these elements of beauty are real the whole thing simply appeals to our sense of dramatic effect. Suddenly we find that we are no longer the actors but the spectators of the play. Or rather we are both. We watch ourselves, and the mere wonder of the spectacle enthrals us.

When a woman finds out that her husband is absolutely indifferent to her, she either becomes dreadfully dowdy or wears very smart bonnets that some other woman's husband has to pay for.

It is immoral to use private property in order to alleviate the horrible evils that result from the institution of private property.

It is a mistake to think that the passion one feels in creation is ever really shown in the work one creates. Art is always more abstract than we fancy. Form and colour tell us of form and colour-that is all.

It is sometimes said that the tragedy of an artist's life is that he cannot realise his ideal. But the true tragedy that dogs the steps of most artists is that they realise their ideal too absolutely. For when the ideal is realised it is robbed of its wonder and its mystery, and becomes simply a new starting-point for an ideal that is other than itself.

People who go in for being consistent have just as many moods as others have. The only difference is that their moods are rather meaningless.

It is only shallow people who require years to get rid of an emotion. A man who is master of himself can end a sorrow as easily as he can invent a pleasure.

Good women have such a limited view of life, their horizon is so small, their interests so petty. The fact is they are not modern, and to be modern is the only thing worth being nowadays.

Discontent is the first step in the progress of a man or a nation.

Men marry because they are tired, women because they are curious. Both are disappointed.

All men are married women's property. That is the only true definition of what married women's property really is.

I am not in favour of this modern mania for turning bad people into good people at a moment's notice. As a man sows so let him reap.

Nothing refines but the intellect.

It is very painful for me to be forced to speak the truth. It is the first time in my life that I have ever been reduced to such a painful position, and I am really quite inexperienced in doing anything of the kind.

The man who regards his past is a man who deserves to have no future to look forward to.

Just as it is only by contact with the art of foreign nations that the art of a country gains that individual and separate life that we call nationality, so, by curious inversion, it is only by intensifying his own personality that the critic can interpret the personality of others; and the more strongly this personality enters into the interpretation the more real the interpretation becomes, the more satisfying, the more convincing, and the more true.

Man is least himself when he talks in his own person. Give him a mask, and he will tell you the truth.

All women become like their mothers: that is their tragedy. No man does: that is his.

Women are a fascinatingly wilful sex. Every woman is a rebel, and usually in wild revolt against herself.

One should always be in love. That is the reason one should never marry.

No man came across two ideal things. Few come across one.

To become the spectator of one's own life is to escape the suffering of life.

The state is to make what is useful. The individual is to make what is beautiful.

A community is infinitely more brutalised by the habitual employment of punishment than it is by the occasional occurrence of crime.

The systems that fail are those that rely on the permanency of human nature and not on its growth and development.

Jealousy, which is an extraordinary source of crime in modern life, is an emotion closely bound up with our conceptions of property, and under socialism and individualism will die out. It is remarkable that in communistic tribes jealousy is entirely unknown.

All art is immoral.

He to whom the present is the only thing that is present knows nothing of the age in which he lives. To realise the nineteenth century one must realise every century that has preceded it and that has contributed to its making.

Few parents nowadays pay any regard to what their children say to them. The old-fashioned respect for the young is fast dying out.

The history of woman is the history of the worst form of tyranny the world has ever known; the tyranny of the weak over the strong. It is the only tyranny that lasts.

The happiness of a married man depends on the people he has not married.

There is no one type for man. There are as many perfections as there are imperfect men. And while to the claims of charity a man may yield and yet be free, to the claims of conformity no man may yield and remain free at all.

A practical scheme is either a scheme that is already in existence or a scheme that could be carried out under existing conditions.

All imitation in morals and in life is wrong.

The world has been made by fools that wise men may live in it.

Women love us for our defects. If we have enough of them they will forgive us everything, even our gigantic intellects.

Society is a necessary thing. No man has any real success in this world unless he has got women to back him—and women rule society. If you have not got women on your side you are quite over. You might just as well be a barrister or a stockbroker or a journalist at once.

The worship of the senses has often, and with much justice, been decried; men feeling a natural instinct of terror about passions and sensations that seem stronger than themselves, and that they are conscious of sharing with the less highly organised forms of existence. But it is probable the true nature of the senses has never been understood, and that they have remained savage and animal merely because the world has sought to starve them into submission or to kill them by pain instead of aiming at making them elements of a new spirituality, of which a fine instinct for beauty will be the dominant characteristic.

Women appreciate cruelty more than anything else. They have wonderfully primitive instincts. We have emancipated them, but they remain slaves, looking for their master all the same. They love being dominated.

Those who try to lead the people can only do so by following the mob. It is through the voice of one crying in the wilderness that the way of the gods must be prepared.

Circumstances are the lashes laid on to us by life. Some of us have to receive them with bared ivory backs, and others are permitted to keep on a coat—that is the only difference.

Criticism is itself an art.... It is no more to be judged by any low standard of imitation or resemblance than is the work of poet or sculptor. The critic occupies the same relation to the work of art that he criticises as the artist does to the visible world of form and colour or the unseen world of passion and thought. He does not even require for the perfection of his art the finest materials. Anything will serve his purpose.

It is very much more difficult to talk about a thing than to do it. In the sphere of actual life that is, of course, obvious. Anybody can make history, only a great man can write it.

If we lived long enough to see the results of our actions it may be that those who call themselves good would be filled with a wild remorse and those whom the world calls evil stirred with a noble joy. Each little thing that we do passes into the great machine of life, which may grind our virtues to powder and make them worthless or transform our sins into elements of a new civilisation more marvellous and more splendid than any that has gone before.

Children begin by loving their parents; as they grow older they judge them, sometimes they forgive them.

We live in an age that reads too much to be wise and that thinks too much to be beautiful.

One should absorb the colour of life, but one should never remember its details. Details are always vulgar.

It will be a marvellous thing—the true personality of man—when we see it. It will grow naturally and simply flowerlike, or as a tree grows. It will not be at discord. It will never argue or dispute. It will not prove things. It will know everything, and yet it will not busy itself about knowledge. It will have wisdom. Its value will not be measured by material things. It will have nothing, and yet it will have everything, and whatever one takes from it it will still have, so rich it will be. It will not be always meddling with others or asking them to be like itself. It will love them because they will be different. And yet, while it will not meddle with others, it will help all, as a beautiful thing helps us, by being what it is. The personality of man will be very wonderful. It will be as wonderful as the personality of a child.

Cynicism is merely the art of seeing things as they are instead of as they ought to be.

Three addresses always inspire confidence, even in tradesmen.

If one doesn't talk about a thing it has never happened. It is simply expression that gives reality to things.

No man is able who is unable to get on, just as no woman is clever who can't succeed in obtaining that worst and most necessary of evils, a husband.

The one charm of the past is that it is the past. But women never know when the curtain has fallen. They always want a sixth act, and as soon as the interest of the play is entirely over they propose to continue it. If they were allowed their way every comedy would have a tragic ending and every tragedy would culminate in a farce. They are charmingly artificial, but they have no sense of art.

Each time that one loves is the only time that one has ever loved. Difference of object does not alter singleness of passion. It merely intensifies it.

The real tragedy of the poor is that they can afford nothing but self-denial. Beautiful sins, like beautiful things, are the privilege of the rich.

Human life is the one thing worth investigating. Compared to it there is nothing else of any value. It is true that as one watches life in its curious crucible of pain and pleasure one cannot wear over one's face a mask of glass nor keep the sulphurous fumes from troubling the brain and making the imagination turbid with monstrous fancies and misshapen dreams. There are poisons so subtle that to know their properties one has to sicken of them. There are maladies so strange that one has to pass through them if one seeks to understand their nature. And yet what a great reward one receives! How wonderful the whole world becomes to one! To note the curious, hard logic of passion and the emotional, coloured life of the intellect—to observe where they meet, and where they separate, at what point they are in unison and at what point they are in discord—there is a delight in that! What matter what the cost is? One can never pay too high a price for any sensation.

There is only one class in the community that thinks more about money than the rich, and that is the poor. The poor can think of nothing else. That is the misery of being poor.

To live is the rarest thing in the world. Most people exist—that is all.

Personality is a very mysterious thing. A man cannot always be estimated by what he does. He may keep the law, and yet be worthless. He may break the law, and yet be fine. He may be bad without ever doing anything bad. He may commit a sin against society, and yet realise through that sin his true perfection.

Mediæval art is charming, but mediæval emotions are out of date. One can use them in fiction, of course; but then the only things that one can use in fiction are the only things that one has ceased to use in fact.

Man is complete in himself.

What is a cynic? A man who knows the price of everything and the value of nothing.

It's the old, old story. Love—well, not at first sight—but love at the end of the season, which is so much more satisfactory.

No nice girl should ever waltz with such particularly younger sons! It looks so fast!

Good resolutions are useless attempts to interfere with scientific laws. Their origin is pure vanity. Their result is absolutely nil. They give us now and then some of those luxurious, sterile emotions that have a certain charm for the weak. That is all that can be said for them. They are simply cheques that men draw on a bank where they have no account.

What is the difference between literature and journalism? Journalism is unreadable and literature is unread.

I hope you have not been leading a double life, pretending to be wicked and being really good all the time. That would be hypocrisy.

My husband is a sort of promissory note; I am tired of meeting him.

Conscience makes egotists of us all.

Never trust a woman who wears mauve, whatever her age may be, or a woman over thirty-five who is fond of pink ribbons. It always means that they have a history.

There is a fatality about good resolutions-they are always made too late.

We can have in life but one great experience at best, and the secret of life is to reproduce that experience as often as possible.

Anybody can be good in the country. There are no temptations there. That is the reason why people who live out of town are so absolutely uncivilised. Civilisation is not by any means an easy thing to attain to. There are only two ways by which man can reach it. One is by being cultured, the other by being corrupt. Country people have no opportunity of being either, so they stagnate.

What nonsense people talk about happy marriages! A man can be happy with any woman so long as he does not love her.

The things one feels absolutely certain about are never true. That is the fatality of faith and the lesson of romance.

In the common world of fact the wicked are not punished nor the good rewarded. Success is given to the strong, failure thrust upon the weak.

Nothing should be able to harm a man except himself. Nothing should be able to rob a man at all. What a man really has is what is in him. What is outside of him should be a matter of no importance.

Modern morality consists in accepting the standard of one's age. I consider that for any man of culture to accept the standard of his age is a form of the grossest immorality.

Perplexity and mistrust fan affection into passion, and so bring about those beautiful tragedies that alone make life worth living. Women once felt this, while men did not, and so women once ruled the world.

Sin is a thing that writes itself across a man's, face. It cannot be concealed. People talk sometimes of secret vices. There are no such things.

If a wretched man has a vice it shows itself in the lines of his mouth, the drop of his eyelids, the moulding of his hands even.

There are sins whose fascination is more in the memory than in the doing of them, strange triumphs that gratify the pride more than the passions and give to the intellect a quickened sense of joy, greater than they bring or can ever bring to the senses.

No civilised man ever regrets a pleasure, and no uncivilised man ever knows what a pleasure is.

As for a spoiled life, no life is spoiled but one whose growth is arrested. If you want to mar a nature you have merely to reform it.

Socialism itself will be of value simply because it will lead to individualism.

Some years ago people went about the country saying that property has duties. It is perfectly true. Property not merely has duties, but has so many duties that its possession to any large extent is a bore. If property had simply pleasures we could stand it, but its duties make it unbearable.

It is through joy that the individualism of the future will develop itself. Christ made no attempt to reconstruct society, and consequently the individualism that He preached to man could be realised only through pain or in solitude.

Most people become bankrupt through having invested too heavily in the prose of life. To have ruined oneself over poetry is an honour.

The only artists I have ever known who are personally delightful are bad artists. Good artists exist simply on what they make, and consequently are perfectly uninteresting in what they are.

What are the virtues? Nature, Renan tells us, cares little about chastity, and it may be that it is to the shame of the Magdalen, and not to their own purity, that the Lucretias of modern life owe their freedom from stain. Charity, as even those of whose religion it makes a formal part have been compelled to acknowledge, creates a multitude of evils. The mere existence of conscience, that faculty of which people prate so much nowadays, and are so ignorantly proud, is a sign of our imperfect development. It must be merged in instinct before we become fine. Self-denial is simply a method by which man arrests his progress, and self-sacrifice a survival of the mutilation of the savage, part of that old worship of pain which is so terrible a factor in the history of the world, and which even now makes its victims day by day and has its altars in the land. Virtues! Who knows what the virtues are? Not you. Not I. Not anyone. It is well for our vanity that we slay the criminal, for if we suffered him to live he might show us what we had gained by his crime. It is well for his peace that the saint goes to his martyrdom. He is spared the sight of the horror of his harvest.

Nowadays all the married men live like bachelors and all the bachelors like married men.

The higher education of men is what I should like to see. Men need it so sadly.

The world is perfectly packed with good women. To know them is a middle-class education.

Hesitation of any kind is a sign of mental decay in the young, of physical weakness in the old.

Our husbands never appreciate anything in us. We have to go to others for that.

Most women in London nowadays seem to furnish their rooms with nothing but orchids, foreigners and French novels.

The canons of good society are, or should be, the same as the canons of art. Form is absolutely essential to it. It should have the dignity of a ceremony as well as its unreality, and should combine the insincere character of a romantic play with the wit and beauty that make such plays delightful to us. Is sincerity such a terrible thing? I think not. It is merely a method by which we can multiply our personalities.

The tragedy of old age is not that one is old but that one is young.

A great poet, a really great poet, is the most unpoetical of all creatures. But inferior poets are absolutely fascinating. The worse their rhymes are the more picturesque they look. The mere fact of having published a book of second-rate sonnets makes a man quite irresistible. He lives the poetry that he cannot write. The others write the poetry that they dare not realise.

Being adored is a nuisance. Women treat us just as humanity treats its gods. They worship us, and are always bothering us to do something for them.

If a man treats life artistically his brain is his heart.

The 'Peerage' is the one book a young man about town should know thoroughly, and it is the best thing in fiction the English have ever done.

The world has always laughed at its own tragedies, that being the only way in which it has been able to bear them. Consequently whatever the world has treated seriously belongs to the comedy side of things.

The only difference between the saint and the sinner is that every saint has a past and every sinner has a future.

What is termed sin is an essential element of progress. Without it the world would stagnate or grow old or becomes colourless. By its curiosity it increases the experience of the race. Through its intensified assertion of individualism it saves us from the commonplace. In its rejection of the current notions about morality it is one with the higher ethics.

Formerly we used to canonise our heroes. The modern method is to vulgarise them. Cheap editions of great books may be delightful, but cheap editions of great men are absolutely detestable.

Individualism does not come to man with any claims upon him at all. It comes naturally and inevitably out of man. It is the point to which all development tends. It is the differentiation to which all organisms grow. It is the perfection that is inherent in every mode of life and toward which every mode of life quickens. Individualism exercises no compulsion over man. On the contrary, it says to man that he should suffer no compulsion to be exercised over him. It does not try to force people to be good. It knows that people are good when they are let alone. Man will develop individualism out of himself. Man is now so developing individualism. To ask whether individualism is practical is like asking whether evolution is practical. Evolution is the law of life, and there is no evolution except towards individualism.

The longer I live the more keenly I feel that whatever was good enough for our fathers is not good enough for us. In art, as in politics, 'les grand pères ont toujours tort.'

No woman is a genius. Women are a decorative sex. They never have anything to say but they say it charmingly.

Humanity takes itself too seriously. It is the world's original sin. If the cave men had known how to laugh history would have been different.

I wonder who it was defined man as a rational animal. It was the most premature definition ever given. Man is many things, but he is not rational.

Thought and language are to the artist instruments of an art.

To get into the best society nowadays one has either to feed people, amuse people, or shock people—that is all.

51

You should never try to understand women. Women are pictures, men are problems. If you want to know what a woman really means—which, by the way, is always a dangerous thing to do—look at her, don't listen to her.

Ordinary women never appeal to one's imagination. They are limited to their century. No glamour ever transfigures them. One knows their minds as easily as one knows their bonnets. One can always find them. There is no mystery in any of them. They ride in the park in the morning and chatter at tea parties in the afternoon. They have their stereotyped smile and their fashionable mauve.

Don't run down dyed hair and painted faces. There is an extraordinary charm in them—sometimes.

To have been well brought up is a great drawback nowadays. It shuts one out from so much.

The people who have adored me—there have not been very many, but there have been some—have always insisted on living on long after I had ceased to care for them or they to care for me. They have become stout and tedious, and when I meet them they go in at once for reminiscences. That awful memory of women! What a fearful thing it is! And what an utter intellectual stagnation it reveals!

Examinations are pure humbug from beginning to end. If a man is a gentleman he knows quite enough, and if he is not a gentleman whatever he knows is bad for him.

Credit is the capital of a younger son, and he can live charmingly on it.

The object of art is not simply truth but complex beauty. Art itself is really a form of exaggeration, and selection, which is the very spirit of art, is nothing more than an intensified mode of over-emphasis.

The popular cry of our time is: 'Let us return to Life and Nature, they will recreate Art for us and send the red blood coursing through her veins; they will shoe her feet with swiftness and make her hand strong.' But, alas! we are mistaken in our amiable and well-meant efforts. Nature is always behind the age. And as for life, she is the solvent that breaks up Art, the enemy that lays waste her house.

There are only two kinds of women—the plain and the coloured. The plain women are very useful. If you want to gain a reputation for respectability you have merely to take them down to supper. The other women are very charming. They commit one mistake, however—they paint in order to try and look young.

The way of paradoxes is the way of truth. To test reality we must see it on the tight-rope. When the verities become acrobats we can judge them.

Life imitates art far more than art imitates life.... The Greeks with their quick, artistic instinct understood this, and set in the bride's chamber the statue of Hermes or of Apollo, that she might bear children as lovely as the works of art that she looked at in her rapture or her pain. They knew that life gains from art not merely spirituality, depth of thought and feeling, soul-turmoil or soul-peace, but that she can form herself on the very lines and colours of art, and can reproduce the dignity of Pheidias as well as the grace of Praxiteles. Hence came this objection to realism. They disliked it on purely social grounds. They felt that it inevitably makes people ugly, and they were perfectly right.

Faithfulness is to the emotional life what consistency is to the life of the intellect—simply a confession of failure.

There are many things that we would throw away if we were not afraid that others might pick them up.

What a fuss people make about fidelity! Why, even in love it is purely a question for physiology. It has nothing to do with our own will. Young men want to be faithful and are not; old men want to be faithless and cannot—that is all one can say.

Modernity of form and modernity of subject-matter are entirely and absolutely wrong. We have mistaken the common livery of the age for the vesture of the muses, and spent our days in the sordid streets and hideous suburbs of our vile cities when we should be out on the hillside with Apollo.

53

Certainly we are a degraded race, and have sold our birthright for a mess of facts.

Nothing can cure the soul but the senses, just as nothing can cure the senses but the soul.

I can stand brute force, but brute reason is quite unbearable. There is something unfair about its use. It is hitting below the intellect.

Those who live in marble or on painted panel know of life but a single exquisite instant, eternal, indeed, in its beauty but limited to one note of passion or one mood of calm. Those whom the poet makes live have their myriad emotions of joy and terror, of courage and despair, of pleasure and of suffering. The seasons come and go in glad or saddening pageant, and with winged or leaden feet the years pass by before them. They have their youth and their manhood, they are children, and they grow old. It is always dawn for St Helena as Veronese saw her at the window. Through the still morning air the angels bring her the symbol of God's pain. The cool breezes of the morning lift the gilt threads from her brow. On that little hill by the city of Florence, where the lovers of Giorgione are lying, it is always the solstice of noon—of noon made so languorous by summer suns that hardly can the slim, naked girl dip into the marble tank the round bubble of clear glass, and the long fingers of the lute player rest idly upon the chords. It is twilight always for the dancing nymphs whom Corot set free among the silver poplars of France. In eternal twilight they move, those frail, diaphanous figures, whose tremulous, white feet seem not to touch the dew-drenched grass they tread on. But those who walk in epos, drama, or romance see through the labouring months the young moons wax and wane, and watch the night from evening into morning star, and from sunrise into sun-setting can note the shifting day with all its gold and shadow. For them, as for us, the flowers bloom and wither, and the earth, that green-tressed goddess, as Coleridge calls her, alters her raiment for their pleasure. The statue is concentrated to one moment of perfection. The image stained upon the canvas possesses no spiritual element of growth or change. If they know nothing of death it is because they know little of life, for the secrets of life and death belong to those, and to those only, whom the sequence of time affects, and who possess not merely the present but the future, and can rise or fall from a past of glory or of shame. Movement, that problem of the visible arts, can be truly realised by literature alone. It is literature that shows us the body in its swiftness and the soul in its unrest.

Behind every exquisite thing that exists there is something tragic. Worlds have to be in travail that the merest flower may blow.

Beauty is a form of genius—is higher, indeed, than genius, as it needs no explanation. It is one of the great facts of the world, like sunlight, or spring-time, or the reflection in dark water of that silver shell we call the moon. It cannot be questioned, it has its divine right of sovereignty.

The only way to get rid of a temptation is to yield to it. Resist it and your soul grows sick with longing for the things it has forbidden to itself.

Women spoil every romance by trying to make it last for ever.

He's sure to be a wonderful success. He thinks like a Tory and talks like a Radical, and that's so important nowadays.

Nowadays to be intelligible is to be found out.

We make gods of men and they leave us. Others make brutes of them and they fawn and are faithful.

The husbands of very beautiful women belong to the criminal classes.

To me beauty is the Wonder of wonders. It is only shallow people who do not judge by appearances.

The true mystery of the world is the visible, not the invisible.

The thoroughly well-informed man is the modern ideal. And the mind of the thoroughly well-informed man is a dreadful thing. It is like a bric-a-brac shop, all monsters and dust, with everything priced above its proper value.

Women have no appreciation of good looks in men—at least good women have none.

To influence a person is to give him one's own soul. He does not think his natural thoughts or burn with his natural passions. His virtues are not real to him. His sins, if there are such things as sins, are borrowed. He becomes an echo of someone else's music, an actor of a part that has not been written for him.

Those who are faithful know only the trivial side of love; it is the faithless who know love's tragedies.

An artist should create beautiful things, but should put nothing of his own life into them. We live in an age when men treat art as if it were meant to be a form of autobiography. We have lost the abstract sense of beauty.

A man cannot be too careful in the choice of his enemies. I have not got one who is a fool. They are all men of some intellectual power, and consequently they all appreciate me.

The value of an idea has nothing whatever to do with the sincerity of the man who expresses it.

I like persons better than principles, and I like persons with no principles better than anything else in the world.

He who would lead a Christ-like life is he who is perfectly and absolutely himself. He may be a great poet, or a great man of science; or a young student at the university, or one who watches sheep upon a moor; or a maker of dramas, like Shakespeare, or a thinker about God, like Spinoza; or a child who plays in a garden, or a fisherman who throws his nets into the sea. It does not matter what he is as long as he realises the perfection of the soul that is within him.

The aim of life is self-development. To realise one's nature perfectly— that is what each of us is here for.

There is no such thing as a good influence. All influence is immoral— immoral from the scientific point of view.

Words have not merely music as sweet as that of viol and lute, colour as rich and vivid as any that makes lovely for us the canvas of the Venetian or the Spaniard, and plastic form no less sure and certain than that which reveals itself in marble or in bronze, but thought and passion and spirituality are theirs also—are theirs, indeed, alone.

There is nothing so absolutely pathetic as a really fine paradox. The pun is the clown among jokes, the well-turned paradox is the polished comedian, and the highest comedy verges upon tragedy, just as the keenest edge of tragedy is often tempered by a subtle humour. Our minds are shot with moods as a fabric is shot with colours, and our moods often seem inappropriate. Everything that is true is inappropriate.

The longer one studies life and literature the more strongly one feels that behind everything that is wonderful stands the individual, and that it is not the moment that makes the man but the man who creates the age.

To know the vintage and quality of a wine one need not drink the whole cask.

It is a sad thing to think of, but there is no doubt that genius lasts longer than beauty. That accounts for the fact that we all take such pains to over-educate ourselves.

The ugly and the stupid have the best of it in this world. They can sit at their ease and gape at the play. If they know nothing of victory they are at least spared the knowledge of defeat.

To have a capacity for a passion, and not to realise it is to make oneself incomplete and limited.

Even in actual life egotism is not without its attractions. When people talk to us about others they are usually dull. When they talk to us about themselves they are nearly always interesting, and if one could shut them up when they become wearisome as easily as one can shut up a book of which one has grown wearied they would be perfect absolutely.

Every great man nowadays has his disciples and it is invariably Judas who writes the biography.

Art finds her own perfection within, and not outside of, herself. She is not to be judged by any external standard of resemblance. She is a veil rather than a mirror. She has flowers that no forest knows of, birds that no woodland possesses. She makes and unmakes many worlds, and can draw the moon from heaven with a scarlet thread. Hers are the 'forms more real than living man,' and hers the great archetypes, of which things that have existence are but unfinished copies. Nature has, in her eyes, no laws, no uniformity. She can work miracles at her will, and when she calls monsters from the deep they come. She can bid the almond-tree blossom in winter and send the snow upon the ripe cornfield. At her word the frost lays its silver finger on the burning mouth of June, and the winged lions creep out from the hollows of the Lydian hills. The dryads peer from the thicket as she passes by, and the brown fauns smile strangely at her when she comes near them. She has hawk-faced gods that worship her, and the centaurs gallop at her side.

In literature mere egotism is delightful.

If we live for aims we blunt our emotions. If we live for aims we live for one minute, for one day, for one year, instead of for every minute, every day, every year. The moods of one's life are life's beauties. To yield to all one's moods is to really live.

Many a young man starts in life with a natural gift for exaggeration which, if nurtured in congenial and sympathetic surroundings, or by the imitations of the best models, might grow into something really great and wonderful. But, as a rule, he comes to nothing. He either falls into careless habits of accuracy or takes to frequenting the society of the aged and the well-informed. Both things are equally fatal to his imagination.

The spirit of an age may be best expressed in the abstract ideal arts, for the spirit itself is abstract and ideal.

As for believing things, I can believe anything provided that it is quite incredible.

'Know thyself' was written over the portal of the antique world. Over the portal of the new world 'Be thyself' shall be written. And the message of Christ to man was simply: 'Be thyself.' That is the secret of Christ.

London is full of women who trust their husbands. One can always recognise them, they look so thoroughly unhappy.

For those who are not artists, and to whom there is no mode of life but the actual life of fact, pain is the only door to perfection.

The English public always feels perfectly at its ease when a mediocrity is talking to it.

Men always fall into the absurdity of endeavouring to develop the mind, to push it violently forward in this direction or in that. The mind should be receptive, a harp waiting to catch the winds, a pool ready to be ruffled, not a bustling busybody for ever trotting about on the pavement looking for a new bun shop.

There is nothing more beautiful than to forget, except, perhaps, to be forgotten.

All bad art comes from returning to life and nature, and elevating them into ideals. Life and nature may sometimes be used as part of art's rough material, but before they are of any real service to art they must be translated into artistic conventions. The moment art surrenders its imaginative medium it surrenders everything. As a method realism is a complete failure, and the two things that every artist should avoid are modernity of form and modernity of subject-matter.

Men may have women's minds just as women may have the minds of men.

London is too full of fogs and serious people. Whether the fogs produce the serious people or whether the serious people produce the fogs I don't know.

How marriage ruins a man! It's as demoralising as cigarettes, and far more expensive.

He must be quite respectable. One has never heard his name before in the whole course of one's life, which speaks volumes for a man nowadays.

Literature always anticipates life. It does not copy it, but moulds it to its purpose.

As long as a thing is useful or necessary to us or affects us in any way, either for pain or pleasure, or appeals strongly to our sympathies or is a vital part of the environment in which we live, it is outside the proper sphere of art.

I couldn't have a scene in this bonnet: it is far too fragile. A harsh word would ruin it.

Music creates for one a past of which one has been ignorant and fills one with a sense of sorrows that have been hidden from one's tears.

Nothing is so fatal to personality as deliberation.

I adore London dinner parties. The clever people never listen and the stupid people never talk.

Learned conversation is either the affection of the ignorant or the profession of the mentally unemployed.

The Academy is too large and too vulgar. Whenever I have gone there, there have been either so many people that I have not been able to see the pictures—which was dreadful, or so many pictures that I have not been able to see the people—which was worse.

All art is quite useless.

Beauty, real beauty, ends where an intellectual expression begins. Intellect is in itself a mode of exaggeration and destroys the harmony of any face. The moment one sits down to think one becomes all nose or all forehead or something horrid.

The one charm of marriage is that it makes a life of deception absolutely necessary for both parties.

Secrecy seems to be the one thing that can make modern life mysterious or marvellous to us. The commonest thing is delightful if one only hides it.

Conceit is one of the greatest of the virtues, yet how few people recognise it as a thing to aim at and to strive after. In conceit many a man and woman has found salvation, yet the average person goes on all-fours grovelling after modesty.

It is difficult not to be unjust to what one loves.

Humanity will always love Rousseau for having confessed his sins not to a friend but to the world.

Just as those who do not love Plato more than truth cannot pass beyond the threshold of the Academe, so those who do not love beauty more than truth never know the inmost shrine of art.

There is a fatality about all physical and intellectual distinction: the sort of fatality that seems to dog, through history, the faltering steps of kings. It is better not to be different from one's fellows.

To be born, or at any rate bred, in a handbag, whether it had handles or not, seems to me to display a contempt for the ordinary decencies of family life that reminds one of the worst excesses of the French Revolution.

Vice and virtue are to the artist materials for an art.

There must be a new Hedonism that shall recreate life and save it from that harsh, uncomely Puritanism that is having, in our own day, its curious revival. It must have its service of the intellect, certainly, yet it must never accept any theory or system that will involve the sacrifice of any mode of passionate experience. Its aim, indeed, is to be experience itself and not the fruits of experience, bitter or sweet as they may be. Of the æstheticism that deadens the senses, as of the vulgar profligacy that dulls them, it is to know nothing. But it is to teach man to concentrate himself upon the moments of a life that is itself but a moment.

Art never expresses anything but itself. It has an independent life, just as thought has, and develops purely on its own lines. It is not necessarily realistic in an age of realism nor spiritual in an age of faith. So far from being the creation of its time it is usually in direct opposition to it, and the only history that it preserves for us is the history of its own progress.

People who mean well always do badly. They are like the ladies who wear clothes that don't fit them in order to show their piety. Good intentions are invariably ungrammatical.

Man can believe the impossible, but man can never believe the improbable.

When art is more varied nature will, no doubt, be more varied also.

If a man is sufficiently imaginative to produce evidence in support of a lie he might just as well speak the truth at once.

The ancient historians gave us delightful fiction in the form of fact; the modern novelist presents us with dull facts under the guise of fiction.

Nature is no great mother who has home us. She is our own creation. It is in our brain that she quickens to life. Things are because we see them, and what we see and how we see it depends on the arts that have influenced us. To look at a thing is very different from seeing a thing. One does not see anything until one sees its beauty.

The proper school to learn art in is not life but art.

I won't tell you that the world matters nothing, or the world's voice, or the voice of society. They matter a good deal. They matter far too much.

I wouldn't marry a man with a future before him for anything under the sun.

I am the only person in the world I should like to know thoroughly, but I don't see any chance of it just at present.

Modern memoirs are generally written by people who have entirely lost their memories and have never done anything worth recording.

Education is an admirable thing, but it is well to remember from time to time that nothing that is worth knowing can be taught.

Women are like minors, they live upon their expectations.

Twisted minds are as natural to some people as twisted bodies.

62

It is the very passions about whose origin we deceive ourselves that tyrannise most strongly over us. Our weakest motives are those of whose nature we are conscious. It often happens that when we think we are experimenting on others we are really experimenting on ourselves.

Whenever a man does a thoroughly stupid thing it is always from the noblest motives.

I thought I had no heart. I find I have, and a heart doesn't suit me. Somehow it doesn't go with modern dress. It makes one look old, and it spoils one's career at critical moments.

I don't play accurately—anyone can play accurately—but I play with wonderful expression. As far as the piano is concerned sentiment is my forte. I keep science for life.

I delight in men over seventy. They always offer one the devotion of a lifetime.

Everybody who is incapable of learning has taken to teaching—that is really what our enthusiasm for education has come to.

Nature hates mind.

From the point of view of form the type of all the arts is the art of the musician. From the point of view of feeling the actor's craft is the type.

Where we differ from each other is purely in accidentals—in dress, manner, tone of voice, religious opinions, personal appearance, tricks of habit, and the like.

The more we study art the less we care for Nature. What art really reveals to us is Nature's lack of design, her curious crudities, her extraordinary monotony, her absolutely unfinished condition.... It is fortunate for us, however, that nature is so imperfect, as otherwise we should have had no art at all. Art is our spirited protest, our gallant attempt to teach Nature her proper place. As for the infinite variety of nature, that is a pure myth. It is not to be found in Nature herself. It resides in the imagination or fancy or cultivated blindness of the man who looks at her.

Facts are not merely finding a footing-place in history but they are usurping the domain of fancy and have invaded the kingdom of romance. Their chilling touch is over everything. They are vulgarising mankind.

Ordinary people wait till life discloses to them its secrets, but to the few, to the elect, the mysteries of life are revealed before the veil is drawn away. Sometimes this is the effect of art, and chiefly of the art of literature which deals immediately with the passions and the intellect. But now and then a complex personality takes the place and assumes the office of art, is, indeed, in its way a real work of art, Life having its elaborate masterpieces just as poetry has, or sculpture, or painting.

Thinking is the most unhealthy thing in the world, and people die of it just as they die of any other disease.

A cigarette is the perfect type of a perfect pleasure. It is exquisite and it leaves one unsatisfied.

The aim of the liar is simply to charm, to delight, to give pleasure. He is the very basis of civilised society.

It is quite a mistake to believe, as many people do, that the mind shows itself in the face. Vice may sometimes write itself in lines and changes of contour, but that is all. Our faces are really masks given to us to conceal our minds with.

What on earth should we men do going about with purity and innocence? A carefully thought-out buttonhole is much more effective.

The only difference between a caprice and a lifelong passion is that the caprice lasts a little longer.

People say sometimes that beauty is only superficial. That may be so, but at least it is not so superficial as thought is.

It is the spectator and not life that art really mirrors.

Nowadays people know the price of everything and the value of nothing.

Conscience and cowardice are really the same things. Conscience is the trade name of the firm—that is all.

In every sphere of life form is the beginning of things. The rhythmic, harmonious gestures of dancing convey, Plato tells us, both rhythm and harmony into the mind. Forms are the food of faith, cried Newman, in one of those great moments of sincerity that make us admire and know the man. He was right, though he may not have known how terribly right he was. The creeds are believed not because they are rational but because they are repeated. Yes; form is everything. It is the secret of life. Find expression for a sorrow and it will become dear to you. Find expression for a joy and you intensify its ecstasy. Do you wish to love? Use love's litany and the words will create the yearning from which the world fancies that they spring. Have you a grief that corrodes your heart? Learn its utterance from Prince Hamlet and Queen Constance and you will find that mere expression is a mode of consolation and that form, which is the birth of passion, is also the death of pain. And so, to return to the sphere of art, it is form that creates not merely the critical temperament but also the æsthetic instinct that reveals to one all things under the condition of beauty. Start with the worship of form and there is no secret in art that will not be revealed to you.

It is only the intellectually lost who ever argue.

Nowadays most people die of a sort of creeping common-sense, and discover when it is too late that the only things one never regrets are one's mistakes.

Lady Henry Wotton was a curious woman, whose dresses always looked as if they had been designed in a rage and put on in a tempest. She was usually in love with somebody, and, as her passion was never returned, she had kept all her illusions. She tried to look picturesque but only succeeded in being untidy.

Those who go beneath the surface do so at their peril.

With an evening coat and a white tie anybody, even a stockbroker, can gain a reputation for being civilised.

There is nothing so interesting as telling a good man or woman how bad one has been. It is intellectually fascinating. One of the greatest pleasures of having been wicked is that one has so much to say to the good.

Laws are made in order that people in authority may not remember them, just as marriages are made in order that the divorce court may not play about idly.

To get back one's youth one has merely to repeat one's follies.

Never marry a woman with straw-coloured hair. They are so sentimental.

The reason we all like to think so well of others is that we are all afraid for ourselves. The basis of optimism is sheer terror. We think that we are generous because we credit our neighbours with the possession of those virtues that are likely to be a benefit to us. We praise the banker that we may overdraw our account, and find good qualities in the high-wayman in the hope that he may spare our pockets. I have the greatest contempt for optimism.

Art begins with abstract decoration, with purely imaginative and pleasureable work dealing with what is unreal and non-existent. This is the first stage. Then life becomes fascinated with this new wonder, and asks to be admitted into the charmed circle. Art takes life as part of her rough material, recreates it and refashions it in fresh form; is absolutely indifferent to facts; invents, imagines, dreams, and keeps between herself and reality the impenetrable barrier of beautiful style, of decorative or ideal treatment. The third stage is when Life gets the upper hand and drives Art out into the wilderness. This is the true decadence, and it is from this that we are now suffering.

Good intentions have been the ruin of the world. The only people who have achieved anything have been those who have had no intentions at all.

I never take any notice of what common people say, and I never interfere with what charming people do.

You know I am not a champion of marriage. The real drawback to marriage is that it makes one unselfish, and unselfish people are colourless— they lack individuality. Still there are certain temperaments that marriage makes more complex. They retain their egotism, and add to it many other egos. They are forced to have more than one life. They become more highly organised, and to be highly organised is, I should fancy, the object of man's existence. Besides, every experience is of value, and whatever one may say against marriage it is certainly an experience.

Those who read the symbol do so at their peril.

I never talk during music—at least not during good music. If anyone hears bad music it is one's duty to drown it in conversation.

When critics disagree the artist is in accord with himself.

Faith is the most plural thing I know. We are all supposed to believe in the same thing in different ways. It is like eating out of the same dish with different coloured spoons.

Experience is of no ethical value. It is merely the name men give to their mistakes. Moralists have, as a rule, regarded it as a mode of warning, have claimed for it a certain ethical efficacy in the formation of character, have praised it as something that teaches us what to follow and shows us what to avoid. But there is no motive power in experience. It is as little of an active cause as conscience itself. All that it really demonstrates is that our future will be the same as our past and that the sin we have done once, and with loathing, we shall do many times, and with joy.

Sensations are the details that build up the stories of our lives.

No artist has ethical sympathies. An ethical sympathy in an artist is an unpardonable mannerism of style.

She looks like an 'edition de luxe' of a wicked French novel meant specially for the English market.

I never knew what terror was before; I know it now. It is as if a hand of ice were laid upon one's heart. It is as if one's heart were beating itself to death in some empty hollow.

We can forgive a man for making a useful thing as long as he does not admire it. The only excuse for making a useless thing is that one admires it intensely.

No artist desires to prove anything. Even things that are true can be proved.

One knows so well the popular idea of health. The English country gentleman galloping along after a fox—the unspeakable in pursuit of the uneatable.

People seldom tell the truths that are worth telling. We ought to choose our truths as carefully as we choose our lies and to select our virtues with as much thought as we bestow upon the selection of our enemies.

Soul and body, body and soul—how mysterious they are! There is animalism in the soul, and the body has its moments of spirituality. The senses can refine and the intellect can degrade. Who can say where the fleshly impulse ceases or the psychical impulse begins? How shallow are the arbitrary definitions of ordinary psychologists! And yet how difficult to decide between the claims of the various schools! Is the soul a shadow seated in the house of sin? Or is the body really in the soul, as Giordano Bruno thought? The separation of spirit from matter is a mystery, and the unison of spirit with matter is a mystery also.

Those who find beautiful meanings in beautiful things are the cultivated. For these there is hope.

There is no such thing as a moral or an immoral book. Books are well written or badly written-that is all.

Marriage is a sort of forcing house. It brings strange sins to fruit, and sometimes strange renunciations.

The moral life of man forms part of the subject-matter of the artist, but the morality of art consists in the perfect use of an imperfect medium.

A sense of duty is like some horrible disease. It destroys the tissues of the mind, as certain complaints destroy the tissues of the body. The catechism has a great deal to answer for.

They are the elect to whom beautiful things mean only beauty.

Those who find ugly meanings in beautiful things are corrupt without being charming. This is a fault.

Few people have sufficient strength to resist the preposterous claims of orthodoxy.

She wore far too much rouge last night and not quite enough clothes. That is always a sign of despair in a woman.

A virtue is like a city set upon a hill—it cannot be hid. We can conceal our vices if we care to—for a time at least—but a virtue will out.

Can't make out how you stand London society. The thing has gone to the dogs: a lot of damned nobodies talking about nothing.

You don't know what an existence they lead down there. It is pure, unadulterated country life. They get up early because they have so much to do, and go to bed early because they have so little to think about.

Nothing is so fatal to a personality as the keeping of promises, unless it be telling the truth.

Who cares whether Mr Ruskin's views on Turner are sound or not? What does it matter? That mighty and majestic prose of his, so fervid and so fiery coloured in its noble eloquence, so rich in its elaborate symphonic music, so sure and certain, at its best, in subtle choice of word and epithet, is, at least, as great a work of art as any of those wonderful sunsets that bleach or rot on their corrupted canvases in England's gallery—greater, indeed, one is apt to think at times, not merely because its equal beauty is more enduring but on account of the fuller variety of its appeal—soul speaking to soul in those long, cadenced lines, not through form and colour alone, though through these, indeed, completely and without loss, but with intellectual and emotional utterance, with lofty passion and with loftier thought, with imaginative insight and with poetic aim—greater, I always think, even as literature is the greater art.

Laughter is not at all a bad beginning for a friendship, and it is far the best ending for one.

Mrs Cheveley is one of those very modern women of our time who find a new scandal as becoming as a new bonnet, and air them both in the Park every afternoon at 5.30. I am sure she adores scandals, and that the sorrow of her life at present is that she can't manage to have enough of them.

The world divides actions into three classes: good actions, bad actions that you may do, and bad actions that you may not do. If you stick to the good actions you are respected by the good. If you stick to the bad actions that you may do you are respected by the bad. But if you perform the bad actions that no one may do then the good and the bad set upon you and you are lost indeed.

I choose my friends for their good looks, my acquaintances for their good characters, and my enemies for their good intellects.

The artist is the creator of beautiful things.

To me the word 'natural' means all that is middle class, all that is of the essence of Jingoism, all that is colourless and without form and void. It might be a beautiful word, but it is the most debased coin in the currency of language.

I pity any woman who is married to a man called John. She would probably never be allowed to know the entrancing pleasure of a single moment's solitude.

It is only when we have learned to love forgetfulness that we have learned the art of living.

To reveal art and conceal the artist is art's aim.

The world taken 'en masse' is a monster, crammed with prejudices, packed with prepossessions, cankered with what it calls virtues, a Puritan, a prig. And the art of life is the art of defiance. To defy—that is what we ought to live for, instead of living, as we do, to acquiesce.

Some resemblance the creative work of the critic will have to the work that has stirred him to creation, but it will be such resemblance as exists, not between nature and the mirror that the painter of landscape or figure may be supposed to hold up to her, but between nature and the work of the decorative artist. Just as on the flowerless carpets of Persia tulip and rose blossom indeed, and are lovely to look on, though they are not reproduced in visible shape or line; just as the pearl and purple of the sea shell is echoed in the church of St Mark at Venice; just as the vaulted ceiling of the wondrous chapel at Ravenna is made gorgeous by the gold and green and sapphire of the peacock's tail, though the birds of Juno fly not across it; so the critic reproduces the work that he criticises in a mode that is never imitative, and part of whose charm may really consist in the rejection of resemblance, and shows us in this way not merely the meaning but also the mystery of beauty, and by transforming each art into literature solves once for all the problem of art's unity.

Diversity of opinion about a work of art shows that the work is new, complex, and vital.

Nothing is more painful to me than to come across virtue in a person in whom I have never suspected its existence. It is like finding a needle in a bundle of hay. It pricks you. If we have virtue we should warn people of it.

The critic is he who can translate into another manner or a new material his impression of beautiful things.

Hopper is one of nature's gentlemen—the worst type of gentleman I know.

If one intends to be good one must take it up as a profession. It is quite the most engrossing one in the world.

I like Wagner's music better than anybody's. It is so loud that one can talk the whole time without other people hearing what one says.

All art is at once surface and symbol.

Childhood is one long career of innocent eavesdropping, of hearing what one ought not to hear.

The highest as the lowest form of criticism is a mode of autobiography.

The only things worth saying are those that we forget, just as the only things worth doing are those that the world is surprised at.

Maturity is one long career of saying what one ought not to say. That is the art of conversation.

Virtue is generally merely a form of deficiency, just as vice is an assertion of intellect.

People teach in order to conceal their ignorance, as people smile in order to conceal their tears.

To be unnatural is often to be great. To be natural is generally to be stupid.

To lie finely is an art, to tell the truth is to act according to nature.

People who talk sense are like people who break stones in the road: they cover one with dust and splinters.

Jesus said to man: You have a wonderful personality. Develop it. Be yourself. Don't imagine that your perfection lies in accumulating or possessing external things. Your perfection is inside of you. If only you could realise that you would not want to be rich. Ordinary riches can be stolen from a man, real riches cannot. In the treasury-house of your soul there are infinitely precious things that may not be taken from you. Try to so shape your life that external things will not harm you, and try also to get rid of personal property. It involves sordid preoccupation, endless industry, continual wrong. Personal property hinders individualism at every step.

When Jesus talks about the poor He simply means personalities, just as when He talks about the rich He simply means people who have not developed their personalities.

An echo is often more beautiful than the voice it repeats.

THE SOUL OF MAN

The chief advantage that would result from the establishment of Socialism is, undoubtedly, the fact that Socialism would relieve us from that sordid necessity of living for others which, in the present condition of things, presses so hardly upon almost everybody. In fact, scarcely anyone at all escapes.

Now and then, in the course of the century, a great man of science, like Darwin; a great poet, like Keats; a fine critical spirit, like M, Renan; a supreme artist, like Flaubert, has been able to isolate himself, to keep himself out of reach of the clamorous claims of others, to stand 'under the shelter of the wall,' as Plato puts it, and so to realise the perfection of what was in him, to his own incomparable gain, and to the incomparable and lasting gain of the whole world. These, however, are exceptions. The majority of people spoil their lives by an unhealthy and exaggerated altruism—are forced, indeed, so to spoil them. They find themselves surrounded by hideous poverty, by hideous ugliness, by hideous starvation. It is inevitable that they should be strongly moved by all this. The emotions of man are stirred more quickly than man's intelligence; and, as I pointed out some time ago in an article on the function of criticism, it is much more easy to have sympathy with suffering than it is to have sympathy with thought. Accordingly, with admirable, though misdirected intentions, they very seriously and very sentimentally set themselves to the task of remedying the evils that they see. But their remedies do not cure the disease: they merely prolong it. Indeed, their remedies are part of the disease.

They try to solve the problem of poverty, for instance, by keeping the poor alive; or, in the case of a very advanced school, by amusing the poor.

But this is not a solution: it is an aggravation of the difficulty. The proper aim is to try and reconstruct society on such a basis that poverty will be impossible. And the altruistic virtues have really prevented the carrying out of this aim. Just as the worst slave-owners were those who were kind to their slaves, and so prevented the horror of the system being realised by those who suffered from it, and understood by those who contemplated it, so, in the present state of things in England, the people who do most harm are the people who try to do most good; and at last we have had the spectacle of men who have really studied the problem and know the life-educated men who live in the East End—coming forward and imploring the community to restrain its altruistic impulses of charity, benevolence, and the like. They do so on the ground that such charity degrades and demoralises. They are perfectly right. Charity creates a multitude of sins.

There is also this to be said. It is immoral to use private property in order to alleviate the horrible evils that result from the institution of private property. It is both immoral and unfair.

Under Socialism all this will, of course, be altered. There will be no people living in fetid dens and fetid rags, and bringing up unhealthy, hunger-pinched children in the midst of impossible and absolutely repulsive surroundings. The security of society will not depend, as it does now, on the state of the weather. If a frost comes we shall not have a hundred thousand men out of work, tramping about the streets in a state of disgusting misery, or whining to their neighbours for alms, or crowding round the doors of loathsome shelters to try and secure a hunch of bread and a night's unclean lodging. Each member of the society will share in the general prosperity and happiness of the society, and if a frost comes no one will practically be anything the worse.

Upon the other hand, Socialism itself will be of value simply because it will lead to Individualism.

Socialism, Communism, or whatever one chooses to call it, by converting private property into public wealth, and substituting co-operation for competition, will restore society to its proper condition of a thoroughly healthy organism, and insure the material well-being of each member of the community. It will, in fact, give Life it's proper basis and its proper environment. But for the full development of Life to its highest mode of perfection, something more is needed. What is needed is Individualism. If the

Socialism is Authoritarian; if there are Governments armed with economic power as they are now with political power; if, in a word, we are to have Industrial Tyrannies, then the last state of man will be worse than the first. At present, in consequence of the existence of private property, a great many people are enabled to develop a certain very limited amount of Individualism. They are either under no necessity to work for their living, or are enabled to choose the sphere of activity that is really congenial to them, and gives them pleasure. These are the poets, the philosophers, the men of science, the men of culture—in a word, the real men, the men who have realised themselves, and in whom all Humanity gains a partial realisation. Upon the other hand, there are a great many people who, having no private property of their own, and being always on the brink of sheer starvation, are compelled to do the work of beasts of burden, to do work that is quite uncongenial to them, and to which they are forced by the peremptory, unreasonable, degrading Tyranny of want. These are the poor, and amongst them there is no grace of manner, or charm of speech, or civilisation, or culture, or refinement in pleasures, or joy of life. From their collective force Humanity gains much in material prosperity. But it is only the material result that it gains, and the man who is poor is in himself absolutely of no importance. He is merely the infinitesimal atom of a force that, so far from regarding him, crushes him: indeed, prefers him crushed, as in that case he is far more obedient.

Of course, it might be said that the Individualism generated under conditions of private property is not always, or even as a rule, of a fine or wonderful type, and that the poor, if they have not culture and charm, have still many virtues. Both these statements would be quite true. The possession of private property is very often extremely demoralising, and that is, of course, one of the reasons why Socialism wants to get rid of the institution. In fact, property is really a nuisance. Some years ago people went about the country saying that property has duties. They said it so often and so tediously that, at last, the Church has begun to say it. One hears it now from every pulpit. It is perfectly true. Property not merely has duties, but has so many duties that its possession to any large extent is a bore. It involves endless claims upon one, endless attention to business, endless bother. If property had simply pleasures, we could stand it; but its duties make it unbearable. In the interest of the rich we must get rid of it. The virtues of the poor may be readily admitted, and are much to be regretted. We are often told that the poor are grateful for charity. Some of them are, no doubt, but the best amongst the poor are never grateful. They are ungrateful, discontented, disobedient, and rebellious. They are quite right to be so. Charity they feel to be a ridiculously inadequate mode of partial restitution, or a sentimental dole, usually accompanied by some impertinent attempt on the part of the sentimentalist to tyrannise over their private lives. Why should they be grateful for the crumbs that fall from the rich man's table? They should be seated at the board, and are beginning to know it. As for being discontented, a man who would not be discontented with such surroundings and such a low mode of life would be a perfect brute. Disobedience, in the eyes of anyone who has read history, is man's original virtue. It is through disobedience that progress has been made, through disobedience and through rebellion. Sometimes the poor are praised for being thrifty. But to recommend thrift to the poor is both grotesque and insulting. It is like advising a man who is starving to eat less. For a town or country labourer to practise thrift would be absolutely immoral. Man should not be ready to show that he can live like a badly-fed animal. He should decline to live like that, and should either steal or go on the rates, which is considered by many to be a form of stealing. As for begging, it is safer to beg than to take, but it is finer to take than to beg. No: a poor man who is ungrateful, unthrifty, discontented, and rebellious, is probably a real personality, and has much in him. He is at any rate a healthy protest. As for the virtuous poor, one can pity them, of course, but one cannot possibly admire them; They have made private terms with the enemy, and sold their birthright for very bad pottage. They must also be extraordinarily stupid. I can quite understand a man accepting laws that protect private property, and admit of its accumulation, as long as he himself is able under those conditions to realise some form of beautiful and intellectual life. But it is almost incredible to me how a man whose life is marred and made hideous by such laws can possibly acquiesce in their continuance.

However, the explanation is not really difficult to find. It is simply this. Misery and poverty are so absolutely degrading, and exercise such a paralysing effect over the nature of men, that no class is ever really conscious of its own suffering. They have to be told of it by other people, and they often entirely disbelieve them. What is said by great employers of labour against agitators is unquestionably true. Agitators are a set of interfering, meddling people, who come down to some perfectly contented class of the community, and sow the seeds of discontent amongst them. That is the reason why agitators are so absolutely necessary. Without them, in our incomplete state, there would be no advance towards civilisation. Slavery was put down in America, not in consequence of any action on the part of the slaves, or even any express desire on their part that they should be free. It was put down entirely through the grossly illegal conduct of certain agitators in Boston and elsewhere, who were not slaves themselves, nor owners of slaves, nor had anything to do with the question really. It was, undoubtedly, the Abolitionists who set the torch alight, who began the whole thing. And it is curious to note that from the slaves themselves they received, not merely very little assistance, but hardly any sympathy even; and when at the close of the war the slaves found themselves free, found themselves indeed so absolutely free that they were free to starve, many of them bitterly regretted the new state of things. To the thinker, the most tragic fact in the whole of the French Revolution is not that Marie Antoinette was killed for being a queen, but that the starved peasant of the Vendée voluntarily went out to die for the hideous cause of feudalism.

It is clear, then, that no Authoritarian Socialism will do. For while under the present system a very large number of people can lead lives of a certain amount of freedom and expression and happiness, under an industrial-barrack system, or a system of economic tyranny, nobody would be able to have any such freedom at all. It is to be regretted that a portion of our community should be practically in slavery, but to propose to solve the problem by enslaving the entire community is childish. Every man must be left quite free to choose his own work. No form of compulsion must be exercised over him. If there is, his work will not be good for him, will not be good in itself, and will not be good for others. And by work I simply mean activity of any kind.

I hardly think that any Socialist, nowadays, would seriously propose that an inspector should call every morning at each house to see that each citizen rose up and did manual labour for eight hours. Humanity has got beyond that stage, and reserves such a form of life for the people whom, in a very arbitrary manner, it chooses to call criminals. But I confess that many of the socialistic views that I have come across seem to me to be tainted with ideas of authority, if not of actual compulsion. Of course, authority and compulsion are out of the question. All association must be quite voluntary. It is only in voluntary associations that man is fine.

But it may be asked how Individualism, which is now more or less dependent on the existence of private property for its development, will benefit by the abolition of such private property. The answer is very simple. It is true that, under existing conditions, a few men who have had private means of their own, such as Byron, Shelley, Browning, Victor Hugo, Baudelaire, and others, have been able to realise their personality more or less completely. Not one of these men ever did a single day's work for hire. They were relieved from poverty. They had an immense advantage. The question is whether it would be for the good of Individualism that such an advantage should be taken away. Let us suppose that it is taken away. What happens then to Individualism? How will it benefit?

It will benefit in this way, under the new conditions Individualism will be far freer, far finer, and far more intensified than it is now. I am not talking of the great imaginatively-realised Individualism of such poets as I have mentioned, but of the great actual Individualism latent and potential in mankind generally. For the recognition of private property has really harmed Individualism, and obscured it, by confusing a man with what he possesses. It has led Individualism entirely astray. It has made gain not growth its aim. So that man thought that the important thing was to have, and did not know that the important thing is to be. The true perfection of man lies, not in what man has, but in what man is. Private property has crushed true Individualism, and set up an Individualism that is false. It has debarred one part of the community from being individual by starving them. It has debarred the other part of the community from being individual by putting them on the wrong road, and encumbering them. Indeed, so completely has man's personality been absorbed by his possessions that the English law has always treated offences against a man's property with far more severity than offences

78

against his person, and property is still the test of complete citizenship. The industry necessary for the making of money is also very demoralising. In a community like ours, where property confers immense distinction, social position, honour, respect, titles, and other pleasant things of the kind, man, being naturally ambitious, makes it his aim to accumulate this property, and goes on wearily and tediously accumulating it long after he has got far more than he wants, or can use, or enjoy, or perhaps even know of. Man will kill himself by overwork in order to secure property, and really, considering the enormous advantages that property brings, one is hardly surprised. One's regret is that society should be constructed on such a basis that man has been forced into a groove in which he cannot freely develop what is wonderful, and fascinating, and delightful in him—in which, in fact, he misses the true pleasure and joy of living. He is also, under existing conditions, very insecure. An enormously wealthy merchant may be—often is—at every moment of his life at the mercy of things that are not under his control. If the wind blows an extra point or so, or the weather suddenly changes, or some trivial thing happens, his ship may go down, his speculations may go wrong, and he finds himself a poor man, with his social position quite gone. Now, nothing should be able to harm a man except himself. Nothing should be able to rob a man at all. What a man really has, is what is in him. What is outside of him should be a matter of no importance.

With the abolition of private property, then, we shall have true, beautiful, healthy Individualism. Nobody will waste his life in accumulating things, and the symbols for things. One will live. To live is the rarest thing in the world. Most people exist, that is all.

It is a question whether we have ever seen the full expression of a personality, except on the imaginative plane of art. In action, we never have. Cæsar, says Mommsen, was the complete and perfect man. But how tragically insecure was Cæsar! Wherever there is a man who exercises authority, there is a man who resists authority. Cæsar was very perfect, but his perfection travelled by too dangerous a road. Marcus Aurelius was the perfect man, says Renan. Yes; the great emperor was a perfect man. But how intolerable were the endless claims upon him! He staggered under the burden of the empire.

He was conscious how inadequate one man was to bear the weight of that Titan and too vast orb. What I mean by a perfect man is one who develops under perfect conditions; one who is not wounded, or worried or maimed, or in danger. Most personalities have been obliged to be rebels. Half their strength has been wasted in friction. Byron's personality, for instance, was terribly wasted in its battle with the stupidity, and hypocrisy, and Philistinism of the English. Such battles do not always intensify strength: they often exaggerate weakness. Byron was never able to give us what he might have given us. Shelley escaped better. Like Byron, he got out of England as soon as possible. But he was not so well known. If the English had had any idea of what a great poet he really was, they would have fallen on him with tooth and nail, and made his life as unbearable to him as they possibly could. But he was not a remarkable figure in society, and consequently he escaped, to a certain degree. Still, even in Shelley the note of rebellion is sometimes too strong. The note of the perfect personality is not rebellion, but peace.

It will be a marvellous thing—the true personality of man—when we see it. It will grow naturally and simply, flowerlike, or as a tree grows. It will not be at discord. It will never argue or dispute. It will not prove things. It will know everything. And yet it will not busy itself about knowledge. It will have wisdom. Its value will not be measured by material things. It will have nothing. And yet it will have everything, and whatever one takes from it, it will still have, so rich will it he. It will not be always meddling with others, or asking them to be like itself. It will love them because they will be different. And yet while it will not meddle with others, it will help all, as a beautiful thing helps us, by being what it is. The personality of man will be very wonderful. It will be as wonderful as the personality of a child.

In its development it will be assisted by Christianity, if men desire that; but if men do not desire that, it will develop none the less surely. For it will not worry itself about the past, nor care whether things happened or did not happen. Nor will it admit any laws but its own laws; nor any authority but its own authority. Yet it will love those who sought to intensity it, and speak often of them. And of these Christ was one.

'Know thyself' was written over the portal of the antique world. Over the portal of the new world, 'Be thyself' shall be written. And the message of Christ to man was simply 'Be thyself.' That is the secret of Christ.

When Jesus talks about the poor he simply means personalities, just as when he talks about the rich he simply means people who have not developed their personalities. Jesus moved in a community that allowed the accumulation of private property just as ours does, and the gospel that he preached was not that in such a community it is an advantage for a man to live on scanty, unwholesome food, to wear ragged, unwholesome clothes, to sleep in horrid, unwholesome dwellings, and a disadvantage for a man to live under healthy, pleasant, and decent conditions. Such a view would have been wrong there and then, and would, of course, be still more wrong now and in England; for as man moves northward the material necessities of life become of more vital importance, and our society is infinitely more complex, and displays far greater extremes of luxury and pauperism than any society of the antique world. What Jesus meant, was this. He said to man, 'You have a wonderful personality. Develop it. Be yourself. Don't imagine that your perfection lies in accumulating or possessing external things. Your perfection is inside of you. If only you could realise that, you would not want to be rich. Ordinary riches can be stolen from a man. Real riches cannot. In the treasury-house of your soul, there are infinitely precious things, that may not be taken from you. And so, try to so shape your life that external things will not harm you. And try also to get rid of personal property. It involves sordid preoccupation, endless industry, continual wrong. Personal property hinders Individualism at every step. It is to be noted that Jesus never says that impoverished people are necessarily good, or wealthy people necessarily bad. That would not have been true. Wealthy people are, as a class, better than impoverished people, more moral, more intellectual, more well-behaved. There is only one class in the community that thinks more about money than the rich, and that is the poor. The poor can think of nothing else. That is the misery of being poor. What Jesus does say is that man reaches his perfection, not through what he has, not even through what he does, but entirely through what he is. And so the wealthy young man who comes to Jesus is represented as a thoroughly good citizen, who has broken none of the laws of his state, none of the commandments of his religion. He is quite respectable, in the ordinary sense of that extraordinary word. Jesus says to him, 'You should give up private property. It hinders you from realising your perfection. It is a drag upon you. It is a burden. Your personality does not need it. It is within you, and not outside of you, that you will find what you really are, and what you really want.' To his own friends he says the same thing. He tells them to be themselves, and not to be always worrying about other things. What do other things matter? Man is complete in himself. When they go into the world, the world will disagree with them. That is inevitable. The world hates Individualism. But that is not to trouble them. They are to be calm and self-centred. If a man takes their cloak, they are to give him their coat, just to show that material things are of no importance. If people abuse them, they are not to answer back. What does it signify? The things people say of a man do not alter a man. He is what he is. Public opinion is of no value whatsoever. Even if people employ actual violence, they are not to be violent in turn. That would be to fall to the same low level. After all, even in prison, a man can be quite free. His soul can be free. His personality can be untroubled. He can be at peace. And, above all things, they are not to interfere with other people or judge them in any way. Personality is a very mysterious thing. A man cannot always be estimated by what he does. He may keep the law, and yet be worthless. He may break the law, and yet be fine. He may be bad, without ever doing anything bad. He may commit a sin against society, and yet realise through that sin his true perfection.

There was a woman who was taken in adultery. We are not told the history of her love, but that love must have been very great; for Jesus said that her sins were forgiven her, not because she repented, but because her love was so intense and wonderful. Later on, a short time before his death, as he sat at a feast, the woman came in and poured costly perfumes on his hair. His friends tried to interfere with her, and said that it was an extravagance, and that the money that the perfume cost should have been expended on charitable relief of people in want, or something of that kind. Jesus did not accept that view. He pointed out that the material needs of Man were great and very permanent, but that the spiritual needs of Man were greater still, and that in one divine moment, and by selecting its own mode of expression, a personality might make itself perfect. The world worships the woman, even now, as a saint.

Yes; there are suggestive things in Individualism. Socialism annihilates family life, for instance. With the abolition of private property, marriage in its present form must disappear. This is part of the programme. Individualism accepts this and makes it fine. It converts the abolition of legal restraint into a form of freedom that will help the full development of personality, and make the love of man and woman more wonderful, more beautiful, and more ennobling. Jesus knew this. He rejected the claims of family life, although they existed in his day and community in a very marked form. 'Who is my mother? Who are my brothers?' he said, when he was told that they wished to speak to him. When one of his followers asked leave to go and bury his father, 'Let the dead bury the dead,' was his terrible answer. He would allow no claim whatsoever to be made on personality.

And so he who would lead a Christ-like like life is he who is perfectly and absolutely himself. He may be a great poet, or a great man of science; or a young student at a University, or one who watches sheep upon a moor; or a maker of dramas, like Shakespeare, or a thinker about God, like Spinoza; or a child who plays in a garden, or a fisherman who throws his net into the sea. It does not matter what he is, as long as he realises the perfection of the soul that is within him. All imitation in morals and in life is wrong. Through the streets of Jerusalem at the present day crawls one who is mad and carries a wooden cross on his shoulders. He is a symbol of the lives that are marred by imitation. Father Damien was Christ-like when he went out to live with the lepers, because in such service he realised fully what was best in him. But he was not more Christ-like than Wagner when he realised his soul in music; or than Shelley, when he realised his soul in song. There is no one type for man. There are as many perfections as there are imperfect men. And while to the claims of charity a man may yield and yet be free, to the claims of conformity no man may yield and remain free at all.

Individualism, then, is what through Socialism we are to attain to. As a natural result the State must give up all idea of government. It must give it up because, as a wise man once said many centuries before Christ, there is such a thing as leaving mankind alone; there is no such thing as governing mankind. All modes of government are failures. Despotism is unjust to everybody, including the despot, who was probably made for better things. Oligarchies are unjust to the many, and ochlocracies are unjust to the few. High hopes were once formed of democracy; but democracy means simply the bludgeoning of the people by the people for the people. It has been found out. I must say that it was high time, for all authority is quite degrading. It degrades those who exercise it, and degrades those over whom it is exercised. When it is violently, grossly, and cruelly used, it produces a good effect, by creating, or at any rate bringing out, the spirit of revolt and Individualism that is to kill it. When it is used with a certain amount of kindness, and accompanied by prizes and rewards, it is dreadfully demoralising. People, in that case, are less conscious of the horrible pressure that is being put on them, and so go through their lives in a sort of coarse comfort, like petted animals, without ever realising that they are probably thinking other people's thoughts, living by other people's standards, wearing practically what one may call other people's second-hand clothes, and never being themselves for a single moment. 'He who would be free,' says a fine thinker, 'must not conform.' And authority, by bribing people to conform, produces a very gross kind of over-fed barbarism amongst us.

With authority, punishment will pass away. This will be a great gain—a gain, in fact, of incalculable value. As one reads history, not in the expurgated editions written for schoolboys and passmen, but in the original authorities of each time, one is absolutely sickened, not by the crimes that the wicked have committed, but by the punishments that the good have inflicted; and a community is infinitely more brutalised by the habitual employment of punishment, than it is by the occurrence of crime. It obviously follows that the more punishment is inflicted the more crime is produced, and most modern legislation has clearly recognised this, and has made it its task to diminish punishment as far as it thinks it can. Wherever it has really diminished it, the results have always been extremely good. The less punishment, the less crime. When there is no punishment at all, crime will either cease to exist, or, if it occurs, will be treated by physicians as a very distressing form of dementia, to be cured by care and kindness. For what are called criminals nowadays are not criminals at all. Starvation, and not sin, is the parent of modern crime. That indeed is the reason why our criminals are, as a class, so absolutely uninteresting from any psychological point of view. They are not marvellous Macbeths and terrible Vautrins. They are merely what ordinary, respectable, commonplace people would be if they had not got enough to eat. When private property is abolished there will be no necessity for crime, no demand for it; it will cease to exist. Of course, all crimes are not crimes against property, though such are the crimes that the English law, valuing what a man has more than what a man is, punishes with the harshest and most horrible severity, if we except the crime of murder, and regard death as worse than penal servitude, a point on which our criminals, I believe, disagree. But though a crime may not be against property, it may spring from the misery and rage and depression produced by our wrong system of property-holding, and so, when that system is abolished, will disappear. When each member of the community has sufficient for his wants, and is not interfered with by his neighbour, it will not be an object of any interest to him to interfere with anyone else. Jealousy, which is an extraordinary source of crime in modern life, is an emotion closely bound up with our conceptions of property, and under Socialism and Individualism will die out. It is remarkable that in communistic tribes jealousy is entirely unknown.

Now as the State is not to govern, it may be asked what the State is to do. The State is to be a voluntary association that will organise labour, and be the manufacturer and distributor of necessary commodities. The State is to make what is useful. The individual is to make what is beautiful. And as I have mentioned the word labour. I cannot help saying that a great deal of nonsense is being written and talked nowadays about the dignity of manual labour. There is nothing necessarily dignified about manual labour at all, and most of it is absolutely degrading. It is mentally and morally injurious to man to do anything in which he does not find pleasure, and many forms of labour are quite pleasureless activities, and should be regarded as such. To sweep a slushy crossing for eight hours on a day when the east wind is blowing is a disgusting occupation. To sweep it with mental, moral, or physical dignity seems to me to be impossible. To sweep it with joy would be appalling. Man is made for something better than disturbing dirt. All work of that kind should be done by a machine.

And I have no doubt that it will be so. Up to the present, man has been, to a certain extent, the slave of machinery, and there is something tragic in the fact that as soon as man had invented a machine to do his work he began to starve. This, however, is, of course, the result of our property system and our system of competition. One man owns a machine which does the work of five hundred men. Five hundred men are, in consequence, thrown out of employment, and, having no work to do, become hungry and take to thieving. The one man secures the produce of the machine and keeps it, and has five hundred times as much as he should have, and probably, which is of much more importance, a great deal more than he really wants. Were that machine the property of all, everyone would benefit by it. It would be an immense advantage to the community. All unintellectual labour, all monotonous, dull labour, all labour that deals with dreadful things, and involves unpleasant conditions, must be done by machinery. Machinery must work for us in coal mines, and do all sanitary services, and be the stoker of steamers, and clean the streets, and run messages on wet days, and do anything that is tedious or distressing. At present machinery competes against man. Under proper conditions machinery will serve man. There is no doubt at all that this is the future of machinery, and just as trees grow while the country gentleman is asleep, so while Humanity will be amusing itself, or enjoying cultivated leisure—which, and not labour, is the aim of man—or making beautiful things, or reading beautiful things, or simply contemplating the world with admiration and delight, machinery will be doing all the necessary and unpleasant work. The fact is, that civilisation requires slaves. The Greeks were quite right there. Unless there are slaves to do the ugly, horrible, uninteresting work, culture and contemplation become almost impossible. Human slavery is wrong, insecure, and demoralising. On mechanical slavery, on the slavery of the machine, the future of the world depends. And when scientific men are no longer called upon to go down to a depressing East End and distribute bad cocoa and worse blankets to starving people, they will have delightful leisure in which to devise wonderful and marvellous things for their own joy and the joy of everyone else. There will be great storages of force for every city, and for every house if required, and this force man will convert into heat, light, or motion, according to his needs. Is this Utopian? A map of the world that does not include Utopia is not worth even glancing at, for it leaves out the one country at which Humanity is always landing. And when Humanity lands there, it looks out, and, seeing a better country, sets sail. Progress is the realisation of Utopias.

Now, I have said that the community by means of organisation of machinery will supply the useful things, and that the beautiful things will be made by the individual. This is not merely necessary, but it is the only possible way by which we can get either the one or the other. An individual who has to make things for the use of others, and with reference to their wants and their wishes, does not work with interest, and consequently cannot put into his work what is best in him. Upon the other hand, whenever a community or a powerful section of a community, or a government of any kind, attempts to dictate to the artist what he is to do, Art either entirely vanishes, or becomes stereotyped, or degenerates into a low and ignoble form of craft. A work of art is the unique result of a unique temperament. Its beauty comes from the fact that the author is what he is. It has nothing to do with the fact that other people want what they want. Indeed, the moment that an artist takes notice of what other people want, and tries to supply the demand, he ceases to be an artist, and becomes a dull or an amusing craftsman, an honest or a dishonest tradesman. He has no further claim to be considered as an artist. Art is the most intense mode of Individualism that the world has known. I am inclined to say that it is the only real mode of Individualism that the world has known. Crime, which, under certain conditions, may seem to have created Individualism, must take cognisance of other people and interfere with them. It belongs to the sphere of action. But alone, without any reference to his neighbours, without any interference, the artist can fashion a beautiful thing; and if he does not do it solely for his own pleasure, he is not an artist at all.

And it is to be noted that it is the fact that Art is this intense form of Individualism that makes the public try to exercise over it an authority that is as immoral as it is ridiculous, and as corrupting as it is contemptible. It is not quite their fault. The public has always, and in every age, been badly brought up. They are continually asking Art to be popular, to please their want of taste, to flatter their absurd vanity, to tell them what they have been told before, to show them what they ought to be tired of seeing, to amuse them when they feel heavy after eating too much, and to distract their thoughts when they are wearied of their own stupidity. Now Art should never try to be popular. The public should try to make itself artistic. There is a very wide difference. If a man of science were told that the results of his experiments, and the conclusions that he arrived at, should be of such a character that they would not upset the received popular notions on the subject, or disturb popular prejudice, or hurt the sensibilities of people who knew nothing about science; if a philosopher were told that he had a perfect right to speculate in the highest spheres of thought, provided that he arrived at the same conclusions as were held by those who had never thought in any sphere at all—well, nowadays the man of science and the philosopher would be considerably amused. Yet it is really a very few years since both philosophy and science were subjected to brutal popular control, to authority in fact—the authority of either the general ignorance of the community, or the terror and greed for power of an ecclesiastical or governmental class. Of course, we have to a very great extent got rid of any attempt on the part of the community, or the Church, or the Government, to interfere with the individualism of speculative thought, but the attempt to interfere with the individualism of imaginative art still lingers. In fact, it does more than linger; it is aggressive, offensive, and brutalising.

In England, the arts that have escaped best are the arts in which the public take no interest. Poetry is an instance of what I mean. We have been able to have fine poetry in England because the public do not read it, and consequently do not influence it. The public like to insult poets because they are individual, but once they have insulted them, they leave them alone. In the case of the novel and the drama, arts in which the public do take an interest, the result of the exercise of popular authority has been absolutely ridiculous. No country produces such badly-written fiction, such tedious, common work in the novel form, such silly, vulgar plays as England. It must necessarily be so. The popular standard is of such a character that no artist can get to it. It is at once too easy and too difficult to be a popular novelist. It is too easy, because the requirements of the public as far as plot, style, psychology, treatment of life, and treatment of literature are concerned are within the reach of the very meanest capacity and the most uncultivated mind. It is too difficult, because to meet such requirements the artist would have to do violence to his temperament, would have to write not for the artistic joy of writing, but for the amusement of half-educated people, and so would have to suppress his individualism, forget his culture, annihilate his style, and surrender everything that is valuable in him. In the case of the drama, things are a little better: the theatre-going public like the obvious, it is true, but they do not like the tedious; and burlesque and farcical comedy, the two most popular forms, are distinct forms of art. Delightful work may be produced under burlesque and farcical conditions, and in work of this kind the artist in England is allowed very great freedom. It is when one comes to the higher forms of the drama that the result of popular control is seen. The one thing that the public dislike is novelty. Any attempt to extend the subject-matter of art is extremely distasteful to the public; and yet the vitality and progress of art depend in a large measure on the continual extension of subject-matter. The public dislike novelty because they are afraid of it. It represents to them a mode of Individualism, an assertion on the part of the artist that he selects his own subject, and treats it as he chooses. The public are quite right in their attitude. Art is Individualism, and Individualism is a disturbing and disintegrating force. Therein lies its immense value. For what it seeks to disturb is monotony of type, slavery of custom, tyranny of habit, and the reduction of man to the level of a machine. In Art, the public accept what has been, because they cannot alter it, not because they appreciate it. They swallow their classics whole, and never taste them. They endure them as the inevitable, and as they cannot mar them, they mouth about them. Strangely enough, or not strangely, according to one's own views, this acceptance of the classics does a great deal of harm. The uncritical admiration of the Bible and Shakespeare in England is an instance of what I mean. With regard to the Bible, considerations of ecclesiastical authority enter into the matter, so that I need not dwell upon the point.

But in the case of Shakespeare it is quite obvious that the public really see neither the beauties nor the defects of his plays. If they saw the beauties, they would not object to the development of the drama; and if they saw the defects, they would not object to the development of the drama either. The fact is, the public make use of the classics of a country as a means of checking the progress of Art. They degrade the classics into authorities. They use them as bludgeons for preventing the free expression of Beauty in new forms. They are always asking a writer why he does not write like somebody else, or a painter why he does not paint like somebody else, quite oblivious of the fact that if either of them did anything of the kind he would cease to be an artist. A fresh mode of Beauty is absolutely distasteful to them, and whenever it appears they get so angry and bewildered, that they always use two stupid expressions—one is that the work of art is grossly unintelligible; the other, that the work of art is grossly immoral. What they mean by these words seems to me to be this. When they say a work is grossly unintelligible, they mean that the artist has said or made a beautiful thing that is new; when they describe a work as grossly immoral, they mean that the artist has said or made a beautiful thing that is true. The former expression has reference to style; the latter to subject-matter. But they probably use the words very vaguely, as an ordinary mob will use ready-made paving-stones. There is not a single real poet or prose-writer of this century, for instance, on whom the British public have not solemnly conferred diplomas of immorality, and these diplomas practically take the place, with us, of what in France, is the formal recognition of an Academy of Letters, and fortunately make the establishment of such an institution quite unnecessary in England. Of course, the public are very reckless in their use of the word. That they should have called Wordsworth an immoral poet, was only to be expected. Wordsworth was a poet. But that they should have called Charles Kingsley an immoral novelist is extraordinary. Kingsley's prose was not of a very fine quality. Still, there is the word, and they use it as best they can. An artist is, of course, not disturbed by it. The true artist is a man who believes absolutely in himself, because he is absolutely himself. But I can fancy that if an artist produced a work of art in England that immediately on its appearance was recognised by the public, through their medium, which is the public press, as a work that was quite intelligible and highly moral, he would begin to seriously question whether in its creation he had really been himself at all, and consequently whether the work was not quite unworthy of him, and either of a thoroughly second-rate order, or of no artistic value whatsoever.

Perhaps, however, I have wronged the public in limiting them to such words as 'immoral,' 'unintelligible,' 'exotic,' and 'unhealthy.' There is one other word that they use. That word is 'morbid.' They do not use it often. The meaning of the word is so simple that they are afraid of using it. Still, they use it sometimes, and, now and then, one comes across it in popular newspapers. It is, of course, a ridiculous word to apply to a work of art. For what is morbidity but a mood of emotion or a mode of thought that one cannot express? The public are all morbid, because the public can never find expression for anything. The artist is never morbid. He expresses everything. He stands outside his subject, and through its medium produces incomparable and artistic effects. To call an artist morbid because he deals with morbidity as his subject-matter is as silly as if one called Shakespeare mad because he wrote 'King Lear.'

On the whole, an artist in England gains something by being attacked. His individuality is intensified. He becomes more completely himself. Of course, the attacks are very gross, very impertinent, and very contemptible. But then no artist expects grace from the vulgar mind, or style from the suburban intellect. Vulgarity and stupidity are two very vivid facts in modern life. One regrets them, naturally. But there they are. They are subjects for study, like everything else. And it is only fair to state, with regard to modern journalists, that they always apologise to one in private for what they have written against one in public.

Within the last few years two other adjectives, it may be mentioned, have been added to the very limited vocabulary of art-abuse that is at the disposal of the public. One is the word 'unhealthy,' the other is the word 'exotic.' The latter merely expresses the rage of the momentary mushroom against the immortal, entrancing, and exquisitely lovely orchid. It is a tribute, but a tribute of no importance. The word 'unhealthy,' however, admits of analysis. It is a rather interesting word. In fact, it is so interesting that the people who use it do not know what it means.

What does it mean? What is a healthy, or an unhealthy work of art? All terms that one applies to a work of art, provided that one applies them rationally, have reference to either its style or its subject, or to both together. From the point of view of style, a healthy work of art is one whose style recognises the beauty of the material it employs, be that material one of words or of bronze, of colour or of ivory, and uses that beauty as a factor in producing the æsthetic effect. From the point of view of subject, a healthy work of art is one the choice of whose subject is conditioned by the temperament of the artist, and comes directly out of it. In fine, a healthy work of art is one that has both perfection and personality. Of course, form and substance cannot be separated in a work of art; they are always one. But for purposes of analysis, and setting the wholeness of æsthetic impression aside for a moment, we can intellectually so separate them. An unhealthy work of art, on the other hand, is a work whose style is obvious, old-fashioned, and common, and whose subject is deliberately chosen, not because the artist has any pleasure in it, but because he thinks that the public will pay him for it. In fact, the popular novel that the public calls healthy is always a thoroughly unhealthy production; and what the public call an unhealthy novel is always a beautiful and healthy work of art.

I need hardly say that I am not, for a single moment, complaining that the public and the public press misuse these words. I do not see how, with their lack of comprehension of what Art is, they could possibly use them in the proper sense. I am merely pointing out the misuse; and as for the origin of the misuse and the meaning that lies behind it all, the explanation is very simple. It comes from the barbarous conception of authority. It comes from the natural inability of a community corrupted by authority to understand or appreciate Individualism. In a word, it comes from that monstrous and ignorant thing that is called Public Opinion, which, bad and well-meaning as it is when it tries to control action, is infamous and of evil meaning when it tries to control Thought or Art.

Indeed, there is much more to be said in favour of the physical force of the public than there is in favour of the public's opinion. The former may be fine. The latter must be foolish. It is often said that force is no argument. That, however, entirely depends on what one wants to prove. Many of the most important problems of the last few centuries, such as the continuance of personal government in England, or of feudalism in France, have been solved entirely by means of physical force. The very violence of a revolution may make the public grand and splendid for a moment. It was a fatal day when the public discovered that the pen is mightier than the paving-stone, and can be made as offensive as the brickbat. They at once sought for the journalist, found him, developed him, and made him their industrious and well-paid servant. It is greatly to be regretted, for both their sakes. Behind the barricade there may be much that is noble and heroic. But what is there behind the leading-article but prejudice, stupidity, cant, and twaddle? And when these four are joined together they make a terrible force, and constitute the new authority.

In old days men had the rack. Now they have the press. That is an improvement certainly. But still it is very bad, and wrong, and demoralising. Somebody—was it Burke?—called journalism the fourth estate. That was true at the time, no doubt. But at the present moment it really is the only estate. It has eaten up the other three. The Lords Temporal say nothing, the Lords Spiritual have nothing to say, and the House of Commons has nothing to say and says it. We are dominated by Journalism. In America the President reigns for four years, and Journalism governs for ever and ever. Fortunately in America Journalism has carried its authority to the grossest and most brutal extreme. As a natural consequence it has begun to create a spirit of revolt. People are amused by it, or disgusted by it, according to their temperaments. But it is no longer the real force it was. It is not seriously treated. In England, Journalism, not, except in a few well-known instances, having been carried to such excesses of brutality, is still a great factor, a really remarkable power. The tyranny that it proposes to exercise over people's private lives seems to me to be quite extraordinary. The fact is, that the public have an insatiable curiosity to know everything, except what is worth knowing. Journalism, conscious of this, and having tradesman-like habits, supplies their demands. In centuries before ours the public nailed the ears of journalists to the pump. That was quite hideous. In this century journalists have nailed their own ears to the keyhole. That is much worse. And what aggravates the mischief is that the journalists who are most to blame are not the amusing journalists who write for what are called Society papers. The harm is done by the serious, thoughtful, earnest journalists, who solemnly, as they are doing at present, will drag before the eyes of the public some incident in the private life of a great statesman, of a man who is a leader of political thought as he is a creator of political force, and invite the public to discuss the incident, to exercise authority in the matter, to give their views, and not merely to give their views, but to carry them into action, to dictate to the man upon all other points, to dictate to his party, to dictate to his country; in fact, to make themselves ridiculous, offensive, and harmful. The private lives of men and women should not be told to the public. The public have nothing to do with them at all. In Prance they manage these things better. There they do not allow the details of the trials that take place in the divorce courts to be published for the amusement or criticism of the public. All that the public are allowed to know is that the divorce has taken place and was granted on petition of one or other or both of the married parties concerned. In France, in fact, they limit the journalist, and allow the artist almost perfect freedom. Here we allow absolute freedom to the journalist, and entirely limit the artist. English public opinion, that is to say, tries to constrain and impede and warp the man who makes things that are beautiful in effect, and compels the journalist to retail things that are ugly, or disgusting, or revolting in fact, so that we have the most serious journalists in the world, and the most indecent newspapers. It is no exaggeration to talk of compulsion. There are possibly some journalists who take a real pleasure in publishing horrible things, or who, being poor, look to scandals as forming a sort of permanent basis for an income. But there are other journalists, I feel certain, men of education and cultivation, who really dislike publishing these things, who know that it is wrong to do so, and only do it because the unhealthy conditions under which their occupation is carried on oblige them to supply the public with what the public wants, and to compete with other journalists in making that supply as full and satisfying to the gross popular appetite as possible. It is a very degrading position for any body of educated men to be placed in, and I have no doubt that most of them feel it acutely.

However, let us leave what is really a very sordid side of the subject, and return to the question of popular control in the matter of Art, by which I mean Public Opinion dictating to the artist the form which he is to use, the mode in which he is to use it, and the materials with which he is to work. I have pointed out that the arts which have escaped best in England are the arts in which the public have not been interested. They are, however, interested in the drama, and as a certain advance has been made in the drama within the last ten or fifteen years, it is important to point out that this advance is entirely due to a few individual artists refusing to accept the popular want of taste as their standard, and refusing to regard Art as a mere matter of demand and supply. With his marvellous and vivid personality, with a style that has really a true colour-element in it, with his extraordinary power, not over mere mimicry but over imaginative and intellectual creation, Mr Irving, had his sole object been to give the public what they wanted, could have produced the commonest plays in the commonest manner, and made as much success and money as a man could possibly desire. But his object was not that. His object was to realise his own perfection as an artist, under certain conditions, and in certain forms of Art. At first he appealed to the few; now he has educated the many. He has created in the public both taste and temperament. The public appreciate his artistic success immensely. I often wonder, however, whether the public understand that that success is entirely due to the fact that he did not accept their standard, but realised his own. With their standard the Lyceum would have been a sort of second-rate booth, as some of the popular theatres in London are at present. Whether they understand it or not the fact however remains, that taste and temperament have, to a certain extent, been created in the public, and that the public is capable of developing these qualities. The problem then is, why do not the public become more civilised? They have the capacity. What stops them?

The thing that stops them, it must be said again, is their desire to exercise authority over the artist and over works of art. To certain theatres, such as the Lyceum and the Haymarket, the public seem to come in a proper mood. In both of these theatres there have been individual artists, who have succeeded in creating in their audiences—and every theatre in London has its own audience—the temperament to which Art appeals. And what is that temperament? It is the temperament of receptivity. That is all.

If a man approaches a work of art with any desire to exercise authority over it and the artist, he approaches it in such a spirit that he cannot receive any artistic impression from it at all. The work of art is to dominate the

95

spectator: the spectator is not to dominate the work of art. The spectator is to be receptive. He is to be the violin on which the master is to play. And the more completely he can suppress his own silly views, his own foolish prejudices, his own absurd ideas of what Art should be, or should not be, the more likely he is to understand and appreciate the work of art in question. This is, of course, quite obvious in the case of the vulgar theatre-going public of English men and women. But it is equally true of what are called educated people. For an educated person's ideas of Art are drawn naturally from what Art has been, whereas the new work of art is beautiful by being what Art has never been; and to measure it by the standard of the past is to measure it by a standard on the rejection of which its real perfection depends. A temperament capable of receiving, through an imaginative medium, and under imaginative conditions, new and beautiful impressions, is the only temperament that can appreciate a work of art. And true as this is in the case of the appreciation of sculpture and painting, it is still more true of the appreciation of such arts as the drama. For a picture and a statue are not at war with Time. They take no count of its succession. In one moment their unity may be apprehended. In the case of literature it is different. Time must be traversed before the unity of effect is realised. And so, in the drama, there may occur in the first act of the play something whose real artistic value may not be evident to the spectator till the third or fourth act is reached. Is the silly fellow to get angry and call out, and disturb the play, and annoy the artists? No, the honest man is to sit quietly, and know the delightful emotions of wonder, curiosity, and suspense. He is not to go to the play to lose a vulgar temper. He is to go to the play to realise an artistic temperament. He is to go to the play to gain an artistic temperament. He is not the arbiter of the work of art. He is one who is admitted to contemplate the work of art, and, if the work be fine, to forget in its contemplation all, the egotism that mars him—the egotism of his ignorance, or the egotism of his information. This point about the drama is hardly, I think, sufficiently recognised. I can quite understand that were 'Macbeth' produced for the first time before a modern London audience, many of the people present would strongly and vigorously object to the introduction of the witches in the first act, with their grotesque phrases and their ridiculous words. But when the play is over one realises that the laughter of the witches in 'Macbeth' is as terrible as the laughter of madness in 'Lear,' more terrible than the daughter of Iago in the tragedy of the Moor. No spectator of art needs a more perfect mood of receptivity than the spectator of a play. The moment he seeks to exercise authority he becomes the avowed enemy of Art and of himself. Art does not mind. It is he who suffers.

With the novel it is the same thing. Popular authority and the recognition of popular authority are fatal. Thackeray's 'Esmond' is a beautiful work of art because he wrote it to please himself. In his other novels, in 'Pendennis,' in 'Philip,' in 'Vanity Fair' even, at times, he is too conscious of the public, and spoils his work by appealing directly to the sympathies of the public, or by directly mocking at them. A true artist takes no notice whatever of the public. The public are to him non-existent. He has no poppied or honeyed cakes through which to give the monster sleep or sustenance. He leaves that to the popular novelist. One incomparable novelist we have now in England, Mr George Meredith. There are better artists in France, but France has no one whose view of life is so large, so varied, so imaginatively true. There are tellers of stories in Russia who have a more vivid sense of what pain in fiction may be. But to him belongs philosophy in fiction. His people not merely live, but they live in thought. One can see them from myriad points of view. They are suggestive. There is soul in them and around them. They are interpretative and symbolic. And he who made them, those wonderful quickly-moving figures, made them for his own pleasure, and has never asked the public what they wanted, has never cared to know what they wanted, has never allowed the public to dictate to him or influence him in any way, but has gone on intensifying his own personality, and producing his own individual work. At first none came to him. That did not matter. Then the few came to him. That did not change him. The many have come now. He is still the same. He's an incomparable novelist.

With the decorative arts it is not different. The public clung with really pathetic tenacity to what I believe were the direct traditions of the Great Exhibition of international vulgarity, traditions that were so appalling that the houses in which people lived were only fit for blind people to live in. Beautiful things began to be made, beautiful colours came from the dyer's hand, beautiful patterns from the artist's brain, and the use of beautiful things and their value and importance were set forth. The public were really very indignant. They lost their temper. They said silly things. No one minded. No one was a whit the worse. No one accepted the authority of public opinion. And now it is almost impossible to enter any modern house without seeing some recognition of good taste, some recognition of the value of lovely surroundings, some sign of appreciation of beauty. In fact, people's houses are, as a rule, quite charming nowadays. People have been to a very great extent civilised. It is only fair to state, however, that the extraordinary success of the revolution in house-decoration and furniture and the like has not really been due to the majority of the public developing a very fine taste in such matters. It has been chiefly due to the fact that the craftsmen of things so appreciated the pleasure of making what was beautiful, and woke to such a vivid consciousness of the hideousness and vulgarity of what the public had previously wanted, that they simply starved the public out. It would be quite impossible at the present moment to furnish a room as rooms were furnished a few years ago, without going for everything to an auction of second-hand furniture from some third-rate lodging-house. The things are no longer made. However they may object to it, people must nowadays have something charming in their surroundings. Fortunately for them, their assumption of authority in these art-matters came to entire grief.

It is evident, then, that all authority in such things is bad. People sometimes inquire what form of government is most suitable for an artist to live under. To this question there is only one answer. The form of government that is most suitable to the artist is no government at all. Authority over him and his art is ridiculous. It has been stated that under despotisms artists have produced lovely work. This is not quite so. Artists have visited despots, not as subjects to be tyrannised over, but as wandering wonder-makers, as fascinating vagrant personalities, to be entertained and charmed and suffered to be at peace, and allowed to create. There is this to be said in favour of the despot, that he, being an individual, may have culture, while the mob, being a monster, has none. One who is an Emperor and King may stoop down to pick up a brush for a painter, but when the democracy stoops down it is merely to throw mud. And yet the democracy have not so far to stoop as the emperor. In fact, when they want to throw mud they have not to stoop at all. But there is no necessity to separate the monarch from the mob; all authority is equally bad.

There are three kinds of despots. There is the despot who tyrannises over the body. There is the despot who tyrannises over the soul. There is the despot who tyrannises over the soul and body alike. The first is called the Prince. The second is called the Pope The third is called the People. The Prince may be cultivated. Many Princes have been. Yet in the Prince there is danger. One thinks of Dante at the bitter feast in Verona, of Tasso in Ferrara's madman's cell. It is better for the artist not to live with Princes. The Pope may be cultivated. Many Popes have been; the bad Popes have been. The bad Popes loved Beauty, almost as passionately, nay, with as much passion as the good Popes hated Thought. To the wickedness of the Papacy humanity owes much. The goodness of the Papacy owes a terrible debt to humanity. Yet, though the Vatican has kept the rhetoric of its thunders, and lost the rod of its lightning, it is better for the artist not to live with Popes. It was a Pope who said of Cellini to a conclave of Cardinals that common laws and common authority were not made for men such as he; but it was a Pope who thrust Cellini into prison, and kept him there till he sickened with rage, and created unreal visions for himself, and saw the gilded sun enter his room, and grew so enamoured of it that he sought to escape, and crept out from tower to tower, and falling through dizzy air at dawn, maimed himself, and was by a vine-dresser covered with vine leaves, and carried in a cart to one who, loving beautiful things, had care of him. There is danger in Popes. And as for the People, what of them and their authority? Perhaps of them and their authority one has spoken enough. Their authority is a thing blind, deaf, hideous, grotesque, tragic, amusing, serious, and obscene. It is impossible for the artist to live with the People. All despots bribe. The people bribe and brutalise. Who told them to exercise authority? They were made to live, to listen, and to love. Someone has done them a great wrong. They have marred themselves by imitation of their inferiors. They have taken the sceptre of the Prince. How should they use it? They have taken the triple tiara of the Pope. How should they carry its burden? They are as a clown whose heart is broken. They are as a priest whose soul is not yet born. Let all who love Beauty pity them. Though they themselves love not Beauty, yet let them pity themselves. Who taught them the trick of tyranny?

There are many other things that one might point out. One might point out how the Renaissance was great, because it sought to solve no social problem, and busied itself not about such things, but suffered the individual to develop freely, beautifully, and naturally, and so had great and individual artists, and great and individual men. One might point out how Louis XIV., by creating the modern state, destroyed the individualism of the artist, and made things monstrous in their monotony of repetition, and contemptible in their conformity to rule, and destroyed throughout all France all those fine freedoms of expression that had made tradition new in beauty, and new modes one with antique form. But the past is of no importance. The present is of no importance. It is with the future that we have to deal. For the past is what man should not have been. The present is what man ought not to be. The future is what artists are.

It will, of course, be said that such a scheme as is set forth here is quite unpractical, and goes against human nature. This is perfectly true. It is unpractical, and it goes against human nature. This is why it is worth carrying out, and that is why one proposes it. For what is a practical scheme? A practical scheme is either a scheme that is already in existence, or a scheme that could be carried out under existing conditions. But it is exactly the existing conditions that one objects to; and any scheme that could accept these conditions is wrong and foolish. The conditions will be done away with, and human nature will change. The only thing that one really knows about human nature is that it changes. Change is the one quality we can predicate of it. The systems that fail are those that rely on the permanency of human nature, and not on its growth and development. The error of Louis XIV. was that he thought human nature would always be the same. The result of his error was the French Revolution. It was an admirable result. All the results of the mistakes of governments are quite admirable.

It is to be noted also that Individualism does not come to man with any sickly cant about duty, which merely means doing what other people want because they want it; or any hideous cant about self-sacrifice, which is merely

100

a survival of savage mutilation. In fact, it does not come to man with any claims upon him at all. It comes naturally and inevitably out of man. It is the point to which all development tends. It is the differentiation to which all organisms grow. It is the perfection that is inherent in every mode of life, and towards which every mode of life quickens. And so Individualism exercises no compulsion over man. On the contrary, it says to man that he should suffer no compulsion to be exercised over him. It does not try to force people to be good. It knows that people are good when they are let alone. Man will develop Individualism out of himself. Man is now so developing Individualism. To ask whether Individualism is practical is like asking whether Evolution is practical. Evolution is the law of life, and there is no evolution except towards Individualism. Where this tendency is not expressed, it is a case of artificially-arrested growth, or of disease, or of death.

Individualism will also be unselfish and unaffected. It has been pointed out that one of the results of the extraordinary tyranny of authority is that words are absolutely distorted from their proper and simple meaning, and are used to express the obverse of their right signification. What is true about Art is true about Life. A man is called affected, nowadays, if he dresses as he likes to dress. But in doing that he is acting in a perfectly natural manner. Affectation, in such matters, consists in dressing according to the views of one's neighbour, whose views, as they are the views of the majority, will probably be extremely stupid. Or a man is called selfish if he lives in the manner that seems to him most suitable for the full realisation of his own personality; if, in fact, the primary aim of his life is self-development. But this is the way in which everyone should live. Selfishness is not living as one wishes to live, it is asking others to live as one wishes to live. And unselfishness is letting other people's lives alone, not interfering with them. Selfishness always aims at creating around it an absolute uniformity of type. Unselfishness recognises infinite variety of type as a delightful thing, accepts it, acquiesces in it, enjoys it. It is not selfish to think for oneself. A man who does not think for himself does not think at all. It is grossly selfish to require of one's neighbour that he should think in the same way, and hold the same opinions. Why should he? If he can think, he will probably think differently. If he cannot think, it is monstrous to require thought of any kind from him. A red rose is not selfish because it wants to be a red rose. It would be horribly selfish if it wanted all the other flowers in the garden to be both red and roses. Under Individualism people will be quite natural and absolutely unselfish, and will know the meanings of the words, and realise them in their free, beautiful lives. Nor will men be egotistic as they are now. For the egotist is he who makes claims upon others, and the Individualist will not desire to do that. It will not give him pleasure. When man has realised Individualism, he will also realise sympathy and exercise it freely and spontaneously. Up to the present man has hardly cultivated sympathy at all. He has merely sympathy with pain, and sympathy with pain is not the highest form of sympathy. All sympathy is fine, but sympathy with suffering is the least fine mode. It is tainted with egotism. It is apt to become morbid. There is in it a certain element of terror for our own safety. We become afraid that we ourselves might be as the leper or as the blind, and that no man would have care of us. It is curiously limiting, too. One should sympathise with the entirety of life, not with life's sores and maladies merely, but with life's joy and beauty and energy and health and freedom. The wider sympathy is, of course, the more difficult. It requires more unselfishness. Anybody can sympathise with the sufferings of a friend, but it requires a very fine nature—it requires, in fact, the nature of a true Individualist—to sympathise with a friend's success.

In the modern stress of competition and struggle for place, such sympathy is naturally rare, and is also very much stifled by the immoral ideal of uniformity of type and conformity to rule which is so prevalent everywhere, and is perhaps most obnoxious in England.

Sympathy with pain there will, of course, always be. It is one of the first instincts of man. The animals which are individual, the higher animals, that is to say, share it with us. But it must be remembered that while sympathy with joy intensifies the sum of joy in the world, sympathy with pain does not really diminish the amount of pain. It may make man better able to endure evil, but the evil remains. Sympathy with consumption does not cure consumption; that is what Science does. And when Socialism has solved the problem of poverty, and Science solved the problem of disease, the area of the sentimentalists will be lessened, and the sympathy of man will be large, healthy, and spontaneous. Man will have joy in the contemplation of the joyous life of others.

For it is through joy that the Individualism of the future will develop itself. Christ made no attempt to reconstruct society, and consequently the Individualism that he preached to man could be realised only through pain or in solitude. The ideals that we owe to Christ are the ideals of the man who abandons society entirely, or of the man who resists society absolutely. But man is naturally social. Even the Thebaid became peopled at last. And though the cenobite realises his personality, it is often an impoverished personality that he so realises. Upon the other hand, the terrible truth that pain is a mode through which man may realise himself exercises a wonderful fascination over the world. Shallow speakers and shallow thinkers in pulpits and on platforms often talk about the world's worship of pleasure, and whine against it. But it is rarely in the world's history that its ideal has been one of joy and beauty. The worship of pain has far more often dominated the world. Mediævalism, with its saints and martyrs, its love of self-torture, its wild passion for wounding itself, its gashing with knives, and its whipping with rods—Mediævalism is real Christianity, and the mediæval Christ is the real Christ. When the Renaissance dawned upon the world, and brought with it the new ideals of the beauty of life and the joy of living, men could not understand Christ. Even Art shows us that. The painters of the Renaissance drew Christ as a little boy playing with another boy in a palace or a garden, or lying back in his mother's arms, smiling at her, or at a flower, or at a bright bird; or as a noble, stately figure moving nobly through the world; or as a wonderful figure rising in a sort of ecstasy from death to life. Even when they drew him crucified they drew him as a beautiful God on whom evil men had inflicted suffering. But he did not preoccupy them much. What delighted them was to paint the men and women whom they admired, and to show the loveliness of this lovely earth. They painted many religious pictures—in fact, they painted far too many, and the monotony of type and motive is wearisome, and was bad for art. It was the result of the authority of the public in art-matters, and is to be deplored. But their soul was not in the subject Raphael was a great artist when he painted his portrait of the Pope. When he painted his Madonnas and infant Christs, he is not a great artist at all. Christ had no message for the Renaissance, which was wonderful because it brought an ideal at variance with his, and to find the presentation of the real Christ we must go to mediæval art. There he is one maimed and marred; one who is not comely to look on, because Beauty is a joy; one who is not in fair raiment, because that may be a joy also: he is a beggar who has a marvellous soul; he is a leper whose soul is divine; he needs neither property nor health; he is a God realising his perfection through pain.

The evolution of man is slow. The injustice of men is great. It was necessary that pain should be put forward as a mode of self-realisation. Even now, in some places in the world, the message of Christ is necessary. No one who lived in modern Russia could possibly realise his perfection except by pain. A few Russian artists have realised themselves in Art; in a fiction that is mediæval in character, hecauae its dominant note is the realisation of men through suffering. But for those who are not artists, and to whom there is no mode of life but the actual life of fact, pain is the only door to perfection. A Russian who lives happily under the present system of government in Russia must either believe that man has no soul, or that, if he has, it is not worth developing. A Nihilist who rejects all authority, because he knows authority to be evil, and welcomes all pain, because through that he realises his personality, is a real Christian. To him the Christian ideal is a true thing.

And yet, Christ did not revolt against authority. He accepted the imperial authority of the Roman Empire and paid tribute. He endured the ecclesiastical authority of the Jewish Church, and would not repel its violence by any violence of his own. He had, as I said before, no scheme for the reconstruction of society. But the modern world has schemes. It proposes to do away with poverty and the suffering that it entails. It desires to get rid of pain, and the suffering that pain entails. It trusts to Socialism and to Science as its methods. What it aims at is an Individualism expressing itself through joy. This Individualism will be larger, fuller, lovelier than any Individualism has ever been. Pain is not the ultimate mode of perfection. It is merely provisional and a protest. It has reference to wrong, unhealthy, unjust surroundings. When the wrong, and the disease, and the injustice are removed, it will have no further place. It will have done its work. It was a great

104

work, but it is almost over. Its sphere lessens every day.

Nor will man miss it. For what man has sought for is, indeed, neither pain nor pleasure, but simply Life. Man has sought to live intensely, fully, perfectly. When he can do so without exercising restraint on others, or suffering it ever, and his activities are all pleasurable to him, he will be saner, healthier, more civilised, more himself. Pleasure is Nature's test, her sign of approval. When man is happy, he is in harmony with himself and his environment. The new Individualism, for whose service Socialism, whether it wills it or not, is working, will be perfect harmony. It will be what the Greeks sought for, but could not, except in Thought, realise completely, because they had slaves, and fed them; it will be what the Renaissance sought for, but could not realise completely except in Art, because they had slaves, and starved them. It will be complete, and through it each man will attain to his perfection. The new Individualism is the new Hellenism.

MISCELLANIES

DEDICATION: TO WALTER LEDGER

Since these volumes are sure of a place in your marvellous library I trust that with your unrivalled knowledge of the various editions of Wilde you may not detect any grievous error whether of taste or type, of omission or commission. But should you do so you must blame the editor, and not those who so patiently assisted him, the proof readers, the printers, or the publishers. Some day, however, I look forward to your bibliography of the author, in which you will be at liberty to criticise my capacity for anything except regard and friendship for yourself.—Sincerely yours,

ROBERT ROSS

May 25, 1908.

INTRODUCTION

The concluding volume of any collected edition is unavoidably fragmentary and desultory. And if this particular volume is no exception to a general tendency, it presents points of view in the author's literary career which may have escaped his greatest admirers and detractors. The wide range of his knowledge and interests is more apparent than in some of his finished work.

What I believed to be only the fragment of an essay on Historical Criticism was already in the press, when accidentally I came across the remaining portions, in Wilde's own handwriting; it is now complete though unhappily divided in this edition. {0a} Any doubt as to its authenticity, quite apart from the calligraphy, would vanish on reading such a characteristic passage as the following:—' . . . For, it was in vain that the middle ages strove to guard the buried spirit of progress. When the dawn of the Greek spirit arose, the sepulchre was empty, the grave clothes laid aside. Humanity had risen from the dead.' It was only Wilde who could contrive a literary conceit of that description; but readers will observe with different feelings, according to their temperament, that he never followed up the particular trend of thought developed in the essay. It is indeed more the work of the Berkeley Gold Medallist at Dublin, or the brilliant young Magdalen Demy than of the dramatist who was to write Salomé. The composition belongs to his Oxford days when he was the unsuccessful competitor for the Chancellor's English Essay Prize. Perhaps Magdalen, which has never forgiven herself for nurturing the author of Ravenna, may be felicitated on having escaped the further intolerable honour that she might have suffered by seeing crowned again with paltry academic parsley the most highly gifted of all her children in the last century. Compared with the crude criticism on The Grosvenor Gallery (one of the earliest of Wilde's published prose writings), Historical Criticism is singularly advanced and mature. Apart from his mere scholarship Wilde developed his literary and dramatic talent slowly. He told me that he was never regarded as a particularly precocious or clever youth. Indeed many old family friends and contemporary journalists maintain sturdily that the talent of his elder brother William was much more remarkable. In this opinion they are fortified, appropriately enough, by the late Clement Scott. I record this interesting view because it symbolises the familiar phenomenon that those nearest the mountain cannot appreciate its height.

The exiguous fragment of La Sainte Courtisane is the next unpublished work of importance. At the time of Wilde's trial the nearly completed drama was entrusted to Mrs. Leverson, who in 1897 went to Paris on purpose to restore it to the author. Wilde immediately left the manuscript in a cab. A few days later he laughingly informed me of the loss, and added that a cab was a very proper place for it. I have explained elsewhere that he looked on his plays with disdain in his last years, though he was always full of schemes for writing others. All my attempts to recover the lost work failed. The passages here reprinted are from some odd leaves of a first draft. The play is of course not unlike Salome, though it was written in English. It expanded Wilde's favourite theory that when you convert some one to an idea, you lose your faith in it; the same motive runs through Mr. W. H. Honorius the hermit, so far as I recollect the story, falls in love with the courtesan who has come to tempt him, and he reveals to her the secret of the Love of God. She immediately becomes a Christian, and is murdered by robbers; Honorius the hermit goes back to Alexandria to pursue a life of pleasure. Two other similar plays Wilde invented in prison, Ahab and Isabel and Pharaoh; he would never write them down, though often importuned to do so. Pharaoh was intensely dramatic and perhaps more original than any of the group. None of these works must be confused with the manuscripts stolen from 16 Tite Street in 1895—namely the enlarged version of Mr. W. H., the completed form of A Florentine Tragedy, and The Duchess of Padua (which existing in a prompt copy was of less importance than the others); nor with The Cardinal of Arragon, the manuscript of which I never saw. I scarcely think it ever existed, though Wilde used to recite proposed passages for it.

In regard to printing the lectures I have felt some diffidence: the majority of them were delivered from notes, and the same lectures were repeated in different towns in England and America. The reports of them in the papers are never trustworthy; they are often grotesque travesties, like the reports of after-dinner speeches in the London press of today. I have included only those lectures of which I possess or could obtain manuscript.

The aim of this edition has been completeness; and it is complete so far as human effort can make it; but besides the lost manuscripts there must be buried in the contemporary press many anonymous reviews which I have failed to identify. The remaining contents of this book do not call for further comment, other than a reminder that Wilde would hardly have consented to their republication. But owing to the number of anonymous works wrongly attributed to him, chiefly in America, and spurious works published in his name, I found it necessary to violate the laws of friendship by rejecting nothing I knew to be authentic. It will be seen on reference to the letters on The Ethics of Journalism that Wilde's name appearing at the end of poems and articles was not always a proof of authenticity even in his lifetime.

Of the few letters Wilde wrote to the press, those addressed to Whistler I have included with greater misgiving than anything else in this volume. They do not seem to me more amusing than those to which they were the intended rejoinders. But the dates are significant. Wilde was at one time always accused of plagiarising his ideas and his epigrams from Whistler, especially those with which he decorated his lectures, the accusation being brought by Whistler himself and his various disciples. It should be noted that all the works by which Wilde is known throughout Europe were written after the two friends quarrelled. That Wilde derived a great deal from the older man goes without saying, just as he derived much in a greater degree from Pater, Ruskin, Arnold and Burne-Jones. Yet the tedious attempt to recognise in every jest of his some original by Whistler induces the criticism that it seems a pity the great painter did not get them off on the public before he was forestalled. Reluctance from an appeal to publicity was never a weakness in either of the men. Some of Wilde's more frequently quoted sayings were made at the Old Bailey (though their provenance is often forgotten) or on his death-bed.

As a matter of fact, the genius of the two men was entirely different. Wilde was a humourist and a humanist before everything; and his wittiest

113

jests have neither the relentlessness nor the keenness characterising those of the clever American artist. Again, Whistler could no more have obtained the Berkeley Gold Medal for Greek, nor have written The Importance of Being Earnest, nor The Soul of Man, than Wilde, even if equipped as a painter, could ever have evinced that superb restraint distinguishing the portraits of 'Miss Alexander,' 'Carlyle,' and other masterpieces. Wilde, though it is not generally known, was something of a draughtsman in his youth. I possess several of his drawings.

A complete bibliography including all the foreign translations and American piracies would make a book of itself much larger than the present one. In order that Wilde collectors (and there are many, I believe) may know the authorised editions and authentic writings from the spurious, Mr. Stuart Mason, whose work on this edition I have already acknowledged, has supplied a list which contains every genuine and authorised English edition. This of course does not preclude the chance that some of the American editions are authorised, and that some of Wilde's genuine works even are included in the pirated editions.

I am indebted to the Editors and Proprietors of the Queen for leave to reproduce the article on 'English Poetesses'; to the Editor and Proprietors of the Sunday Times for the article entitled 'Art at Willis's Rooms'; and to Mr. William Waldorf Astor for those from the Pall Mall Gazette.

ROBERT ROSS

THE TOMB OF KEATS

(*Irish Monthly*, July 1877.)

As one enters Rome from the Via Ostiensis by the Porta San Paolo, the first object that meets the eye is a marble pyramid which stands close at hand on the left.

There are many Egyptian obelisks in Rome—tall, snakelike spires of red sandstone, mottled with strange writings, which remind us of the pillars of flame which led the children of Israel through the desert away from the land of the Pharaohs; but more wonderful than these to look upon is this gaunt, wedge-shaped pyramid standing here in this Italian city, unshattered amid the ruins and wrecks of time, looking older than the Eternal City itself, like terrible impassiveness turned to stone. And so in the Middle Ages men supposed this to be the sepulchre of Remus, who was slain by his own brother at the founding of the city, so ancient and mysterious it appears; but we have now, perhaps unfortunately, more accurate information about it, and know that it is the tomb of one Caius Cestius, a Roman gentleman of small note, who died about 30 B.C.

Yet though we cannot care much for the dead man who lies in lonely state beneath it, and who is only known to the world through his sepulchre, still this pyramid will be ever dear to the eyes of all English-speaking people, because at evening its shadows fall on the tomb of one who walks with Spenser, and Shakespeare, and Byron, and Shelley, and Elizabeth Barrett Browning in the great procession of the sweet singers of England.

For at its foot there is a green, sunny slope, known as the Old Protestant Cemetery, and on this a common-looking grave, which bears the following inscription:

> This grave contains all that was mortal of a young English poet, who on his deathbed, in the bitterness of his heart, desired these words to be engraven on his tombstone: HERE LIES ONE WHOSE NAME WAS

WRIT IN WATER. February 24, 1821.

And the name of the young English poet is John Keats.

Lord Houghton calls this cemetery 'one of the most beautiful spots on which the eye and heart of man can rest,' and Shelley speaks of it as making one 'in love with death, to think that one should be buried in so sweet a place'; and indeed when I saw the violets and the daisies and the poppies that overgrow the tomb, I remembered how the dead poet had once told his friend that he thought the 'intensest pleasure he had received in life was in watching the growth of flowers,' and how another time, after lying a while quite still, he murmured in some strange prescience of early death, 'I feel the flowers growing over me.'

But this time-worn stone and these wildflowers are but poor memorials {3} of one so great as Keats; most of all, too, in this city of Rome, which pays such honour to her dead; where popes, and emperors, and saints, and cardinals lie hidden in 'porphyry wombs,' or couched in baths of jasper and chalcedony and malachite, ablaze with precious stones and metals, and tended with continual service. For very noble is the site, and worthy of a noble monument; behind looms the grey pyramid, symbol of the world's age, and filled with memories of the sphinx, and the lotus leaf, and the glories of old Nile; in front is the Monte Testaccio, built, it is said, with the broken fragments of the vessels in which all the nations of the East and the West brought their tribute to Rome; and a little distance off, along the slope of the hill under the Aurelian wall, some tall gaunt cypresses rise, like burnt-out funeral torches, to mark the spot where Shelley's heart (that 'heart of hearts'!) lies in the earth; and, above all, the soil on which we tread is very Rome!

As I stood beside the mean grave of this divine boy, I thought of him as of a Priest of Beauty slain before his time; and the vision of Guido's St. Sebastian came before my eyes as I saw him at Genoa, a lovely brown boy, with crisp, clustering hair and red lips, bound by his evil enemies to a tree, and though pierced by arrows, raising his eyes with divine, impassioned gaze towards the Eternal Beauty of the opening heavens. And thus my thoughts shaped themselves to rhyme:

HEU MISERANDE PUER

Rid of the world's injustice and its pain,

He rests at last beneath God's veil of blue;

Taken from life while life and love were new

The youngest of the martyrs here is lain,

Fair as Sebastian and as foully slain.

No cypress shades his grave, nor funeral yew,

But red-lipped daisies, violets drenched with dew,

And sleepy poppies, catch the evening rain.

O proudest heart that broke for misery!

O saddest poet that the world hath seen!

O sweetest singer of the English land!

Thy name was writ in water on the sand,

But our tears shall keep thy memory green,

And make it flourish like a Basil-tree.

Borne, 1877.

Note.—A later version of this sonnet, under the title of 'The Grave of Keats,' is given in the Poems, page 157.

THE GROSVENOR GALLERY, 1877

(*Dublin University Magazine*, July 1877.)

That 'Art is long and life is short' is a truth which every one feels, or ought to feel; yet surely those who were in London last May, and had in one week the opportunities of hearing Rubenstein play the Sonata Impassionata, of seeing Wagner conduct the Spinning-Wheel Chorus from the Flying Dutchman, and of studying art at the Grosvenor Gallery, have very little to complain of as regards human existence and art-pleasures.

Descriptions of music are generally, perhaps, more or less failures, for music is a matter of individual feeling, and the beauties and lessons that one draws from hearing lovely sounds are mainly personal, and depend to a large extent on one's own state of mind and culture. So leaving Rubenstein and Wagner to be celebrated by Franz Hüffer, or Mr. Haweis, or any other of our picturesque writers on music, I will describe some of the pictures now being shown in the Grosvenor Gallery.

The origin of this Gallery is as follows: About a year ago the idea occurred to Sir Coutts Lindsay of building a public gallery, in which, untrammelled by the difficulties or meannesses of 'Hanging Committees,' he could exhibit to the lovers of art the works of certain great living artists side by side: a gallery in which the student would not have to struggle through an endless monotony of mediocre works in order to reach what was worth looking at; one in which the people of England could have the opportunity of judging of the merits of at least one great master of painting, whose pictures had been kept from public exhibition by the jealousy and ignorance of rival artists. Accordingly, last May, in New Bond Street, the Grosvenor Gallery was opened to the public.

As far as the Gallery itself is concerned, there are only three rooms, so there is no fear of our getting that terrible weariness of mind and eye which comes on after the 'Forced Marches' through ordinary picture galleries. The walls are hung with scarlet damask above a dado of dull green and gold; there are luxurious velvet couches, beautiful flowers and plants, tables of gilded and inlaid marbles, covered with Japanese china and the latest 'Minton,' globes of 'rainbow glass' like large soap-bubbles, and, in fine, everything in decoration that is lovely to look on, and in harmony with the surrounding works of art.

Burne-Jones and Holman Hunt are probably the greatest masters of colour that we have ever had in England, with the single exception of Turner, but their styles differ widely. To draw a rough distinction, Holman Hunt studies and reproduces the colours of natural objects, and deals with historical subjects, or scenes of real life, mostly from the East, touched occasionally with a certain fancifulness, as in the Shadow of the Cross. Burne-Jones, on the contrary, is a dreamer in the land of mythology, a seer of fairy visions, a symbolical painter. He is an imaginative colourist too, knowing that all colour is no mere delightful quality of natural things, but a 'spirit upon them by which they become expressive to the spirit,' as Mr. Pater says. Watts's power, on the other hand, lies in his great originative and imaginative genius, and he reminds us of Æschylus or Michael Angelo in the startling vividness of his conceptions. Although these three painters differ much in aim and in result, they yet are one in their faith, and love, and reverence, the three golden keys to the gate of the House Beautiful.

On entering the West Gallery the first picture that meets the eye is Mr. Watts's Love and Death, a large painting, representing a marble doorway, all overgrown with white-starred jasmine and sweet brier-rose. Death, a giant form, veiled in grey draperies, is passing in with inevitable and mysterious power, breaking through all the flowers. One foot is already on the threshold, and one relentless hand is extended, while Love, a beautiful boy with lithe brown limbs and rainbow-coloured wings, all shrinking like a crumpled leaf, is trying, with vain hands, to bar the entrance. A little dove, undisturbed by the agony of the terrible conflict, waits patiently at the foot of the steps for her playmate; but will wait in vain, for though the face of Death is hidden from us, yet we can see from the terror in the boy's eyes and quivering lips, that, Medusa-like, this grey phantom turns all it looks upon to stone; and the wings of Love are rent and crushed. Except on the ceiling of the Sistine

119

Chapel in Rome, there are perhaps few paintings to compare with this in intensity of strength and in marvel of conception. It is worthy to rank with Michael Angelo's God Dividing the Light from the Darkness.

Next to it are hung five pictures by Millais. Three of them are portraits of the three daughters of the Duke of Westminster, all in white dresses, with white hats and feathers; the delicacy of the colour being rather injured by the red damask background. These pictures do not possess any particular merit beyond that of being extremely good likenesses, especially the one of the Marchioness of Ormonde. Over them is hung a picture of a seamstress, pale and vacant-looking, with eyes red from tears and long watchings in the night, hemming a shirt. It is meant to illustrate Hood's familiar poem. As we look on it, a terrible contrast strikes us between this miserable pauper-seamstress and the three beautiful daughters of the richest duke in the world, which breaks through any artistic reveries by its awful vividness.

The fifth picture is a profile head of a young man with delicate aquiline nose, thoughtful oval face, and artistic, abstracted air, which will be easily recognised as a portrait of Lord Ronald Gower, who is himself known as an artist and sculptor. But no one would discern in these five pictures the genius that painted the Home at Bethlehem and the portrait of John Ruskin which is at Oxford.

Then come eight pictures by Alma Tadema, good examples of that accurate drawing of inanimate objects which makes his pictures so real from an antiquarian point of view, and of the sweet subtlety of colouring which gives to them a magic all their own. One represents some Roman girls bathing in a marble tank, and the colour of the limbs in the water is very perfect indeed; a dainty attendant is tripping down a flight of steps with a bundle of towels, and in the centre a great green sphinx in bronze throws forth a shower of sparkling water for a very pretty laughing girl, who stoops gleefully beneath it. There is a delightful sense of coolness about the picture, and one can almost imagine that one hears the splash of water, and the girls' chatter. It is wonderful what a world of atmosphere and reality may be condensed into a very small space, for this picture is only about eleven by two and a half inches.

The most ambitious of these pictures is one of Phidias Showing the

Frieze of the Parthenon to his Friends. We are supposed to be on a high scaffolding level with the frieze, and the effect of great height produced by glimpses of light between the planking of the floor is very cleverly managed. But there is a want of individuality among the connoisseurs clustered round Phidias, and the frieze itself is very inaccurately coloured. The Greek boys who are riding and leading the horses are painted Egyptian red, and the whole design is done in this red, dark blue, and black. This sombre colouring is un-Greek; the figures of these boys were undoubtedly tinted with flesh colour, like the ordinary Greek statues, and the whole tone of the colouring of the original frieze was brilliant and light; while one of its chief beauties, the reins and accoutrements of burnished metal, is quite omitted. This painter is more at home in the Greco-Roman art of the Empire and later Republic than he is in the art of the Periclean age.

The most remarkable of Mr. Richmond's pictures exhibited here is his Electra at the Tomb of Agamemnon—a very magnificent subject, to which, however, justice is not done. Electra and her handmaidens are grouped gracefully around the tomb of the murdered King; but there is a want of humanity in the scene: there is no trace of that passionate Asiatic mourning for the dead to which the Greek women were so prone, and which Æschylus describes with such intensity; nor would Greek women have come to pour libations to the dead in such bright-coloured dresses as Mr. Richmond has given them; clearly this artist has not studied Æschylus' play of the Choëphori, in which there is an elaborate and pathetic account of this scene. The tall, twisted tree-stems, however, that form the background are fine and original in effect, and Mr. Richmond has caught exactly that peculiar opal-blue of the sky which is so remarkable in Greece; the purple orchids too, and daffodil and narcissi that are in the foreground are all flowers which I have myself seen at Argos.

Sir Coutts Lindsay sends a life-size portrait of his wife, holding a violin, which has some good points of colour and position, and four other pictures, including an exquisitely simple and quaint little picture of the Dower House at Balcarres, and a Daphne with rather questionable flesh-painting, and in whom we miss the breathlessness of flight.

I saw the blush come o'er her like a rose;

The half-reluctant crimson comes and goes;

Her glowing limbs make pause, and she is stayed

Wondering the issue of the words she prayed.

It is a great pity that Holman Hunt is not represented by any of his really great works, such as the Finding of Christ in the Temple, or Isabella Mourning over the Pot of Basil, both of which are fair samples of his powers. Four pictures of his are shown here: a little Italian child, painted with great love and sweetness, two street scenes in Cairo full of rich Oriental colouring, and a wonderful work called the Afterglow in Egypt. It represents a tall swarthy Egyptian woman, in a robe of dark and light blue, carrying a green jar on her shoulder, and a sheaf of grain on her head; around her comes fluttering a flock of beautiful doves of all colours, eager to be fed. Behind is a wide flat river, and across the river a stretch of ripe corn, through which a gaunt camel is being driven; the sun has set, and from the west comes a great wave of red light like wine poured out on the land, yet not crimson, as we see the Afterglow in Northern Europe, but a rich pink like that of a rose. As a study of colour it is superb, but it is difficult to feel a human interest in this Egyptian peasant.

Mr. Albert Moore sends some of his usual pictures of women, which as studies of drapery and colour effects are very charming. One of them, a tall maiden, in a robe of light blue clasped at the neck with a glowing sapphire, and with an orange headdress, is a very good example of the highest decorative art, and a perfect delight in colour.

Mr. Spencer Stanhope's picture of Eve Tempted is one of the remarkable pictures of the Gallery. Eve, a fair woman, of surpassing loveliness, is leaning against a bank of violets, underneath the apple tree; naked, except for the rich thick folds of gilded hair which sweep down from her head like the bright rain in which Zeus came to Danae. The head is drooped a little forward as a flower droops when the dew has fallen heavily, and her eyes are dimmed with the haze that comes in moments of doubtful thought. One arm falls

122

idly by her side; the other is raised high over her head among the branches, her delicate fingers just meeting round one of the burnished apples that glow amidst the leaves like 'golden lamps in a green night.' An amethyst-coloured serpent, with a devilish human head, is twisting round the trunk of the tree and breathes into the woman's ear a blue flame of evil counsel. At the feet of Eve bright flowers are growing, tulips, narcissi, lilies, and anemones, all painted with a loving patience that reminds us of the older Florentine masters; after whose example, too, Mr. Stanhope has used gilding for Eve's hair and for the bright fruits.

Next to it is another picture by the same artist, entitled Love and the Maiden. A girl has fallen asleep in a wood of olive trees, through whose branches and grey leaves we can see the glimmer of sky and sea, with a little seaport town of white houses shining in the sunlight. The olive wood is ever sacred to the Virgin Pallas, the Goddess of Wisdom; and who would have dreamed of finding Eros hidden there? But the girl wakes up, as one wakes from sleep one knows not why, to see the face of the boy Love, who, with outstretched hands, is leaning towards her from the midst of a rhododendron's crimson blossoms. A rose-garland presses the boy's brown curls, and he is clad in a tunic of oriental colours, and delicately sensuous are his face and his bared limbs. His boyish beauty is of that peculiar type unknown in Northern Europe, but common in the Greek islands, where boys can still be found as beautiful as the Charmides of Plato. Guido's St. Sebastian in the Palazzo Rosso at Genoa is one of those boys, and Perugino once drew a Greek Ganymede for his native town, but the painter who most shows the influence of this type is Correggio, whose lily-bearer in the Cathedral at Parma, and whose wild-eyed, open-mouthed St. Johns in the 'Incoronata Madonna' of St. Giovanni Evangelista, are the best examples in art of the bloom and vitality and radiance of this adolescent beauty. And so there is extreme loveliness in this figure of Love by Mr. Stanhope, and the whole picture is full of grace, though there is, perhaps, too great a luxuriance of colour, and it would have been a relief had the girl been dressed in pure white.

Mr. Frederick Burton, of whom all Irishmen are so justly proud, is represented by a fine water-colour portrait of Mrs. George Smith; one would almost believe it to be in oils, so great is the lustre on this lady's raven-black hair, and so rich and broad and vigorous is the painting of a Japanese scarf she is wearing. Then as we turn to the east wall of the gallery we see the three great pictures of Burne-Jones, the Beguiling of Merlin, the Days of Creation, and the Mirror of Venus. The version of the legend of Merlin's Beguiling that Mr. Burne-Jones has followed differs from Mr. Tennyson's and from the account in the Morte d'Arthur. It is taken from the Romance of Merlin, which tells the story in this wise:

> It fell on a day that they went through the forest of Breceliande, and found a bush that was fair and high, of white hawthorn, full of flowers, and there they sat in the shadow. And Merlin fell on sleep; and when she felt that he was on sleep she arose softly, and began her enchantments, such as Merlin had taught her, and made the ring nine times, and nine times the enchantments.

> . . . . .

> And then he looked about him, and him seemed he was in the fairest tower of the world, and the most strong; neither of iron was it fashioned, nor steel, nor timber, nor of stone, but of the air, without any other thing; and in sooth so strong it is that it may never be undone while the world endureth.

So runs the chronicle; and thus Mr. Burne-Jones, the 'Archimage of the esoteric unreal,' treats the subject. Stretched upon a low branch of the tree, and encircled with the glory of the white hawthorn-blossoms, half sits, half lies, the great enchanter. He is not drawn as Mr. Tennyson has described him, with the 'vast and shaggy mantle of a beard,' which youth gone out had left in ashes; smooth and clear-cut and very pale is his face; time has not seared him with wrinkles or the signs of age; one would hardly know him to be old were it not that he seems very weary of seeking into the mysteries of the world, and that the great sadness that is born of wisdom has cast a shadow on him. But now what availeth him his wisdom or his arts? His eyes, that saw once so clear, are dim and glazed with coming death, and his white and delicate hands that wrought of old such works of marvel, hang listlessly. Vivien, a tall, lithe woman, beautiful and subtle to look on, like a snake, stands in front of him, reading the fatal spell from the enchanted book; mocking the utter helplessness of him whom once her lying tongue had called

> Her lord and liege,
>
> Her seer, her bard, her silver star of eve,
>
> Her god, her Merlin, the one passionate love
>
> Of her whole life.

In her brown crisp hair is the gleam of a golden snake, and she is clad in a silken robe of dark violet that clings tightly to her limbs, more expressing than hiding them; the colour of this dress is like the colour of a purple sea-shell, broken here and there with slight gleams of silver and pink and azure; it has a strange metallic lustre like the iris-neck of the dove. Were this Mr. Burne-Jones's only work it would be enough of itself to make him rank as a great painter. The picture is full of magic; and the colour is truly a spirit dwelling on things and making them expressive to the spirit, for the delicate tones of grey, and green, and violet seem to convey to us the idea of languid sleep, and even the hawthorn-blossoms have lost their wonted brightness, and are more like the pale moonlight to which Shelley compared them, than the sheet of summer snow we see now in our English fields.

The next picture is divided into six compartments, each representing a day in the Creation of the World, under the symbol of an angel holding a crystal globe, within which is shown the work of a day. In the first compartment stands the lonely angel of the First Day, and within the crystal ball Light is being separated from Darkness. In the fourth compartment are four angels, and the crystal glows like a heated opal, for within it the creation of the Sun, Moon, and Stars is passing; the number of the angels increases, and the colours grow more vivid till we reach the sixth compartment, which shines afar off like a rainbow. Within it are the six angels of the Creation, each holding its crystal ball; and within the crystal of the sixth angel one can see Adam's strong brown limbs and hero form, and the pale, beautiful body of Eve. At the feet also of these six winged messengers of the Creator is sitting the angel of the Seventh Day, who on a harp of gold is singing the glories of that coming day which we have not yet seen. The faces of the angels are pale and oval-shaped, in their eyes is the light of Wisdom and Love, and their lips seem as if they would speak to us; and strength and beauty are in their wings. They stand with naked feet, some on shell-strewn sands whereon tide has never washed nor storm broken, others it seems on pools of water, others on strange flowers; and their hair is like the bright glory round a saint's head.

The scene of the third picture is laid on a long green valley by the sea; eight girls, handmaidens of the Goddess of Love, are collected by the margin of a long pool of clear water, whose surface no wandering wind or flapping bird has ruffled; but the large flat leaves of the water-lily float on it undisturbed, and clustering forget-me-nots rise here and there like heaps of scattered turquoise.

In this Mirror of Venus each girl is reflected as in a mirror of polished steel. Some of them bend over the pool in laughing wonder at their own beauty, others, weary of shadows, are leaning back, and one girl is standing straight up; and nothing of her is reflected in the pool but a glimmer of white feet. This picture, however, has not the intense pathos and tragedy of the Beguiling of Merlin, nor the mystical and lovely symbolism of the Days of the Creation. Above these three pictures are hung five allegorical studies of figures by the same artist, all worthy of his fame.

Mr. Walter Crane, who has illustrated so many fairy tales for children, sends an ambitious work called the Renaissance of Venus, which in the dull colour of its 'sunless dawn,' and in its general want of all the glow and beauty and passion that one associates with this scene reminds one of Botticelli's picture of the same subject. After Mr. Swinburne's superb description of the sea-birth of the goddess in his Hymn to Proserpine, it is very strange to find a cultured artist of feeling producing such a vapid Venus as this. The best thing in it is the painting of an apple tree: the time of year is spring, and the leaves have not yet come, but the tree is laden with pink and white blossoms, which stand out in beautiful relief against the pale blue of the sky, and are very true to nature.

M. Alphonse Legros sends nine pictures, and there is a natural curiosity to see the work of a gentleman who holds at Cambridge the same professorship

126

as Mr. Ruskin does at Oxford. Four of these are studies of men's heads, done in two hours each for his pupils at the Slade Schools. There is a good deal of vigorous, rough execution about them, and they are marvels of rapid work. His portrait of Mr. Carlyle is unsatisfactory; and even in No. 79, a picture of two scarlet-robed bishops, surrounded by Spanish monks, his colour is very thin and meagre. A good bit of painting is of some metal pots in a picture called Le Chaudronnier.

Mr. Leslie, unfortunately, is represented only by one small work, called Palm-blossom. It is a picture of a perfectly lovely child that reminds one of Sir Joshua's cherubs in the National Gallery, with a mouth like two petals of a rose; the under-lip, as Rossetti says quaintly somewhere, 'sucked in, as if it strove to kiss itself.'

Then we come to the most abused pictures in the whole Exhibition—the 'colour symphonies' of the 'Great Dark Master,' Mr. Whistler, who deserves the name of 'Ο σκοτεινος as much as Heraclitus ever did. Their titles do not convey much information. No. 4 is called Nocturne in Black and Gold, No. 6A Nocturne in Blue and Silver, and so on. The first of these represents a rocket of golden rain, with green and red fires bursting in a perfectly black sky, two large black smudges on the picture standing, I believe, for a tower which is in 'Cremorne Gardens' and for a crowd of lookers-on. The other is rather prettier; a rocket is breaking in a pale blue sky over a large dark blue bridge and a blue and silver river. These pictures are certainly worth looking at for about as long as one looks at a real rocket, that is, for somewhat less than a quarter of a minute.

No. 7 is called Arrangement in Black No. 3, apparently some pseudonym for our greatest living actor, for out of black smudgy clouds comes looming the gaunt figure of Mr. Henry Irving, with the yellow hair and pointed beard, the ruff, short cloak, and tight hose in which he appeared as Philip II. in Tennyson's play Queen Mary. One hand is thrust into his breast, and his legs are stuck wide apart in a queer stiff position that Mr. Irving often adopts preparatory to one of his long, wolflike strides across the stage. The figure is life-size, and, though apparently one-armed, is so ridiculously like the original that one cannot help almost laughing when one sees it. And we may imagine that any one who had the misfortune to be shut up at night in the Grosvenor Gallery would hear this Arrangement in Black No. 3 murmuring in the well-known Lyceum accents:

By St. James, I do protest,

Upon the faith and honour of a Spaniard,

I am vastly grieved to leave your Majesty.

Simon, is supper ready?

Nos. 8 and 9 are life-size portraits of two young ladies, evidently caught in a black London fog; they look like sisters, but are not related probably, as one is a Harmony in Amber and Black, the other only an Arrangement in Brown.

Mr. Whistler, however, sends one really good picture to this exhibition, a portrait of Mr. Carlyle, which is hung in the entrance hall; the expression on the old man's face, the texture and colour of his grey hair, and the general sympathetic treatment, show Mr. Whistler {19} to be an artist of very great power when he likes.

There is not so much in the East Gallery that calls for notice. Mr. Leighton is unfortunately represented only by two little heads, one of an Italian girl, the other called A Study. There is some delicate flesh painting of red and brown in these works that reminds one of a russet apple, but of course they are no samples of this artist's great strength. There are two good portraits—one of Mrs. Burne-Jones, by Mr. Poynter. This lady has a very delicate, artistic face, reminding us, perhaps, a little of one of the angels her husband has painted. She is represented in a white dress, with a perfectly gigantic old-fashioned watch hung to her waist, drinking tea from an old blue china cup. The other is a head of the Duchess of Westminster by Mr. Forbes-Robertson, who both as an actor and an artist has shown great cleverness. He has succeeded very well in reproducing the calm, beautiful profile and lustrous golden hair, but the shoulders are ungraceful, and very unlike the original. The figure of a girl leaning against a wonderful screen, looking terribly 'misunderstood,' and surrounded by any amount of artistic china and furniture, by Mrs. Louise Jopling, is worth looking at too. It is called It Might Have Been, and the girl is quite fit to be the heroine of any sentimental novel.

The two largest contributors to this gallery are Mr. Ferdinand Heilbuth and Mr. James Tissot. The first of these two artists sends some delightful pictures from Rome, two of which are particularly pleasing. One is of an old Cardinal in the Imperial scarlet of the Cæsars meeting a body of young Italian boys in purple soutanes, students evidently in some religious college, near the Church of St. John Lateran. One of the boys is being presented to the Cardinal, and looks very nervous under the operation; the rest gaze in wonder at the old man in his beautiful dress. The other picture is a view in the gardens of the Villa Borghese; a Cardinal has sat down on a marble seat in the shade of the trees, and is suspending his meditation for a moment to smile at a pretty child to whom a French bonne is pointing out the gorgeously dressed old gentleman; a flunkey in attendance on the Cardinal looks superciliously on.

Nearly all of Mr. Tissot's pictures are deficient in feeling and depth; his young ladies are too fashionably over-dressed to interest the artistic eye, and he has a hard unscrupulousness in painting uninteresting objects in an uninteresting way. There is some good colour and drawing, however, in his painting of a withered chestnut tree, with the autumn sun glowing through the yellow leaves, in a picnic scene, No. 23; the remainder of the picture being something in the photographic style of Frith.

What a gap in art there is between such a picture as the Banquet of the Civic Guard in Holland, with its beautiful grouping of noble-looking men, its exquisite Venetian glass aglow with light and wine, and Mr. Tissot's over-dressed, common-looking people, and ugly, painfully accurate representation of modern soda-water bottles!

Mr. Tissot's Widower, however, shines in qualities which his other pictures lack; it is full of depth and suggestiveness; the grasses and wild, luxuriant growth of the foreground are a revel of natural life.

We must notice besides in this gallery Mr. Watts's two powerful portraits of Mr. Burne-Jones and Lady Lindsay.

To get to the Water-Colour Room we pass through a small sculpture gallery, which contains some busts of interest, and a pretty terra-cotta figure of a young sailor, by Count Gleichen, entitled Cheeky, but it is not remarkable in any way, and contrasts very unfavourably with the Exhibition of Sculpture at the Royal Academy, in which are three really fine works of art—Mr. Leighton's Man Struggling with a Snake, which may be thought worthy of being looked on side by side with the Laocoon of the Vatican, and Lord Ronald Gower's two statues, one of a dying French Guardsman at the Battle of Waterloo, the other of Marie Antoinette being led to execution with bound hands, Queenlike and noble to the last.

The collection of water-colours is mediocre; there is a good effect of Mr. Poynter's, the east wind seen from a high cliff sweeping down on the sea like the black wings of some god; and some charming pictures of Fairy Land by Mr. Richard Doyle, which would make good illustrations for one of Mr. Allingham's Fairy-Poems, but the tout-ensemble is poor.

Taking a general view of the works exhibited here, we see that this dull land of England, with its short summer, its dreary rains and fogs, its mining districts and factories, and vile deification of machinery, has yet produced very great masters of art, men with a subtle sense and love of what is beautiful, original, and noble in imagination.

Nor are the art-treasures of this country at all exhausted by this Exhibition; there are very many great pictures by living artists hidden away in different places, which those of us who are yet boys have never seen, and which our elders must wish to see again.

Holman Hunt has done better work than the Afterglow in Egypt; neither Millais, Leighton, nor Poynter has sent any of the pictures on which his fame rests; neither Burne-Jones nor Watts shows us here all the glories of his art; and the name of that strange genius who wrote the Vision of Love revealed in Sleep, and the names of Dante Rossetti and of the Marchioness of Waterford, cannot be found in the catalogue. And so it is to be hoped that this is not the only exhibition of paintings that we shall see in the Grosvenor Gallery; and Sir Coutts Lindsay, in showing us great works of art, will be most materially aiding that revival of culture and love of beauty which in great part owes its birth to Mr. Ruskin, and which Mr. Swinburne, and Mr. Pater, and Mr. Symonds, and Mr. Morris, and many others, are fostering and keeping alive, each in his own peculiar fashion.

THE GROSVENOR GALLERY 1879

(*Saunders' Irish Daily News*, May 5, 1879.)

While the yearly exhibition of the Royal Academy may be said to present us with the general characteristics of ordinary English art at its most commonplace level, it is at the Grosvenor Gallery that we are enabled to see the highest development of the modern artistic spirit as well as what one might call its specially accentuated tendencies.

Foremost among the great works now exhibited at this gallery are Mr. Burne-Jones's Annunciation and his four pictures illustrating the Greek legend of Pygmalion—works of the very highest importance in our æsthetic development as illustrative of some of the more exquisite qualities of modern culture. In the first the Virgin Mary, a passionless, pale woman, with that mysterious sorrow whose meaning she was so soon to learn mirrored in her wan face, is standing, in grey drapery, by a marble fountain, in what seems the open courtyard of an empty and silent house, while through the branches of a tall olive tree, unseen by the Virgin's tear-dimmed eyes, is descending the angel Gabriel with his joyful and terrible message, not painted as Angelico loved to do, in the varied splendour of peacock-like wings and garments of gold and crimson, but somewhat sombre in colour, set with all the fine grace of nobly-fashioned drapery and exquisitely ordered design. In presence of what may be called the mediæval spirit may be discerned both the idea and the technique of the work, and even still more so in the four pictures of the story of Pygmalion, where the sculptor is represented in dress and in looks rather as a Christian St. Francis, than as a pure Greek artist in the first morning tide of art, creating his own ideal, and worshipping it. For delicacy and melody of colour these pictures are beyond praise, nor can anything exceed the idyllic loveliness of Aphrodite waking the statue into sensuous life: the world above her head like a brittle globe of glass, her feet resting on a drift of the blue sky, and a choir of doves fluttering around her like a fall of white snow. Following in the same school of ideal and imaginative painting is Miss Evelyn Pickering, whose picture of St. Catherine, in the Dudley of some years ago, attracted such great attention. To the present gallery she has contributed a large picture of Night and Sleep, twin brothers floating over the world in indissoluble embrace, the one spreading the cloak of darkness, while from the other's listless hands the Leathean poppies fall in a scarlet shower. Mr. Strudwich sends a picture of Isabella, which realises in some measure the pathos of Keats's poem, and another of the lover in the lily garden from the Song of Solomon, both works full of delicacy of design and refinement of detail, yet essentially weak in colour, and in comparison with the splendid Giorgione-like work of Mr. Fairfax Murray, are more like the coloured drawings of the modern German school than what we properly call a painting. The last-named artist, while essentially weak in draughtsmanship, yet possesses the higher quality of noble colour in the fullest degree.

The draped figures of men and women in his Garland Makers, and Pastoral, some wrought in that single note of colour which the earlier Florentines loved, others with all the varied richness and glow of the Venetian school, show what great results may be brought about by a youth spent in Italian cities. And finally I must notice the works contributed to this Gallery by that most powerful of all our English artists, Mr. G. F. Watts, the extraordinary width and reach of whose genius were never more illustrated than by the various pictures bearing his name which are here exhibited. His Paolo and Francesca, and his Orpheus and Eurydice, are creative visions of the very highest order of imaginative painting; marked as it is with all the splendid vigour of nobly ordered design, the last-named picture possesses qualities of colour no less great. The white body of the dying girl, drooping like a pale lily, and the clinging arms of her lover, whose strong brown limbs seem filled with all the sensuous splendour of passionate life, form a melancholy and wonderful note of colour to which the eye continually returns as indicating the motive of the conception. Yet here I would dwell rather on two pictures which show the splendid simplicity and directness of his strength, the one a portrait of himself, the other that of a little child called Dorothy, who has all that sweet gravity and look of candour which we like to associate with that old-fashioned name: a child with bright rippling hair, tangled like floss silk, open brown eyes and flower-like mouth; dressed in faded claret, with little lace about the neck and throat, toned down to a delicate grey—the hands simply clasped before her. This is the picture; as truthful and lovely as any of those Brignoli children which Vandyke has painted in Genoa. Nor is his own picture of himself—styled in the catalogue merely A Portrait—less wonderful, especially the luminous treatment of the various shades of black as shown in the hat and cloak. It would be quite impossible, however, to give any adequate account or criticism of the work now exhibited in the Grosvenor Gallery within the limits of a single notice. Richmond's noble picture of Sleep and Death Bearing the Slain Body of Sarpedon, and his bronze statue of the Greek athlete, are works of the very highest order of artistic excellence, but I will reserve for another occasion the qualities of his power. Mr. Whistler, whose wonderful and eccentric genius is better appreciated in France than in England, sends a very wonderful picture entitled The Golden Girl, a life-size study in amber, yellow and browns, of a child dancing with a skipping-rope, full of birdlike grace and exquisite motion; as well as some delightful specimens of etching (an art of which he is the consummate master), one of which, called The Little Forge, entirely done with the dry point, possesses extraordinary merit; nor have the philippics of the Fors Clavigera deterred him from exhibiting some more of his 'arrangements in colour,' one of which, called a Harmony in Green and Gold, I would especially mention as an extremely good example of what ships lying at anchor on a summer evening are from the 'Impressionist point of view.'

Mr. Eugene Benson, one of the most cultured of those many Americans who seem to have found their Mecca in modern Rome, has sent a picture of Narcissus, a work full of the true Theocritean sympathy for the natural picturesqueness of shepherd life, and entirely delightful to all who love the peculiar qualities of Italian scenery. The shadows of the trees drifting across the grass, the crowding together of the sheep, and the sense of summer air and light which fills the picture, are full of the highest truth and beauty; and Mr. Forbes-Robertson, whose picture of Phelps as Cardinal Wolsey has just been bought by the Garrick Club, and who is himself so well known as a young actor of the very highest promise, is represented by a portrait of Mr. Hermann Vezin which is extremely clever and certainly very lifelike. Nor amongst the minor works must I omit to notice Miss Stuart-Wortley's view on the

134

river Cherwell, taken from the walks of Magdalen College, Oxford,—a little picture marked by great sympathy for the shade and coolness of green places and for the stillness of summer waters; or Mrs. Valentine Bromley's Misty Day, remarkable for the excellent drawing of a breaking wave, as well as for a great delicacy of tone. Besides the Marchioness of Waterford, whose brilliant treatment of colour is so well known, and Mr. Richard Doyle, whose water-colour drawings of children and of fairy scenes are always so fresh and bright, the qualities of the Irish genius in the field of art find an entirely adequate exponent in Mr. Wills, who as a dramatist and a painter has won himself such an honourable name. Three pictures of his are exhibited here: the Spirit of the Shell, which is perhaps too fanciful and vague in design; the Nymph and Satyr, where the little goat-footed child has all the sweet mystery and romance of the woodlands about him; and the Parting of Ophelia and Laertes, a work not only full of very strong drawing, especially in the modelling of the male figure, but a very splendid example of the power of subdued and reserved colour, the perfect harmony of tone being made still more subtle by the fitful play of reflected light on the polished armour.

I shall reserve for another notice the wonderful landscapes of Mr. Cecil Lawson, who has caught so much of Turner's imagination and mode of treatment, as well as a consideration of the works of Herkomer, Tissot and Legros, and others of the modern realistic school.

Note.—The other notice mentioned above did not appear.

L'ENVOI

An Introduction to *Rose Leaf and Apple Leaf* by Rennell Rodd, published by J. M. Stoddart and Co., Philadelphia, 1882.

Amongst the many young men in England who are seeking along with me to continue and to perfect the English Renaissance—jeunes guerriers du drapeau romantique, as Gautier would have called us—there is none whose love of art is more flawless and fervent, whose artistic sense of beauty is more subtle and more delicate—none, indeed, who is dearer to myself—than the young poet whose verses I have brought with me to America; verses full of sweet sadness, and yet full of joy; for the most joyous poet is not he who sows the desolate highways of this world with the barren seed of laughter, but he who makes his sorrow most musical, this indeed being the meaning of joy in art—that incommunicable element of artistic delight which, in poetry, for instance, comes from what Keats called the 'sensuous life of verse,' the element of song in the singing, made so pleasurable to us by that wonder of motion which often has its origin in mere musical impulse, and in painting is to be sought for, from the subject never, but from the pictorial charm only— the scheme and symphony of the colour, the satisfying beauty of the design: so that the ultimate expression of our artistic movement in painting has been, not in the spiritual visions of the Pre-Raphaelites, for all their marvel of Greek legend and their mystery of Italian song, but in the work of such men as Whistler and Albert Moore, who have raised design and colour to the ideal level of poetry and music. For the quality of their exquisite painting comes from the mere inventive and creative handling of line and colour, from a certain form and choice of beautiful workmanship, which, rejecting all literary reminiscence and all metaphysical idea, is in itself entirely satisfying to the æsthetic sense—is, as the Greeks would say, an end in itself; the effect of their work being like the effect given to us by music; for music is the art in which form and matter are always one—the art whose subject cannot be separated from the method of its expression; the art which most completely realises for us the artistic ideal, and is the condition to which all the other arts are constantly aspiring.

Now, this increased sense of the absolutely satisfying value of beautiful workmanship, this recognition of the primary importance of the sensuous element in art, this love of art for art's sake, is the point in which we of the younger school have made a departure from the teaching of Mr. Ruskin,—a departure definite and different and decisive.

Master indeed of the knowledge of all noble living and of the wisdom of all spiritual things will he be to us ever, seeing that it was he who by the magic of his presence and the music of his lips taught us at Oxford that enthusiasm for beauty which is the secret of Hellenism, and that desire for creation which is the secret of life, and filled some of us, at least, with the lofty and passionate ambition to go forth into far and fair lands with some message for the nations and some mission for the world, and yet in his art criticism, his estimate of the joyous element of art, his whole method of approaching art, we are no longer with him; for the keystone to his æsthetic system is ethical always. He would judge of a picture by the amount of noble moral ideas it expresses; but to us the channels by which all noble work in painting can touch, and does touch, the soul are not those of truths of life or metaphysical truths. To him perfection of workmanship seems but the symbol of pride, and incompleteness of technical resource the image of an imagination too limitless to find within the limits of form its complete expression, or of a love too simple not to stammer in its tale. But to us the rule of art is not the rule of morals. In an ethical system, indeed, of any gentle mercy good intentions will, one is fain to fancy, have their recognition; but of those that would enter the serene House of Beauty the question that we ask is not what they had ever meant to do, but what they have done. Their pathetic intentions are of no value to us, but their realised creations only. *Pour moi je préfère les poètes qui font des vers, les médecins qui sachent guérir, les peintres qui sachent peindre.*

Nor, in looking at a work of art, should we be dreaming of what it symbolises, but rather loving it for what it is. Indeed, the transcendental spirit is alien to the spirit of art. The metaphysical mind of Asia may create for itself the monstrous and many-breasted idol, but to the Greek, pure artist, that work is most instinct with spiritual life which conforms most closely to the perfect facts of physical life also. Nor, in its primary aspect, has a painting, for instance, any more spiritual message or meaning for us than a blue tile from the wall of Damascus, or a Hitzen vase. It is a beautifully coloured surface, nothing more, and affects us by no suggestion stolen from philosophy, no pathos pilfered from literature, no feeling filched from a poet, but by its own incommunicable artistic essence—by that selection of truth which we call style, and that relation of values which is the draughtsmanship of painting, by the whole quality of the workmanship, the arabesque of the design, the splendour of the colour, for these things are enough to stir the most divine and remote of the chords which make music in our soul, and colour, indeed, is of itself a mystical presence on things, and tone a kind of sentiment.

This, then—the new departure of our younger school—is the chief characteristic of Mr. Rennell Rodd's poetry; for, while there is much in his work that may interest the intellect, much that will excite the emotions, and many-cadenced chords of sweet and simple sentiment—for to those who love Art for its own sake all other things are added—yet, the effect which they pre-eminently seek to produce is purely an artistic one. Such a poem as The Sea-King's Grave, with all its majesty of melody as sonorous and as strong as the sea by whose pine-fringed shores it was thus nobly conceived and nobly fashioned; or the little poem that follows it, whose cunning workmanship, wrought with such an artistic sense of limitation, one might liken to the rare chasing of the mirror that is its motive; or In a Church, pale flower of one of those exquisite moments when all things except the moment itself seem so curiously real, and when the old memories of forgotten days are touched and made tender, and the familiar place grows fervent and solemn suddenly with a vision of the undying beauty of the gods that died; or the scene in Chartres Cathedral, sombre silence brooding on vault and arch, silent people kneeling on the dust of the desolate pavement as the young priest lifts Lord Christ's body in a crystal star, and then the sudden beams of scarlet light that break through the blazoned window and smite on the carven screen, and sudden organ peals of mighty music rolling and echoing from choir to canopy, and from spire to shaft, and over all the clear glad voice of a singing boy, affecting one as a thing over-sweet, and striking just the right artistic keynote for one's emotions; or At Lanuvium, through the music of whose lines one seems to hear again the murmur of the Mantuan bees straying down from their own green valleys and inland streams to find what honeyed amber the sea-flowers might be hiding; or the poem written In the Coliseum, which gives one the same artistic joy that one gets watching a handicraftsman at his work, a goldsmith hammering out his gold into those thin plates as delicate as the petals of a yellow rose, or drawing it out into the long wires like tangled sunbeams, so perfect and precious is the mere handling of it; or the little lyric interludes that break in here and there like the singing of a thrush, and are as swift and as sure as the beating of a bird's wing, as light and bright as the apple-blossoms that flutter fitfully down to the orchard grass after a spring shower, and look the lovelier for the rain's tears lying on their dainty veinings of pink and pearl; or the sonnets—for Mr. Rodd is one of those qui sonnent le sonnet, as the Ronsardists used to say—that one called On the Border Hills, with its fiery wonder of imagination and the strange beauty of its eighth line; or the one which tells of the sorrow of the great king for the little dead child—well, all these poems aim, as I said, at producing a purely artistic effect, and have the rare and exquisite quality that belongs to work of that kind; and I feel that the entire subordination in our æsthetic movement of all merely emotional and intellectual motives to the vital informing poetic principle is the surest sign of our strength.

But it is not enough that a work of art should conform to the æsthetic demands of the age: there should be also about it, if it is to give us any permanent delight, the impress of a distinct individuality. Whatever work we have in the nineteenth century must rest on the two poles of personality and perfection. And so in this little volume, by separating the earlier and more simple work from the work that is later and stronger and possesses increased technical power and more artistic vision, one might weave these disconnected poems, these stray and scattered threads, into one fiery-coloured strand of life, noting first a boy's mere gladness of being young, with all its simple joy in field and flower, in sunlight and in song, and then the bitterness of sudden sorrow at the ending by Death of one of the brief and beautiful friendships of one's youth, with all those unanswered longings and questionings unsatisfied by which we vex, so uselessly, the marble face of death; the artistic contrast between the discontented incompleteness of the spirit and the complete perfection of the style that expresses it forming the chief element of the æsthetic charm of these particular poems;—and then the birth of Love, and all the wonder and the fear and the perilous delight of one on whose boyish brows the little wings of love have beaten for the first time; and the love-songs, so dainty and delicate, little swallow-flights of music, and full of such fragrance and freedom that they might all be sung in the open air and across moving water; and then autumn, coming with its choirless woods and odorous decay and ruined loveliness, Love lying dead; and the sense of the mere pity of it.

One might stop there, for from a young poet one should ask for no deeper chords of life than those that love and friendship make eternal for us; and the best poems in the volume belong clearly to a later time, a time when these real experiences become absorbed and gathered up into a form which seems from such real experiences to be the most alien and the most remote; when the simple expression of joy or sorrow suffices no longer, and lives rather in the stateliness of the cadenced metre, in the music and colour of the linked words, than in any direct utterance; lives, one might say, in the perfection of the form more than in the pathos of the feeling. And yet, after the broken music of love and the burial of love in the autumn woods, we can trace that wandering among strange people, and in lands unknown to us, by which we try so pathetically to heal the hurts of the life we know, and that pure and passionate devotion to Art which one gets when the harsh reality of life has too suddenly wounded one, and is with discontent or sorrow marring one's youth, just as often, I think, as one gets it from any natural joy of living; and that curious intensity of vision by which, in moments of overmastering sadness and despair ungovernable, artistic things will live in one's memory with a vivid realism caught from the life which they help one to forget—an old grey tomb in Flanders with a strange legend on it, making one think how, perhaps, passion does live on after death; a necklace of blue and amber beads and a broken mirror found in a girl's grave at Rome, a marble image of a boy habited like Erôs, and with the pathetic tradition of a great king's sorrow lingering about it like a purple shadow,—over all these the tired spirit broods with that calm and certain joy that one gets when one has found something that the ages never dull and the world cannot harm; and with it comes that desire of Greek things which is often an artistic method of expressing one's desire for perfection; and that longing for the old dead days which is so modern, so incomplete, so touching, being, in a way, the inverted torch of Hope, which burns the hand it should guide; and for many things a little sadness, and for all things a great love; and lastly, in the pinewood by the sea, once more the quick and vital pulse of joyous youth leaping and laughing in every line, the frank and fearless freedom of wave and wind waking into fire life's burnt-out ashes and into song the silent lips of pain,—how clearly one seems to see it all, the long colonnade of pines with sea and sky peeping in here and there like a flitting of silver; the open place in the green, deep heart of the wood with the little moss-grown altar to the old Italian god in it; and the flowers all about, cyclamen in the shadowy places, and the stars of the white narcissus lying like snow-flakes over the grass, where the quick, bright-eyed lizard starts by the stone, and the snake lies coiled lazily in the sun on the hot sand, and overhead the gossamer floats from the branches like thin, tremulous threads of gold,—the scene is so perfect for its motive, for surely here, if anywhere, the real gladness of life might be revealed to one's youth— the gladness that comes, not from the rejection, but from the absorption, of all passion, and is like that serene calm that dwells in the faces of the Greek statues, and which despair and sorrow cannot touch, but intensify only.

In some such way as this we could gather up these strewn and scattered petals of song into one perfect rose of life, and yet, perhaps, in so doing, we might be missing the true quality of the poems; one's real life is so often the life that one does not lead; and beautiful poems, like threads of beautiful silks, may be woven into many patterns and to suit many designs, all wonderful and all different: and romantic poetry, too, is essentially the poetry of impressions, being like that latest school of painting, the school of Whistler and Albert Moore, in its choice of situation as opposed to subject; in its dealing with the exceptions rather than with the types of life; in its brief intensity; in what one might call its fiery-coloured momentariness, it being indeed the momentary situations of life, the momentary aspects of nature, which poetry and painting now seek to render for us. Sincerity and constancy will the artist, indeed, have always; but sincerity in art is merely that plastic perfection of execution without which a poem or a painting, however noble its sentiment or human its origin, is but wasted and unreal work, and the constancy of the artist cannot be to any definite rule or system of living, but to that principle of beauty only through which the inconstant shadows of his life are in their most fleeting moment arrested and made permanent. He will not, for instance, in intellectual matters acquiesce in that facile orthodoxy of our day which is so reasonable and so artistically uninteresting, nor yet will he desire that fiery faith of the antique time which, while it intensified, yet limited the vision; still less will he allow the calm of his culture to be marred by the discordant despair of doubt or the sadness of a sterile scepticism; for the Valley Perilous, where ignorant armies clash by night, is no resting-place meet for her to whom the gods have assigned the clear upland, the serene height, and the sunlit air,—rather will he be always curiously testing new forms of belief, tinging his nature with the sentiment that still lingers about some beautiful creeds, and searching for experience itself, and not for the fruits of experience; when he has got its secret, he will leave without regret much that was once very precious to him. 'I am always insincere,' says Emerson somewhere, 'as knowing that there are other moods': 'Les émotions,' wrote Théophile Gautier once in a review of Arsène Houssaye, 'Les émotions ne se ressemblent pas, mais être ému—voilà l'important.'

Now, this is the secret of the art of the modern romantic school, and gives one the right keynote for its apprehension; but the real quality of all work which, like Mr. Rodd's, aims, as I said, at a purely artistic effect, cannot be described in terms of intellectual criticism; it is too intangible for that. One can perhaps convey it best in terms of the other arts, and by reference to them; and, indeed, some of these poems are as iridescent and as exquisite as a lovely fragment of Venetian glass; others as delicate in perfect workmanship and as single in natural motive as an etching by Whistler is, or one of those beautiful little Greek figures which in the olive woods round Tanagra men can still find, with the faint gilding and the fading crimson not yet fled from hair and lips and raiment; and many of them seem like one of Corot's twilights just passing into music; for not merely in visible colour, but in sentiment also—which is the colour of poetry—may there be a kind of tone.

But I think that the best likeness to the quality of this young poet's work I ever saw was in the landscape by the Loire. We were staying once, he and I, at Amboise, that little village with its grey slate roofs and steep streets and gaunt, grim gateway, where the quiet cottages nestle like white pigeons into the sombre clefts of the great bastioned rock, and the stately Renaissance houses stand silent and apart—very desolate now, but with some memory of the old days still lingering about the delicately-twisted pillars, and the carved doorways, with their grotesque animals, and laughing masks, and quaint heraldic devices, all reminding one of a people who could not think life real till they had made it fantastic. And above the village, and beyond the bend of the river, we used to go in the afternoon, and sketch from one of the big barges that bring the wine in autumn and the wood in winter down to the sea, or lie in the long grass and make plans *pour la gloire, et pour ennuyer les philistins,* or wander along the low, sedgy banks, 'matching our reeds in sportive rivalry,' as comrades used in the old Sicilian days; and the land was an ordinary land enough, and bare, too, when one thought of Italy, and how the oleanders were robing the hillsides by Genoa in scarlet, and the cyclamen filling with its purple every valley from Florence to Rome; for there was not much real beauty, perhaps, in it, only long, white dusty roads and straight rows of formal poplars; but, now and then, some little breaking gleam of broken light would lend to the grey field and the silent barn a secret and a mystery that were hardly their own, would transfigure for one exquisite moment the peasants passing down through the vineyard, or the shepherd watching on the hill, would tip the willows with silver and touch the river into gold; and the wonder of the effect, with the strange simplicity of the material, always seemed to me to be a little like the quality of these the verses of my friend.

MRS. LANGTRY AS HESTER GRAZEBROOK

(*New York World*, November 7, 1882.)

It is only in the best Greek gems, on the silver coins of Syracuse, or among the marble figures of the Parthenon frieze, that one can find the ideal representation of the marvellous beauty of that face which laughed through the leaves last night as Hester Grazebrook.

Pure Greek it is, with the grave low forehead, the exquisitely arched brow; the noble chiselling of the mouth, shaped as if it were the mouthpiece of an instrument of music; the supreme and splendid curve of the cheek; the augustly pillared throat which bears it all: it is Greek, because the lines which compose it are so definite and so strong, and yet so exquisitely harmonised that the effect is one of simple loveliness purely: Greek, because its essence and its quality, as is the quality of music and of architecture, is that of beauty based on absolutely mathematical laws.

But while art remains dumb and immobile in its passionless serenity, with the beauty of this face it is different: the grey eyes lighten into blue or deepen into violet as fancy succeeds fancy; the lips become flower-like in laughter or, tremulous as a bird's wing, mould themselves at last into the strong and bitter moulds of pain or scorn. And then motion comes, and the statue wakes into life. But the life is not the ordinary life of common days; it is life with a new value given to it, the value of art: and the charm to me of Hester Grazebrook's acting in the first scene of the play {43} last night was that mingling of classic grace with absolute reality which is the secret of all beautiful art, of the plastic work of the Greeks and of the pictures of Jean François Millet equally.

I do not think that the sovereignty and empire of women's beauty has at all passed away, though we may no longer go to war for them as the Greeks did for the daughter of Leda. The greatest empire still remains for them— the empire of art. And, indeed, this wonderful face, seen last night for the first time in America, has filled and permeated with the pervading image of its type the whole of our modern art in England. Last century it was the romantic type which dominated in art, the type loved by Reynolds and Gainsborough, of wonderful contrasts of colour, of exquisite and varying charm of expression, but without that definite plastic feeling which divides classic from romantic work. This type degenerated into mere facile prettiness in the hands of lesser masters, and, in protest against it, was created by the hands of the Pre-Raphaelites a new type, with its rare combination of Greek form with Florentine mysticism. But this mysticism becomes over-strained and a burden, rather than an aid to expression, and a desire for the pure Hellenic joy and serenity came in its place; and in all our modern work, in the paintings of such men as Albert Moore and Leighton and Whistler, we can trace the influence of this single face giving fresh life and inspiration in the form of a new artistic ideal.

As regards Hester Grazebrook's dresses, the first was a dress whose grace depended entirely on the grace of the person who wore it. It was merely the simple dress of a village girl in England. The second was a lovely combination of blue and creamy lace. But the masterpiece was undoubtedly the last, a symphony in silver-grey and pink, a pure melody of colour which I feel sure Whistler would call a Scherzo, and take as its visible motive the moonlight wandering in silver mist through a rose-garden; unless indeed he saw this dress, in which case he would paint it and nothing else, for it is a dress such as Velasquez only could paint, and Whistler very wisely always paints those things which are within reach of Velasquez only.

The scenery was, of course, prepared in a hurry. Still, much of it was very good indeed: the first scene especially, with its graceful trees and open forge and cottage porch, though the roses were dreadfully out of tone and, besides their crudity of colour, were curiously badly grouped. The last scene was exceedingly clever and true to nature as well, being that combination of lovely scenery and execrable architecture which is so specially characteristic of a German spa. As for the drawing-room scene, I cannot regard it as in any way a success. The heavy ebony doors are entirely out of keeping with the satin panels; the silk hangings and festoons of black and yellow are quite meaningless in their position and consequently quite ugly; the carpet is out of all colour relation with the rest of the room, and the table-cover is mauve. Still, to have decorated ever so bad a room in six days must, I suppose, be a subject of respectful wonder, though I should have fancied that Mr. Wallack had many very much better sets in his own stock.

But I am beginning to quarrel generally with most modern scene-painting. A scene is primarily a decorative background for the actors, and should always be kept subordinate, first to the players, their dress, gesture, and action; and secondly, to the fundamental principle of decorative art, which is not to imitate but to suggest nature. If the landscape is given its full realistic value, the value of the figures to which it serves as a background is impaired and often lost, and so the painted hangings of the Elizabethan age were a far more artistic, and so a far more rational form of scenery than most modern scene-painting is. From the same master-hand which designed the curtain of Madison Square Theatre I should like very much to see a good decorative landscape in scene-painting; for I have seen no open-air scene in any theatre which did not really mar the value of the actors. One must either, like Titian, make the landscape subordinate to the figures, or, like Claude, the figures subordinate to the landscape; for if we desire realistic acting we cannot have realistic scene-painting.

I need not describe, however, how the beauty of Hester Grazebrook survived the crude roses and the mauve tablecloth triumphantly. That it is a beauty that will be appreciated to the full in America I do not doubt for a moment, for it is only countries which possess great beauty that can appreciate beauty at all. It may also influence the art of America as it has influenced the art of England, for of the rare Greek type it is the most absolutely perfect example.

The Philistine may, of course, object that to be absolutely perfect is impossible. Well, that is so: but then it is only the impossible things that are worth doing nowadays!

WOMAN'S DRESS

(*Pall Mall Gazette*, October 14, 1884.)

Mr. Oscar Wilde, who asks us to permit him 'that most charming of all pleasures, the pleasure of answering one's critics,' sends us the following remarks:—

The 'Girl Graduate' must of course have precedence, not merely for her sex but for her sanity: her letter is extremely sensible. She makes two points: that high heels are a necessity for any lady who wishes to keep her dress clean from the Stygian mud of our streets, and that without a tight corset 'the ordinary number of petticoats and etceteras' cannot be properly or conveniently held up. Now, it is quite true that as long as the lower garments are suspended from the hips a corset is an absolute necessity; the mistake lies in not suspending all apparel from the shoulders. In the latter case a corset becomes useless, the body is left free and unconfined for respiration and motion, there is more health, and consequently more beauty. Indeed all the most ungainly and uncomfortable articles of dress that fashion has ever in her folly prescribed, not the tight corset merely, but the farthingale, the vertugadin, the hoop, the crinoline, and that modern monstrosity the so-called 'dress improver' also, all of them have owed their origin to the same error, the error of not seeing that it is from the shoulders, and from the shoulders only, that all garments should be hung.

And as regards high heels, I quite admit that some additional height to the shoe or boot is necessary if long gowns are to be worn in the street; but what I object to is that the height should be given to the heel only, and not to the sole of the foot also. The modern high-heeled boot is, in fact, merely the clog of the time of Henry VI., with the front prop left out, and its inevitable effect is to throw the body forward, to shorten the steps, and consequently to produce that want of grace which always follows want of freedom.

Why should clogs be despised? Much art has been expended on clogs.

They have been made of lovely woods, and delicately inlaid with ivory, and with mother-of-pearl. A clog might be a dream of beauty, and, if not too high or too heavy, most comfortable also. But if there be any who do not like clogs, let them try some adaptation of the trouser of the Turkish lady, which is loose round the limb and tight at the ankle.

The 'Girl Graduate,' with a pathos to which I am not insensible, entreats me not to apotheosise 'that awful, befringed, beflounced, and bekilted divided skirt.' Well, I will acknowledge that the fringes, the flounces, and the kilting do certainly defeat the whole object of the dress, which is that of ease and liberty; but I regard these things as mere wicked superfluities, tragic proofs that the divided skirt is ashamed of its own division. The principle of the dress is good, and, though it is not by any means perfection, it is a step towards it.

Here I leave the 'Girl Graduate,' with much regret, for Mr. Wentworth Huyshe. Mr. Huyshe makes the old criticism that Greek dress is unsuited to our climate, and, to me the somewhat new assertion, that the men's dress of a hundred years ago was preferable to that of the second part of the seventeenth century, which I consider to have been the exquisite period of English costume.

Now, as regards the first of these two statements, I will say, to begin with, that the warmth of apparel does not depend really on the number of garments worn, but on the material of which they are made. One of the chief faults of modern dress is that it is composed of far too many articles of clothing, most of which are of the wrong substance; but over a substratum of pure wool, such as is supplied by Dr. Jaeger under the modern German system, some modification of Greek costume is perfectly applicable to our climate, our country and our century. This important fact has already been pointed out by Mr. E. W. Godwin in his excellent, though too brief, handbook on Dress, contributed to the Health Exhibition. I call it an important fact because it makes almost any form of lovely costume perfectly practicable in our cold climate. Mr. Godwin, it is true, points out that the English ladies of the thirteenth century abandoned after some time the flowing garments of the early Renaissance in favour of a tighter mode, such as Northern Europe seems to demand. This I quite admit, and its significance; but what I contend, and what I am sure Mr. Godwin would agree with me in, is that the principles, the laws of Greek dress may be perfectly realised, even in a moderately tight gown with sleeves: I mean the principle of suspending all apparel from the shoulders, and of relying for beauty of effect not on the stiff ready-made ornaments of the modern milliner—the bows where there should be no bows, and the flounces where there should be no flounces—but on the exquisite play of light and line that one gets from rich and rippling folds. I am not proposing any antiquarian revival of an ancient costume, but trying merely to point out the right laws of dress, laws which are dictated by art and not by archæology, by science and not by fashion; and just as the best work of art in our days is that which combines classic grace with absolute reality, so from a continuation of the Greek principles of beauty with the German principles of health will come, I feel certain, the costume of the future.

And now to the question of men's dress, or rather to Mr. Huyshe's claim of the superiority, in point of costume, of the last quarter of the eighteenth century over the second quarter of the seventeenth. The broad-brimmed hat of 1640 kept the rain of winter and the glare of summer from the face; the same cannot be said of the hat of one hundred years ago, which, with its comparatively narrow brim and high crown, was the precursor of the modern 'chimney-pot': a wide turned-down collar is a healthier thing than a strangling stock, and a short cloak much more comfortable than a sleeved overcoat, even though the latter may have had 'three capes'; a cloak is easier to put on and off, lies lightly on the shoulder in summer, and wrapped round one in winter keeps one perfectly warm. A doublet, again, is simpler than a coat and waistcoat; instead of two garments one has one; by not being open also it protects the chest better.

Short loose trousers are in every way to be preferred to the tight knee-breeches which often impede the proper circulation of the blood; and finally, the soft leather boots which could be worn above or below the knee, are more supple, and give consequently more freedom, than the stiff Hessian which Mr. Huyshe so praises. I say nothing about the question of grace and picturesqueness, for I suppose that no one, not even Mr. Huyshe, would prefer a maccaroni to a cavalier, a Lawrence to a Vandyke, or the third George to the first Charles; but for ease, warmth and comfort this seventeenth-century dress is infinitely superior to anything that came after it, and I do not think it is excelled by any preceding form of costume. I sincerely trust that we may soon see in England some national revival of it.

MORE RADICAL IDEAS UPON DRESS REFORM

(*Pall Mall Gazette*, November 11, 1884.)

I have been much interested at reading the large amount of correspondence that has been called forth by my recent lecture on Dress. It shows me that the subject of dress reform is one that is occupying many wise and charming people, who have at heart the principles of health, freedom, and beauty in costume, and I hope that 'H. B. T.' and 'Materfamilias' will have all the real influence which their letters—excellent letters both of them—certainly deserve.

I turn first to Mr. Huyshe's second letter, and the drawing that accompanies it; but before entering into any examination of the theory contained in each, I think I should state at once that I have absolutely no idea whether this gentleman wears his hair longer short, or his cuffs back or forward, or indeed what he is like at all. I hope he consults his own comfort and wishes in everything which has to do with his dress, and is allowed to enjoy that individualism in apparel which he so eloquently claims for himself, and so foolishly tries to deny to others; but I really could not take Mr. Wentworth Huyshe's personal appearance as any intellectual basis for an investigation of the principles which should guide the costume of a nation. I am not denying the force, or even the popularity, of the ''Eave arf a brick' school of criticism, but I acknowledge it does not interest me. The gamin in the gutter may be a necessity, but the gamin in discussion is a nuisance. So I will proceed at once to the real point at issue, the value of the late eighteenth-century costume over that worn in the second quarter of the seventeenth: the relative merits, that is, of the principles contained in each. Now, as regards the eighteenth-century costume, Mr. Wentworth Huyshe acknowledges that he has had no practical experience of it at all; in fact, he makes a pathetic appeal to his friends to corroborate him in his assertion, which I do not question for a moment, that he has never been 'guilty of the eccentricity' of wearing himself the dress which he proposes for general adoption by others.

There is something so naïve and so amusing about this last passage in Mr. Huyshe's letter that I am really in doubt whether I am not doing him a wrong in regarding him as having any serious, or sincere, views on the question of a possible reform in dress; still, as irrespective of any attitude of Mr. Huyshe's in the matter, the subject is in itself an interesting one, I think it is worth continuing, particularly as I have myself worn this late eighteenth-century dress many times, both in public and in private, and so may claim to have a very positive right to speak on its comfort and suitability. The particular form of the dress I wore was very similar to that given in Mr. Godwin's handbook, from a print of Northcote's, and had a certain elegance and grace about it which was very charming; still, I gave it up for these reasons:—After a further consideration of the laws of dress I saw that a doublet is a far simpler and easier garment than a coat and waistcoat, and, if buttoned from the shoulder, far warmer also, and that tails have no place in costume, except on some Darwinian theory of heredity; from absolute experience in the matter I found that the excessive tightness of knee-breeches is not really comfortable if one wears them constantly; and, in fact, I satisfied myself that the dress is not one founded on any real principles. The broad-brimmed hat and loose cloak, which, as my object was not, of course, historical accuracy but modern ease, I had always worn with the costume in question, I have still retained, and find them most comfortable.

Well, although Mr. Huyshe has no real experience of the dress he proposes, he gives us a drawing of it, which he labels, somewhat prematurely, 'An ideal dress.' An ideal dress of course it is not; 'passably picturesque,' he says I may possibly think it; well, passably picturesque it may be, but not beautiful, certainly, simply because it is not founded on right principles, or, indeed, on any principles at all. Picturesqueness one may get in a variety of ways; ugly things that are strange, or unfamiliar to us, for instance, may be picturesque, such as a late sixteenth-century costume, or a Georgian house. Ruins, again, may be picturesque, but beautiful they never can be, because their lines are meaningless. Beauty, in fact, is to be got only from the perfection of principles; and in 'the ideal dress' of Mr. Huyshe there are no ideas or principles at all, much less the perfection of either. Let us examine it, and see its faults; they are obvious to any one who desires more than a

'Fancy-dress ball' basis for costume. To begin with, the hat and boots are all wrong. Whatever one wears on the extremities, such as the feet and head, should, for the sake of comfort, be made of a soft material, and for the sake of freedom should take its shape from the way one chooses to wear it, and not from any stiff, stereotyped design of hat or boot maker. In a hat made on right principles one should be able to turn the brim up or down according as the day is dark or fair, dry or wet; but the hat brim of Mr. Huyshe's drawing is perfectly stiff, and does not give much protection to the face, or the possibility of any at all to the back of the head or the ears, in case of a cold east wind; whereas the bycocket, a hat made in accordance with the right laws, can be turned down behind and at the sides, and so give the same warmth as a hood. The crown, again, of Mr. Huyshe's hat is far too high; a high crown diminishes the stature of a small person, and in the case of any one who is tall is a great inconvenience when one is getting in and out of hansoms and railway carriages, or passing under a street awning: in no case is it of any value whatsoever, and being useless it is of course against the principles of dress.

As regards the boots, they are not quite so ugly or so uncomfortable as the hat; still they are evidently made of stiff leather, as otherwise they would fall down to the ankle, whereas the boot should be made of soft leather always, and if worn high at all must be either laced up the front or carried well over the knee: in the latter case one combines perfect freedom for walking together with perfect protection against rain, neither of which advantages a short stiff boot will ever give one, and when one is resting in the house the long soft boot can be turned down as the boot of 1640 was. Then there is the overcoat: now, what are the right principles of an overcoat? To begin with, it should be capable of being easily put on or off, and worn over any kind of dress; consequently it should never have narrow sleeves, such as are shown in Mr. Huyshe's drawing. If an opening or slit for the arm is required it should be made quite wide, and may be protected by a flap, as in that excellent overall the modern Inverness cape; secondly, it should not be too tight, as otherwise all freedom of walking is impeded. If the young gentleman in the drawing buttons his overcoat he may succeed in being statuesque, though that I doubt very strongly, but he will never succeed in being swift; his super-totus is made for him on no principle whatsoever; a super-totus, or overall,

153

should be capable of being worn long or short, quite loose or moderately tight, just as the wearer wishes; he should be able to have one arm free and one arm covered, or both arms free or both arms covered, just as he chooses for his convenience in riding, walking, or driving; an overall again should never be heavy, and should always be warm: lastly, it should be capable of being easily carried if one wants to take it off; in fact, its principles are those of freedom and comfort, and a cloak realises them all, just as much as an overcoat of the pattern suggested by Mr. Huyshe violates them.

The knee-breeches are of course far too tight; any one who has worn them for any length of time—any one, in fact, whose views on the subject are not purely theoretical—will agree with me there; like everything else in the dress, they are a great mistake. The substitution of the jacket for the coat and waistcoat of the period is a step in the right direction, which I am glad to see; it is, however, far too tight over the hips for any possible comfort. Whenever a jacket or doublet comes below the waist it should be slit at each side. In the seventeenth century the skirt of the jacket was sometimes laced on by points and tags, so that it could be removed at will, sometimes it was merely left open at the sides: in each case it exemplified what are always the true principles of dress, I mean freedom and adaptability to circumstances.

Finally, as regards drawings of this kind, I would point out that there is absolutely no limit at all to the amount of 'passably picturesque' costumes which can be either revived or invented for us; but that unless a costume is founded on principles and exemplified laws, it never can be of any real value to us in the reform of dress. This particular drawing of Mr. Huyshe's, for instance, proves absolutely nothing, except that our grandfathers did not understand the proper laws of dress. There is not a single rule of right costume which is not violated in it, for it gives us stiffness, tightness and discomfort instead of comfort, freedom and ease.

Now here, on the other hand, is a dress which, being founded on principles, can serve us as an excellent guide and model; it has been drawn for me, most kindly, by Mr. Godwin from the Duke of Newcastle's delightful book on horsemanship, a book which is one of our best authorities on our best era of costume. I do not of course propose it necessarily for absolute imitation; that is not the way in which one should regard it; it is not, I mean, a revival of a dead costume, but a realisation of living laws. I give it as an example of a particular application of principles which are universally right. This rationally dressed young man can turn his hat brim down if it rains, and his loose trousers and boots down if he is tired—that is, he can adapt his costume to circumstances; then he enjoys perfect freedom, the arms and legs are not made awkward or uncomfortable by the excessive tightness of narrow sleeves and knee-breeches, and the hips are left quite untrammelled, always an important point; and as regards comfort, his jacket is not too loose for warmth, nor too close for respiration; his neck is well protected without being strangled, and even his ostrich feathers, if any Philistine should object to them, are not merely dandyism, but fan him very pleasantly, I am sure, in summer, and when the weather is bad they are no doubt left at home, and his cloak taken out. The value of the dress is simply that every separate article of it expresses a law. My young man is consequently apparelled with ideas, while Mr. Huyshe's young man is stiffened with facts; the latter teaches one nothing; from the former one learns everything. I need hardly say that this dress is good, not because it is seventeenth century, but because it is constructed on the true principles of costume, just as a square lintel or a pointed arch is good, not because one may be Greek and the other Gothic, but because each of them is the best method of spanning a certain-sized opening, or resisting a certain weight. The fact, however, that this dress was generally worn in England two centuries and a half ago shows at least this, that the right laws of dress have been understood and realised in our country, and so in our country may be realised and understood again. As regards the absolute beauty of this dress and its meaning, I should like to say a few words more. Mr. Wentworth Huyshe solemnly announces that 'he and those who think with him' cannot permit this question of beauty to be imported into the question of dress; that he and those who think with him take 'practical views on the subject,' and so on. Well, I will not enter here into a discussion as to how far any one who does not take beauty and the value of beauty into account can claim to be practical at all. The word practical is nearly always the last refuge of the uncivilised. Of all misused words it is the most evilly treated. But what I want to point out is that beauty is essentially organic; that is, it comes, not from without, but from within, not from any added prettiness, but from the perfection of its own being; and that consequently, as the body is beautiful, so all apparel that rightly clothes it must be beautiful also in its construction and in its lines.

I have no more desire to define ugliness than I have daring to define beauty; but still I would like to remind those who mock at beauty as being an unpractical thing of this fact, that an ugly thing is merely a thing that is badly made, or a thing that does not serve its purpose; that ugliness is want of fitness; that ugliness is failure; that ugliness is uselessness, such as ornament in the wrong place, while beauty, as some one finely said, is the purgation of all superfluities. There is a divine economy about beauty; it gives us just what is needful and no more, whereas ugliness is always extravagant; ugliness is a spendthrift and wastes its material; in fine, ugliness—and I would commend this remark to Mr. Wentworth Huyshe—ugliness, as much in costume as in anything else, is always the sign that somebody has been unpractical. So the costume of the future in England, if it is founded on the true laws of freedom, comfort, and adaptability to circumstances, cannot fail to be most beautiful also, because beauty is the sign always of the rightness of principles, the mystical seal that is set upon what is perfect, and upon what is perfect only.

As for your other correspondent, the first principle of dress that all garments should be hung from the shoulders and not from the waist seems to me to be generally approved of, although an 'Old Sailor' declares that no sailors or athletes ever suspend their clothes from the shoulders, but always from the hips. My own recollection of the river and running ground at Oxford—those two homes of Hellenism in our little Gothic town—is that the best runners and rowers (and my own college turned out many) wore always a tight jersey, with short drawers attached to it, the whole costume being woven in one piece. As for sailors it is true, I admit, and the bad custom seems to involve that constant 'hitching up' of the lower garments which, however popular in transpontine dramas, cannot, I think, but be considered an extremely awkward habit; and as all awkwardness comes from discomfort of some kind, I trust that this point in our sailor's dress will be looked to in the coming reform of our navy, for, in spite of all protests, I hope we are about to reform everything, from torpedoes to top-hats, and from crinolettes to cruises.

Then as regards clogs, my suggestion of them seems to have aroused a great deal of terror. Fashion in her high-heeled boots has screamed, and the dreadful word 'anachronism' has been used. Now, whatever is useful cannot be an anachronism. Such a word is applicable only to the revival of some folly; and, besides, in the England of our own day clogs are still worn in many of our manufacturing towns, such as Oldham. I fear that in Oldham they may not be dreams of beauty; in Oldham the art of inlaying them with ivory and with pearl may possibly be unknown; yet in Oldham they serve their purpose. Nor is it so long since they were worn by the upper classes of this country generally. Only a few days ago I had the pleasure of talking to a lady who remembered with affectionate regret the clogs of her girlhood; they were, according to her, not too high nor too heavy, and were provided, besides, with some kind of spring in the sole so as to make them the more supple for the foot in walking. Personally, I object to all additional height being given to a boot or shoe; it is really against the proper principles of dress, although, if any such height is to be given it should be by means of two props, not one; but what I should prefer to see is some adaptation of the divided skirt or long and moderately loose knickerbockers. If, however, the divided skirt is to be of any positive value, it must give up all idea of 'being identical in appearance with an ordinary skirt'; it must diminish the moderate width of each of its divisions, and sacrifice its foolish frills and flounces; the moment it imitates a dress it is lost; but let it visibly announce itself as what it actually is, and it will go far towards solving a real difficulty. I feel sure that there will be found many graceful and charming girls ready to adopt a costume founded on these principles, in spite of Mr. Wentworth Huyshe's terrible threat that he will not propose to them as long as they wear it, for all charges of a want of womanly character in these forms of dress are really meaningless; every right article of apparel belongs equally to both sexes, and there is absolutely no such thing as a definitely feminine garment. One word of warning I should like to be allowed to give: The over-tunic should be made full and moderately loose; it may, if desired, be shaped more or less to the figure, but in no case should it be confined at the waist by any straight band or belt; on the contrary, it should fall from the shoulder to the knee, or below it, in fine curves and vertical lines, giving more freedom and consequently more grace. Few garments are so absolutely unbecoming as a belted tunic that reaches to the knees, a fact which I wish some of our Rosalinds would consider when they don doublet and hose; indeed, to the disregard of this artistic principle is due the ugliness, the want of proportion, in the Bloomer costume, a costume which in other respects is sensible.

MR. WHISTLER'S TEN O'CLOCK

(*Pall Mall Gazette*, February 21, 1885.)

Last night, at Prince's Hall, Mr. Whistler made his first public appearance as a lecturer on art, and spoke for more than an hour with really marvellous eloquence on the absolute uselessness of all lectures of the kind. Mr. Whistler began his lecture with a very pretty aria on prehistoric history, describing how in earlier times hunter and warrior would go forth to chase and foray, while the artist sat at home making cup and bowl for their service. Rude imitations of nature they were first, like the gourd bottle, till the sense of beauty and form developed and, in all its exquisite proportions, the first vase was fashioned. Then came a higher civilisation of architecture and armchairs, and with exquisite design, and dainty diaper, the useful things of life were made lovely; and the hunter and the warrior lay on the couch when they were tired, and, when they were thirsty, drank from the bowl, and never cared to lose the exquisite proportion of the one, or the delightful ornament of the other; and this attitude of the primitive anthropophagous Philistine formed the text of the lecture and was the attitude which Mr. Whistler entreated his audience to adopt towards art. Remembering, no doubt, many charming invitations to wonderful private views, this fashionable assemblage seemed somewhat aghast, and not a little amused, at being told that the slightest appearance among a civilised people of any joy in beautiful things is a grave impertinence to all painters; but Mr. Whistler was relentless, and, with charming ease and much grace of manner, explained to the public that the only thing they should cultivate was ugliness, and that on their permanent stupidity rested all the hopes of art in the future.

The scene was in every way delightful; he stood there, a miniature Mephistopheles, mocking the majority! He was like a brilliant surgeon lecturing to a class composed of subjects destined ultimately for dissection, and solemnly assuring them how valuable to science their maladies were, and how absolutely uninteresting the slightest symptoms of health on their part would be. In fairness to the audience, however, I must say that they seemed extremely gratified at being rid of the dreadful responsibility of admiring anything, and nothing could have exceeded their enthusiasm when they were told by Mr. Whistler that no matter how vulgar their dresses were, or how hideous their surroundings at home, still it was possible that a great painter, if there was such a thing, could, by contemplating them in the twilight and half closing his eyes, see them under really picturesque conditions, and produce a picture which they were not to attempt to understand, much less dare to enjoy. Then there were some arrows, barbed and brilliant, shot off, with all the speed and splendour of fireworks, and the archæologists, who spend their lives in verifying the birthplaces of nobodies, and estimate the value of a work of art by its date or its decay; at the art critics who always treat a picture as if it were a novel, and try and find out the plot; at dilettanti in general and amateurs in particular; and (O mea culpa!) at dress reformers most of all. 'Did not Velasquez paint crinolines? What more do you want?'

Having thus made a holocaust of humanity, Mr. Whistler turned to nature, and in a few moments convicted her of the Crystal Palace, Bank holidays, and a general overcrowding of detail, both in omnibuses and in landscapes, and then, in a passage of singular beauty, not unlike one that occurs in Corot's letters, spoke of the artistic value of dim dawns and dusks, when the mean facts of life are lost in exquisite and evanescent effects, when common things are touched with mystery and transfigured with beauty, when the warehouses become as palaces and the tall chimneys of the factory seem like campaniles in the silver air.

Finally, after making a strong protest against anybody but a painter judging of painting, and a pathetic appeal to the audience not to be lured by the æsthetic movement into having beautiful things about them, Mr. Whistler concluded his lecture with a pretty passage about Fusiyama on a fan, and made his bow to an audience which he had succeeded in completely fascinating by his wit, his brilliant paradoxes, and, at times, his real eloquence. Of course, with regard to the value of beautiful surroundings I differ entirely from Mr. Whistler. An artist is not an isolated fact; he is the resultant of a certain milieu and a certain entourage, and can no more be born of a nation that is devoid of any sense of beauty than a fig can grow from a thorn or a rose blossom from a thistle. That an artist will find beauty in ugliness, le beau dans l'horrible, is now a commonplace of the schools, the argot of the atelier, but I strongly deny that charming people should be condemned to live with magenta ottomans and Albert-blue curtains in their rooms in order that some painter may observe the side-lights on the one and the values of the other. Nor do I accept the dictum that only a painter is a judge of painting. I say that only an artist is a judge of art; there is a wide difference. As long as a painter is a painter merely, he should not be allowed to talk of anything but mediums and megilp, and on those subjects should be compelled to hold his tongue; it is only when he becomes an artist that the secret laws of artistic creation are revealed to him. For there are not many arts, but one art merely—poem, picture and Parthenon, sonnet and statue—all are in their essence the same, and he who knows one knows all. But the poet is the supreme artist, for he is the master of colour and of form, and the real musician besides, and is lord over all life and all arts; and so to the poet beyond all others are these mysteries known; to Edgar Allan Poe and to Baudelaire, not to Benjamin West and Paul Delaroche. However, I should not enjoy anybody else's lectures unless in a few points I disagreed with them, and Mr. Whistler's lecture last night was, like everything that he does, a masterpiece. Not merely for its clever satire and amusing jests will it be remembered, but for the pure and perfect beauty of many of its passages—passages delivered with an earnestness which seemed to amaze those who had looked on Mr. Whistler as a master of persiflage merely, and had not known him as we do, as a master of painting also. For that he is indeed one of the very greatest masters of painting is my opinion. And I may add that in this opinion Mr. Whistler himself entirely concurs.

THE RELATION OF DRESS TO ART: A NOTE IN BLACK AND WHITE ON MR. WHISTLER'S LECTURE

(*Pall Mall Gazette*, February 28, 1885.)

'How can you possibly paint these ugly three-cornered hats?' asked a reckless art critic once of Sir Joshua Reynolds. 'I see light and shade in them,' answered the artist. '*Les grands coloristes*,' says Baudelaire, in a charming article on the artistic value of frock coats, '*les grands coloristes savent faire de la couleur avec un habit noir, une cravate blanche, et un fond gris.*'

'Art seeks and finds the beautiful in all times, as did her high priest Rembrandt, when he saw the picturesque grandeur of the Jews' quarter of Amsterdam, and lamented not that its inhabitants were not Greeks,' were the fine and simple words used by Mr. Whistler in one of the most valuable passages of his lecture. The most valuable, that is, to the painter: for there is nothing of which the ordinary English painter needs more to be reminded than that the true artist does not wait for life to be made picturesque for him, but sees life under picturesque conditions always—under conditions, that is to say, which are at once new and delightful. But between the attitude of the painter towards the public and the attitude of a people towards art, there is a wide difference. That, under certain conditions of light and shade, what is ugly in fact may in its effect become beautiful, is true; and this, indeed, is the real modernité of art: but these conditions are exactly what we cannot be always sure of, as we stroll down Piccadilly in the glaring vulgarity of the noonday, or lounge in the park with a foolish sunset as a background. Were we able to carry our chiaroscuro about with us, as we do our umbrellas, all would be well; but this being impossible, I hardly think that pretty and delightful people will continue to wear a style of dress as ugly as it is useless and as meaningless as it is monstrous, even on the chance of such a master as Mr. Whistler spiritualising them into a symphony or refining them into a mist. For the arts are made for life, and not life for the arts.

Nor do I feel quite sure that Mr. Whistler has been himself always true to the dogma he seems to lay down, that a painter should paint only the dress of his age and of his actual surroundings: far be it from me to burden a butterfly with the heavy responsibility of its past: I have always been of opinion that consistency is the last refuge of the unimaginative: but have we not all seen, and most of us admired, a picture from his hand of exquisite English girls strolling by an opal sea in the fantastic dresses of Japan? Has not Tite Street been thrilled with the tidings that the models of Chelsea were posing to the master, in peplums, for pastels?

Whatever comes from Mr Whistler's brush is far too perfect in its loveliness to stand or fall by any intellectual dogmas on art, even by his own: for Beauty is justified of all her children, and cares nothing for explanations: but it is impossible to look through any collection of modern pictures in London, from Burlington House to the Grosvenor Gallery, without feeling that the professional model is ruining painting and reducing it to a condition of mere pose and pastiche.

Are we not all weary of him, that venerable impostor fresh from the steps of the Piazza di Spagna, who, in the leisure moments that he can spare from his customary organ, makes the round of the studios and is waited for in Holland Park? Do we not all recognise him, when, with the gay insouciance of his nation, he reappears on the walls of our summer exhibitions as everything that he is not, and as nothing that he is, glaring at us here as a patriarch of Canaan, here beaming as a brigand from the Abruzzi? Popular is he, this poor peripatetic professor of posing, with those whose joy it is to paint the posthumous portrait of the last philanthropist who in his lifetime had neglected to be photographed,—yet he is the sign of the decadence, the symbol of decay.

For all costumes are caricatures. The basis of Art is not the Fancy Ball. Where there is loveliness of dress, there is no dressing up. And so, were our national attire delightful in colour, and in construction simple and sincere; were dress the expression of the loveliness that it shields and of the swiftness and motion that it does not impede; did its lines break from the shoulder instead of bulging from the waist; did the inverted wineglass cease to be the ideal of form; were these things brought about, as brought about they will be, then would painting be no longer an artificial reaction against the ugliness of life, but become, as it should be, the natural expression of life's beauty. Nor would painting merely, but all the other arts also, be the gainers by a change such as that which I propose; the gainers, I mean, through the increased atmosphere of Beauty by which the artists would be surrounded and in which they would grow up. For Art is not to be taught in Academies. It is what one looks at, not what one listens to, that makes the artist. The real schools should be the streets. There is not, for instance, a single delicate line, or delightful proportion, in the dress of the Greeks, which is not echoed exquisitely in their architecture. A nation arrayed in stove-pipe hats and dress-improvers might have built the Pantechnicon possibly, but the Parthenon never. And finally, there is this to be said: Art, it is true, can never have any other claim but her own perfection, and it may be that the artist, desiring merely to contemplate and to create, is wise in not busying himself about change in others: yet wisdom is not always the best; there are times when she sinks to the level of common-sense; and from the passionate folly of those—and there are many—who desire that Beauty shall be confined no longer to the bric-à-brac of the collector and the dust of the museum, but shall be, as it should be, the natural and national inheritance of all,—from this noble unwisdom, I say, who knows what new loveliness shall be given to life, and, under these more exquisite conditions, what perfect artist born? Le milieu se renouvelant, l'art se renouvelle.

Speaking, however, from his own passionless pedestal, Mr. Whistler, in pointing out that the power of the painter is to be found in his power of vision, not in his cleverness of hand, has expressed a truth which needed expression, and which, coming from the lord of form and colour, cannot fail to have its influence. His lecture, the Apocrypha though it be for the people, yet remains from this time as the Bible for the painter, the masterpiece of masterpieces, the song of songs. It is true he has pronounced the panegyric of the Philistine, but I fancy Ariel praising Caliban for a jest: and, in that he has read the Commination Service over the critics, let all men thank him, the critics themselves, indeed, most of all, for he has now relieved them from the necessity of a tedious existence. Considered, again, merely as an orator, Mr. Whistler seems to me to stand almost alone. Indeed, among all our public speakers I know but few who can combine so felicitously as he does the mirth and malice of Puck with the style of the minor prophets.

KEATS'S SONNET ON BLUE

(*Century Guild Hobby Horse*, July 1886.)

During my tour in America I happened one evening to find myself in Louisville, Kentucky. The subject I had selected to speak on was the Mission of Art in the Nineteenth Century, and in the course of my lecture I had occasion to quote Keats's Sonnet on Blue as an example of the poet's delicate sense of colour-harmonies. When my lecture was concluded there came round to see me a lady of middle age, with a sweet gentle manner and a most musical voice. She introduced herself to me as Mrs. Speed, the daughter of George Keats, and invited me to come and examine the Keats manuscripts in her possession. I spent most of the next day with her, reading the letters of Keats to her father, some of which were at that time unpublished, poring over torn yellow leaves and faded scraps of paper, and wondering at the little Dante in which Keats had written those marvellous notes on Milton. Some months afterwards, when I was in California, I received a letter from Mrs. Speed asking my acceptance of the original manuscript of the sonnet which I had quoted in my lecture. This manuscript I have had reproduced here, as it seems to me to possess much psychological interest. It shows us the conditions that preceded the perfected form, the gradual growth, not of the conception but of the expression, and the workings of that spirit of selection which is the secret of style. In the case of poetry, as in the case of the other arts, what may appear to be simply technicalities of method are in their essence spiritual, not mechanical, and although, in all lovely work, what concerns us is the ultimate form, not the conditions that necessitate that form, yet the preference that precedes perfection, the evolution of the beauty, and the mere making of the music, have, if not their artistic value, at least their value to the artist.

It will be remembered that this sonnet was first published in 1848 by Lord Houghton in his Life, Letters, and Literary Remains of John Keats. Lord Houghton does not definitely state where he found it, but it was probably among the Keats manuscripts belonging to Mr. Charles Brown. It is evidently taken from a version later than that in my possession, as it accepts all the corrections, and makes three variations. As in my manuscript the first line is torn away, I give the sonnet here as it appears in Lord Houghton's edition.

ANSWER TO A SONNET ENDING THUS:

Dark eyes are dearer far

Than those that make the hyacinthine bell. {74}

By J. H. REYNOLDS.

Blue! 'Tis the life of heaven,—the domain

Of Cynthia,—the wide palace of the sun,—

The tent of Hesperus and all his train,—

The bosomer of clouds, gold, grey and dun.

Blue! 'Tis the life of waters—ocean

And all its vassal streams: pools numberless

May rage, and foam, and fret, but never can

Subside if not to dark-blue nativeness.

Blue! gentle cousin of the forest green,

Married to green in all the sweetest flowers,

Forget-me-not,—the blue-bell,—and, that queen

Of secrecy, the violet: what strange powers

Hast thou, as a mere shadow! But how great,

When in an Eye thou art alive with fate!

Feb. 1818.

In the Athenæum of the 3rd of June 1876, appeared a letter from Mr. A. J. Horwood, stating that he had in his possession a copy of The Garden of Florence in which this sonnet was transcribed. Mr. Horwood, who was unaware that the sonnet had been already published by Lord Houghton, gives the transcript at length. His version reads hue for life in the first line, and bright for wide in the second, and gives the sixth line thus:

> With all his tributary streams, pools numberless,

a foot too long: it also reads to for of in the ninth line. Mr. Buxton Forman is of opinion that these variations are decidedly genuine, but indicative of an earlier state of the poem than that adopted in Lord Houghton's edition. However, now that we have before us Keats's first draft of his sonnet, it is difficult to believe that the sixth line in Mr. Horwood's version is really a genuine variation. Keats may have written,

> Ocean

> His tributary streams, pools numberless,

and the transcript may have been carelessly made, but having got his line right in his first draft, Keats probably did not spoil it in his second. The Athenæum version inserts a comma after art in the last line, which seems to me a decided improvement, and eminently characteristic of Keats's method. I am glad to see that Mr. Buxton Forman has adopted it.

As for the corrections that Lord Houghton's version shows Keats to have made in the eighth and ninth lines of this sonnet, it is evident that they sprang from Keats's reluctance to repeat the same word in consecutive lines, except in cases where a word's music or meaning was to be emphasised. The substitution of 'its' for 'his' in the sixth line is more difficult of explanation. It was due probably to a desire on Keats's part not to mar by any echo the fine personification of Hesperus.

It may be noticed that Keats's own eyes were brown, and not blue, as stated by Mrs. Proctor to Lord Houghton. Mrs. Speed showed me a note to that effect written by Mrs. George Keats on the margin of the page in Lord Houghton's Life (p. 100, vol. i.), where Mrs. Proctor's description is given. Cowden Clarke made a similar correction in his Recollections, and in some of the later editions of Lord Houghton's book the word 'blue' is struck out.

In Severn's portraits of Keats also the eyes are given as brown.

The exquisite sense of colour expressed in the ninth and tenth lines may be paralleled by

The Ocean with its vastness, its blue green,

of the sonnet to George Keats.

THE AMERICAN INVASION

(*Court and Society Review*, March 23, 1887.)

A terrible danger is hanging over the Americans in London. Their future and their reputation this season depend entirely on the success of Buffalo Bill and Mrs. Brown-Potter. The former is certain to draw; for English people are far more interested in American barbarism than they are in American civilisation. When they sight Sandy Hook they look to their rifles and ammunition; and, after dining once at Delmonico's, start off for Colorado or California, for Montana or the Yellow Stone Park. Rocky Mountains charm them more than riotous millionaires; they have been known to prefer buffaloes to Boston. Why should they not? The cities of America are inexpressibly tedious. The Bostonians take their learning too sadly; culture with them is an accomplishment rather than an atmosphere; their 'Hub,' as they call it, is the paradise of prigs. Chicago is a sort of monster-shop, full of bustle and bores. Political life at Washington is like political life in a suburban vestry. Baltimore is amusing for a week, but Philadelphia is dreadfully provincial; and though one can dine in New York one could not dwell there. Better the Far West with its grizzly bears and its untamed cow-boys, its free open-air life and its free open-air manners, its boundless prairie and its boundless mendacity! This is what Buffalo Bill is going to bring to London; and we have no doubt that London will fully appreciate his show.

With regard to Mrs. Brown-Potter, as acting is no longer considered absolutely essential for success on the English stage, there is really no reason why the pretty bright-eyed lady who charmed us all last June by her merry laugh and her nonchalant ways, should not—to borrow an expression from her native language—make a big boom and paint the town red. We sincerely hope she will; for, on the whole, the American invasion has done English society a great deal of good. American women are bright, clever, and wonderfully cosmopolitan. Their patriotic feelings are limited to an admiration for Niagara and a regret for the Elevated Railway; and, unlike the men, they never bore us with Bunkers Hill. They take their dresses from Paris and their manners from Piccadilly, and wear both charmingly. They have a quaint pertness, a delightful conceit, a native self-assertion. They insist on being paid compliments and have almost succeeded in making Englishmen eloquent. For our aristocracy they have an ardent admiration; they adore titles and are a permanent blow to Republican principles. In the art of amusing men they are adepts, both by nature and education, and can actually tell a story without forgetting the point—an accomplishment that is extremely rare among the women of other countries. It is true that they lack repose and that their voices are somewhat harsh and strident when they land first at Liverpool; but after a time one gets to love these pretty whirlwinds in petticoats that sweep so recklessly through society and are so agitating to all duchesses who have daughters. There is something fascinating in their funny, exaggerated gestures and their petulant way of tossing the head. Their eyes have no magic nor mystery in them, but they challenge us for combat; and when we engage we are always worsted. Their lips seem made for laughter and yet they never grimace. As for their voices, they soon get them into tune. Some of them have been known to acquire a fashionable drawl in two seasons; and after they have been presented to Royalty they all roll their R's as vigorously as a young equerry or an old lady-in-waiting. Still, they never really lose their accent; it keeps peeping out here and there, and when they chatter together they are like a bevy of peacocks. Nothing is more amusing than to watch two American girls greeting each other in a drawing-room or in the Row. They are like children with their shrill staccato cries of wonder, their odd little exclamations. Their conversation sounds like a series of exploding crackers; they are exquisitely incoherent and use a sort of primitive, emotional language. After five minutes they are left beautifully breathless and look at each other half in amusement and half in affection. If a stolid young Englishman is fortunate enough to be introduced to them he is amazed at their extraordinary vivacity, their electric quickness of repartee, their inexhaustible store of curious catchwords. He never really understands them, for their thoughts flutter about with the sweet irresponsibility of butterflies; but he is pleased and amused and feels as if he were in an aviary. On the whole, American girls have a wonderful charm and, perhaps, the chief secret of their charm is that they never talk seriously except about amusements. They have, however, one grave fault—their mothers. Dreary as were those old Pilgrim Fathers who left our shores more than two centuries ago to found a New England beyond seas, the Pilgrim Mothers who have returned to us in the nineteenth century are drearier still.

Here and there, of course, there are exceptions, but as a class they are either dull, dowdy or dyspeptic. It is only fair to the rising generation of America to state that they are not to blame for this. Indeed, they spare no pains at all to bring up their parents properly and to give them a suitable, if somewhat late, education. From its earliest years every American child spends most of its time in correcting the faults of its father and mother; and no one who has had the opportunity of watching an American family on the deck of an Atlantic steamer, or in the refined seclusion of a New York boarding-house, can fail to have been struck by this characteristic of their civilisation. In America the young are always ready to give to those who are older than themselves the full benefits of their inexperience. A boy of only eleven or twelve years of age will firmly but kindly point out to his father his defects of manner or temper; will never weary of warning him against extravagance, idleness, late hours, unpunctuality, and the other temptations to which the aged are so particularly exposed; and sometimes, should he fancy that he is monopolising too much of the conversation at dinner, will remind him, across the table, of the new child's adage, 'Parents should be seen, not heard.' Nor does any mistaken idea of kindness prevent the little American girl from censuring her mother whenever it is necessary. Often, indeed, feeling that a rebuke conveyed in the presence of others is more truly efficacious than one merely whispered in the quiet of the nursery, she will call the attention of perfect strangers to her mother's general untidiness, her want of intellectual Boston conversation, immoderate love of iced water and green corn, stinginess in the matter of candy, ignorance of the usages of the best Baltimore society, bodily ailments and the like. In fact, it may be truly said that no American child is ever blind to the deficiencies of its parents, no matter how much it may love them.

Yet, somehow, this educational system has not been so successful as it deserved. In many cases, no doubt, the material with which the children had to deal was crude and incapable of real development; but the fact remains that the American mother is a tedious person. The American father is better, for he is never seen in London. He passes his life entirely in Wall Street and communicates with his family once a month by means of a telegram in cipher. The mother, however, is always with us, and, lacking the quick imitative faculty of the younger generation, remains uninteresting and provincial to the last. In spite of her, however, the American girl is always welcome. She brightens our dull dinner parties for us and makes life go pleasantly by for a season. In the race for coronets she often carries off the prize; but, once she has gained the victory, she is generous and forgives her English rivals everything, even their beauty.

Warned by the example of her mother that American women do not grow old gracefully, she tries not to grow old at all and often succeeds. She has exquisite feet and hands, is always bien chaussée et bien gantée and can talk brilliantly upon any subject, provided that she knows nothing about it.

Her sense of humour keeps her from the tragedy of a grande passion, and, as there is neither romance nor humility in her love, she makes an excellent wife. What her ultimate influence on English life will be it is difficult to estimate at present; but there can be no doubt that, of all the factors that have contributed to the social revolution of London, there are few more important, and none more delightful, than the American Invasion.

SERMONS IN STONES AT BLOOMSBURY: THE NEW SCULPTURE ROOM AT THE BRITISH MUSEUM

(*Pall Mall Gazette*, October 15, 1887.)

Through the exertions of Sir Charles Newton, to whom every student of classic art should be grateful, some of the wonderful treasures so long immured in the grimy vaults of the British Museum have at last been brought to light, and the new Sculpture Room now opened to the public will amply repay the trouble of a visit, even from those to whom art is a stumbling-block and a rock of offence. For setting aside the mere beauty of form, outline and mass, the grace and loveliness of design and the delicacy of technical treatment, here we have shown to us what the Greeks and Romans thought about death; and the philosopher, the preacher, the practical man of the world, and even the Philistine himself, cannot fail to be touched by these 'sermons in stones,' with their deep significance, their fertile suggestion, their plain humanity. Common tombstones they are, most of them, the work not of famous artists but of simple handicraftsmen, only they were wrought in days when every handicraft was an art. The finest specimens, from the purely artistic point of view, are undoubtedly the two stelai found at Athens. They are both the tombstones of young Greek athletes. In one the athlete is represented handing his strigil to his slave, in the other the athlete stands alone, strigil in hand. They do not belong to the greatest period of Greek art, they have not the grand style of the Phidian age, but they are beautiful for all that, and it is impossible not to be fascinated by their exquisite grace and by the treatment which is so simple in its means, so subtle in its effect. All the tombstones, however, are full of interest. Here is one of two ladies of Smyrna who were so remarkable in their day that the city voted them honorary crowns; here is a Greek doctor examining a little boy who is suffering from indigestion; here is the memorial of Xanthippus who, probably, was a martyr to gout, as he is holding in his hand the model of a foot, intended, no doubt, as a votive offering to some god. A lovely stele from Rhodes gives us a family group. The husband is on horseback and is bidding farewell to his wife, who seems as if she would follow him but is being held back by a little child. The pathos of parting from those we love is the central motive of Greek funeral art. It is repeated in every possible form, and each mute marble stone seems to murmur χαιρε. Roman art is different. It introduces vigorous and realistic portraiture and deals with pure family life far more frequently than Greek art does. They are very ugly, those stern-looking Roman men and women whose portraits are exhibited on their tombs, but they seem to have been loved and respected by their children and their servants. Here is the monument of Aphrodisius and Atilia, a Roman gentleman and his wife, who died in Britain many centuries ago, and whose tombstone was found in the Thames; and close by it stands a stele from Rome with the busts of an old married couple who are certainly marvellously ill-favoured. The contrast between the abstract Greek treatment of the idea of death and the Roman concrete realisation of the individuals who have died is extremely curious.

Besides the tombstones, the new Sculpture Room contains some most fascinating examples of Roman decorative art under the Emperors. The most wonderful of all, and this alone is worth a trip to Bloomsbury, is a bas-relief representing a marriage scene. Juno Pronuba is joining the hands of a handsome young noble and a very stately lady. There is all the grace of Perugino in this marble, all the grace of Raphael even. The date of it is uncertain, but the particular cut of the bridegroom's beard seems to point to the time of the Emperor Hadrian. It is clearly the work of Greek artists and is one of the most beautiful bas-reliefs in the whole Museum. There is something in it which reminds one of the music and the sweetness of Propertian verse. Then we have delightful friezes of children. One representing children playing on musical instruments might have suggested much of the plastic art of Florence. Indeed, as we view these marbles it is not difficult to see whence the Renaissance sprang and to what we owe the various forms of Renaissance art. The frieze of the Muses, each of whom wears in her hair a feather plucked from the wings of the vanquished sirens, is extremely fine; there is a lovely little bas-relief of two cupids racing in chariots; and the frieze of recumbent Amazons has some splendid qualities of design. A frieze of children playing with the armour of the god Mars should also be mentioned. It is full of fancy and delicate humour.

On the whole, Sir Charles Newton and Mr. Murray are warmly to be congratulated on the success of the new room. We hope, however, that some more of the hidden treasures will shortly be catalogued and shown. In the vaults at present there is a very remarkable bas-relief of the marriage of Cupid and Psyche, and another representing the professional mourners weeping over the body of the dead. The fine cast of the Lion of Chæronea should also be brought up, and so should the stele with the marvellous portrait of the Roman slave. Economy is an excellent public virtue, but the parsimony that allows valuable works of art to remain in the grime and gloom of a damp cellar is little short of a detestable public vice.

THE UNITY OF THE ARTS: A LECTURE AND A FIVE O'CLOCK

(*Pall Mall Gazette*, December 12, 1887.)

Last Saturday afternoon, at Willis's Rooms, Mr. Selwyn Image delivered the first of a series of four lectures on Modern Art before a select and distinguished audience. The chief point on which he dwelt was the absolute unity of all the arts and, in order to convey this idea, he framed a definition wide enough to include Shakespeare's King Lear and Michael Angelo's Creation, Paul Veronese's picture of Alexander and Darius, and Gibbon's description of the entry of Heliogabalus into Rome. All these he regarded as so many expressions of man's thoughts and emotions on fine things, conveyed through visible or audible modes; and starting from this point he approached the question of the true relation of literature to painting, always keeping in view the central motive of his creed, Credo in unam artem multipartitam, indivisibilem, and dwelling on resemblances rather than differences. The result at which he ultimately arrived was this: the Impressionists, with their frank artistic acceptance of form and colour as things absolutely satisfying in themselves, have produced very beautiful work, but painting has something more to give us than the mere visible aspect of things. The lofty spiritual visions of William Blake, and the marvellous romance of Dante Gabriel Rossetti, can find their perfect expression in painting; every mood has its colour and every dream has its form. The chief quality of Mr. Image's lecture was its absolute fairness, but this was, to a certain portion of the audience, its chief defect. 'Sweet reasonableness,' said one, 'is always admirable in a spectator, but from a leader we want something more.' 'It is only an auctioneer who should admire all schools of art,' said another; while a third sighed over what he called 'the fatal sterility of the judicial mind,' and expressed a perfectly groundless fear that the Century Guild was becoming rational. For, with a courtesy and a generosity that we strongly recommend to other lecturers, Mr. Image provided refreshments for his audience after his address was over, and it was extremely interesting to listen to the various opinions expressed by the great Five-o'clock-tea School of Criticism which was largely represented.

For our own part, we found Mr. Image's lecture extremely suggestive. It was sometimes difficult to understand in what exact sense he was using the word 'literary,' and we do not think that a course of drawing from the plaster cast of the Dying Gaul would in the slightest degree improve the ordinary art critic. The true unity of the arts is to be found, not in any resemblance of one art to another, but in the fact that to the really artistic nature all the arts have the same message and speak the same language though with different tongues. No amount of daubing on a cellar wall will make a man understand the mystery of Michael Angelo's Sybils, nor is it necessary to write a blank verse drama before one can appreciate the beauty of Hamlet. It is essential that an art critic should have a nature receptive of beautiful impressions, and sufficient intuition to recognise style when he meets with it, and truth when it is shown to him; but, if he does not possess these qualities, a reckless career of water-colour painting will not give them to him, for, if from the incompetent critic all things be hidden, to the bad painter nothing shall be revealed.

ART AT WILLIS'S ROOMS

(*Sunday Times*, December 25, 1887.)

Accepting a suggestion made by a friendly critic last week, Mr. Selwyn Image began his second lecture by explaining more fully what he meant by literary art, and pointed out the difference between an ordinary illustration to a book and such creative and original works as Michael Angelo's fresco of The Expulsion from Eden and Rossetti's Beata Beatrix. In the latter case the artist treats literature as if it were life itself, and gives a new and delightful form to what seer or singer has shown us; in the former we have merely a translation which misses the music and adds no marvel. As for subject, Mr. Image protested against the studio-slang that no subject is necessary, defining subject as the thought, emotion or impression which a man desires to embody in form and colour, and admitting Mr. Whistler's fireworks as readily as Giotto's angels, and Van Huysum's roses no less than Mantegna's gods. Here, we think that Mr. Image might have pointed out more clearly the contrast between the purely pictorial subject and the subject that includes among its elements such things as historical associations or poetic memories; the contrast, in fact, between impressive art and the art that is expressive also. However, the topics he had to deal with were so varied that it was, no doubt, difficult for him to do more than suggest. From subject he passed to style, which he described as 'that masterful but restrained individuality of manner by which one artist is differentiated from another.' The true qualities of style he found in restraint which is submission to law; simplicity which is unity of vision; and severity, for le beau est toujours sévère.

The realist he defined as one who aims at reproducing the external phenomena of nature, while the idealist is the man who 'imagines things of fine interest.' Yet, while he defined them he would not separate them. The true artist is a realist, for he recognises an external world of truth; an idealist, for he has selection, abstraction and the power of individualisation. To stand apart from the world of nature is fatal, but it is no less fatal merely to reproduce facts.

Art, in a word, must not content itself simply with holding the mirror up to nature, for it is a re-creation more than a reflection, and not a repetition but rather a new song. As for finish, it must not be confused with elaboration. A picture, said Mr. Image, is finished when the means of form and colour employed by the artist are adequate to convey the artist's intention; and, with this definition and a peroration suitable to the season, he concluded his interesting and intellectual lecture.

Light refreshments were then served to the audience, and the five-o'clock-tea school of criticism came very much to the front. Mr. Image's entire freedom from dogmatism and self-assertion was in some quarters rather severely commented on, and one young gentleman declared that such virtuous modesty as the lecturer's might easily become a most vicious mannerism. Everybody, however, was extremely pleased to learn that it is no longer the duty of art to hold the mirror up to nature, and the few Philistines who dissented from this view received that most terrible of all punishments— the contempt of the highly cultured.

Mr. Image's third lecture will be delivered on January 21 and will, no doubt, be largely attended, as the subjects advertised are full of interest, and though 'sweet reasonableness' may not convert, it always charms.

MR. MORRIS ON TAPESTRY

(*Pall Mall Gazette*, November 2, 1888.)

Yesterday evening Mr. William Morris delivered a most interesting and fascinating lecture on Carpet and Tapestry Weaving at the Arts and Crafts Exhibition now held at the New Gallery. Mr. Morris had small practical models of the two looms used, the carpet loom where the weaver sits in front of his work; the more elaborate tapestry loom where the weaver sits behind, at the back of the stuff, has his design outlined on the upright threads and sees in a mirror the shadow of the pattern and picture as it grows gradually to perfection. He spoke at much length on the question of dyes—praising madder and kermes for reds, precipitate of iron or ochre for yellows, and for blue either indigo or woad. At the back of the platform hung a lovely Flemish tapestry of the fourteenth century, and a superb Persian carpet about two hundred and fifty years old. Mr. Morris pointed out the loveliness of the carpet—its delicate suggestion of hawthorn blossom, iris and rose, its rejection of imitation and shading; and showed how it combined the great quality of decorative design—being at once clear and well defined in form: each outline exquisitely traced, each line deliberate in its intention and its beauty, and the whole effect being one of unity, of harmony, almost of mystery, the colours being so perfectly harmonised together and the little bright notes of colour being so cunningly placed either for tone or brilliancy.

Tapestries, he said, were to the North of Europe what fresco was to the South—our climate, amongst other reasons, guiding us in our choice of material for wall-covering. England, France, and Flanders were the three great tapestry countries—Flanders with its great wool trade being the first in splendid colours and superb Gothic design. The keynote of tapestry, the secret of its loveliness, was, he told the audience, the complete filling up of every corner and square inch of surface with lovely and fanciful and suggestive design. Hence the wonder of those great Gothic tapestries where the forest trees rise in different places, one over the other, each leaf perfect in its shape and colour and decorative value, while in simple raiment of beautiful design knights and ladies wandered in rich flower gardens, and rode with hawk on wrist through long green arcades, and sat listening to lute and viol in blossom-starred bowers or by cool gracious water springs. Upon the other hand, when the Gothic feeling died away, and Boucher and others began to design, they gave us wide expanses of waste sky, elaborate perspective, posing nymphs and shallow artificial treatment. Indeed, Boucher met with scant mercy at Mr. Morris's vigorous hands and was roundly abused, and modern Gobelins, with M. Bougereau's cartoons, fared no better.

Mr. Morris told some delightful stories about old tapestry work from the days when in the Egyptian tombs the dead were laid wrapped in picture cloths, some of which are now in the South Kensington Museum, to the time of the great Turk Bajazet who, having captured some Christian knights, would accept nothing for their ransom but the 'storied tapestries of France' and gerfalcons. As regards the use of tapestry in modern days, he pointed out that we were richer than the middle ages, and so should be better able to afford this form of lovely wall-covering, which for artistic tone is absolutely without rival. He said that the very limitation of material and form forced the imaginative designer into giving us something really beautiful and decorative. 'What is the use of setting an artist in a twelve-acre field and telling him to design a house? Give him a limited space and he is forced by its limitation to concentrate, and to fill with pure loveliness the narrow surface at his disposal.' The worker also gives to the original design a very perfect richness of detail, and the threads with their varying colours and delicate reflections convey into the work a new source of delight. Here, he said, we found perfect unity between the imaginative artist and the handicraftsman. The one was not too free, the other was not a slave. The eye of the artist saw, his brain conceived, his imagination created, but the hand of the weaver had also its opportunity for wonderful work, and did not copy what was already made, but re-created and put into a new and delightful form a design that for its perfection needed the loom to aid, and had to pass into a fresh and marvellous material before its beauty came to its real flower and blossom of absolutely right expression and artistic effect. But, said Mr. Morris in conclusion, to have great work we must be worthy of it. Commercialism, with its vile god cheapness, its callous

181

indifference to the worker, its innate vulgarity of temper, is our enemy. To gain anything good we must sacrifice something of our luxury—must think more of others, more of the State, the commonweal: 'We cannot have riches and wealth both,' he said; we must choose between them.

The lecture was listened to with great attention by a very large and distinguished audience, and Mr. Morris was loudly applauded.

The next lecture will be on Sculpture by Mr. George Simonds, and if it is half so good as Mr. Morris it will well repay a visit to the lecture-room. Mr. Crane deserves great credit for his exertions in making this exhibition what it should be, and there is no doubt but that it will exercise an important and a good influence on all the handicrafts of our country.

SCULPTURE AT THE ARTS AND CRAFTS

(*Pall Mall Gazette*, November 9, 1888.)

The most satisfactory thing in Mr. Simonds' lecture last night was the peroration, in which he told the audience that 'an artist cannot be made.' But for this well-timed warning some deluded people might have gone away under the impression that sculpture was a sort of mechanical process within the reach of the meanest capabilities. For it must be confessed that Mr. Simonds' lecture was at once too elementary and too elaborately technical. The ordinary art student, even the ordinary studio-loafer, could not have learned anything from it, while the 'cultured person,' of whom there were many specimens present, could not but have felt a little bored at the careful and painfully clear descriptions given by the lecturer of very well-known and uninteresting methods of work. However, Mr. Simonds did his best. He described modelling in clay and wax; casting in plaster and in metal; how to enlarge and how to diminish to scale; bas-reliefs and working in the round; the various kinds of marble, their qualities and characteristics; how to reproduce in marble the plaster or clay bust; how to use the point, the drill, the wire and the chisel; and the various difficulties attending each process. He exhibited a clay bust of Mr. Walter Crane on which he did some elementary work; a bust of Mr. Parsons; a small statuette; several moulds, and an interesting diagram of the furnace used by Balthasar Keller for casting a great equestrian statue of Louis XIV. in 1697-8.

What his lecture lacked were ideas. Of the artistic value of each material; of the correspondence between material or method and the imaginative faculty seeking to find expression; of the capacities for realism and idealism that reside in each material; of the historical and human side of the art—he said nothing. He showed the various instruments and how they are used, but he treated them entirely as instruments for the hand. He never once brought his subject into any relation either with art or with life. He explained forms of labour and forms of saving labour. He showed the various methods as they might be used by an artisan. Mr. Morris, last week, while explaining the technical processes of weaving, never forgot that he was lecturing on an art. He not merely taught his audience, but he charmed them. However, the audience gathered together last night at the Arts and Crafts Exhibition seemed very much interested; at least, they were very attentive; and Mr. Walter Crane made a short speech at the conclusion, in which he expressed his satisfaction that in spite of modern machinery sculpture had hardly altered one of its tools. For our own part we cannot help regretting the extremely commonplace character of the lecture. If a man lectures on poets he should not confine his remarks purely to grammar.

Next week Mr. Emery Walker lectures on Printing. We hope—indeed we are sure, that he will not forget that it is an art, or rather it was an art once, and can be made so again.

PRINTING AND PRINTERS

(*Pall Mall Gazette*, November 16, 1888.)

Nothing could have been better than Mr. Emery Walker's lecture on Letterpress Printing and Illustration, delivered last night at the Arts and Crafts. A series of most interesting specimens of old printed books and manuscripts was displayed on the screen by means of the magic-lantern, and Mr. Walker's explanations were as clear and simple as his suggestions were admirable. He began by explaining the different kinds of type and how they are made, and showed specimens of the old block-printing which preceded the movable type and is still used in China. He pointed out the intimate connection between printing and handwriting—as long as the latter was good the printers had a living model to go by, but when it decayed printing decayed also. He showed on the screen a page from Gutenberg's Bible (the first printed book, date about 1450-5) and a manuscript of Columella; a printed Livy of 1469, with the abbreviations of handwriting, and a manuscript of the History of Pompeius by Justin of 1451. The latter he regarded as an example of the beginning of the Roman type. The resemblance between the manuscripts and the printed books was most curious and suggestive. He then showed a page out of John of Spier's edition of Cicero's Letters, the first book printed at Venice, an edition of the same book by Nicholas Jansen in 1470, and a wonderful manuscript Petrarch of the sixteenth century. He told the audience about Aldus, who was the first publisher to start cheap books, who dropped abbreviations and had his type cut by Francia pictor et aurifex, who was said to have taken it from Petrarch's handwriting. He exhibited a page of the copy-book of Vicentino, the great Venetian writing-master, which was greeted with a spontaneous round of applause, and made some excellent suggestions about improving modern copy-books and avoiding slanting writing.

A superb Plautus printed at Florence in 1514 for Lorenzo di Medici, Polydore Virgil's History with the fine Holbein designs, printed at Basle in 1556, and other interesting books, were also exhibited on the screen, the size, of course, being very much enlarged. He spoke of Elzevir in the seventeenth century when handwriting began to fall off, and of the English printer Caslon, and of Baskerville whose type was possibly designed by Hogarth, but is not very good. Latin, he remarked, was a better language to print than English, as the tails of the letters did not so often fall below the line. The wide spacing between lines, occasioned by the use of a lead, he pointed out, left the page in stripes and made the blanks as important as the lines. Margins should, of course, be wide except the inner margins, and the headlines often robbed the page of its beauty of design. The type used by the Pall Mall was, we are glad to say, rightly approved of.

With regard to illustration, the essential thing, Mr. Walker said, is to have harmony between the type and the decoration. He pleaded for true book ornament as opposed to the silly habit of putting pictures where they are not wanted, and pointed out that mechanical harmony and artistic harmony went hand in hand. No ornament or illustration should be used in a book which cannot be printed in the same way as the type. For his warnings he produced Rogers's Italy with a steel-plate engraving, and a page from an American magazine which being florid, pictorial and bad, was greeted with some laughter. For examples we had a lovely Boccaccio printed at Ulm, and a page out of La Mer des Histoires printed in 1488. Blake and Bewick were also shown, and a page of music designed by Mr. Horne.

The lecture was listened to with great attention by a large audience, and was certainly most attractive. Mr. Walker has the keen artistic instinct that comes out of actually working in the art of which he spoke. His remarks about the pictorial character of modern illustration were well timed, and we hope that some of the publishers in the audience will take them to heart.

Next Thursday Mr. Cobden-Sanderson lectures on Bookbinding, a subject on which few men in England have higher qualifications for speaking. We are glad to see these lectures are so well attended.

THE BEAUTIES OF BOOKBINDING

(*Pall Mall Gazette*, November 23, 1888.)

'The beginning of art,' said Mr. Cobden-Sanderson last night in his charming lecture on Bookbinding, 'is man thinking about the universe.' He desires to give expression to the joy and wonder that he feels at the marvels that surround him, and invents a form of beauty through which he utters the thought or feeling that is in him. And bookbinding ranks amongst the arts: 'through it a man expresses himself.'

This elegant and pleasantly exaggerated exordium preceded some very practical demonstrations. 'The apron is the banner of the future!' exclaimed the lecturer, and he took his coat off and put his apron on. He spoke a little about old bindings for the papyrus roll, about the ivory or cedar cylinders round which old manuscripts were wound, about the stained covers and the elaborate strings, till binding in the modern sense began with literature in a folded form, with literature in pages. A binding, he pointed out, consists of two boards, originally of wood, now of mill-board, covered with leather, silk or velvet. The use of these boards is to protect the 'world's written wealth.' The best material is leather, decorated with gold. The old binders used to be given forests that they might always have a supply of the skins of wild animals; the modern binder has to content himself with importing morocco, which is far the best leather there is, and is very much to be preferred to calf.

Mr. Sanderson mentioned by name a few of the great binders such as Le Gascon, and some of the patrons of bookbinding like the Medicis, Grolier, and the wonderful women who so loved books that they lent them some of the perfume and grace of their own strange lives. However, the historical part of the lecture was very inadequate, possibly necessarily so through the limitations of time. The really elaborate part of the lecture was the practical exposition. Mr. Sanderson described and illustrated the various processes of smoothing, pressing, cutting, paring, and the like. He divided bindings into two classes, the useful and the beautiful. Among the former he reckoned paper covers such as the French use, paper boards and cloth boards, and half leather or calf bindings. Cloth he disliked as a poor material, the gold on which soon fades away. As for beautiful bindings, in them 'decoration rises into enthusiasm.' A beautiful binding is 'a homage to genius.' It has its ethical value, its spiritual effect. 'By doing good work we raise life to a higher plane,' said the lecturer, and he dwelt with loving sympathy on the fact that a book is 'sensitive by nature,' that it is made by a human being for a human being, that the design must 'come from the man himself, and express the moods of his imagination, the joy of his soul.' There must, consequently, be no division of labour. 'I make my own paste and enjoy doing it,' said Mr. Sanderson as he spoke of the necessity for the artist doing the whole work with his own hands. But before we have really good bookbinding we must have a social revolution. As things are now, the worker diminished to a machine is the slave of the employer, and the employer bloated into a millionaire is the slave of the public, and the public is the slave of its pet god, cheapness. The bookbinder of the future is to be an educated man who appreciates literature and has freedom for his fancy and leisure for his thought.

All this is very good and sound. But in treating bookbinding as an imaginative, expressive human art we must confess that we think that Mr. Sanderson made something of an error. Bookbinding is essentially decorative, and good decoration is far more often suggested by material and mode of work than by any desire on the part of the designer to tell us of his joy in the world. Hence it comes that good decoration is always traditional. Where it is the expression of the individual it is usually either false or capricious. These handicrafts are not primarily expressive arts; they are impressive arts. If a man has any message for the world he will not deliver it in a material that always suggests and always conditions its own decoration. The beauty of bookbinding is abstract decorative beauty. It is not, in the first instance, a mode of expression for a man's soul. Indeed, the danger of all these lofty claims for handicraft is simply that they show a desire to give crafts the province and motive of arts such as poetry, painting and sculpture. Such province and such motive they have not got. Their aim is different. Between the arts that aim at annihilating their material and the arts that aim at glorifying it there is a wide gulf.

188

However, it was quite right of Mr. Cobden-Sanderson to extol his own art, and though he seemed often to confuse expressive and impressive modes of beauty, he always spoke with great sincerity.

Next week Mr. Crane delivers the final lecture of this admirable 'Arts and Crafts' series and, no doubt, he will have much to say on a subject to which he has devoted the whole of his fine artistic life. For ourselves, we cannot help feeling that in bookbinding art expresses primarily not the feeling of the worker but simply itself, its own beauty, its own wonder.

THE CLOSE OF THE ARTS AND CRAFTS

(*Pall Mall Gazette*, November 30, 1888.)

Mr. Walter Crane, the President of the Society of Arts and Crafts, was greeted last night by such an enormous audience that at one time the honorary secretary became alarmed for the safety of the cartoons, and many people were unable to gain admission at all. However, order was soon established, and Mr. Cobden-Sanderson stepped up on to the platform and in a few pleasantly sententious phrases introduced Mr. Crane as one who had always been 'the advocate of great and unpopular causes,' and the aim of whose art was 'joy in widest commonalty spread.' Mr. Crane began his lecture by pointing out that Art had two fields, aspect and adaptation, and that it was primarily with the latter that the designer was concerned, his object being not literal fact but ideal beauty. With the unstudied and accidental effects of Nature the designer had nothing to do. He sought for principles and proceeded by geometric plan and abstract line and colour. Pictorial art is isolated and unrelated, and the frame is the last relic of the old connection between painting and architecture. But the designer does not desire primarily to produce a picture. He aims at making a pattern and proceeds by selection; he rejects the 'hole in the wall' idea, and will have nothing to do with the 'false windows of a picture.'

Three things differentiate designs. First, the spirit of the artist, that mode and manner by which Dürer is separated from Flaxman, by which we recognise the soul of a man expressing itself in the form proper to it. Next comes the constructive idea, the filling of spaces with lovely work. Last is the material which, be it leather or clay, ivory or wood, often suggests and always controls the pattern. As for naturalism, we must remember that we see not with our eyes alone but with our whole faculties. Feeling and thought are part of sight. Mr. Crane then drew on a blackboard the naturalistic oak-tree of the landscape painter and the decorative oak-tree of the designer. He showed that each artist is looking for different things, and that the designer always makes appearance subordinate to decorative motive. He showed also the field daisy as it is in Nature and the same flower treated for panel decoration. The designer systematises and emphasises, chooses and rejects, and decorative work bears the same relation to naturalistic presentation that the imaginative language of the poetic drama bears to the language of real life. The decorative capabilities of the square and the circle were then shown on the board, and much was said about symmetry, alternation and radiation, which last principle Mr. Crane described as 'the Home Rule of design, the perfection of local self-government,' and which, he pointed out, was essentially organic, manifesting itself in the bird's wing as well as in the Tudor vaulting of Gothic architecture. Mr. Crane then passed to the human figure, 'that expressive unit of design,' which contains all the principles of decoration, and exhibited a design of a nude figure with an axe couched in an architectural spandrel, a figure which he was careful to explain was, in spite of the axe, not that of Mr. Gladstone. The designer then leaving chiaroscuro, shading and other 'superficial facts of life' to take care of themselves, and keeping the idea of space limitation always before him, then proceeds to emphasise the beauty of his material, be it metal with its 'agreeable bossiness,' as Ruskin calls it, or leaded glass with its fine dark lines, or mosaic with its jewelled tesseræ, or the loom with its crossed threads, or wood with its pleasant crispness. Much bad art comes from one art trying to borrow from another. We have sculptors who try to be pictorial, painters who aim at stage effects, weavers who seek for pictorial motives, carvers who make Life and not Art their aim, cotton printers 'who tie up bunches of artificial flowers with streamers of artificial ribbons' and fling them on the unfortunate textile.

Then came the little bit of Socialism, very sensible and very quietly put. 'How can we have fine art when the worker is condemned to monotonous and mechanical labour in the midst of dull or hideous surroundings, when cities and nature are sacrificed to commercial greed, when cheapness is the god of Life?' In old days the craftsman was a designer; he had his 'prentice days of quiet study; and even the painter began by grinding colours. Some little old ornament still lingers, here and there, on the brass rosettes of cart-horses, in the common milk-cans of Antwerp, in the water-vessels of Italy. But even this is disappearing. 'The tourist passes by' and creates a demand that commerce satisfies in an unsatisfactory manner. We have not yet arrived at a healthy state of things. There is still the Tottenham Court Road and a threatened revival of Louis Seize furniture, and the 'popular pictorial print struggles through the meshes of the antimacassar.' Art depends on Life. We cannot get it from machines. And yet machines are bad only when they are our masters. The printing press is a machine that Art values because it obeys her. True art must have the vital energy of life itself, must take its colours from life's good or evil, must follow angels of light or angels of darkness. The art of the past is not to be copied in a servile spirit. For a new age we require a new form.

Mr. Crane's lecture was most interesting and instructive. On one point only we would differ from him. Like Mr. Morris he quite underrates the art of Japan, and looks on the Japanese as naturalists and not as decorative artists. It is true that they are often pictorial, but by the exquisite finesse of their touch, the brilliancy and beauty of their colour, their perfect knowledge of how to make a space decorative without decorating it (a point on which Mr. Crane said nothing, though it is one of the most important things in decoration), and by their keen instinct of where to place a thing, the Japanese are decorative artists of a high order. Next year somebody must lecture the Arts and Crafts on Japanese art. In the meantime, we congratulate Mr. Crane and Mr. Cobden-Sanderson on the admirable series of lectures that has been delivered at this exhibition. Their influence for good can hardly be over-estimated. The exhibition, we are glad to hear, has been a financial success. It closes tomorrow, but is to be only the first of many to come.

ENGLISH POETESSES

(*Queen*, December 8, 1888.)

England has given to the world one great poetess, Elizabeth Barrett Browning. By her side Mr. Swinburne would place Miss Christina Rossetti, whose New Year hymn he describes as so much the noblest of sacred poems in our language, that there is none which comes near it enough to stand second. 'It is a hymn,' he tells us, 'touched as with the fire, and bathed as in the light of sunbeams, tuned as to chords and cadences of refluent sea-music beyond reach of harp and organ, large echoes of the serene and sonorous tides of heaven.' Much as I admire Miss Rossetti's work, her subtle choice of words, her rich imagery, her artistic naïveté, wherein curious notes of strangeness and simplicity are fantastically blended together, I cannot but think that Mr. Swinburne has, with noble and natural loyalty, placed her on too lofty a pedestal. To me, she is simply a very delightful artist in poetry. This is indeed something so rare that when we meet it we cannot fail to love it, but it is not everything. Beyond it and above it are higher and more sunlit heights of song, a larger vision, and an ampler air, a music at once more passionate and more profound, a creative energy that is born of the spirit, a winged rapture that is born of the soul, a force and fervour of mere utterance that has all the wonder of the prophet, and not a little of the consecration of the priest.

Mrs. Browning is unapproachable by any woman who has ever touched lyre or blown through reed since the days of the great Æolian poetess. But Sappho, who, to the antique world was a pillar of flame, is to us but a pillar of shadow. Of her poems, burnt with other most precious work by Byzantine Emperor and by Roman Pope, only a few fragments remain. Possibly they lie mouldering in the scented darkness of an Egyptian tomb, clasped in the withered hands of some long-dead lover. Some Greek monk at Athos may even now be poring over an ancient manuscript, whose crabbed characters conceal lyric or ode by her whom the Greeks spoke of as 'the Poetess' just as they termed Homer 'the Poet,' who was to them the tenth Muse, the flower of the Graces, the child of Erôs, and the pride of Hellas—Sappho, with the sweet voice, the bright, beautiful eyes, the dark hyacinth-coloured hair. But, practically, the work of the marvellous singer of Lesbos is entirely lost to us.

We have a few rose-leaves out of her garden, that is all. Literature nowadays survives marble and bronze, but in old days, in spite of the Roman poet's noble boast, it was not so. The fragile clay vases of the Greeks still keep for us pictures of Sappho, delicately painted in black and red and white; but of her song we have only the echo of an echo.

Of all the women of history, Mrs. Browning is the only one that we could name in any possible or remote conjunction with Sappho.

Sappho was undoubtedly a far more flawless and perfect artist. She stirred the whole antique world more than Mrs. Browning ever stirred our modern age. Never had Love such a singer. Even in the few lines that remain to us the passion seems to scorch and burn. But, as unjust Time, who has crowned her with the barren laurels of fame, has twined with them the dull poppies of oblivion, let us turn from the mere memory of a poetess to one whose song still remains to us as an imperishable glory to our literature; to her who heard the cry of the children from dark mine and crowded factory, and made England weep over its little ones; who, in the feigned sonnets from the Portuguese, sang of the spiritual mystery of Love, and of the intellectual gifts that Love brings to the soul; who had faith in all that is worthy, and enthusiasm for all that is great, and pity for all that suffers; who wrote the Vision of Poets and Casa Guidi Windows and Aurora Leigh.

As one, to whom I owe my love of poetry no less than my love of country, has said of her:

> Still on our ears
>
> The clear 'Excelsior' from a woman's lip
>
> Rings out across the Apennines, although
>
> The woman's brow lies pale and cold in death
>
> With all the mighty marble dead in Florence.

For while great songs can stir the hearts of men,

Spreading their full vibrations through the world

In ever-widening circles till they reach

The Throne of God, and song becomes a prayer,

And prayer brings down the liberating strength

That kindles nations to heroic deeds,

She lives—the great-souled poetess who saw

From Casa Guidi windows Freedom dawn

On Italy, and gave the glory back

In sunrise hymns to all Humanity!

She lives indeed, and not alone in the heart of Shakespeare's England, but in the heart of Dante's Italy also. To Greek literature she owed her scholarly culture, but modern Italy created her human passion for Liberty. When she crossed the Alps she became filled with a new ardour, and from that fine, eloquent mouth, that we can still see in her portraits, broke forth such a noble and majestic outburst of lyrical song as had not been heard from woman's lips for more than two thousand years. It is pleasant to think that an English poetess was to a certain extent a real factor in bringing about that unity of Italy that was Dante's dream, and if Florence drove her great singer into exile, she at least welcomed within her walls the later singer that England had sent to her.

If one were asked the chief qualities of Mrs. Browning's work, one would say, as Mr. Swinburne said of Byron's, its sincerity and its strength. Faults it, of course, possesses. 'She would rhyme moon to table,' used to be said of her in jest; and certainly no more monstrous rhymes are to be found in all literature than some of those we come across in Mrs. Browning's poems. But her ruggedness was never the result of carelessness. It was deliberate, as her letters to Mr. Horne show very clearly. She refused to sandpaper her muse. She disliked facile smoothness and artificial polish. In her very rejection of art she was an artist. She intended to produce a certain effect by certain means, and she succeeded; and her indifference to complete assonance in rhyme often gives a splendid richness to her verse, and brings into it a pleasurable element of surprise.

In philosophy she was a Platonist, in politics an Opportunist. She attached herself to no particular party. She loved the people when they were king-like, and kings when they showed themselves to be men. Of the real value and motive of poetry she had a most exalted idea. 'Poetry,' she says, in the preface of one of her volumes, 'has been as serious a thing to me as life itself; and life has been a very serious thing. There has been no playing at skittles for me in either. I never mistook pleasure for the final cause of poetry, nor leisure for the hour of the poet. I have done my work so far, not as mere hand and head work apart from the personal being, but as the completest expression of that being to which I could attain.'

It certainly is her completest expression, and through it she realises her fullest perfection. 'The poet,' she says elsewhere, 'is at once richer and poorer than he used to be; he wears better broadcloth, but speaks no more oracles.' These words give us the keynote to her view of the poet's mission. He was to utter Divine oracles, to be at once inspired prophet and holy priest; and as such we may, I think, without exaggeration, conceive her. She was a Sibyl delivering a message to the world, sometimes through stammering lips, and once at least with blinded eyes, yet always with the true fire and fervour of lofty and unshaken faith, always with the great raptures of a spiritual nature, the high ardours of an impassioned soul. As we read her best poems we feel that, though Apollo's shrine be empty and the bronze tripod overthrown, and the vale of Delphi desolate, still the Pythia is not dead. In our own age she has sung for us, and this land gave her new birth. Indeed, Mrs. Browning is the wisest of the Sibyls, wiser even than that mighty figure whom Michael Angelo has painted on the roof of the Sistine Chapel at Rome, poring over the scroll of mystery, and trying to decipher the secrets of Fate; for she realised that, while knowledge is power, suffering is part of knowledge.

To her influence, almost as much as to the higher education of women, I would be inclined to attribute the really remarkable awakening of woman's song that characterises the latter half of our century in England. No country has ever had so many poetesses at once. Indeed, when one remembers that the Greeks had only nine muses, one is sometimes apt to fancy that we have too many. And yet the work done by women in the sphere of poetry is really of a very high standard of excellence. In England we have always been prone to underrate the value of tradition in literature. In our eagerness to find a new voice and a fresh mode of music, we have forgotten how beautiful Echo may be. We look first for individuality and personality, and these are, indeed, the chief characteristics of the masterpieces of our literature, either in prose or verse; but deliberate culture and a study of the best models, if united to an artistic temperament and a nature susceptible of exquisite impressions, may produce much that is admirable, much that is worthy of praise. It would be quite impossible to give a complete catalogue of all the women who since Mrs. Browning's day have tried lute and lyre. Mrs. Pfeiffer, Mrs. Hamilton King, Mrs. Augusta Webster, Graham Tomson, Miss Mary Robinson, Jean Ingelow, Miss May Kendall, Miss Nesbit, Miss May Probyn, Mrs. Craik, Mrs. Meynell, Miss Chapman, and many others have done really good work in poetry, either in the grave Dorian mode of thoughtful and intellectual verse, or in the light and graceful forms of old French song, or in the romantic manner of antique ballad, or in that 'moment's monument,' as Rossetti called it, the intense and concentrated sonnet. Occasionally one is tempted to wish that the quick, artistic faculty that women undoubtedly possess developed itself somewhat more in prose and somewhat less in verse. Poetry is for our highest moods, when we wish to be with the gods, and in our poetry nothing but the very best should satisfy us; but prose is for our daily bread, and the lack of good prose is one of the chief blots on our culture. French prose, even in the hands of the most ordinary writers, is always readable, but English prose is detestable. We have a few, a very few, masters, such as they are. We have Carlyle, who should not be imitated; and Mr. Pater, who, through the subtle perfection of his form, is inimitable absolutely; and Mr. Froude, who is useful; and Matthew Arnold, who is a model; and Mr. George Meredith, who is a warning; and Mr. Lang, who is the divine amateur; and Mr. Stevenson, who is the humane artist; and Mr. Ruskin, whose rhythm and colour and fine rhetoric and marvellous music of words are entirely unattainable. But the general prose that one reads in magazines and in newspapers is terribly dull and cumbrous, heavy in movement and uncouth or exaggerated in expression. Possibly some day our women of letters will apply themselves more definitely to prose.

Their light touch, and exquisite ear, and delicate sense of balance and proportion would be of no small service to us. I can fancy women bringing a new manner into our literature.

However, we have to deal here with women as poetesses, and it is interesting to note that, though Mrs. Browning's influence undoubtedly contributed very largely to the development of this new song-movement, if I may so term it, still there seems to have been never a time during the last three hundred years when the women of this kingdom did not cultivate, if not the art, at least the habit, of writing poetry.

Who the first English poetess was I cannot say. I believe it was the Abbess Juliana Berners, who lived in the fifteenth century; but I have no doubt that Mr. Freeman would be able at a moment's notice to produce some wonderful Saxon or Norman poetess, whose works cannot be read without a glossary, and even with its aid are completely unintelligible. For my own part, I am content with the Abbess Juliana, who wrote enthusiastically about hawking; and after her I would mention Anne Askew, who in prison and on the eve of her fiery martyrdom wrote a ballad that has, at any rate, a pathetic and historical interest. Queen Elizabeth's 'most sweet and sententious ditty' on Mary Stuart is highly praised by Puttenham, a contemporary critic, as an example of 'Exargasia, or the Gorgeous in Literature,' which somehow seems a very suitable epithet for such a great Queen's poems. The term she applies to the unfortunate Queen of Scots, 'the daughter of debate,' has, of course, long since passed into literature. The Countess of Pembroke, Sir Philip Sidney's sister, was much admired as a poetess in her day.

In 1613 the 'learned, virtuous, and truly noble ladie,' Elizabeth Carew, published a Tragedie of Marian, the Faire Queene of Jewry, and a few years later the 'noble ladie Diana Primrose' wrote A Chain of Pearl, which is a panegyric on the 'peerless graces' of Gloriana. Mary Morpeth, the friend and admirer of Drummond of Hawthornden; Lady Mary Wroth, to whom Ben Jonson dedicated The Alchemist; and the Princess Elizabeth, the sister of Charles I., should also be mentioned.

After the Restoration women applied themselves with still greater ardour to the study of literature and the practice of poetry. Margaret, Duchess of Newcastle, was a true woman of letters, and some of her verses are extremely pretty and graceful. Mrs. Aphra Behn was the first Englishwoman who adopted literature as a regular profession. Mrs. Katharine Philips, according to Mr. Gosse, invented sentimentality. As she was praised by Dryden, and mourned by Cowley, let us hope she may be forgiven. Keats came across her poems at Oxford when he was writing Endymion, and found in one of them 'a most delicate fancy of the Fletcher kind'; but I fear nobody reads the Matchless Orinda now. Of Lady Winchelsea's Nocturnal Reverie Wordsworth said that, with the exception of Pope's Windsor Forest, it was the only poem of the period intervening between Paradise Lost and Thomson's Seasons that contained a single new image of external nature. Lady Rachel Russell, who may be said to have inaugurated the letter-writing literature of England; Eliza Haywood, who is immortalised by the badness of her work, and has a niche in The Dunciad; and the Marchioness of Wharton, whose poems Waller said he admired, are very remarkable types, the finest of them being, of course, the first named, who was a woman of heroic mould and of a most noble dignity of nature.

Indeed, though the English poetesses up to the time of Mrs. Browning cannot be said to have produced any work of absolute genius, they are certainly interesting figures, fascinating subjects for study. Amongst them we find Lady Mary Wortley Montague, who had all the caprice of Cleopatra, and whose letters are delightful reading; Mrs. Centlivre, who wrote one brilliant comedy; Lady Anne Barnard, whose Auld Robin Gray was described by Sir Walter Scott as 'worth all the dialogues Corydon and Phillis have together spoken from the days of Theocritus downwards,' and is certainly a very beautiful and touching poem; Esther Vanhomrigh and Hester Johnson, the Vanessa and the Stella of Dean Swift's life; Mrs. Thrale, the friend of the great lexicographer; the worthy Mrs. Barbauld; the excellent Mrs. Hannah

More; the industrious Joanna Baillie; the admirable Mrs. Chapone, whose Ode to Solitude always fills me with the wildest passion for society, and who will at least be remembered as the patroness of the establishment at which Becky Sharp was educated; Miss Anna Seward, who was called 'The Swan of Lichfield'; poor L. E. L., whom Disraeli described in one of his clever letters to his sister as 'the personification of Brompton—pink satin dress, white satin shoes, red cheeks, snub nose, and her hair à la Sappho'; Mrs. Ratcliffe, who introduced the romantic novel, and has consequently much to answer for; the beautiful Duchess of Devonshire, of whom Gibbon said that she was 'made for something better than a Duchess'; the two wonderful sisters, Lady Dufferin and Mrs. Norton; Mrs. Tighe, whose Psyche Keats read with pleasure; Constantia Grierson, a marvellous blue-stocking in her time; Mrs. Hemans; pretty, charming 'Perdita,' who flirted alternately with poetry and the Prince Regent, played divinely in the Winter's Tale, was brutally attacked by Gifford, and has left us a pathetic little poem on the Snowdrop; and Emily Brontë, whose poems are instinct with tragic power, and seem often on the verge of being great.

Old fashions in literature are not so pleasant as old fashions in dress. I like the costume of the age of powder better than the poetry of the age of Pope. But if one adopts the historical standpoint—and this is, indeed, the only standpoint from which we can ever form a fair estimate of work that is not absolutely of the highest order—we cannot fail to see that many of the English poetesses who preceded Mrs. Browning were women of no ordinary talent, and that if the majority of them looked upon poetry simply as a department of belles lettres, so in most cases did their contemporaries. Since Mrs. Browning's day our woods have become full of singing birds, and if I venture to ask them to apply themselves more to prose and less to song, it is not that I like poetical prose, but that I love the prose of poets.

LONDON MODELS

(English Illustrated Magazine, January 1889.)

Professional models are a purely modern invention. To the Greeks, for instance, they were quite unknown. Mr. Mahaffy, it is true, tells us that Pericles used to present peacocks to the great ladies of Athenian society in order to induce them to sit to his friend Phidias, and we know that Polygnotus introduced into his picture of the Trojan women the face of Elpinice, the celebrated sister of the great Conservative leader of the day, but these grandes dames clearly do not come under our category. As for the old masters, they undoubtedly made constant studies from their pupils and apprentices, and even their religious pictures are full of the portraits of their friends and relations, but they do not seem to have had the inestimable advantage of the existence of a class of people whose sole profession is to pose. In fact the model, in our sense of the word, is the direct creation of Academic Schools.

Every country now has its own models, except America. In New York, and even in Boston, a good model is so great a rarity that most of the artists are reduced to painting Niagara and millionaires. In Europe, however, it is different. Here we have plenty of models, and of every nationality. The Italian models are the best. The natural grace of their attitudes, as well as the wonderful picturesqueness of their colouring, makes them facile—often too facile—subjects for the painter's brush. The French models, though not so beautiful as the Italian, possess a quickness of intellectual sympathy, a capacity, in fact, of understanding the artist, which is quite remarkable. They have also a great command over the varieties of facial expression, are peculiarly dramatic, and can chatter the argot of the atelier as cleverly as the critic of the Gil Bias. The English models form a class entirely by themselves. They are not so picturesque as the Italian, nor so clever as the French, and they have absolutely no tradition, so to speak, of their order. Now and then some old veteran knocks at a studio door, and proposes to sit as Ajax defying the lightning, or as King Lear upon the blasted heath. One of them some time ago called on a popular painter who, happening at the moment to require his services, engaged him, and told him to begin by kneeling down in the attitude of prayer. 'Shall I be Biblical or Shakespearean, sir?' asked the veteran. 'Well—Shakespearean,' answered the artist, wondering by what subtle nuance of expression the model would convey the difference. 'All right, sir,' said the professor of posing, and he solemnly knelt down and began to wink with his left eye! This class, however, is dying out. As a rule the model, nowadays, is a pretty girl, from about twelve to twenty-five years of age, who knows nothing about art, cares less, and is merely anxious to earn seven or eight shillings a day without much trouble. English models rarely look at a picture, and never venture on any æsthetic theories. In fact, they realise very completely Mr. Whistler's idea of the function of an art critic, for they pass no criticisms at all. They accept all schools of art with the grand catholicity of the auctioneer, and sit to a fantastic young impressionist as readily as to a learned and laborious academician. They are neither for the Whistlerites nor against them; the quarrel between the school of facts and the school of effects touches them not; idealistic and naturalistic are words that convey no meaning to their ears; they merely desire that the studio shall be warm, and the lunch hot, for all charming artists give their models lunch.

As to what they are asked to do they are equally indifferent. On Monday they will don the rags of a beggar-girl for Mr. Pumper, whose pathetic pictures of modern life draw such tears from the public, and on Tuesday they will pose in a peplum for Mr. Phœbus, who thinks that all really artistic subjects are necessarily B.C. They career gaily through all centuries and through all costumes, and, like actors, are interesting only when they are not themselves. They are extremely good-natured, and very accommodating. 'What do you sit for?' said a young artist to a model who had sent him in her card (all models, by the way, have cards and a small black bag). 'Oh, for anything you like, sir,' said the girl, 'landscape if necessary!'

Intellectually, it must be acknowledged, they are Philistines, but physically they are perfect—at least some are. Though none of them can talk Greek, many can look Greek, which to a nineteenth-century painter is naturally of great importance. If they are allowed, they chatter a great deal, but they never say anything. Their observations are the only banalités heard in Bohemia. However, though they cannot appreciate the artist as artist, they are quite ready to appreciate the artist as a man. They are very sensitive to kindness, respect and generosity. A beautiful model who had sat for two years to one of our most distinguished English painters, got engaged to a street vendor of penny ices. On her marriage the painter sent her a pretty wedding present, and received in return a nice letter of thanks with the following remarkable postscript: 'Never eat the green ices!'

When they are tired a wise artist gives them a rest. Then they sit in a chair and read penny dreadfuls, till they are roused from the tragedy of literature to take their place again in the tragedy of art. A few of them smoke cigarettes. This, however, is regarded by the other models as showing a want of seriousness, and is not generally approved of. They are engaged by the day and by the half-day. The tariff is a shilling an hour, to which great artists usually add an omnibus fare. The two best things about them are their extraordinary prettiness, and their extreme respectability. As a class they are very well behaved, particularly those who sit for the figure, a fact which is curious or natural according to the view one takes of human nature. They usually marry well, and sometimes they marry the artist. For an artist to marry his model is as fatal as for a gourmet to marry his cook: the one gets no sittings, and the other gets no dinners.

On the whole the English female models are very naïve, very natural, and very good-humoured. The virtues which the artist values most in them are prettiness and punctuality. Every sensible model consequently keeps a diary of her engagements, and dresses neatly. The bad season is, of course, the summer, when the artists are out of town. However, of late years some artists have engaged their models to follow them, and the wife of one of our most charming painters has often had three or four models under her charge in the country, so that the work of her husband and his friends should not be interrupted. In France the models migrate en masse to the little seaport villages or forest hamlets where the painters congregate. The English models, however, wait patiently in London, as a rule, till the artists come back. Nearly all of them live with their parents, and help to support the house. They have every qualification for being immortalised in art except that of beautiful hands. The hands of the English model are nearly always coarse and red.

As for the male models, there is the veteran whom we have mentioned above. He has all the traditions of the grand style, and is rapidly disappearing with the school he represents. An old man who talks about Fuseli is, of course, unendurable, and, besides, patriarchs have ceased to be fashionable subjects. Then there is the true Academy model. He is usually a man of thirty, rarely good-looking, but a perfect miracle of muscles. In fact he is the apotheosis of anatomy, and is so conscious of his own splendour that he tells you of his tibia and his thorax, as if no one else had anything of the kind. Then come the Oriental models. The supply of these is limited, but there are always about a dozen in London. They are very much sought after as they can remain immobile for hours, and generally possess lovely costumes. However, they have a very poor opinion of English art, which they regard as something between a vulgar personality and a commonplace photograph. Next we have the Italian youth who has come over specially to be a model, or takes to it when his organ is out of repair. He is often quite charming with his large melancholy eyes, his crisp hair, and his slim brown figure. It is true he eats garlic, but then he can stand like a faun and couch like a leopard, so he is forgiven. He is always full of pretty compliments, and has been known to have kind words of encouragement for even our greatest artists. As for the English lad of the same age, he never sits at all. Apparently he does not regard the career of a model as a serious profession. In any case he is rarely, if ever, to be got hold of. English boys, too, are difficult to find. Sometimes an ex-model who has a son will curl his hair, and wash his face, and bring him the round of the studios, all soap and shininess. The young school don't like him, but the older school do, and when he appears on the walls of the Royal Academy he is called The Infant Samuel. Occasionally also an artist catches a couple of gamins in the gutter and asks them to come to his studio. The first time they always appear, but after that they don't keep their appointments. They dislike sitting still, and have a strong and perhaps natural objection to looking pathetic. Besides, they are always under the impression that the artist is laughing at them. It is a sad fact, but there is no doubt that the poor are completely unconscious of their own picturesqueness. Those of them who can be induced to sit do so with the idea that the artist is merely a benevolent philanthropist who has chosen an eccentric method of distributing alms to the undeserving. Perhaps the School Board will teach the London gamin his own artistic value, and then they will be better models than they are now. One remarkable privilege belongs to the Academy model, that of extorting a sovereign from any newly elected Associate or R.A. They wait at Burlington House till the announcement is made, and then race to the hapless artist's house. The one who arrives first receives the money. They have of late been much troubled at the long distances they have had to run, and they look with disfavour on the election of artists who live at Hampstead or at Bedford Park, for it is considered a point of honour not to employ the underground railway, omnibuses, or any artificial means of locomotion. The race is to the swift.

Besides the professional posers of the studio there are posers of the Row, the posers at afternoon teas, the posers in politics and the circus posers. All four classes are delightful, but only the last class is ever really decorative. Acrobats and gymnasts can give the young painter infinite suggestions, for they bring into their art an element of swiftness of motion and of constant change that the studio model necessary lacks. What is interesting in these 'slaves of the ring' is that with them Beauty is an unconscious result not a conscious aim, the result in fact of the mathematical calculation of curves and distances, of absolute precision of eye, of the scientific knowledge of the equilibrium of forces, and of perfect physical training. A good acrobat is always graceful, though grace is never his object; he is graceful because he does what he has to do in the best way in which it can be done—graceful because he is natural. If an ancient Greek were to come to life now, which considering the probable severity of his criticisms would be rather trying to our conceit, he would be found far oftener at the circus than at the theatre. A good circus is an oasis of Hellenism in a world that reads too much to be wise, and thinks too much to be beautiful. If it were not for the running-ground at Eton, the towing-path at Oxford, the Thames swimming-baths, and the yearly circuses, humanity would forget the plastic perfection of its own form, and degenerate into a race of short-sighted professors and spectacled précieuses. Not that the circus proprietors are, as a rule, conscious of their high mission. Do they not bore us with the haute école, and weary us with Shakespearean clowns?—Still, at least, they give us acrobats, and the acrobat is an artist. The mere fact that he never speaks to the audience shows how well he appreciates the great truth that the aim of art is not to reveal personality but to please. The clown may be blatant, but the acrobat is always beautiful. He is an interesting combination of the spirit of Greek sculpture with the spangles of the modern costumier. He has even had his niche in the novels of our age, and if Manette Salomon be the unmasking of the model, Les Frères Zemganno is the apotheosis of the acrobat.

As regards the influence of the ordinary model on our English school of painting, it cannot be said that it is altogether good. It is, of course, an advantage for the young artist sitting in his studio to be able to isolate 'a little corner of life,' as the French say, from disturbing surroundings, and to study it under certain effects of light and shade. But this very isolation leads often to mere mannerism in the painter, and robs him of that broad acceptance of the general facts of life which is the very essence of art. Model-painting, in a word, while it may be the condition of art, is not by any means its aim. It is simply practice, not perfection. Its use trains the eye and the hand of the painter, its abuse produces in his work an effect of mere posing and prettiness. It is the secret of much of the artificiality of modern art, this constant posing of pretty people, and when art becomes artificial it becomes monotonous. Outside the little world of the studio, with its draperies and its bric-à-brac, lies the world of life with its infinite, its Shakespearean variety. We must, however, distinguish between the two kinds of models, those who sit for the figure and those who sit for the costume. The study of the first is always excellent, but the costume-model is becoming rather wearisome in modern pictures. It is really of very little use to dress up a London girl in Greek draperies and to paint her as a goddess. The robe may be the robe of Athens, but the face is usually the face of Brompton. Now and then, it is true, one comes across a model whose face is an exquisite anachronism, and who looks lovely and natural in the dress of any century but her own. This, however, is rather rare. As a rule models are absolutely de notre siècle, and should be painted as such. Unfortunately they are not, and, as a consequence, we are shown every year a series of scenes from fancy dress balls which are called historical pictures, but are little more than mediocre representations of modern people masquerading. In France they are wiser. The French painter uses the model simply for study; for the finished picture he goes direct to life.

However, we must not blame the sitters for the shortcomings of the artists. The English models are a well-behaved and hard-working class, and if they are more interested in artists than in art, a large section of the public is in the same condition, and most of our modern exhibitions seem to justify its choice.

LETTER TO JOAQUIN MILLER

Written to Mr. Joaquin Miller in reply to a letter, dated February 9, 1882, in reference to the behaviour of a section of the audience at Wilde's lecture on the English Renaissance at the Grand Opera House, Rochester, New York State, on February 7. It was first published in a volume called Decorative Art in America, containing unauthorised reprints of certain reviews and letters contributed by Wilde to English newspapers. (New York: Brentano's, 1906.)

St. Louis, *February* 28, 1882.

MY DEAR JOAQUIN MILLER,—I thank you for your chivalrous and courteous letter. Believe me, I would as lief judge of the strength and splendour of sun and sea by the dust that dances in the beam and the bubble that breaks on the wave, as take the petty and profitless vulgarity of one or two insignificant towns as any test or standard of the real spirit of a sane, strong and simple people, or allow it to affect my respect for the many noble men or women whom it has been my privilege in this great country to know.

For myself and the cause which I represent I have no fears as regards the future. Slander and folly have their way for a season, but for a season only; while, as touching the few provincial newspapers which have so vainly assailed me, or that ignorant and itinerant libeller of New England who goes lecturing from village to village in such open and ostentatious isolation, be sure I have no time to waste on them. Youth being so glorious, art so godlike, and the very world about us so full of beautiful things, and things worthy of reverence, and things honourable, how should one stop to listen to the lucubrations of a literary gamin, to the brawling and mouthing of a man whose praise would be as insolent as his slander is impotent, or to the irresponsible and irrepressible chatter of the professionally unproductive?

It is a great advantage, I admit, to have done nothing, but one must not abuse even that advantage.

Who, after all, that I should write of him, is this scribbling anonymuncule in grand old Massachusetts who scrawls and screams so glibly about what he cannot understand? This apostle of inhospitality, who delights to defile, to desecrate, and to defame the gracious courtesies he is unworthy to enjoy? Who are these scribes who, passing with purposeless alacrity from the Police News to the Parthenon, and from crime to criticism, sway with such serene incapacity the office which they so lately swept? 'Narcissuses of imbecility,' what should they see in the clear waters of Beauty and in the well undefiled of Truth but the shifting and shadowy image of their own substantial stupidity? Secure of that oblivion for which they toil so laboriously and, I must acknowledge, with such success, let them peer at us through their telescopes and report what they like of us. But, my dear Joaquin, should we put them under the microscope there would be really nothing to be seen.

I look forward to passing another delightful evening with you on my return to New York, and I need not tell you that whenever you visit England you will be received with that courtesy with which it is our pleasure to welcome all Americans, and that honour with which it is our privilege to greet all poets.—Most sincerely and affectionately yours,

OSCAR WILDE.

NOTES ON WHISTLER

I.

(World, November 14, 1883.)

From Oscar Wilde, Exeter, to J. M'Neill Whistler, Tite Street.—Punch too ridiculous—when you and I are together we never talk about anything except ourselves.

II.

(World, February 25, 1885.)

DEAR BUTTERFLY,—By the aid of a biographical dictionary I made the discovery that there were once two painters, called Benjamin West and Paul Delaroche, who rashly lectured upon Art. As of their works nothing at all remains, I conclude that they explained themselves away.

Be warned in time, James; and remain, as I do, incomprehensible. To be great is to be misunderstood.—Tout à vous, OSCAR WILDE.

III.

(World, November 24,1886.)

ATLAS,—This is very sad! With our James vulgarity begins at home, and should be allowed to stay there.—À vous, OSCAR WILDE.

REPLY TO WHISTLER

(*Truth*, January 9, 1890.)

To the Editor of Truth.

SIR,—I can hardly imagine that the public is in the very smallest degree interested in the shrill shrieks of 'Plagiarism' that proceed from time to time out of the lips of silly vanity or incompetent mediocrity.

However, as Mr. James Whistler has had the impertinence to attack me with both venom and vulgarity in your columns, I hope you will allow me to state that the assertions contained in his letter are as deliberately untrue as they are deliberately offensive.

The definition of a disciple as one who has the courage of the opinions of his master is really too old even for Mr. Whistler to be allowed to claim it, and as for borrowing Mr. Whistler's ideas about art, the only thoroughly original ideas I have ever heard him express have had reference to his own superiority as a painter over painters greater than himself.

It is a trouble for any gentleman to have to notice the lucubrations of so ill-bred and ignorant a person as Mr. Whistler, but your publication of his insolent letter left me no option in the matter.—I remain, sir, faithfully yours, OSCAR WILDE.

16 TITE STREET, CHELSEA, S. W.

LETTERS ON DORIAN GRAY

I. MR. WILDE'S BAD CASE

(*St. James's Gazette*, June 26, 1890.)

To the Editor of the *St. James's Gazette*.

SIR,—I have read your criticism of my story, The Picture of Dorian Gray; and I need hardly say that I do not propose to discuss its merits or demerits, its personalities or its lack of personality. England is a free country, and ordinary English criticism is perfectly free and easy. Besides, I must admit that, either from temperament or taste, or from both, I am quite incapable of understanding how any work of art can be criticised from a moral standpoint. The sphere of art and the sphere of ethics are absolutely distinct and separate; and it is to the confusion between the two that we owe the appearance of Mrs. Grundy, that amusing old lady who represents the only original form of humour that the middle classes of this country have been able to produce.

What I do object to most strongly is that you should have placarded the town with posters on which was printed in large letters:—

MR. OSCAR WILDE'S

LATEST ADVERTISEMENT:

A BAD CASE.

Whether the expression 'A Bad Case' refers to my book or to the present position of the Government, I cannot tell. What was silly and unnecessary was the use of the term 'advertisement.'

I think I may say without vanity—though I do not wish to appear to run vanity down—that of all men in England I am the one who requires least advertisement. I am tired to death of being advertised—I feel no thrill when I see my name in a paper. The chronicle does not interest me any more. I wrote this book entirely for my own pleasure, and it gave me very great pleasure to write it. Whether it becomes popular or not is a matter of absolute indifference to me. I am afraid, Sir, that the real advertisement is your cleverly written article. The English public, as a mass, takes no interest in a work of art until it is told that the work in question is immoral, and your réclame will, I have no doubt, largely increase the sale of the magazine; in which sale I may mention with some regret, I have no pecuniary interest.—I remain, Sir, your obedient servant, OSCAR WILDE.

16 TITE STREET, CHELSEA, June 25.

II. MR. OSCAR WILDE AGAIN

(*St. James's Gazette*, June 27, 1890.)

SIR,—In your issue of today you state that my brief letter published in your columns is the 'best reply' I can make to your article upon Dorian Gray. This is not so. I do not propose to discuss fully the matter here, but I feel bound to say that your article contains the most unjustifiable attack that has been made upon any man of letters for many years.

The writer of it, who is quite incapable of concealing his personal malice, and so in some measure destroys the effect he wishes to produce, seems not to have the slightest idea of the temper in which a work of art should be approached. To say that such a book as mine should be 'chucked into the fire' is silly. That is what one does with newspapers.

Of the value of pseudo-ethical criticism in dealing with artistic work I have spoken already. But as your writer has ventured into the perilous grounds of literary criticism I ask you to allow me, in fairness not merely to myself but to all men to whom literature is a fine art, to say a few words about his critical method.

He begins by assailing me with much ridiculous virulence because the chief personages in my story are puppies. They are puppies. Does he think that literature went to the dogs when Thackeray wrote about puppydom? I think that puppies are extremely interesting from an artistic as well as from a psychological point of view.

They seem to me to be certainly far more interesting than prigs; and

I am of opinion that Lord Henry Wotton is an excellent corrective of the tedious ideal shadowed forth in the semi-theological novels of our age.

He then makes vague and fearful insinuations about my grammar and my erudition. Now, as regards grammar, I hold that, in prose at any rate, correctness should always be subordinate to artistic effect and musical cadence; and any peculiarities of syntax that may occur in Dorian Gray are deliberately intended, and are introduced to show the value of the artistic theory in question. Your writer gives no instance of any such peculiarity. This I regret, because I do not think that any such instances occur.

As regards erudition, it is always difficult, even for the most modest of us, to remember that other people do not know quite as much as one does one's self. I myself frankly admit I cannot imagine how a casual reference to Suetonius and Petronius Arbiter can be construed into evidence of a desire to impress an unoffending and ill-educated public by an assumption of superior knowledge. I should fancy that the most ordinary of scholars is perfectly well acquainted with the Lives of the Cæsars and with the Satyricon.

The Lives of the Cæsars, at any rate, forms part of the curriculum at Oxford for those who take the Honour School of Literæ Humaniores; and as for the Satyricon it is popular even among pass-men, though I suppose they are obliged to read it in translations.

The writer of the article then suggests that I, in common with that great and noble artist Count Tolstoi, take pleasure in a subject because it is dangerous. About such a suggestion there is this to be said. Romantic art deals with the exception and with the individual. Good people, belonging as they do to the normal, and so, commonplace, type, are artistically uninteresting.

Bad people are, from the point of view of art, fascinating studies. They represent colour, variety and strangeness. Good people exasperate one's reason; bad people stir one's imagination. Your critic, if I must give him so honourable a title, states that the people in my story have no counterpart in life; that they are, to use his vigorous if somewhat vulgar phrase, 'mere catchpenny revelations of the non-existent.' Quite so.

If they existed they would not be worth writing about. The function of the artist is to invent, not to chronicle. There are no such people. If there were I would not write about them. Life by its realism is always spoiling the subject-matter of art.

The superior pleasure in literature is to realise the non-existent.

And finally, let me say this. You have reproduced, in a journalistic form, the comedy of Much Ado about Nothing and have, of course, spoilt it in your reproduction.

The poor public, hearing, from an authority so high as your own, that this is a wicked book that should be coerced and suppressed by a Tory Government, will, no doubt, rush to it and read it. But, alas! they will find that it is a story with a moral. And the moral is this: All excess, as well as all renunciation, brings its own punishment.

The painter, Basil Hallward, worshipping physical beauty far too much, as most painters do, dies by the hand of one in whose soul he has created a monstrous and absurd vanity. Dorian Gray, having led a life of mere sensation and pleasure, tries to kill conscience, and at that moment kills himself. Lord Henry Wotton seeks to be merely the spectator of life. He finds that those who reject the battle are more deeply wounded than those who take part in it.

Yes, there is a terrible moral in Dorian Gray—a moral which the prurient will not be able to find in it, but it will be revealed to all whose minds are healthy. Is this an artistic error? I fear it is. It is the only error in the book.—I remain, Sir, your obedient servant, OSCAR WILDE.

16 TITE STREET, CHELSEA, June 26.

III. MR. OSCAR WILDE'S DEFENCE

(*St. James's Gazette*, June 28, 1890.)

To the Editor of the *St. James's Gazette*.

SIR,—As you still keep up, though in a somewhat milder form than before, your attacks on me and my book, you not only confer on me the right, but you impose upon me the duty of reply.

You state, in your issue of today, that I misrepresented you when I said that you suggested that a book so wicked as mine should be 'suppressed and coerced by a Tory Government.' Now, you did not propose this, but you did suggest it. When you declare that you do not know whether or not the Government will take action about my book, and remark that the authors of books much less wicked have been proceeded against in law, the suggestion is quite obvious.

In your complaint of misrepresentation you seem to me, Sir, to have been not quite candid.

However, as far as I am concerned, this suggestion is of no importance. What is of importance is that the editor of a paper like yours should appear to countenance the monstrous theory that the Government of a country should exercise a censorship over imaginative literature. This is a theory against which I, and all men of letters of my acquaintance, protest most strongly; and any critic who admits the reasonableness of such a theory shows at once that he is quite incapable of understanding what literature is, and what are the rights that literature possesses. A Government might just as well try to teach painters how to paint, or sculptors how to model, as attempt to interfere with the style, treatment and subject-matter of the literary artist, and no writer, however eminent or obscure, should ever give his sanction to a theory that would degrade literature far more than any didactic or so-called immoral book could possibly do.

You then express your surprise that 'so experienced a literary gentleman' as myself should imagine that your critic was animated by any feeling of personal malice towards him. The phrase 'literary gentleman' is a vile phrase, but let that pass.

I accept quite readily your assurance that your critic was simply criticising a work of art in the best way that he could, but I feel that I was fully justified in forming the opinion of him that I did. He opened his article by a gross personal attack on myself. This, I need hardly say, was an absolutely unpardonable error of critical taste.

There is no excuse for it except personal malice; and you, Sir, should

216

not have sanctioned it. A critic should be taught to criticise a work of art without making any reference to the personality of the author. This, in fact, is the beginning of criticism. However, it was not merely his personal attack on me that made me imagine that he was actuated by malice. What really confirmed me in my first impression was his reiterated assertion that my book was tedious and dull.

Now, if I were criticising my book, which I have some thoughts of doing, I think I would consider it my duty to point out that it is far too crowded with sensational incident, and far too paradoxical in style, as far, at any rate, as the dialogue goes. I feel that from a standpoint of art these are true defects in the book. But tedious and dull the book is not.

Your critic has cleared himself of the charge of personal malice, his denial and yours being quite sufficient in the matter; but he has done so only by a tacit admission that he has really no critical instinct about literature and literary work, which, in one who writes about literature, is, I need hardly say, a much graver fault than malice of any kind.

Finally, Sir, allow me to say this. Such an article as you have published really makes me despair of the possibility of any general culture in England. Were I a French author, and my book brought out in Paris, there is not a single literary critic in France on any paper of high standing who would think for a moment of criticising it from an ethical standpoint. If he did so he would stultify himself, not merely in the eyes of all men of letters, but in the eyes of the majority of the public.

You have yourself often spoken against Puritanism. Believe me, Sir, Puritanism is never so offensive and destructive as when it deals with art matters. It is there that it is radically wrong. It is this Puritanism, to which your critic has given expression, that is always marring the artistic instinct of the English. So far from encouraging it, you should set yourself against it, and should try to teach your critics to recognise the essential difference between art and life.

The gentleman who criticised my book is in a perfectly hopeless confusion about it, and your attempt to help him out by proposing that the subject-matter of art should be limited does not mend matters. It is proper that limitation should be placed on action. It is not proper that limitation should be placed on art. To art belong all things that are and all things that are not, and even the editor of a London paper has no right to restrain the freedom of art in the selection of subject-matter. I now trust, Sir, that these attacks on me and on my book will cease. There are forms of advertisement that are unwarranted and unwarrantable.—I am, Sir, your obedient servant,

OSCAR WILDE.

16 TITE STREET, S. W., June 27.

IV. (St. James's Gazette, June 30, 1890.)

To the Editor of the *St. James's Gazette.*

SIR,—In your issue of this evening you publish a letter from 'A London Editor' which clearly insinuates in the last paragraph that I have in some way sanctioned the circulation of an expression of opinion, on the part of the proprietors of Lippincott's Magazine, of the literary and artistic value of my story of The Picture of Dorian Gray.

Allow me, Sir, to state that there are no grounds for this insinuation. I was not aware that any such document was being circulated; and I have written to the agents, Messrs. Ward and Lock—who cannot, I feel sure, be primarily responsible for its appearance—to ask them to withdraw it at once. No publisher should ever express an opinion of the value of what he publishes. That is a matter entirely for the literary critic to decide.

I must admit, as one to whom contemporary literature is constantly submitted for criticism, that the only thing that ever prejudices me against a book is the lack of literary style; but I can quite understand how any ordinary critic would be strongly prejudiced against a work that was accompanied by a premature and unnecessary panegyric from the publisher. A publisher is simply a useful middleman. It is not for him to anticipate the verdict of criticism.

I may, however, while expressing my thanks to the 'London Editor' for drawing my attention to this, I trust, purely American method of procedure, venture to differ from him in one of his criticisms. He states that he regards the expression 'complete' as applied to a story, as a specimen of the 'adjectival exuberance of the puffer.' Here, it seems to me, he sadly exaggerates. What my story is is an interesting problem. What my story is not is a 'novelette'—a term which you have more than once applied to it. There is no such word in the English language as novelette. It should not be used. It is merely part of the slang of Fleet Street.

In another part of your paper, Sir, you state that I received your assurance of the lack of malice in your critic 'somewhat grudgingly.' This is not so. I frankly said that I accepted that assurance 'quite readily,' and that your own denial and that of your own critic were 'sufficient.'

Nothing more generous could have been said. What I did feel was that you saved your critic from the charge of malice by convicting him of the unpardonable crime of lack of literary instinct. I still feel that. To call my book an ineffective attempt at allegory, that in the hands of Mr. Anstey might have been made striking, is absurd.

Mr. Anstey's sphere in literature and my sphere are different.

You then gravely ask me what rights I imagine literature possesses. That is really an extraordinary question for the editor of a newspaper such as yours to ask. The rights of literature, Sir, are the rights of intellect.

I remember once hearing M. Renan say that he would sooner live under a military despotism than under the despotism of the Church, because the former merely limited the freedom of action, while the latter limited the freedom of mind.

You say that a work of art is a form of action. It is not. It is the highest mode of thought.

In conclusion, Sir, let me ask you not to force on me this continued correspondence by daily attacks. It is a trouble and a nuisance.

As you assailed me first, I have a right to the last word. Let that last word be the present letter, and leave my book, I beg you, to the immortality that it deserves.—I am, Sir, your obedient servant,

OSCAR WILDE.

16 TITE STREET, S.W., June 28.

V. 'DORIAN GRAY'

(*Daily Chronicle*, July 2, 1890.)

To the Editor of the *Daily Chronicle*.

SIR,—Will you allow me to correct some errors into which your critic has fallen in his review of my story, The Picture of Dorian Gray, published in today's issue of your paper?

Your critic states, to begin with, that I make desperate attempts to 'vamp up' a moral in my story. Now, I must candidly confess that I do not know what 'vamping' is. I see, from time to time, mysterious advertisements in the newspapers about 'How to Vamp,' but what vamping really means remains a mystery to me—a mystery that, like all other mysteries, I hope some day to explore.

However, I do not propose to discuss the absurd terms used by modern journalism. What I want to say is that, so far from wishing to emphasise any moral in my story, the real trouble I experienced in writing the story was that of keeping the extremely obvious moral subordinate to the artistic and dramatic effect.

When I first conceived the idea of a young man selling his soul in exchange for eternal youth—an idea that is old in the history of literature, but to which I have given new form—I felt that, from an æsthetic point of view, it would be difficult to keep the moral in its proper secondary place; and even now I do not feel quite sure that I have been able to do so. I think the moral too apparent. When the book is published in a volume I hope to correct this defect.

As for what the moral is, your critic states that it is this—that when a man feels himself becoming 'too angelic' he should rush out and make a 'beast of himself.' I cannot say that I consider this a moral. The real moral of the story is that all excess, as well as all renunciation, brings its punishment, and this moral is so far artistically and deliberately suppressed that it does not enunciate its law as a general principle, but realises itself purely in the lives of individuals, and so becomes simply a dramatic element in a work of art, and not the object of the work of art itself.

Your critic also falls into error when he says that Dorian Gray, having a 'cool, calculating, conscienceless character,' was inconsistent when he destroyed the picture of his own soul, on the ground that the picture did not become less hideous after he had done what, in his vanity, he had considered his first good action. Dorian Gray has not got a cool, calculating, conscienceless character at all. On the contrary, he is extremely impulsive, absurdly romantic, and is haunted all through his life by an exaggerated sense of conscience which mars his pleasures for him and warns him that youth and enjoyment are not everything in the world. It is finally to get rid of the conscience that had dogged his steps from year to year that he destroys the picture; and thus in his attempt to kill conscience Dorian Gray kills himself.

Your critic then talks about 'obtrusively cheap scholarship.' Now, whatever a scholar writes is sure to display scholarship in the distinction of style and the fine use of language; but my story contains no learned or pseudo-learned discussions, and the only literary books that it alludes to are books that any fairly educated reader may be supposed to be acquainted with, such as the Satyricon of Petronius Arbiter, or Gautier's Emaux et Camées. Such books as Le Conso's Clericalis Disciplina belong not to culture, but to curiosity. Anybody may be excused for not knowing them.

Finally, let me say this—the æsthetic movement produced certain curious colours, subtle in their loveliness and fascinating in their almost mystical tone. They were, and are, our reaction against the crude primaries of a doubtless more respectable but certainly less cultivated age. My story is an essay on decorative art. It reacts against the crude brutality of plain realism. It is poisonous if you like, but you cannot deny that it is also perfect, and perfection is what we artists aim at.—I remain, Sir, your obedient servant,

OSCAR WILDE.

16 TITE STREET, June 30.

VI. MR. WILDE'S REJOINDER

(*Scots Observer*, July 12, 1890.)

To the Editor of the *Scots Observer.*

SIR,—You have published a review of my story, The Picture of Dorian Gray. As this review is grossly unjust to me as an artist, I ask you to allow me to exercise in your columns my right of reply.

Your reviewer, Sir, while admitting that the story in question is 'plainly the work of a man of letters,' the work of one who has 'brains, and art, and style,' yet suggests, and apparently in all seriousness, that I have written it in order that it should be read by the most depraved members of the criminal and illiterate classes. Now, Sir, I do not suppose that the criminal and illiterate classes ever read anything except newspapers. They are certainly not likely to be able to understand anything of mine. So let them pass, and on the broad question of why a man of letters writes at all let me say this.

The pleasure that one has in creating a work of art is a purely personal pleasure, and it is for the sake of this pleasure that one creates. The artist works with his eye on the object. Nothing else interests him. What people are likely to say does not even occur to him.

He is fascinated by what he has in hand. He is indifferent to others. I write because it gives me the greatest possible artistic pleasure to write. If my work pleases the few I am gratified. If it does not, it causes me no pain. As for the mob, I have no desire to be a popular novelist. It is far too easy.

Your critic then, Sir, commits the absolutely unpardonable crime of trying to confuse the artist with his subject-matter. For this, Sir, there is no excuse at all.

Of one who is the greatest figure in the world's literature since Greek days, Keats remarked that he had as much pleasure in conceiving the evil as he had in conceiving the good. Let your reviewer, Sir, consider the bearings of Keats's fine criticism, for it is under these conditions that every artist works. One stands remote from one's subject-matter. One creates it and one contemplates it. The further away the subject-matter is, the more freely can the artist work.

Your reviewer suggests that I do not make it sufficiently clear whether I prefer virtue to wickedness or wickedness to virtue. An artist, Sir, has no ethical sympathies at all. Virtue and wickedness are to him simply what the colours on his palette are to the painter. They are no more and they are no less. He sees that by their means a certain artistic effect can be produced and he produces it. Iago may be morally horrible and Imogen stainlessly pure. Shakespeare, as Keats said, had as much delight in creating the one as he had in creating the other.

It was necessary, Sir, for the dramatic development of this story to surround Dorian Gray with an atmosphere of moral corruption. Otherwise the story would have had no meaning and the plot no issue. To keep this atmosphere vague and indeterminate and wonderful was the aim of the artist who wrote the story. I claim, Sir, that he has succeeded. Each man sees his own sin in Dorian Gray. What Dorian Gray's sins are no one knows. He who finds them has brought them.

In conclusion, Sir, let me say how really deeply I regret that you should have permitted such a notice as the one I feel constrained to write on to have appeared in your paper. That the editor of the St. James's Gazette should have employed Caliban as his art-critic was possibly natural. The editor of the Scots Observer should not have allowed Thersites to make mows in his review. It is unworthy of so distinguished a man of letters.—I am, etc.,

OSCAR WILDE.

16 TITE STREET, CHELSEA, July 9.

VII. ART AND MORALITY

(*Scots Observer*, August 2, 1890.)

To the Editor of the *Scots Observer*.

223

SIR,—In a letter dealing with the relations of art to morals recently published in your columns—a letter which I may say seems to me in many respects admirable, especially in its insistence on the right of the artist to select his own subject-matter—Mr. Charles Whibley suggests that it must be peculiarly painful for me to find that the ethical import of Dorian Gray has been so strongly recognised by the foremost Christian papers of England and America that I have been greeted by more than one of them as a moral reformer.

Allow me, Sir, to reassure, on this point, not merely Mr. Charles Whibley himself but also your, no doubt, anxious readers. I have no hesitation in saying that I regard such criticisms as a very gratifying tribute to my story. For if a work of art is rich, and vital and complete, those who have artistic instincts will see its beauty, and those to whom ethics appeal more strongly than æsthetics will see its moral lesson. It will fill the cowardly with terror, and the unclean will see in it their own shame. It will be to each man what he is himself. It is the spectator, and not life, that art really mirrors.

And so in the case of Dorian Gray the purely literary critic, as in the Speaker and elsewhere, regards it as a 'serious' and 'fascinating' work of art: the critic who deals with art in its relation to conduct, as the Christian Leader and the Christian World, regards it as an ethical parable: Light, which I am told is the organ of the English mystics, regards it as a work of high spiritual import; the St. James's Gazette, which is seeking apparently to be the organ of the prurient, sees or pretends to see in it all kinds of dreadful things, and hints at Treasury prosecutions; and your Mr. Charles Whibley genially says that he discovers in it 'lots of morality.'

It is quite true that he goes on to say that he detects no art in it. But I do not think that it is fair to expect a critic to be able to see a work of art from every point of view. Even Gautier had his limitations just as much as Diderot had, and in modern England Goethes are rare. I can only assure Mr. Charles Whibley that no moral apotheosis to which he has added the most modest contribution could possibly be a source of unhappiness to an artist.—I remain, Sir, your obedient servant,

OSCAR WILDE.

16 TITE STREET, CHELSEA, July 1890.

VIII.

(*Scots Observer*, August 16, 1890.)

To the Editor of the *Scots Observer*.

SIR,—I am afraid I cannot enter into any newspaper discussion on the subject of art with Mr. Whibley, partly because the writing of letters is always a trouble to me, and partly because I regret to say that I do not know what qualifications Mr. Whibley possesses for the discussion of so important a topic. I merely noticed his letter because, I am sure without in any way intending it, he made a suggestion about myself personally that was quite inaccurate. His suggestion was that it must have been painful to me to find that a certain section of the public, as represented by himself and the critics of some religious publications, had insisted on finding what he calls 'lots of morality' in my story of The Picture of Dorian Gray.

Being naturally desirous of setting your readers right on a question of such vital interest to the historian, I took the opportunity of pointing out in your columns that I regarded all such criticisms as a very gratifying tribute to the ethical beauty of the story, and I added that I was quite ready to recognise that it was not really fair to ask of any ordinary critic that he should be able to appreciate a work of art from every point of view.

I still hold this opinion. If a man sees the artistic beauty of a thing, he will probably care very little for its ethical import. If his temperament is more susceptible to ethical than to æsthetic influences, he will be blind to questions of style, treatment and the like. It takes a Goethe to see a work of art fully, completely and perfectly, and I thoroughly agree with Mr. Whibley when he says that it is a pity that Goethe never had an opportunity of reading Dorian Gray. I feel quite certain that he would have been delighted by it, and I only hope that some ghostly publisher is even now distributing shadowy copies in the Elysian fields, and that the cover of Gautier's copy is powdered with gilt asphodels.

You may ask me, Sir, why I should care to have the ethical beauty of my story recognised. I answer, Simply because it exists, because the thing is there.

The chief merit of Madame Bovary is not the moral lesson that can be found in it, any more than the chief merit of Salammbô is its archæology; but Flaubert was perfectly right in exposing the ignorance of those who called the one immoral and the other inaccurate; and not merely was he right in the ordinary sense of the word, but he was artistically right, which is everything. The critic has to educate the public; the artist has to educate the critic.

Allow me to make one more correction, Sir, and I will have done with Mr. Whibley. He ends his letter with the statement that I have been indefatigable in my public appreciation of my own work. I have no doubt that in saying this he means to pay me a compliment, but he really overrates my capacity, as well as my inclination for work. I must frankly confess that, by nature and by choice, I am extremely indolent.

Cultivated idleness seems to me to be the proper occupation for man. I dislike newspaper controversies of any kind, and of the two hundred and sixteen criticisms of Dorian Gray that have passed from my library table into the wastepaper basket I have taken public notice of only three. One was that which appeared in the Scots Observer. I noticed it because it made a suggestion, about the intention of the author in writing the book, which needed correction. The second was an article in the St. James's Gazette. It was offensively and vulgarly written, and seemed to me to require immediate and caustic censure. The tone of the article was an impertinence to any man of letters.

The third was a meek attack in a paper called the Daily Chronicle. I think my writing to the Daily Chronicle was an act of pure wilfulness. In fact, I feel sure it was. I quite forget what they said. I believe they said that Dorian Gray was poisonous, and I thought that, on alliterative grounds, it would be kind to remind them that, however that may be, it is at any rate perfect. That was all. Of the other two hundred and thirteen criticisms I have taken no notice. Indeed, I have not read more than half of them. It is a sad thing, but one wearies even of praise.

As regards Mr. Brown's letter, it is interesting only in so far as it

226

exemplifies the truth of what I have said above on the question of the two obvious schools of critics. Mr. Brown says frankly that he considers morality to be the 'strong point' of my story. Mr. Brown means well, and has got hold of a half truth, but when he proceeds to deal with the book from the artistic standpoint he, of course, goes sadly astray. To class Dorian Gray with M. Zola's La Terre is as silly as if one were to class Musset's Fortunio with one of the Adelphi melodramas. Mr. Brown should be content with ethical appreciation. There he is impregnable.

Mr. Cobban opens badly by describing my letter, setting Mr. Whibley right on a matter of fact, as an 'impudent paradox.' The term 'impudent' is meaningless, and the word 'paradox' is misplaced. I am afraid that writing to newspapers has a deteriorating influence on style. People get violent and abusive and lose all sense of proportion, when they enter that curious journalistic arena in which the race is always to the noisiest. 'Impudent paradox' is neither violent nor abusive, but it is not an expression that should have been used about my letter. However, Mr. Cobban makes full atonement afterwards for what was, no doubt, a mere error of manner, by adopting the impudent paradox in question as his own, and pointing out that, as I had previously said, the artist will always look at the work of art from the standpoint of beauty of style and beauty of treatment, and that those who have not got the sense of beauty, or whose sense of beauty is dominated by ethical considerations, will always turn their attention to the subject-matter and make its moral import the test and touchstone of the poem or novel or picture that is presented to them, while the newspaper critic will sometimes take one side and sometimes the other, according as he is cultured or uncultured. In fact, Mr. Cobban converts the impudent paradox into a tedious truism, and, I dare say, in doing so does good service.

The English public likes tediousness, and likes things to be explained to it in a tedious way.

Mr. Cobban has, I have no doubt, already repented of the unfortunate expression with which he has made his début, so I will say no more about it. As far as I am concerned he is quite forgiven.

And finally, Sir, in taking leave of the Scots Observer I feel bound to make a candid confession to you.

It has been suggested to me by a great friend of mine, who is a charming and distinguished man of letters, and not unknown to you personally, that there have been really only two people engaged in this terrible controversy, and that those two people are the editor of the Scots Observer and the author of Dorian Gray. At dinner this evening, over some excellent Chianti, my friend insisted that under assumed and mysterious names you had simply given dramatic expression to the views of some of the semi-educated classes of our community, and that the letters signed 'H.' were your own skilful, if somewhat bitter, caricature of the Philistine as drawn by himself. I admit that something of the kind had occurred to me when I read 'H.'s' first letter—the one in which he proposes that the test of art should be the political opinions of the artist, and that if one differed from the artist on the question of the best way of misgoverning Ireland, one should always abuse his work. Still, there are such infinite varieties of Philistines, and North Britain is so renowned for seriousness, that I dismissed the idea as one unworthy of the editor of a Scotch paper. I now fear that I was wrong, and that you have been amusing yourself all the time by inventing little puppets and teaching them how to use big words. Well, Sir, if it be so—and my friend is strong upon the point— allow me to congratulate you most sincerely on the cleverness with which you have reproduced that lack of literary style which is, I am told, essential for any dramatic and lifelike characterisation. I confess that I was completely taken in; but I bear no malice; and as you have, no doubt, been laughing at me up your sleeve, let me now join openly in the laugh, though it be a little against myself. A comedy ends when the secret is out. Drop your curtain and put your dolls to bed. I love Don Quixote, but I do not wish to fight any longer with marionettes, however cunning may be the master-hand that works their wires. Let them go, Sir, on the shelf. The shelf is the proper place for them. On some future occasion you can re-label them and bring them out for our amusement. They are an excellent company, and go well through their tricks, and if they are a little unreal, I am not the one to object to unreality in art. The jest was really a good one. The only thing that I cannot understand is why you gave your marionettes such extraordinary and improbable names.—I remain, Sir, your obedient servant, OSCAR WILDE.

16 TITE STREET, CHELSEA, August 13.

228

AN ANGLO-INDIAN'S COMPLAINT

(*Times*, September 26, 1891.)

To the Editor of the *Times*.

SIR,—The writer of a letter signed 'An Indian Civilian' that appears in your issue of today makes a statement about me which I beg you to allow me to correct at once.

He says I have described the Anglo-Indians as being vulgar. This is not the case. Indeed, I have never met a vulgar Anglo-Indian. There may be many, but those whom I have had the pleasure of meeting here have been chiefly scholars, men interested in art and thought, men of cultivation; nearly all of them have been exceedingly brilliant talkers; some of them have been exceedingly brilliant writers.

What I did say—I believe in the pages of the Nineteenth Century {158}—was that vulgarity is the distinguishing note of those Anglo-Indians whom Mr. Rudyard Kipling loves to write about, and writes about so cleverly. This is quite true, and there is no reason why Mr. Rudyard Kipling should not select vulgarity as his subject-matter, or as part of it. For a realistic artist, certainly, vulgarity is a most admirable subject. How far Mr. Kipling's stories really mirror Anglo-Indian society I have no idea at all, nor, indeed, am I ever much interested in any correspondence between art and nature. It seems to me a matter of entirely secondary importance. I do not wish, however, that it should be supposed that I was passing a harsh and saugrenu judgment on an important and in many ways distinguished class, when I was merely pointing out the characteristic qualities of some puppets in a prose-play.—I remain, Sir, your obedient servant,

OSCAR WILDE.

September 25.

A HOUSE OF POMEGRANATES

I.

(*Speaker*, December 5, 1891.)

SIR.—I have just purchased, at a price that for any other English sixpenny paper I would have considered exorbitant, a copy of the Speaker at one of the charming kiosks that decorate Paris; institutions, by the way, that I think we should at once introduce into London. The kiosk is a delightful object, and, when illuminated at night from within, as lovely as a fantastic Chinese lantern, especially when the transparent advertisements are from the clever pencil of M. Chéret. In London we have merely the ill-clad newsvendor, whose voice, in spite of the admirable efforts of the Royal College of Music to make England a really musical nation, is always out of tune, and whose rags, badly designed and badly worn, merely emphasise a painful note of uncomely misery, without conveying that impression of picturesqueness which is the only thing that makes the poverty of others at all bearable.

It is not, however, about the establishment of kiosks in London that I wish to write to you, though I am of opinion that it is a thing that the County Council should at once take in hand. The object of my letter is to correct a statement made in a paragraph of your interesting paper.

The writer of the paragraph in question states that the decorative designs that make lovely my book, A House of Pomegranates, are by the hand of Mr. Shannon, while the delicate dreams that separate and herald each story are by Mr. Ricketts. The contrary is the case. Mr. Shannon is the drawer of the dreams, and Mr. Ricketts is the subtle and fantastic decorator. Indeed, it is to Mr. Ricketts that the entire decorative design of the book is due, from the selection of the type and the placing of the ornamentation, to the completely beautiful cover that encloses the whole. The writer of the paragraph goes on to state that he does not 'like the cover.' This is, no doubt, to be regretted, though it is not a matter of much importance, as there are only two people in the world whom it is absolutely necessary that the cover should please. One is Mr. Ricketts, who designed it, the other is myself, whose book it binds. We both admire it immensely! The reason, however, that your critic gives for his failure to gain from the cover any impression of beauty seems to me to show a lack of artistic instinct on his part, which I beg you will allow me to try to correct.

He complains that a portion of the design on the left-hand side of the cover reminds him of an Indian club with a house-painter's brush on top of it, while a portion of the design on the right-hand side suggests to him the idea of 'a chimney-pot hat with a sponge in it.' Now, I do not for a moment dispute that these are the real impressions your critic received. It is the spectator, and the mind of the spectator, as I pointed out in the preface to The Picture of Dorian Gray, that art really mirrors. What I want to indicate is this: the artistic beauty of the cover of my book resides in the delicate tracing, arabesques, and massing of many coral-red lines on a ground of white ivory, the colour effect culminating in certain high gilt notes, and being made still more pleasurable by the overlapping band of moss-green cloth that holds the book together.

What the gilt notes suggest, what imitative parallel may be found to them in that chaos that is termed Nature, is a matter of no importance. They may suggest, as they do sometimes to me, peacocks and pomegranates and splashing fountains of gold water, or, as they do to your critic, sponges and Indian clubs and chimney-pot hats. Such suggestions and evocations have nothing whatsoever to do with the æsthetic quality and value of the design. A thing in Nature becomes much lovelier if it reminds us of a thing in Art, but a thing in Art gains no real beauty through reminding us of a thing in Nature. The primary æsthetic impression of a work of art borrows nothing from recognition or resemblance. These belong to a later and less perfect stage of apprehension.

Properly speaking, they are no part of a real æsthetic impression at all, and the constant preoccupation with subject-matter that characterises nearly all our English art-criticism, is what makes our art-criticisms, especially as regards literature, so sterile, so profitless, so much beside the mark, and of such curiously little account.—I remain, Sir, your obedient servant, OSCAR WILDE.

BOULEVARD DES CAPUCINES, PARIS.

II.

(*Pall Mall Gazette*, December 11, 1891.)

To the Editor of the *Pall Mall Gazette.*

SIR,—I have just had sent to me from London a copy of the Pall Mall Gazette, containing a review of my book A House of Pomegranates. {163} The writer of this review makes a certain suggestion which I beg you will allow me to correct at once.

He starts by asking an extremely silly question, and that is, whether or not I have written this book for the purpose of giving pleasure to the British child. Having expressed grave doubts on this subject, a subject on which I cannot conceive any fairly educated person having any doubts at all, he proceeds, apparently quite seriously, to make the extremely limited vocabulary at the disposal of the British child the standard by which the prose of an artist is to be judged! Now, in building this House of Pomegranates, I had about as much intention of pleasing the British child as I had of pleasing the British public. Mamilius is as entirely delightful as Caliban is entirely detestable, but neither the standard of Mamilius nor the standard of Caliban is my standard. No artist recognises any standard of beauty but that which is suggested by his own temperament. The artist seeks to realise, in a certain material, his immaterial idea of beauty, and thus to transform an idea into an ideal. That is the way an artist makes things. That is why an artist makes things. The artist has no other object in making things. Does your reviewer imagine that Mr. Shannon, for instance, whose delicate and lovely illustrations he confesses himself quite unable to see, draws for the purpose of giving information to the blind?—I remain, Sir, your obedient servant,

OSCAR WILDE.

BOULEVARD DES CAPUCINES, PARIS.

PUPPETS AND ACTORS

(*Daily Telegraph*, February 20, 1892.)

To the Editor of the *Daily Telegraph*.

SIR,—I have just been sent an article that seems to have appeared in your paper some days ago, {164} in which it is stated that, in the course of some remarks addressed to the Playgoers' Club on the occasion of my taking the chair at their last meeting, I laid it down as an axiom that the stage is only 'a frame furnished with a set of puppets.'

Now, it is quite true that I hold that the stage is to a play no more than a picture-frame is to a painting, and that the actable value of a play has nothing whatsoever to do with its value as a work of art. In this century, in England, to take an obvious example, we have had only two great plays—one is Shelley's Cenci, the other Mr. Swinburne's Atalanta in Calydon, and neither of them is in any sense of the word an actable play. Indeed, the mere suggestion that stage representation is any test of a work of art is quite ridiculous. In the production of Browning's plays, for instance, in London and at Oxford, what was being tested was obviously the capacity of the modern stage to represent, in any adequate measure or degree, works of introspective method and strange or sterile psychology. But the artistic value of Strqfford or In a Balcony was settled when Robert Browning wrote their last lines. It is not, Sir, by the mimes that the muses are to be judged.

So far, the writer of the article in question is right. Where he goes wrong is in saying that I describe this frame—the stage—as being furnished with a set of puppets. He admits that he speaks only by report, but he should have remembered, Sir, that report is not merely a lying jade, which, personally, I would willingly forgive her, but a jade who lies without lovely invention is a thing that I, at any rate, can forgive her, never.

What I really said was that the frame we call the stage was 'peopled with either living actors or moving puppets,' and I pointed out briefly, of necessity, that the personality of the actor is often a source of danger in the perfect presentation of a work of art. It may distort. It may lead astray. It may be a discord in the tone or symphony. For anybody can act. Most people in England do nothing else. To be conventional is to be a comedian. To act a particular part, however, is a very different thing, and a very difficult thing as well. The actor's aim is, or should be, to convert his own accidental personality into the real and essential personality of the character he is called upon to personate, whatever that character may be; or perhaps I should say that there are two schools of action—the school of those who attain their effect by exaggeration of personality, and the school of those who attain it by suppression. It would be too long to discuss these schools, or to decide which of them the dramatist loves best. Let me note the danger of personality, and pass to my puppets.

There are many advantages in puppets. They never argue. They have no crude views about art. They have no private lives. We are never bothered by accounts of their virtues, or bored by recitals of their vices; and when they are out of an engagement they never do good in public or save people from drowning, nor do they speak more than is set down for them. They recognise the presiding intellect of the dramatist, and have never been known to ask for their parts to be written up. They are admirably docile, and have no personalities at all. I saw lately, in Paris, a performance by certain puppets of Shakespeare's Tempest, in M. Maurice Boucher's translation. Miranda was the mirage of Miranda, because an artist has so fashioned her; and Ariel was true Ariel, because so had she been made. Their gestures were quite sufficient, and the words that seemed to come from their little lips were spoken by poets who had beautiful voices. It was a delightful performance, and I remember it still with delight, though Miranda took no notice of the flowers I sent her after the curtain fell. For modern plays, however, perhaps we had better have living players, for in modern plays actuality is everything. The charm—the ineffable charm—of the unreal is here denied us, and rightly.

Suffer me one more correction. Your writer describes the author of the brilliant fantastic lecture on 'The Modern Actor' as a protégé of mine. Allow me to state that my acquaintance with Mr. John Gray is, I regret to say, extremely recent, and that I sought it because he had already a perfected mode of expression both in prose and verse. All artists in this vulgar age need protection certainly. Perhaps they have always needed it. But the nineteenth-century artist finds it not in Prince, or Pope, or Patron, but in high indifference of temper, in the pleasure of the creation of beautiful things, and the long contemplation of them, in disdain of what in life is common and ignoble and in such felicitous sense of humour as enables one to see how vain and foolish is all popular opinion, and popular judgment, upon the wonderful things of art. These qualities Mr. John Gray possesses in a marked degree. He needs no other protection, nor, indeed, would he accept it.—I remain, Sir, your obedient servant, OSCAR WILDE.

LADY WINDERMERE'S FAN: AN EXPLANATION

(*St. James's Gazette*, February 27, 1892.)

To the Editor of the *St. James's Gazette*.

SIR,—Allow me to correct a statement put forward in your issue of this evening to the effect that I have made a certain alteration in my play in consequence of the criticism of some journalists who write very recklessly and very foolishly in the papers about dramatic art. This statement is entirely untrue and grossly ridiculous.

The facts are as follows. On last Saturday night, after the play was over, and the author, cigarette in hand, had delivered a delightful and immortal speech, I had the pleasure of entertaining at supper a small number of personal friends; and as none of them was older than myself I, naturally, listened to their artistic views with attention and pleasure. The opinions of the old on matters of Art are, of course, of no value whatsoever. The artistic instincts of the young are invariably fascinating; and I am bound to state that all my friends, without exception, were of opinion that the psychological interest of the second act would be greatly increased by the disclosure of the actual relationship existing between Lady Windermere and Mrs. Erlynne— an opinion, I may add, that had previously been strongly held and urged by Mr. Alexander.

As to those of us who do not look on a play as a mere question of pantomime and clowning psychological interest is everything, I determined, consequently, to make a change in the precise moment of revelation. This determination, however, was entered into long before I had the opportunity of studying the culture, courtesy, and critical faculty displayed in such papers as the Referee, Reynolds', and the Sunday Sun.

When criticism becomes in England a real art, as it should be, and when none but those of artistic instinct and artistic cultivation is allowed to write about works of art, artists will, no doubt, read criticisms with a certain amount of intellectual interest. As things are at present, the criticisms of ordinary newspapers are of no interest whatsoever, except in so far as they display, in its crudest form, the Bœotianism of a country that has produced some Athenians, and in which some Athenians have come to dwell.—I am, Sir, your obedient servant,

OSCAR WILDE.

February 26.

SALOMÉ

(*Times*, March 2, 1893.)

To the Editor of the *Times*.

SIR,—My attention has been drawn to a review of Salomé which was published in your columns last week. {170} The opinions of English critics on a French work of mine have, of course, little, if any, interest for me. I write simply to ask you to allow me to correct a misstatement that appears in the review in question.

The fact that the greatest tragic actress of any stage now living saw in my play such beauty that she was anxious to produce it, to take herself the part of the heroine, to lend to the entire poem the glamour of her personality, and to my prose the music of her flute-like voice—this was naturally, and always will be, a source of pride and pleasure to me, and I look forward with delight to seeing Mme. Bernhardt present my play in Paris, that vivid centre of art, where religious dramas are often performed. But my play was in no sense of the words written for this great actress. I have never written a play for any actor or actress, nor shall I ever do so. Such work is for the artisan in literature—not for the artist.—I remain, Sir, your obedient servant,

OSCAR WILDE.

THE THIRTEEN CLUB

(*Times*, January 16, 1894.)

At a dinner of the Thirteen Club held at the Holborn Restaurant on January 13, 1894, the Chairman (Mr. Harry Furniss) announced that from Mr. Oscar Wilde the following letter had been received:—

I have to thank the members of your Club for their kind invitation, for which convey to them, I beg you, my sincere thanks. But I love superstitions. They are the colour element of thought and imagination. They are the opponents of common sense. Common sense is the enemy of romance. The aim of your Society seems to be dreadful. Leave us some unreality. Do not make us too offensively sane. I love dining out, but with a Society with so wicked an object as yours I cannot dine. I regret it. I am sure you will all be charming, but I could not come, though 13 is a lucky number.

THE ETHICS OF JOURNALISM

I.

(*Pall Mall Gazette*, September 20, 1894.)

To the Editor of the *Pall Mall Gazette*.

SIR,—Will you allow me to draw your attention to a very interesting example of the ethics of modern journalism, a quality of which we have all heard so much and seen so little?

About a month ago Mr. T. P. O'Connor published in the Sunday Sun some doggerel verses entitled 'The Shamrock,' and had the amusing impertinence to append my name to them as their author. As for some years past all kinds of scurrilous personal attacks had been made on me in Mr. O'Connor's newspapers, I determined to take no notice at all of the incident.

Enraged, however, by my courteous silence, Mr. O'Connor returns to the charge this week. He now solemnly accuses me of plagiarising the poem he had the vulgarity to attribute to me. {172}

This seems to me to pass beyond even those bounds of coarse humour and coarser malice that are, by the contempt of all, conceded to the ordinary journalist, and it is really very distressing to find so low a standard of ethics in a Sunday newspaper.—I remain, Sir, your obedient servant,

OSCAR WILDE.

September 18.

II.

(*Pall Mall Gazette*, September 25, 1894.)

To the Editor of the *Pall Mall Gazette*.

SIR,—The assistant editor of the Sunday Sun, on whom seems to devolve the arduous duty of writing Mr. T. P. O'Connor's apologies for him, does not, I observe with regret, place that gentleman's conduct in any more attractive or more honourable light by the attempted explanation that appears in the letter published in your issue of today. For the future it would be much better if Mr. O'Connor would always write his own apologies. That he can do so exceedingly well no one is more ready to admit than myself. I happen to possess one from him.

The assistant editor's explanation, stripped of its unnecessary verbiage, amounts to this: It is now stated that some months ago, somebody, whose name, observe, is not given, forwarded to the office of the Sunday Sun a manuscript in his own handwriting, containing some fifth-rate verses with my name appended to them as their author. The assistant editor frankly admits that they had grave doubts about my being capable of such an astounding production. To me, I must candidly say, it seems more probable that they never for a single moment believed that the verses were really from my pen. Literary instinct is, of course, a very rare thing, and it would be too much to expect any true literary instinct to be found among the members of the staff of an ordinary newspaper; but had Mr. O'Connor really thought that the production, such as it is, was mine, he would naturally have asked my permission before publishing it. Great licence of comment and attack of every kind is allowed nowadays to newspapers, but no respectable editor would dream of printing and publishing a man's work without first obtaining his consent.

Mr. O'Connor's subsequent conduct in accusing me of plagiarism, when it was proved to him on unimpeachable authority that the verses he had vulgarly attributed to me were not by me at all, I have already commented on. It is perhaps best left to the laughter of the gods and the sorrow of men. I would like, however, to point out that when Mr. O'Connor, with the kind help of his assistant editor, states, as a possible excuse for his original sin, that he and the members of his staff 'took refuge' in the belief that the verses in question might conceivably be some very early and useful work of mine, he and the members of his staff showed a lamentable ignorance of the nature of the artistic temperament. Only mediocrities progress. An artist revolves in a cycle of masterpieces, the first of which is no less perfect than the last.

In conclusion, allow me to thank you for your courtesy in opening to me the columns of your valuable paper, and also to express the hope that the painful exposé of Mr. O'Connor's conduct that I have been forced to make will have the good result of improving the standard of journalistic ethics in England.—I remain, Sir, your obedient servant,

OSCAR WILDE.

WORTHING, *September* 22.

THE GREEN CARNATION

(*Pall Mall Gazette*, October 2, 1894.)

To the Editor of the *Pall Mall Gazette*.

SIR,—Kindly allow me to contradict, in the most emphatic manner, the suggestion, made in your issue of Thursday last, and since then copied into many other newspapers, that I am the author of The Green Carnation.

I invented that magnificent flower. But with the middle-class and mediocre book that usurps its strangely beautiful name I have, I need hardly say, nothing whatsoever to do. The flower is a work of art. The book is not.—I remain, Sir, your obedient servant, OSCAR WILDE.

WORTHING, *October* 1.

PHRASES AND PHILOSOPHIES FOR THE USE OF THE YOUNG

(*Chameleon*, December 1894)

The first duty in life is to be as artificial as possible. What the second duty is no one has as yet discovered.

Wickedness is a myth invented by good people to account for the curious attractiveness of others.

If the poor only had profiles there would be no difficulty in solving the problem of poverty.

Those who see any difference between soul and body have neither.

A really well-made buttonhole is the only link between Art and Nature.

Religions die when they are proved to be true. Science is the record of dead religions.

The well-bred contradict other people. The wise contradict themselves.

Nothing that actually occurs is of the smallest importance.

Dulness is the coming of age of seriousness.

In all unimportant matters, style, not sincerity, is the essential. In all important matters, style, not sincerity, is the essential.

If one tells the truth one is sure, sooner or later, to be found out.

Pleasure is the only thing one should live for. Nothing ages like happiness.

It is only by not paying one's bills that one can hope to live in the memory of the commercial classes.

No crime is vulgar, but all vulgarity is crime. Vulgarity is the conduct of others.

Only the shallow know themselves.

Time is waste of money.

One should always be a little improbable.

There is a fatality about all good resolutions. They are invariably made too soon.

The only way to atone for being occasionally a little overdressed is by being always absolutely over-educated.

To be premature is to be perfect.

Any preoccupation with ideas of what is right or wrong in conduct shows an arrested intellectual development.

Ambition is the last refuge of the failure.

A truth ceases to be true when more than one person believes in it.

In examinations the foolish ask questions that the wise cannot answer.

Greek dress was in its essence inartistic. Nothing should reveal the body but the body.

One should either be a work of art, or wear a work of art.

It is only the superficial qualities that last. Man's deeper nature is soon found out.

Industry is the root of all ugliness.

The ages live in history through their anachronisms.

It is only the gods who taste of death. Apollo has passed away, but Hyacinth, whom men say he slew, lives on. Nero and Narcissus are always with us.

The old believe everything: the middle-aged suspect everything: the young know everything.

The condition of perfection is idleness: the aim of perfection is youth.

Only the great masters of style ever succeed in being obscure.

There is something tragic about the enormous number of young men there are in England at the present moment who start life with perfect profiles, and end by adopting some useful profession.

To love oneself is the beginning of a life-long romance.

THE RISE OF HISTORICAL CRITICISM

The first portion of this essay is given at the end of the volume containing *Lord Arthur Savile's Crime and Other Prose Pieces*. Recently the remainder of the original manuscript has been discovered, and is here published for the first time. It was written for the Chancellor's English Essay Prize at Oxford in 1879, the subject being 'Historical Criticism among the Ancients.' The prize was not awarded. To Professor J. W. Mackail thanks are due for revising the proofs.

IV.

It is evident that here Thucydides is ready to admit the variety of manifestations which external causes bring about in their workings on the uniform character of the nature of man. Yet, after all is said, these are perhaps but very general statements: the ordinary effects of peace and war are dwelt on, but there is no real analysis of the immediate causes and general laws of the phenomena of life, nor does Thucydides seem to recognise the truth that if humanity proceeds in circles, the circles are always widening.

Perhaps we may say that with him the philosophy of history is partly in the metaphysical stage, and see, in the progress of this idea from Herodotus to Polybius, the exemplification of the Comtian law of the three stages of thought, the theological, the metaphysical, and the scientific: for truly out of the vagueness of theological mysticism this conception which we call the Philosophy of History was raised to a scientific principle, according to which the past was explained and the future predicted by reference to general laws.

Now, just as the earliest account of the nature of the progress of humanity is to be found in Plato, so in him we find the first explicit attempt to found a universal philosophy of history upon wide rational grounds. Having created an ideally perfect state, the philosopher proceeds to give an elaborate theory of the complex causes which produce revolutions of the moral effects of various forms of government and education, of the rise of the criminal classes and their connection with pauperism, and, in a word, to create history by the deductive method and to proceed from a priori psychological principles to discover the governing laws of the apparent chaos of political life.

There have been many attempts since Plato to deduce from a single philosophical principle all the phenomena which experience subsequently verifies for us. Fichte thought he could predict the world-plan from the idea of universal time. Hegel dreamed he had found the key to the mysteries of life in the development of freedom, and Krause in the categories of being. But the one scientific basis on which the true philosophy of history must rest is the complete knowledge of the laws of human nature in all its wants, its aspirations, its powers and its tendencies: and this great truth, which Thucydides may be said in some measure to have apprehended, was given to us first by Plato.

Now, it cannot be accurately said of this philosopher that either his philosophy or his history is entirely and simply a priori. On est de son siècle même quand on y proteste, and so we find in him continual references to the Spartan mode of life, the Pythagorean system, the general characteristics of Greek tyrannies and Greek democracies. For while, in his account of the method of forming an ideal state, he says that the political artist is indeed to fix his gaze on the sun of abstract truth in the heavens of the pure reason, but is sometimes to turn to the realisation of the ideals on earth: yet, after all, the general character of the Platonic method, which is what we are specially concerned with, is essentially deductive and a priori. And he himself, in the building up of his Nephelococcygia, certainly starts with a καθαρος πιναξ, making a clean sweep of all history and all experience; and it was essentially as an a priori theorist that he is criticised by Aristotle, as we shall see later.

To proceed to closer details regarding the actual scheme of the laws of political revolutions as drawn out by Plato, we must first note that the primary cause of the decay of the ideal state is the general principle, common to the vegetable and animal worlds as well as to the world of history, that all created things are fated to decay—a principle which, though expressed in the terms of a mere metaphysical abstraction, is yet perhaps in its essence scientific. For we too must hold that a continuous redistribution of matter and motion is the inevitable result of the normal persistence of Force, and that perfect equilibrium is as impossible in politics as it certainly is in physics.

The secondary causes which mar the perfection of the Platonic 'city of the sun' are to be found in the intellectual decay of the race consequent on injudicious marriages and in the Philistine elevation of physical achievements over mental culture; while the hierarchical succession of Timocracy and Oligarchy, Democracy and Tyranny, is dwelt on at great length and its causes analysed in a very dramatic and psychological manner, if not in that sanctioned by the actual order of history.

And indeed it is apparent at first sight that the Platonic succession of states represents rather the succession of ideas in the philosophic mind than any historical succession of time.

Aristotle meets the whole simply by an appeal to facts. If the theory of the periodic decay of all created things, he urges, be scientific, it must be universal, and so true of all the other states as well as of the ideal. Besides, a state usually changes into its contrary and not to the form next to it; so the ideal state would not change into Timocracy; while Oligarchy, more often than Tyranny, succeeds Democracy. Plato, besides, says nothing of what a Tyranny would change to. According to the cycle theory it ought to pass into the ideal state again, but as a fact one Tyranny is changed into another as at Sicyon, or into a Democracy as at Syracuse, or into an Aristocracy as at Carthage. The example of Sicily, too, shows that an Oligarchy is often followed by a Tyranny, as at Leontini and Gela. Besides, it is absurd to represent greed as the chief motive of decay, or to talk of avarice as the root of Oligarchy, when in nearly all true oligarchies money-making is forbidden by law. And finally the Platonic theory neglects the different kinds of democracies and of tyrannies.

Now nothing can be more important than this passage in Aristotle's Politics (v. 12.), which may be said to mark an era in the evolution of historical criticism. For there is nothing on which Aristotle insists so strongly as that the generalisations from facts ought to be added to the data of the a priori method—a principle which we know to be true not merely of deductive speculative politics but of physics also: for are not the residual phenomena of chemists a valuable source of improvement in theory?

His own method is essentially historical though by no means empirical. On the contrary, this far-seeing thinker, rightly styled il maestro di color che sanno, may be said to have apprehended clearly that the true method is neither exclusively empirical nor exclusively speculative, but rather a union of both in the process called Analysis or the Interpretation of Facts, which has been defined as the application to facts of such general conceptions as may fix the important characteristics of the phenomena, and present them permanently in their true relations. He too was the first to point out, what even in our own day is incompletely appreciated, that nature, including the development of man, is not full of incoherent episodes like a bad tragedy, that inconsistency and anomaly are as impossible in the moral as they are in the physical world, and that where the superficial observer thinks he sees a revolution the philosophical critic discerns merely the gradual and rational evolution of the inevitable results of certain antecedents.

And while admitting the necessity of a psychological basis for the philosophy of history, he added to it the important truth that man, to be apprehended in his proper position in the universe as well as in his natural powers, must be studied from below in the hierarchical progression of higher function from the lower forms of life. The important maxim, that to obtain a clear conception of anything we must 'study it in its growth from the very beginning' is formally set down in the opening of the Politics, where, indeed, we shall find the other characteristic features of the modern Evolutionary theory, such as the 'Differentiation of Function' and the 'Survival of the Fittest' explicitly set forth.

What a valuable step this was in the improvement of the method of historical criticism it is needless to point out. By it, one may say, the true thread was given to guide one's steps through the bewildering labyrinth of facts. For history (to use terms with which Aristotle has made us familiar) may be looked at from two essentially different standpoints; either as a work of art whose τελος or final cause is external to it and imposed on it from without; or as an organism containing the law of its own development in itself, and working out its perfection merely by the fact of being what it is. Now, if we adopt the former, which we may style the theological view, we shall be in continual danger of tripping into the pitfall of some a priori conclusion—that bourne from which, it has been truly said, no traveller ever returns.

The latter is the only scientific theory and was apprehended in its fulness by Aristotle, whose application of the inductive method to history, and whose employment of the evolutionary theory of humanity, show that he was conscious that the philosophy of history is nothing separate from the facts of history but is contained in them, and that the rational law of the complex phenomena of life, like the ideal in the world of thought, is to be reached through the facts, not superimposed on them— κατα πολλων not παρα πολλα.

And finally, in estimating the enormous debt which the science of historical criticism owes to Aristotle, we must not pass over his attitude towards those two great difficulties in the formation of a philosophy of history on which I have touched above. I mean the assertion of extra-natural interference with the normal development of the world and of the incalculable influence exercised by the power of free will.

Now, as regards the former, he may be said to have neglected it entirely. The special acts of providence proceeding from God's immediate government of the world, which Herodotus saw as mighty landmarks in history, would have been to him essentially disturbing elements in that universal reign of law, the extent of whose limitless empire he of all the great thinkers of antiquity was the first explicitly to recognise.

Standing aloof from the popular religion as well as from the deeper conceptions of Herodotus and the Tragic School, he no longer thought of God as of one with fair limbs and treacherous face haunting wood and glade, nor would he see in him a jealous judge continually interfering in the world's history to bring the wicked to punishment and the proud to a fall. God to him was the incarnation of the pure Intellect, a being whose activity was the contemplation of his own perfection, one whom Philosophy might imitate but whom prayers could never move, to the sublime indifference of whose passionless wisdom what were the sons of men, their desires or their sins? While, as regards the other difficulty and the formation of a philosophy of history, the conflict of free will with general laws appears first in Greek thought in the usual theological form in which all great ideas seem to be cradled at their birth.

It was such legends as those of Œdipus and Adrastus, exemplifying the struggles of individual humanity against the overpowering force of circumstances and necessity, which gave to the early Greeks those same lessons which we of modern days draw, in somewhat less artistic fashion, from the study of statistics and the laws of physiology.

In Aristotle, of course, there is no trace of supernatural influence. The Furies, which drive their victim into sin first and then punishment, are no longer 'viper-tressed goddesses with eyes and mouth aflame,' but those evil thoughts which harbour within the impure soul. In this, as in all other points, to arrive at Aristotle is to reach the pure atmosphere of scientific and modern thought.

But while he rejected pure necessitarianism in its crude form as essentially a reductio ad absurdum of life, he was fully conscious of the fact that the will is not a mysterious and ultimate unit of force beyond which we cannot go and whose special characteristic is inconsistency, but a certain creative attitude of the mind which is, from the first, continually influenced by habits, education and circumstance; so absolutely modifiable, in a word, that the good and the bad man alike seem to lose the power of free will; for the one is morally unable to sin, the other physically incapacitated for reformation.

And of the influence of climate and temperature in forming the nature of man (a conception perhaps pressed too far in modern days when the 'race theory' is supposed to be a sufficient explanation of the Hindoo, and the latitude and longitude of a country the best guide to its morals {188}) Aristotle is completely unaware. I do not allude to such smaller points as the oligarchical tendencies of a horse-breeding country and the democratic influence of the proximity of the sea (important though they are for the consideration of Greek history), but rather to those wider views in the seventh book of his Politics, where he attributes the happy union in the Greek character of intellectual attainments with the spirit of progress to the temperate climate they enjoyed, and points out how the extreme cold of the north dulls the mental faculties of its inhabitants and renders them incapable of social organisation or extended empire; while to the enervating heat of eastern countries was due that want of spirit and bravery which then, as now, was the characteristic of the population in that quarter of the globe.

Thucydides has shown the causal connection between political revolutions and the fertility of the soil, but goes a step farther and points out the psychological influences on a people's character exercised by the various extremes of climate—in both cases the first appearance of a most valuable form of historical criticism.

To the development of Dialectic, as to God, intervals of time are of no account. From Plato and Aristotle we pass direct to Polybius.

The progress of thought from the philosopher of the Academe to the Arcadian historian may be best illustrated by a comparison of the method by which each of the three writers, whom I have selected as the highest expressions of the rationalism of his respective age, attained to his ideal state: for the latter conception may be in a measure regarded as representing the most spiritual principle which they could discern in history.

Now, Plato created his on a priori principles: Aristotle formed his by an analysis of existing constitutions; Polybius found his realised for him in the actual world of fact. Aristotle criticised the deductive speculations of Plato by means of inductive negative instances, but Polybius will not take the 'Cloud City' of the Republic into account at all. He compares it to an athlete who has never run on 'Constitution Hill,' to a statue so beautiful that it is entirely removed from the ordinary conditions of humanity, and consequently from the canons of criticism.

The Roman state had attained in his eyes, by means of the mutual counteraction of three opposing forces, {190} that stable equilibrium in politics which was the ideal of all the theoretical writers of antiquity. And in connection with this point it will be convenient to notice here how much truth there is contained in the accusation so often brought against the ancients that they knew nothing of the idea of Progress, for the meaning of many of their speculations will be hidden from us if we do not try and comprehend first what their aim was, and secondly why it was so.

Now, like all wide generalities, this statement is at least inaccurate. The prayer of Plato's ideal city—εξ αγαθων αμεινους, και εξ ωφελιμωτερους αει τους εκγονους γιγνεσθαι, might be written as a text over the door of the last Temple to Humanity raised by the disciples of Fourier and Saint Simon, but it is certainly true that their ideal principle was order and permanence, not indefinite progress. For, setting aside the artistic prejudices which would have led the Greeks to reject this idea of unlimited improvement, we may note that the modern conception of progress rests partly on the new enthusiasm and worship of humanity, partly on the splendid hopes of material improvements in civilisation which applied science has held out to us, two influences from which ancient Greek thought seems to have been strangely free. For the Greeks marred the perfect humanism of the great men whom they worshipped, by imputing to them divinity and its supernatural powers; while their science was eminently speculative and often almost mystic in its character, aiming at culture and not utility, at higher spirituality and more intense reverence for law, rather than at the increased facilities of locomotion and the cheap production of common things about which our modern scientific school ceases not to boast. And lastly, and perhaps chiefly, we must remember that the 'plague spot of all Greek states,' as one of their own writers has called it, was the terrible insecurity to life and property which resulted from the factions and revolutions which ceased not to trouble Greece at all times, raising a spirit of fanaticism such as religion raised in the middle ages of Europe.

These considerations, then, will enable us to understand first how it was that, radical and unscrupulous reformers as the Greek political theorists were, yet, their end once attained, no modern conservatives raised such outcry against the slightest innovation. Even acknowledged improvements in such things as the games of children or the modes of music were regarded by them

254

with feelings of extreme apprehension as the herald of the *drapeau rouge* of reform. And secondly, it will show us how it was that Polybius found his ideal in the commonwealth of Rome, and Aristotle, like Mr. Bright, in the middle classes. Polybius, however, is not content merely with pointing out his ideal state, but enters at considerable length into the question of those general laws whose consideration forms the chief essential of the philosophy of history.

He starts by accepting the general principle that all things are fated to decay (which I noticed in the case of Plato), and that 'as iron produces rust and as wood breeds the animals that destroy it, so every state has in it the seeds of its own corruption.' He is not, however, content to rest there, but proceeds to deal with the more immediate causes of revolutions, which he says are twofold in nature, either external or internal. Now, the former, depending as they do on the synchronous conjunction of other events outside the sphere of scientific estimation, are from their very character incalculable; but the latter, though assuming many forms, always result from the over-great preponderance of any single element to the detriment of the others, the rational law lying at the base of all varieties of political changes being that stability can result only from the statical equilibrium produced by the counteraction of opposing parts, since the more simple a constitution is the more it is insecure. Plato had pointed out before how the extreme liberty of a democracy always resulted in despotism, but Polybius analyses the law and shows the scientific principles on which it rests.

The doctrine of the instability of pure constitutions forms an important era in the philosophy of history. Its special applicability to the politics of our own day has been illustrated in the rise of the great Napoleon, when the French state had lost those divisions of caste and prejudice, of landed aristocracy and moneyed interest, institutions in which the vulgar see only barriers to Liberty but which are indeed the only possible defences against the coming of that periodic Sirius of politics, the τυραννος εκ προστατικης ριζης

There is a principle which Tocqueville never wearies of explaining, and which has been subsumed by Mr. Herbert Spencer under that general law common to all organic bodies which we call the Instability of the Homogeneous. The various manifestations of this law, as shown in the normal, regular revolutions and evolutions of the different forms of government, {193a} are expounded with great clearness by Polybius, who claimed for his theory in the Thucydidean spirit, that it is a κτημα ες αει, not a mere αγωνισμα ες το παραχρημα, and that a knowledge of it will enable the impartial observer {193b} to discover at any time what period of its constitutional evolution any particular state has already reached and into what form it will be next differentiated, though possibly the exact time of the changes may be more or less uncertain. {193c}

Now in this necessarily incomplete account of the laws of political revolutions as expounded by Polybius enough perhaps has been said to show what is his true position in the rational development of the 'Idea' which I have called the Philosophy of History, because it is the unifying of history. Seen darkly as it is through the glass of religion in the pages of Herodotus, more metaphysical than scientific with Thucydides, Plato strove to seize it by the eagle-flight of speculation, to reach it with the eager grasp of a soul impatient of those slower and surer inductive methods which Aristotle, in his trenchant criticism of his great master, showed were more brilliant than any vague theory, if the test of brilliancy is truth.

What then is the position of Polybius? Does any new method remain for him? Polybius was one of those many men who are born too late to be original. To Thucydides belongs the honour of being the first in the history of Greek thought to discern the supreme calm of law and order underlying the fitful storms of life, and Plato and Aristotle each represents a great new principle. To Polybius belongs the office—how noble an office he made it his writings show—of making more explicit the ideas which were implicit in his predecessors, of showing that they were of wider applicability and perhaps of deeper meaning than they had seemed before, of examining with more minuteness the laws which they had discovered, and finally of pointing out more clearly than any one had done the range of science and the means it offered for analysing the present and predicting what was to come. His office thus was to gather up what they had left, to give their principles new life by a wider application.

Polybius ends this great diapason of Greek thought. When the Philosophy of history appears next, as in Plutarch's tract on 'Why God's anger is delayed,' the pendulum of thought had swung back to where it began. His theory was introduced to the Romans under the cultured style of Cicero, and was welcomed by them as the philosophical panegyric of their state. The last notice of it in Latin literature is in the pages of Tacitus, who alludes to the stable polity formed out of these elements as a constitution easier to commend than to produce and in no case lasting. Yet Polybius had seen the future with no uncertain eye, and had prophesied the rise of the Empire from the unbalanced power of the ochlocracy fifty years and more before there was joy in the Julian household over the birth of that boy who, borne to power as the champion of the people, died wearing the purple of a king.

No attitude of historical criticism is more important than the means by which the ancients attained to the philosophy of history. The principle of heredity can be exemplified in literature as well as in organic life: Aristotle, Plato and Polybius are the lineal ancestors of Fichte and Hegel, of Vico and Cousin, of Montesquieu and Tocqueville.

As my aim is not to give an account of historians but to point out those great thinkers whose methods have furthered the advance of this spirit of historical criticism, I shall pass over those annalists and chroniclers who intervened between Thucydides and Polybius. Yet perhaps it may serve to throw new light on the real nature of this spirit and its intimate connection with all other forms of advanced thought if I give some estimate of the character and rise of those many influences prejudicial to the scientific study of history which cause such a wide gap between these two historians.

Foremost among these is the growing influence of rhetoric and the Isocratean school, which seems to have regarded history as an arena for the display of either pathos or paradoxes, not a scientific investigation into laws.

The new age is the age of style. The same spirit of exclusive attention to form which made Euripides often, like Swinburne, prefer music to meaning and melody to morality, which gave to the later Greek statues that refined effeminacy, that overstrained gracefulness of attitude, was felt in the sphere of history. The rules laid down for historical composition are those relating to the æsthetic value of digressions, the legality of employing more than one metaphor in the same sentence, and the like; and historians are ranked not by their power of estimating evidence but by the goodness of the Greek they write.

I must note also the important influence on literature exercised by Alexander the Great; for while his travels encouraged the more accurate research of geography, the very splendour of his achievements seems to have brought history again into the sphere of romance. The appearance of all great men in the world is followed invariably by the rise of that mythopœic spirit and that tendency to look for the marvellous, which is so fatal to true historical criticism. An Alexander, a Napoleon, a Francis of Assisi and a Mahomet are thought to be outside the limiting conditions of rational law, just as comets were supposed to be not very long ago. While the founding of that city of Alexandria, in which Western and Eastern thought met with such strange result to both, diverted the critical tendencies of the Greek spirit into questions of grammar, philology and the like, the narrow, artificial atmosphere of that University town (as we may call it) was fatal to the development of that independent and speculative spirit of research which strikes out new methods of inquiry, of which historical criticism is one.

The Alexandrines combined a great love of learning with an ignorance of the true principles of research, an enthusiastic spirit for accumulating materials with a wonderful incapacity to use them. Not among the hot sands of Egypt, or the Sophists of Athens, but from the very heart of Greece rises the man of genius on whose influence in the evolution of the philosophy of history I have a short time ago dwelt. Born in the serene and pure air of the clear uplands of Arcadia, Polybius may be said to reproduce in his work the character of the place which gave him birth. For, of all the historians—I do not say of antiquity but of all time—none is more rationalistic than he, none more free from any belief in the 'visions and omens, the monstrous legends, the grovelling superstitions and unmanly craving for the supernatural' (δεισιδαιμουνιας αγεννους και τερατειας γυναικωδους {197a}) which he is compelled to notice himself as the characteristics of some of the historians who preceded him. Fortunate in the land which bore him, he was no less blessed in the wondrous time of his birth. For, representing in himself the spiritual supremacy of the Greek intellect and allied in bonds of chivalrous friendship to the world-conqueror of his day, he seems led as it were by the hand of Fate 'to comprehend,' as has been said, 'more clearly than the Romans themselves the historical position of Rome,' and to discern with greater insight than all other men could those two great resultants of ancient civilisation, the material empire of the city of the seven hills, and the intellectual sovereignty of Hellas.

Before his own day, he says, {197b} the events of the world were unconnected and separate and the histories confined to particular countries. Now, for the first time the universal empire of the Romans rendered a universal history possible. {198a} This, then, is the august motive of his work: to trace the gradual rise of this Italian city from the day when the first legion crossed the narrow strait of Messina and landed on the fertile fields of Sicily to the time when Corinth in the East and Carthage in the West fell before the resistless wave of empire and the eagles of Rome passed on the wings of universal victory from Calpè and the Pillars of Hercules to Syria and the Nile. At the same time he recognised that the scheme of Rome's empire was worked out under the ægis of God's will. {198b} For, as one of the Middle Age scribes most truly says, the τυχη of Polybius is that power which we Christians call God; the second aim, as one may call it, of his history is to point out the rational and human and natural causes which brought this result, distinguishing, as we should say, between God's mediate and immediate government of the world.

With any direct intervention of God in the normal development of Man, he will have nothing to do: still less with any idea of chance as a factor in the phenomena of life. Chance and miracles, he says, are mere expressions for our ignorance of rational causes. The spirit of rationalism which we recognised in Herodotus as a vague uncertain attitude and which appears in Thucydides as a consistent attitude of mind never argued about or even explained, is by Polybius analysed and formulated as the great instrument of historical research.

Herodotus, while believing on principle in the supernatural, yet was sceptical at times. Thucydides simply ignored the supernatural. He did not discuss it, but he annihilated it by explaining history without it. Polybius enters at length into the whole question and explains its origin and the method of treating it. Herodotus would have believed in Scipio's dream. Thucydides would have ignored it entirely. Polybius explains it. He is the culmination of the rational progression of Dialectic. 'Nothing,' he says, 'shows a foolish mind more than the attempt to account for any phenomena on the principle of chance or supernatural intervention. History is a search for rational causes, and there is nothing in the world—even those phenomena which seem to us the most remote from law and improbable—which is not the logical and inevitable result of certain rational antecedents.'

Some things, of course, are to be rejected a priori without entering into the subject: 'As regards such miracles,' he says, {199} 'as that on a certain statue of Artemis rain or snow never falls though the statue stands in the open air, or that those who enter God's shrine in Arcadia lose their natural shadows, I cannot really be expected to argue upon the subject. For these things are not only utterly improbable but absolutely impossible.'

'For us to argue reasonably on an acknowledged absurdity is as vain a task as trying to catch water in a sieve; it is really to admit the possibility of the supernatural, which is the very point at issue.'

What Polybius felt was that to admit the possibility of a miracle is to annihilate the possibility of history: for just as scientific and chemical experiments would be either impossible or useless if exposed to the chance of continued interference on the part of some foreign body, so the laws and principles which govern history, the causes of phenomena, the evolution of progress, the whole science, in a word, of man's dealings with his own race and with nature, will remain a sealed book to him who admits the possibility of extra-natural interference.

The stories of miracles, then, are to be rejected on a priori rational grounds, but in the case of events which we know to have happened the scientific historian will not rest till he has discovered their natural causes which, for instance, in the case of the wonderful rise of the Roman Empire—the most marvellous thing, Polybius says, which God ever brought about {200a}—are to be found in the excellence of their constitution (τη ιδιοτητι της πολιτειας), the wisdom of their advisers, their splendid military arrangements, and their superstition (τη δεισιδαιμονια). For while Polybius regarded the revealed religion as, of course, objective reality of truth, {200b} he laid great stress on its moral subjective influence, going, in one passage on the subject, even so far as almost to excuse the introduction of the supernatural in very small quantities into history on account of the extremely good effect it would have on pious people.

But perhaps there is no passage in the whole of ancient and modern history which breathes such a manly and splendid spirit of rationalism as one preserved to us in the Vatican—strange resting-place for it!—in which he treats of the terrible decay of population which had fallen on his native land in his own day, and which by the general orthodox public was regarded as a special judgment of God, sending childlessness on women as a punishment for the sins of the people. For it was a disaster quite without parallel in the history of the land, and entirely unforeseen by any of its political-economy writers who, on the contrary, were always anticipating that danger would arise from an excess of population overrunning its means of subsistence, and becoming unmanageable through its size. Polybius, however, will have nothing to do with either priest or worker of miracles in this matter. He will not even seek that 'sacred Heart of Greece,' Delphi, Apollo's shrine, whose inspiration even Thucydides admitted and before whose wisdom Socrates bowed. How foolish, he says, were the man who on this matter would pray to God. We must search for the rational causes, and the causes are seen to be clear, and the method of prevention also. He then proceeds to notice how all this arose from the general reluctance to marriage and to bearing the expense of educating a large family which resulted from the carelessness and avarice of the men of his day, and he explains on entirely rational principles the whole of this apparently supernatural judgment.

Now, it is to be borne in mind that while his rejection of miracles as violation of inviolable laws is entirely a priori—for, discussion of such a matter is, of course, impossible for a rational thinker—yet his rejection of supernatural intervention rests entirely on the scientific grounds of the necessity of looking for natural causes. And he is quite logical in maintaining his position on these principles. For, where it is either difficult or impossible to assign any rational cause for phenomena, or to discover their laws, he acquiesces reluctantly in the alternative of admitting some extra-natural interference which his essentially scientific method of treating the matter has logically forced on him, approving, for instance, of prayers for rain, on the express ground that the laws of meteorology had not yet been ascertained. He would, of course, have been the first to welcome our modern discoveries in the matter. The passage in question is in every way one of the most interesting in his whole work, not, of course, as signifying any inclination on his part to acquiesce in the supernatural, but because it shows how essentially logical and rational his method of argument was, and how candid and fair his mind.

Having now examined Polybius's attitude towards the supernatural and the general ideas which guided his research, I will proceed to examine the method he pursued in his scientific investigation of the complex phenomena of life. For, as I have said before in the course of this essay, what is important in all great writers is not so much the results they arrive at as the methods they pursue. The increased knowledge of facts may alter any conclusion in history as in physical science, and the canons of speculative historical credibility must be acknowledged to appeal rather to that subjective attitude of mind which we call the historic sense than to any formulated objective rules. But a scientific method is a gain for all time, and the true if not the only progress of historical criticism consists in the improvement of the instruments of research.

Now first, as regards his conception of history, I have already pointed out that it was to him essentially a search for causes, a problem to be solved, not a picture to be painted, a scientific investigation into laws and tendencies, not a mere romantic account of startling incident and wondrous adventure. Thucydides, in the opening of his great work, had sounded the first note of the scientific conception of history. 'The absence of romance in my pages,' he says, 'will, I fear, detract somewhat from its value, but I have written my work not to be the exploit of a passing hour but as the possession of all time.'

{203} Polybius follows with words almost entirely similar. If, he says, we banish from history the consideration of causes, methods and motives (το δια τι, και πως, και τινος χαριν), and refuse to consider how far the result of anything is its rational consequent, what is left is a mere αγωνισμα, not a μαθημα, an oratorical essay which may give pleasure for the moment, but which is entirely without any scientific value for the explanation of the future. Elsewhere he says that 'history robbed of the exposition of its causes and laws is a profitless thing, though it may allure a fool.' And all through his history the same point is put forward and exemplified in every fashion.

So far for the conception of history. Now for the groundwork. As regards the character of the phenomena to be selected by the scientific investigator, Aristotle had laid down the general formula that nature should be studied in her normal manifestations. Polybius, true to his character of applying explicitly the principles implicit in the work of others, follows out the doctrine of Aristotle, and lays particular stress on the rational and undisturbed character of the development of the Roman constitution as affording special facilities for the discovery of the laws of its progress. Political revolutions result from causes either external or internal. The former are mere disturbing forces which lie outside the sphere of scientific calculation. It is the latter which are important for the establishing of principles and the elucidation of the sequences of rational evolution.

He thus may be said to have anticipated one of the most important truths of the modern methods of investigation: I mean that principle which lays down that just as the study of physiology should precede the study of pathology, just as the laws of disease are best discovered by the phenomena presented in health, so the method of arriving at all great social and political truths is by the investigation of those cases where development has been normal, rational and undisturbed.

The critical canon that the more a people has been interfered with, the more difficult it becomes to generalise the laws of its progress and to analyse the separate forces of its civilisation, is one the validity of which is now generally recognised by those who pretend to a scientific treatment of all history: and while we have seen that Aristotle anticipated it in a general formula, to Polybius belongs the honour of being the first to apply it explicitly in the sphere of history.

I have shown how to this great scientific historian the motive of his work was essentially the search for causes; and true to his analytical spirit he is careful to examine what a cause really is and in what part of the antecedents of any consequent it is to be looked for. To give an illustration: As regards the origin of the war with Perseus, some assigned as causes the expulsion of Abrupolis by Perseus, the expedition of the latter to Delphi, the plot against Eumenes and the seizure of the ambassadors in Bœotia; of these incidents the two former, Polybius points out, were merely the pretexts, the two latter merely the occasions of the war. The war was really a legacy left to Perseus by his father, who was determined to fight it out with Rome. {205}

Here as elsewhere he is not originating any new idea. Thucydides had pointed out the difference between the real and the alleged cause, and the Aristotelian dictum about revolutions, ου περι μικρων αλλ εκ μικρων, draws the distinction between cause and occasion with the brilliancy of an epigram. But the explicit and rational investigation of the difference between αιτια, αρχη and προφασις was reserved for Polybius. No canon of historical criticism can be said to be of more real value than that involved in this distinction, and the overlooking of it has filled our histories with the contemptible accounts of the intrigues of courtiers and of kings and the petty plottings of backstairs influence—particulars interesting, no doubt, to those who would ascribe the Reformation to Anne Boleyn's pretty face, the Persian war to the influence of a doctor or a curtain-lecture from Atossa, or the French Revolution to Madame de Maintenon, but without any value for those who aim at any scientific treatment of history.

But the question of method, to which I am compelled always to return, is not yet exhausted. There is another aspect in which it may be regarded, and I shall now proceed to treat of it.

One of the greatest difficulties with which the modern historian has to contend is the enormous complexity of the facts which come under his notice: D'Alembert's suggestion that at the end of every century a selection of facts should be made and the rest burned (if it was really intended seriously) could not, of course, be entertained for a moment. A problem loses all its value when it becomes simplified, and the world would be all the poorer if the Sybil of History burned her volumes. Besides, as Gibbon pointed out, 'a Montesquieu will detect in the most insignificant fact relations which the vulgar overlook.'

Nor can the scientific investigator of history isolate the particular elements, which he desires to examine, from disturbing and extraneous causes, as the experimental chemist can do (though sometimes, as in the case of lunatic asylums and prisons, he is enabled to observe phenomena in a certain degree of isolation). So he is compelled either to use the deductive mode of arguing from general laws or to employ the method of abstraction which gives a fictitious isolation to phenomena never so isolated in actual existence. And this is exactly what Polybius has done as well as Thucydides. For, as has been well remarked, there is in the works of these two writers a certain plastic unity of type and motive; whatever they write is penetrated through and through with a specific quality, a singleness and concentration of purpose, which we may contrast with the more comprehensive width as manifested not merely in the modern mind, but also in Herodotus. Thucydides, regarding society as influenced entirely by political motives, took no account of forces of a different nature, and consequently his results, like those of most modern political economists, have to be modified largely {207} before they come to correspond with what we know was the actual state of fact. Similarly, Polybius will deal only with those forces which tended to bring the civilised world under the dominion of Rome (ix. 1), and in the Thucydidean spirit points out the want of picturesqueness and romance in his pages which is the result of the abstract method (το μονοειδες της συνταξεως), being careful also to tell us that his rejection of all other forces is essentially deliberate and the result of a preconceived theory and by no means due to carelessness of any kind.

Now, of the general value of the abstract method and the legality of its employment in the sphere of history, this is perhaps not the suitable occasion for any discussion. It is, however, in all ways worthy of note that Polybius is not merely conscious of, but dwells with particular weight on, the fact which is usually urged as the strongest objection to the employment of the abstract method—I mean the conception of a society as a sort of human organism whose parts are indissolubly connected with one another and all affected when one member is in any way agitated. This conception of the organic nature of society appears first in Plato and Aristotle, who apply it to cities. Polybius, as his wont is, expands it to be a general characteristic of all history. It is an idea of the very highest importance, especially to a man like Polybius whose thoughts are continually turned towards the essential unity of history and the impossibility of isolation.

Farther, as regards the particular method of investigating that group of phenomena obtained for him by the abstract method, he will adopt, he tells us, neither the purely deductive nor the purely inductive mode but the union of both. In other words, he formally adopts that method of analysis upon the importance of which I have dwelt before.

And lastly, while, without doubt, enormous simplicity in the elements under consideration is the result of the employment of the abstract method, even within the limit thus obtained a certain selection must be made, and a selection involves a theory. For the facts of life cannot be tabulated with as great an ease as the colours of birds and insects can be tabulated. Now, Polybius points out that those phenomena particularly are to be dwelt on which may serve as a παραδειγμα or sample, and show the character of the tendencies of the age as clearly as 'a single drop from a full cask will be enough to disclose the nature of the whole contents.' This recognition of the importance of single facts, not in themselves but because of the spirit they represent, is extremely scientific; for we know that from the single bone, or tooth even, the anatomist can recreate entirely the skeleton of the primeval horse, and the botanist tell the character of the flora and fauna of a district from a single specimen.

Regarding truth as 'the most divine thing in Nature,' the very 'eye and light of history without which it moves a blind thing,' Polybius spared no pains in the acquisition of historical materials or in the study of the sciences of politics and war, which he considered were so essential to the training of

266

the scientific historian, and the labour he took is mirrored in the many ways in which he criticises other authorities.

There is something, as a rule, slightly contemptible about ancient criticism. The modern idea of the critic as the interpreter, the expounder of the beauty and excellence of the work he selects, seems quite unknown. Nothing can be more captious or unfair, for instance, than the method by which Aristotle criticised the ideal state of Plato in his ethical works, and the passages quoted by Polybius from Timæus show that the latter historian fully deserved the punning name given to him. But in Polybius there is, I think, little of that bitterness and pettiness of spirit which characterises most other writers, and an incidental story he tells of his relations with one of the historians whom he criticised shows that he was a man of great courtesy and refinement of taste—as, indeed, befitted one who had lived always in the society of those who were of great and noble birth.

Now, as regards the character of the canons by which he criticises the works of other authors, in the majority of cases he employs simply his own geographical and military knowledge, showing, for instance, the impossibility in the accounts given of Nabis's march from Sparta simply by his acquaintance with the spots in question; or the inconsistency of those of the battle of Issus; or of the accounts given by Ephorus of the battles of Leuctra and Mantinea. In the latter case he says, if any one will take the trouble to measure out the ground of the site of the battle and then test the manœuvres given, he will find how inaccurate the accounts are.

In other cases he appeals to public documents, the importance of which he was always foremost in recognising; showing, for instance, by a document in the public archives of Rhodes how inaccurate were the accounts given of the battle of Lade by Zeno and Antisthenes. Or he appeals to psychological probability, rejecting, for instance, the scandalous stories told of Philip of Macedon, simply from the king's general greatness of character, and arguing that a boy so well educated and so respectably connected as Demochares (xii. 14) could never have been guilty of that of which evil rumour accused him.

But the chief object of his literary censure is Timæus, who had been so unsparing of his strictures on others. The general point which he makes against him, impugning his accuracy as a historian, is that he derived his knowledge of history not from the dangerous perils of a life of action but in the secure indolence of a narrow scholastic life. There is, indeed, no point on which he is so vehement as this. 'A history,' he says, 'written in a library gives as lifeless and as inaccurate a picture of history as a painting which is copied not from a living animal but from a stuffed one.'

There is more difference, he says in another place, between the history of an eye-witness and that of one whose knowledge comes from books, than there is between the scenes of real life and the fictitious landscapes of theatrical scenery. Besides this, he enters into somewhat elaborate detailed criticism of passages where he thought Timæus was following a wrong method and perverting truth, passages which it will be worth while to examine in detail.

Timæus, from the fact of there being a Roman custom to shoot a war-horse on a stated day, argued back to the Trojan origin of that people. Polybius, on the other hand, points out that the inference is quite unwarrantable, because horse-sacrifices are ordinary institutions common to all barbarous tribes. Timæus here, as was so common with Greek writers, is arguing back from some custom of the present to an historical event in the past. Polybius really is employing the comparative method, showing how the custom was an ordinary step in the civilisation of every early people.

In another place, {211} he shows how illogical is the scepticism of Timæus as regards the existence of the Bull of Phalaris simply by appealing to the statue of the Bull, which was still to be seen in Carthage; pointing out how impossible it was, on any other theory except that it belonged to Phalaris, to account for the presence in Carthage of a bull of this peculiar character with a door between his shoulders. But one of the great points which he uses against this Sicilian historian is in reference to the question of the origin of the Locrian colony. In accordance with the received tradition on the subject, Aristotle had represented the Locrian colony as founded by some Parthenidæ or slaves' children, as they were called, a statement which seems to have roused the indignation of Timæus, who went to a good deal of trouble to confute this theory. He does so on the following grounds:—

268

First of all, he points out that in the ancient days the Greeks had no slaves at all, so the mention of them in the matter is an anachronism; and next he declares that he was shown in the Greek city of Locris certain ancient inscriptions in which their relation to the Italian city was expressed in terms of the position between parent and child, which showed also that mutual rights of citizenship were accorded to each city. Besides this, he appeals to various questions of improbability as regards their international relationship, on which Polybius takes diametrically opposite grounds which hardly call for discussion. And in favour of his own view he urges two points more: first, that the Lacedæmonians being allowed furlough for the purpose of seeing their wives at home, it was unlikely that the Locrians should not have had the same privilege; and next, that the Italian Locrians knew nothing of the Aristotelian version and had, on the contrary, very severe laws against adulterers, runaway slaves and the like. Now, most of these questions rest on mere probability, which is always such a subjective canon that an appeal to it is rarely conclusive. I would note, however, as regards the inscriptions which, if genuine, would of course have settled the matter, that Polybius looks on them as a mere invention on the part of Timæus, who, he remarks, gives no details about them, though, as a rule, he is so over-anxious to give chapter and verse for everything. A somewhat more interesting point is that where he attacks Timæus for the introduction of fictitious speeches into his narrative; for on this point Polybius seems to be far in advance of the opinions held by literary men on the subject not merely in his own day, but for centuries after. Herodotus had introduced speeches avowedly dramatic and fictitious. Thucydides states clearly that, where he was unable to find out what people really said, he put down what they ought to have said. Sallust alludes, it is true, to the fact of the speech he puts into the mouth of the tribune Memmius being essentially genuine, but the speeches given in the senate on the occasion of the Catilinarian conspiracy are very different from the same orations as they appear in Cicero. Livy makes his ancient Romans wrangle and chop logic with all the subtlety of a Hortensius or a Scævola. And even in later days, when shorthand reporters attended the debates of the senate and a Daily News was published in Rome, we find that one of the most celebrated speeches in Tacitus (that in which the Emperor Claudius gives the Gauls their freedom) is shown, by an inscription discovered recently at Lugdunum, to be entirely fabulous.

Upon the other hand, it must be borne in mind that these speeches were not intended to deceive; they were regarded merely as a certain dramatic element which it was allowable to introduce into history for the purpose of giving more life and reality to the narration, and were to be criticised, not as we should, by arguing how in an age before shorthand was known such a report was possible or how, in the failure of written documents, tradition could bring down such an accurate verbal account, but by the higher test of their psychological probability as regards the persons in whose mouths they are placed. An ancient historian in answer to modern criticism would say, probably, that these fictitious speeches were in reality more truthful than the actual ones, just as Aristotle claimed for poetry a higher degree of truth in comparison to history. The whole point is interesting as showing how far in advance of his age Polybius may be said to have been.

The last scientific historian, it is possible to gather from his writings what he considered were the characteristics of the ideal writer of history; and no small light will be thrown on the progress of historical criticism if we strive to collect and analyse what in Polybius are more or less scattered expressions. The ideal historian must be contemporary with the events he describes, or removed from them by one generation only. Where it is possible, he is to be an eye-witness of what he writes of; where that is out of his power he is to test all traditions and stories carefully and not to be ready to accept what is plausible in place of what is true. He is to be no bookworm living aloof from the experiences of the world in the artificial isolation of a university town, but a politician, a soldier, and a traveller, a man not merely of thought but of action, one who can do great things as well as write of them, who in the sphere of history could be what Byron and Æschylus were in the sphere of poetry, at once le chantre et le héros.

He is to keep before his eyes the fact that chance is merely a synonym for our ignorance; that the reign of law pervades the domain of history as much as it does that of political science. He is to accustom himself to look on all occasions for rational and natural causes. And while he is to recognise the practical utility of the supernatural, in an educational point of view, he is not himself to indulge in such intellectual beating of the air as to admit the possibility of the violation of inviolable laws, or to argue in a sphere wherein argument is a priori annihilated. He is to be free from all bias towards friend and country; he is to be courteous and gentle in criticism; he is not to regard history as a mere opportunity for splendid and tragic writing; nor is he to falsify truth for the sake of a paradox or an epigram.

While acknowledging the importance of particular facts as samples of higher truths, he is to take a broad and general view of humanity. He is to deal with the whole race and with the world, not with particular tribes or separate countries. He is to bear in mind that the world is really an organism wherein no one part can be moved without the others being affected also. He is to distinguish between cause and occasion, between the influence of general laws and particular fancies, and he is to remember that the greatest lessons of the world are contained in history and that it is the historian's duty to manifest them so as to save nations from following those unwise policies which always lead to dishonour and ruin, and to teach individuals to apprehend by the intellectual culture of history those truths which else they would have to learn in the bitter school of experience.

Now, as regards his theory of the necessity of the historian's being contemporary with the events he describes, so far as the historian is a mere narrator the remark is undoubtedly true. But to appreciate the harmony and rational position of the facts of a great epoch, to discover its laws, the causes which produced it and the effects which it generates, the scene must be viewed from a certain height and distance to be completely apprehended. A thoroughly contemporary historian such as Lord Clarendon or Thucydides is in reality part of the history he criticises; and, in the case of such contemporary historians as Fabius and Philistus, Polybius is compelled to acknowledge that they are misled by patriotic and other considerations. Against Polybius himself no such accusation can be made. He indeed of all men is able, as from some lofty tower, to discern the whole tendency of the ancient world, the triumph of Roman institutions and of Greek thought which is the last message of the old world and, in a more spiritual sense, has become the Gospel of the new.

One thing indeed he did not see, or if he saw it, he thought but little of it—how from the East there was spreading over the world, as a wave spreads, a spiritual inroad of new religions from the time when the Pessinuntine mother of the gods, a shapeless mass of stone, was brought to the eternal city by her holiest citizen, to the day when the ship Castor and Pollux stood in at Puteoli, and St. Paul turned his face towards martyrdom and victory at Rome. Polybius was able to predict, from his knowledge of the causes of revolutions and the tendencies of the various forms of governments, the uprising of that democratic tone of thought which, as soon as a seed is sown in the murder of the Gracchi and the exile of Marius, culminated as all democratic movements do culminate, in the supreme authority of one man, the lordship of the world under the world's rightful lord, Caius Julius Cæsar. This, indeed, he saw in no uncertain way. But the turning of all men's hearts to the East, the first glimmering of that splendid dawn which broke over the hills of Galilee and flooded the earth like wine, was hidden from his eyes.

There are many points in the description of the ideal historian which one may compare to the picture which Plato has given us of the ideal philosopher. They are both 'spectators of all time and all existence.' Nothing is contemptible in their eyes, for all things have a meaning, and they both walk in august reasonableness before all men, conscious of the workings of God yet free from all terror of mendicant priest or vagrant miracle-worker. But the parallel ends here. For the one stands aloof from the world-storm of sleet and hail, his eyes fixed on distant and sunlit heights, loving knowledge for the sake of knowledge and wisdom for the joy of wisdom, while the other is an eager actor in the world ever seeking to apply his knowledge to useful things. Both equally desire truth, but the one because of its utility, the other for its beauty. The historian regards it as the rational principle of all true history, and no more. To the other it comes as an all-pervading and mystic enthusiasm, 'like the desire of strong wine, the craving of ambition, the passionate love of what is beautiful.'

Still, though we miss in the historian those higher and more spiritual qualities which the philosopher of the Academe alone of all men possessed, we must not blind ourselves to the merits of that great rationalist who seems to have anticipated the very latest words of modern science. Nor yet is he to be regarded merely in the narrow light in which he is estimated by most modern critics, as the explicit champion of rationalism and nothing more. For he is connected with another idea, the course of which is as the course of that great river of his native Arcadia which, springing from some arid and sun-bleached rock, gathers strength and beauty as it flows till it reaches the asphodel meadows of Olympia and the light and laughter of Ionian waters.

For in him we can discern the first notes of that great cult of the seven-hilled city which made Virgil write his epic and Livy his history, which found in Dante its highest exponent, which dreamed of an Empire where the Emperor would care for the bodies and the Pope for the souls of men, and so has passed into the conception of God's spiritual empire and the universal brotherhood of man and widened into the huge ocean of universal thought as the Peneus loses itself in the sea.

Polybius is the last scientific historian of Greece. The writer who seems fittingly to complete the progress of thought is a writer of biographies only. I will not here touch on Plutarch's employment of the inductive method as shown in his constant use of inscription and statue, of public document and building and the like, because they involve no new method. It is his attitude towards miracles of which I desire to treat.

Plutarch is philosophic enough to see that in the sense of a violation of the laws of nature a miracle is impossible. It is absurd, he says, to imagine that the statue of a saint can speak, and that an inanimate object not possessing the vocal organs should be able to utter an articulate sound. Upon the other hand, he protests against science imagining that, by explaining the natural causes of things, it has explained away their transcendental meaning. 'When the tears on the cheek of some holy statue have been analysed into the moisture which certain temperatures produce on wood and marble, it yet by no means follows that they were not a sign of grief and mourning set there by God Himself.' When Lampon saw in the prodigy of the one-horned ram the omen of the supreme rule of Pericles, and when Anaxagoras showed that the abnormal development was the rational resultant of the peculiar formation of the skull, the dreamer and the man of science were both right; it was the business of the latter to consider how the prodigy came about, of the former to show why it was so formed and what it so portended. The progression of thought is exemplified in all particulars. Herodotus had a glimmering sense of the impossibility of a violation of nature. Thucydides ignored the supernatural. Polybius rationalised it. Plutarch raises it to its mystical heights again, though he bases it on law. In a word, Plutarch felt that while science brings the supernatural down to the natural, yet ultimately all that is natural is really supernatural. To him, as to many of our own day, religion was that transcendental attitude of the mind which, contemplating a world resting on inviolable law, is yet comforted and seeks to worship God not in the violation but in the fulfilment of nature.

It may seem paradoxical to quote in connection with the priest of Chæronea such a pure rationalist as Mr. Herbert Spencer; yet when we read as the last message of modern science that 'when the equation of life has been reduced to its lowest terms the symbols are symbols still,' mere signs, that is, of that unknown reality which underlies all matter and all spirit, we may feel how over the wide strait of centuries thought calls to thought and how Plutarch has a higher position than is usually claimed for him in the progress of the Greek intellect.

And, indeed, it seems that not merely the importance of Plutarch himself but also that of the land of his birth in the evolution of Greek civilisation has been passed over by modern critics. To us, indeed, the bare rock to which the Parthenon serves as a crown, and which lies between Colonus and Attica's violet hills, will always be the holiest spot in the land of Greece: and Delphi will come next, and then the meadows of Eurotas where that noble people lived who represented in Hellenic thought the reaction of the law of duty against the law of beauty, the opposition of conduct to culture. Yet, as one stands on the σχιστη οδος of Cithæron and looks out on the great double plain of Bœotia, the enormous importance of the division of Hellas comes to one's mind with great force. To the north is Orchomenus and the Minyan treasure house, seat of those merchant princes of Phœnicia who brought to Greece the knowledge of letters and the art of working in gold. Thebes is at our feet with the gloom of the terrible legends of Greek tragedy still lingering about it, the birthplace of Pindar, the nurse of Epaminondas and the Sacred Band.

And from out of the plain where 'Mars loved to dance,' rises the Muses' haunt, Helicon, by whose silver streams Corinna and Hesiod sang. While far away under the white ægis of those snow-capped mountains lies Chæronea and the Lion plain where with vain chivalry the Greeks strove to check Macedon first and afterwards Rome; Chæronea, where in the Martinmas summer of Greek civilisation Plutarch rose from the drear waste of a dying religion as the aftermath rises when the mowers think they have left the field bare.

Greek philosophy began and ended in scepticism: the first and the last word of Greek history was Faith.

Splendid thus in its death, like winter sunsets, the Greek religion passed away into the horror of night. For the Cimmerian darkness was at hand, and when the schools of Athens were closed and the statue of Athena broken, the Greek spirit passed from the gods and the history of its own land to the subtleties of defining the doctrine of the Trinity and the mystical attempts to bring Plato into harmony with Christ and to reconcile Gethsemane and the Sermon on the Mount with the Athenian prison and the discussion in the woods of Colonus. The Greek spirit slept for wellnigh a thousand years. When it woke again, like Antæus it had gathered strength from the earth where it lay, like Apollo it had lost none of its divinity through its long servitude.

In the history of Roman thought we nowhere find any of those characteristics of the Greek Illumination which I have pointed out are the necessary concomitants of the rise of historical criticism. The conservative respect for tradition which made the Roman people delight in the ritual and formulas of law, and is as apparent in their politics as in their religion, was fatal to any rise of that spirit of revolt against authority the importance of which, as a factor in intellectual progress, we have already seen.

The whitened tables of the Pontifices preserved carefully the records of the eclipses and other atmospherical phenomena, and what we call the art of verifying dates was known to them at an early time; but there was no spontaneous rise of physical science to suggest by its analogies of law and order a new method of research, nor any natural springing up of the questioning spirit of philosophy with its unification of all phenomena and all knowledge. At the very time when the whole tide of Eastern superstition was sweeping into the heart of the Capitol the Senate banished the Greek philosophers from Rome. And of the three systems which did at length take some root in the city those of Zeno and Epicurus were merely used as the rule for the ordering of life, while the dogmatic scepticism of Carneades, by its very principles, annihilated the possibility of argument and encouraged a perfect indifference to research.

Nor were the Romans ever fortunate enough like the Greeks to have to face the incubus of any dogmatic system of legends and myths, the immoralities and absurdities of which might excite a revolutionary outbreak of sceptical criticism. For the Roman religion became as it were crystallised and isolated from progress at an early period of its evolution. Their gods remained mere abstractions of commonplace virtues or uninteresting personifications of the useful things of life. The old primitive creed was indeed always upheld as a state institution on account of the enormous facilities it offered for cheating in politics, but as a spiritual system of belief it was unanimously rejected at a very early period both by the common people and the educated classes, for the sensible reason that it was so extremely dull. The former took refuge in the mystic sensualities of the worship of Isis, the latter in the Stoical rules of life. The Romans classified their gods carefully in their order of precedence, analysed their genealogies in the laborious spirit of modern heraldry, fenced them round with a ritual as intricate as their law, but never quite cared enough about them to believe in them. So it was of no account with them when the philosophers announced that Minerva was merely memory. She had never been much else. Nor did they protest when Lucretius dared to say of Ceres and of Liber that they were only the corn of the field and the fruit of the vine. For they had never mourned for the daughter of Demeter in the asphodel meadows of Sicily, nor traversed the glades of Cithæron with fawn-skin and with spear.

This brief sketch of the condition of Roman thought will serve to prepare us for the almost total want of scientific historical criticism which we shall discern in their literature, and has, besides, afforded fresh corroborations of the conditions essential to the rise of this spirit, and of the modes of thought which it reflects and in which it is always to be found. Roman historical composition had its origin in the pontifical college of ecclesiastical lawyers, and preserved to its close the uncritical spirit which characterised its fountain-head. It possessed from the outset a most voluminous collection of the materials of history, which, however, produced merely antiquarians, not historians. It is so hard to use facts, so easy to accumulate them.

Wearied of the dull monotony of the pontifical annals, which dwelt on little else but the rise and fall in provisions and the eclipses of the sun, Cato wrote out a history with his own hand for the instruction of his child, to which he gave the name of Origines, and before his time some aristocratic families had written histories in Greek much in the same spirit in which the Germans of the eighteenth century used French as the literary language. But the first regular Roman historian is Sallust. Between the extravagant eulogies passed on this author by the French (such as De Closset), and Dr. Mommsen's view of him as merely a political pamphleteer, it is perhaps difficult to reach the via media of unbiassed appreciation. He has, at any rate, the credit of being a purely rationalistic historian, perhaps the only one in Roman literature. Cicero had a good many qualifications for a scientific historian, and (as he usually did) thought very highly of his own powers. On passages of ancient legend, however, he is rather unsatisfactory, for while he is too sensible to believe them he is too patriotic to reject them. And this is really the attitude of Livy, who claims for early Roman legend a certain uncritical homage from the rest of the subject world. His view in his history is that it is not worth while to examine the truth of these stories.

In his hands the history of Rome unrolls before our eyes like some gorgeous tapestry, where victory succeeds victory, where triumph treads on the heels of triumph, and the line of heroes seems never to end. It is not till we pass behind the canvas and see the slight means by which the effect is produced that we apprehend the fact that like most picturesque writers Livy is an indifferent critic. As regards his attitude towards the credibility of early Roman history he is quite as conscious as we are of its mythical and unsound nature. He will not, for instance, decide whether the Horatii were Albans or Romans; who was the first dictator; how many tribunes there were, and the like. His method, as a rule, is merely to mention all the accounts and sometimes to decide in favour of the most probable, but usually not to decide at all. No canons of historical criticism will ever discover whether the Roman women interviewed the mother of Coriolanus of their own accord or at the suggestion of the senate; whether Remus was killed for jumping over his brother's wall or because they quarrelled about birds; whether the ambassadors found Cincinnatus ploughing or only mending a hedge. Livy suspends his judgment over these important facts and history when questioned on their truth is dumb. If he does select between two historians he chooses the one who is nearer to the facts he describes. But he is no critic, only a conscientious writer. It is mere vain waste to dwell on his critical powers, for they do not exist.

* * * * *

In the case of Tacitus imagination has taken the place of history. The past lives again in his pages, but through no laborious criticism; rather through a dramatic and psychological faculty which he specially possessed.

In the philosophy of history he has no belief. He can never make up his mind what to believe as regards God's government of the world. There is no method in him and none elsewhere in Roman literature.

Nations may not have missions but they certainly have functions. And the function of ancient Italy was not merely to give us what is statical in our institutions and rational in our law, but to blend into one elemental creed the spiritual aspirations of Aryan and of Semite. Italy was not a pioneer in intellectual progress, nor a motive power in the evolution of thought. The owl of the goddess of Wisdom traversed over the whole land and found nowhere a resting-place. The dove, which is the bird of Christ, flew straight to the city of Rome and the new reign began. It was the fashion of early Italian painters to represent in mediæval costume the soldiers who watched over the tomb of Christ, and this, which was the result of the frank anachronism of all true art, may serve to us as an allegory. For it was in vain that the middle ages strove

278

to guard the buried spirit of progress. When the dawn of the Greek spirit arose, the sepulchre was empty, the grave-clothes laid aside. Humanity had risen from the dead.

The study of Greek, it has been well said, implies the birth of criticism, comparison and research. At the opening of that education of modern by ancient thought which we call the Renaissance, it was the words of Aristotle which sent Columbus sailing to the New World, while a fragment of Pythagorean astronomy set Copernicus thinking on that train of reasoning which has revolutionised the whole position of our planet in the universe. Then it was seen that the only meaning of progress is a return to Greek modes of thought. The monkish hymns which obscured the pages of Greek manuscripts were blotted out, the splendours of a new method were unfolded to the world, and out of the melancholy sea of mediævalism rose the free spirit of man in all that splendour of glad adolescence, when the bodily powers seem quickened by a new vitality, when the eye sees more clearly than its wont and the mind apprehends what was beforetime hidden from it. To herald the opening of the sixteenth century, from the little Venetian printing press came forth all the great authors of antiquity, each bearing on the title-page the words Αλδος ο Μανουτιος Ρωμαιος και Φιλελλην words which may serve to remind us with what wondrous prescience Polybius saw the world's fate when he foretold the material sovereignty of Roman institutions and exemplified in himself the intellectual empire of Greece.

The course of the study of the spirit of historical criticism has not been a profitless investigation into modes and forms of thought now antiquated and of no account. The only spirit which is entirely removed from us is the mediæval; the Greek spirit is essentially modern. The introduction of the comparative method of research which has forced history to disclose its secrets belongs in a measure to us. Ours, too, is a more scientific knowledge of philology and the method of survival. Nor did the ancients know anything of the doctrine of averages or of crucial instances, both of which methods have proved of such importance in modern criticism, the one adding a most important proof of the statical elements of history, and exemplifying the influences of all physical surroundings on the life of man; the other, as in

279

the single instance of the Moulin Quignon skull, serving to create a whole new science of prehistoric archæology and to bring us back to a time when man was coeval with the stone age, the mammoth and the woolly rhinoceros. But, except these, we have added no new canon or method to the science of historical criticism. Across the drear waste of a thousand years the Greek and the modern spirit join hands.

In the torch race which the Greek boys ran from the Cerameician field of death to the home of the goddess of Wisdom, not merely he who first reached the goal but he also who first started with the torch aflame received a prize. In the Lampadephoria of civilisation and free thought let us not forget to render due meed of honour to those who first lit that sacred flame, the increasing splendour of which lights our footsteps to the far-off divine event of the attainment of perfect truth.

LA SAINTE COURTISANE; OR, THE WOMAN COVERED WITH JEWELS

The scene represents a corner of a valley in the Thebaid. On the right hand of the stage is a cavern. In front of the cavern stands a great crucifix.

On the left [sand dunes].

The sky is blue like the inside of a cup of lapis lazuli. The hills are of red sand. Here and there on the hills there are clumps of thorns.

FIRST MAN. Who is she? She makes me afraid. She has a purple cloak and her hair is like threads of gold. I think she must be the daughter of the Emperor. I have heard the boatmen say that the Emperor has a daughter who wears a cloak of purple.

SECOND MAN. She has birds' wings upon her sandals, and her tunic is of the colour of green corn. It is like corn in spring when she stands still. It is like young corn troubled by the shadows of hawks when she moves. The pearls on her tunic are like many moons.

FIRST MAN. They are like the moons one sees in the water when the wind blows from the hills.

SECOND MAN. I think she is one of the gods. I think she comes from Nubia.

FIRST MAN. I am sure she is the daughter of the Emperor. Her nails are stained with henna. They are like the petals of a rose. She has come here to weep for Adonis.

SECOND MAN. She is one of the gods. I do not know why she has left her temple. The gods should not leave their temples. If she speaks to us let us not answer and she will pass by.

FIRST MAN. She will not speak to us. She is the daughter of the Emperor.

MYRRHINA. Dwells he not here, the beautiful young hermit, he who will not look on the face of woman?

FIRST MAN. Of a truth it is here the hermit dwells.

MYRRHINA. Why will he not look on the face of woman?

SECOND MAN. We do not know.

MYRRHINA. Why do ye yourselves not look at me?

FIRST MAN. You are covered with bright stones, and you dazzle our eyes.

SECOND MAN. He who looks at the sun becomes blind. You are too bright to look at. It is not wise to look at things that are very bright. Many of the priests in the temples are blind, and have slaves to lead them.

MYRRHINA. Where does he dwell, the beautiful young hermit who will not look on the face of woman? Has he a house of reeds or a house of burnt clay or does he lie on the hillside? Or does he make his bed in the rushes?

FIRST MAN. He dwells in that cavern yonder.

MYRRHINA. What a curious place to dwell in.

FIRST MAN. Of old a centaur lived there. When the hermit came the centaur gave a shrill cry, wept and lamented, and galloped away.

SECOND MAN. No. It was a white unicorn who lived in the cave. When it saw the hermit coming the unicorn knelt down and worshipped him. Many people saw it worshipping him.

FIRST MAN. I have talked with people who saw it.

. . . . .

SECOND MAN. Some say he was a hewer of wood and worked for hire. But that may not be true.

. . . . .

MYRRHINA. What gods then do ye worship? Or do ye worship any gods? There are those who have no gods to worship. The philosophers who wear long beards and brown cloaks have no gods to worship. They wrangle with each other in the porticoes. The [ ] laugh at them.

FIRST MAN. We worship seven gods. We may not tell their names. It is a very dangerous thing to tell the names of the gods. No one should ever tell the name of his god. Even the priests who praise the gods all day long, and eat of their food with them, do not call them by their right names.

MYRRHINA. Where are these gods ye worship?

FIRST MAN. We hide them in the folds of our tunics. We do not show them to any one. If we showed them to any one they might leave us.

MYRRHINA. Where did ye meet with them?

FIRST MAN. They were given to us by an embalmer of the dead who had found them in a tomb. We served him for seven years.

MYRRHINA. The dead are terrible. I am afraid of Death.

FIRST MAN. Death is not a god. He is only the servant of the gods.

MYRRHINA. He is the only god I am afraid of. Ye have seen many of the gods?

FIRST MAN. We have seen many of them. One sees them chiefly at night time. They pass one by very swiftly. Once we saw some of the gods at daybreak. They were walking across a plain.

MYRRHINA. Once as I was passing through the market place I heard a sophist from Cilicia say that there is only one God. He said it before many people.

FIRST MAN. That cannot be true. We have ourselves seen many, though we are but common men and of no account. When I saw them I hid myself in a bush. They did me no harm.

MYRRHINA. Tell me more about the beautiful young hermit. Talk to me about the beautiful young hermit who will not look on the face of woman. What is the story of his days? What mode of life has he?

FIRST MAN. We do not understand you.

MYRRHINA. What does he do, the beautiful young hermit? Does he sow or reap? Does he plant a garden or catch fish in a net? Does he weave linen on a loom? Does he set his hand to the wooden plough and walk behind the oxen?

SECOND MAN. He being a very holy man does nothing. We are common men and of no account. We toil all day long in the sun. Sometimes the ground is very hard.

MYRRHINA. Do the birds of the air feed him? Do the jackals share their booty with him?

FIRST MAN. Every evening we bring him food. We do not think that the birds of the air feed him.

MYRRHINA. Why do ye feed him? What profit have ye in so doing?

SECOND MAN. He is a very holy man. One of the gods whom he has offended has made him mad. We think he has offended the moon.

MYRRHINA. Go and tell him that one who has come from Alexandria desires to speak with him.

FIRST MAN. We dare not tell him. This hour he is praying to his God. We pray thee to pardon us for not doing thy bidding.

MYRRHINA. Are ye afraid of him?

FIRST MAN. We are afraid of him.

MYRRHINA. Why are ye afraid of him?

FIRST MAN. We do not know.

MYRRHINA. What is his name?

FIRST MAN. The voice that speaks to him at night time in the cavern calls to him by the name of Honorius. It was also by the name of Honorius that the three lepers who passed by once called to him. We think that his name is Honorius.

MYRRHINA. Why did the three lepers call to him?

FIRST MAN. That he might heal them.

MYRRHINA. Did he heal them?

SECOND MAN. No. They had committed some sin: it was for that reason they were lepers. Their hands and faces were like salt. One of them wore a mask of linen. He was a king's son.

MYRRHINA. What is the voice that speaks to him at night time in his cave?

FIRST MAN. We do not know whose voice it is. We think it is the voice of his God. For we have seen no man enter his cavern nor any come forth from it.

MYRRHINA. Honorius.

HONORIUS (from within). Who calls Honorius?

. . . . .

MYRRHINA. Come forth, Honorius.

. . . . .

My chamber is ceiled with cedar and odorous with myrrh. The pillars of my bed are of cedar and the hangings are of purple. My bed is strewn with purple and the steps are of silver. The hangings are sewn with silver pomegranates and the steps that are of silver are strewn with saffron and with myrrh. My lovers hang garlands round the pillars of my house. At night time they come with the flute players and the players of the harp. They woo me with apples and on the pavement of my courtyard they write my name in wine.

From the uttermost parts of the world my lovers come to me. The kings of the earth come to me and bring me presents.

When the Emperor of Byzantium heard of me he left his porphyry chamber and set sail in his galleys. His slaves bare no torches that none might know of his coming. When the King of Cyprus heard of me he sent me ambassadors. The two Kings of Libya who are brothers brought me gifts of amber.

I took the minion of Cæsar from Cæsar and made him my playfellow. He came to me at night in a litter. He was pale as a narcissus, and his body was like honey.

The son of the Præfect slew himself in my honour, and the Tetrarch of Cilicia scourged himself for my pleasure before my slaves.

The King of Hierapolis who is a priest and a robber set carpets for me to walk on.

Sometimes I sit in the circus and the gladiators fight beneath me. Once a Thracian who was my lover was caught in the net. I gave the signal for him to die and the whole theatre applauded. Sometimes I pass through the gymnasium and watch the young men wrestling or in the race. Their bodies are bright with oil and their brows are wreathed with willow sprays and with myrtle. They stamp their feet on the sand when they wrestle and when they run the sand follows them like a little cloud. He at whom I smile leaves his companions and follows me to my home. At other times I go down to the harbour and watch the merchants unloading their vessels. Those that come from Tyre have cloaks of silk and earrings of emerald. Those that come from Massilia have cloaks of fine wool and earrings of brass. When they see me coming they stand on the prows of their ships and call to me, but I do not answer them. I go to the little taverns where the sailors lie all day long drinking black wine and playing with dice and I sit down with them.

I made the Prince my slave, and his slave who was a Tyrian I made my Lord for the space of a moon.

I put a figured ring on his finger and brought him to my house. I have wonderful things in my house.

The dust of the desert lies on your hair and your feet are scratched with thorns and your body is scorched by the sun. Come with me, Honorius, and I will clothe you in a tunic of silk. I will smear your body with myrrh and pour spikenard on your hair. I will clothe you in hyacinth and put honey in your mouth. Love—

HONORIUS. There is no love but the love of God.

MYRRHINA. Who is He whose love is greater than that of mortal men?

HONORIUS. It is He whom thou seest on the cross, Myrrhina. He is the Son of God and was born of a virgin. Three wise men who were kings brought Him offerings, and the shepherds who were lying on the hills were wakened by a great light.

The Sibyls knew of His coming. The groves and the oracles spake of Him. David and the prophets announced Him. There is no love like the love of God nor any love that can be compared to it.

The body is vile, Myrrhina. God will raise thee up with a new body which will not know corruption, and thou wilt dwell in the Courts of the Lord and see Him whose hair is like fine wool and whose feet are of brass.

MYRRHINA. The beauty . . .

HONORIUS. The beauty of the soul increases till it can see God. Therefore, Myrrhina, repent of thy sins. The robber who was crucified beside Him He brought into Paradise. [Exit.

MYRRHINA. How strangely he spake to me. And with what scorn did he regard me. I wonder why he spake to me so strangely.

. . . . .

HONORIUS. Myrrhina, the scales have fallen from my eyes and I see now clearly what I did not see before. Take me to Alexandria and let me taste of the seven sins.

MYRRHINA. Do not mock me, Honorius, nor speak to me with such bitter words. For I have repented of my sins and I am seeking a cavern in this desert where I too may dwell so that my soul may become worthy to see God.

HONORIUS. The sun is setting, Myrrhina. Come with me to Alexandria.

MYRRHINA. I will not go to Alexandria.

HONORIUS. Farewell, Myrrhina.

MYRRHINA. Honorius, farewell. No, no, do not go.

. . . . .

I have cursed my beauty for what it has done, and cursed the wonder of my body for the evil that it has brought upon you.

Lord, this man brought me to Thy feet. He told me of Thy coming upon earth, and of the wonder of Thy birth, and the great wonder of Thy death also. By him, O Lord, Thou wast revealed to me.

HONORIUS. You talk as a child, Myrrhina, and without knowledge. Loosen your hands. Why didst thou come to this valley in thy beauty?

MYRRHINA. The God whom thou worshippest led me here that I might repent of my iniquities and know Him as the Lord.

HONORIUS. Why didst thou tempt me with words?

MYRRHINA. That thou shouldst see Sin in its painted mask and look on Death in its robe of Shame.

THE ENGLISH RENAISSANCE OF ART

'The English Renaissance of Art' was delivered as a lecture for the first time in the Chickering Hall, New York, on January 9, 1882. A portion of it was reported in the New York Tribune on the following day and in other American papers subsequently. Since then this portion has been reprinted, more or less accurately, from time to time, in unauthorised editions, but not more than one quarter of the lecture has ever been published.

There are in existence no less than four copies of the lecture, the earliest of which is entirely in the author's handwriting. The others are type-written and contain many corrections and additions made by the author in manuscript. These have all been collated and the text here given contains, as nearly as possible, the lecture in its original form as delivered by the author during his tour in the United States.

Among the many debts which we owe to the supreme æsthetic faculty of Goethe is that he was the first to teach us to define beauty in terms the most concrete possible, to realise it, I mean, always in its special manifestations. So, in the lecture which I have the honour to deliver before you, I will not try to give you any abstract definition of beauty—any such universal formula for it as was sought for by the philosophy of the eighteenth century—still less to communicate to you that which in its essence is incommunicable, the virtue by which a particular picture or poem affects us with a unique and special joy; but rather to point out to you the general ideas which characterise the great English Renaissance of Art in this century, to discover their source, as far as that is possible, and to estimate their future as far as that is possible.

I call it our English Renaissance because it is indeed a sort of new birth of the spirit of man, like the great Italian Renaissance of the fifteenth century, in its desire for a more gracious and comely way of life, its passion for physical beauty, its exclusive attention to form, its seeking for new subjects for poetry, new forms of art, new intellectual and imaginative enjoyments: and I call it our romantic movement because it is our most recent expression of beauty.

It has been described as a mere revival of Greek modes of thought, and again as a mere revival of mediæval feeling. Rather I would say that to these forms of the human spirit it has added whatever of artistic value the intricacy and complexity and experience of modern life can give: taking from the one its clearness of vision and its sustained calm, from the other its variety of expression and the mystery of its vision. For what, as Goethe said, is the study of the ancients but a return to the real world (for that is what they did); and what, said Mazzini, is mediævalism but individuality?

It is really from the union of Hellenism, in its breadth, its sanity of purpose, its calm possession of beauty, with the adventive, the intensified individualism, the passionate colour of the romantic spirit, that springs the art of the nineteenth century in England, as from the marriage of Faust and Helen of Troy sprang the beautiful boy Euphorion.

Such expressions as 'classical' and 'romantic' are, it is true, often apt to become the mere catchwords of schools. We must always remember that art has only one sentence to utter: there is for her only one high law, the law of form or harmony—yet between the classical and romantic spirit we may say that there lies this difference at least, that the one deals with the type and the other with the exception. In the work produced under the modern romantic spirit it is no longer the permanent, the essential truths of life that are treated of; it is the momentary situation of the one, the momentary aspect of the other that art seeks to render. In sculpture, which is the type of one spirit, the subject predominates over the situation; in painting, which is the type of the other, the situation predominates over the subject.

There are two spirits, then: the Hellenic spirit and the spirit of romance may be taken as forming the essential elements of our conscious intellectual tradition, of our permanent standard of taste. As regards their origin, in art as in politics there is but one origin for all revolutions, a desire on the part of man for a nobler form of life, for a freer method and opportunity of expression. Yet, I think that in estimating the sensuous and intellectual spirit which presides over our English Renaissance, any attempt to isolate it in any way from the progress and movement and social life of the age that has produced it would be to rob it of its true vitality, possibly to mistake its true meaning. And in disengaging from the pursuits and passions of this crowded modern world those passions and pursuits which have to do with art and the love of art, we must take into account many great events of history which seem to be the most opposed to any such artistic feeling.

Alien then from any wild, political passion, or from the harsh voice of a rude people in revolt, as our English Renaissance must seem, in its passionate cult of pure beauty, its flawless devotion to form, its exclusive and sensitive nature, it is to the French Revolution that we must look for the most primary factor of its production, the first condition of its birth: that great Revolution of which we are all the children, though the voices of some of us be often loud against it; that Revolution to which at a time when even such spirits as Coleridge and Wordsworth lost heart in England, noble messages of love blown across seas came from your young Republic.

It is true that our modern sense of the continuity of history has shown us that neither in politics nor in nature are there revolutions ever but evolutions only, and that the prelude to that wild storm which swept over France in '89 and made every king in Europe tremble for his throne, was first sounded in literature years before the Bastille fell and the Palace was taken. The way for those red scenes by Seine and Loire was paved by that critical spirit of Germany and England which accustomed men to bring all things to the test of reason or utility or both, while the discontent of the people in the streets of Paris was the echo that followed the life of Émile and of Werther. For Rousseau, by silent lake and mountain, had called humanity back to the golden age that still lies before us and preached a return to nature, in passionate eloquence whose music still lingers about our keen northern air. And Goethe and Scott had brought romance back again from the prison she had lain in for so many centuries—and what is romance but humanity?

Yet in the womb of the Revolution itself, and in the storm and terror of that wild time, tendencies were hidden away that the artistic Renaissance bent to her own service when the time came—a scientific tendency first, which has borne in our own day a brood of somewhat noisy Titans, yet in the sphere of poetry has not been unproductive of good. I do not mean merely in its adding to enthusiasm that intellectual basis which is its strength, or that more obvious influence about which Wordsworth was thinking when he said very nobly that poetry was merely the impassioned expression in the face of science, and that when science would put on a form of flesh and blood the poet would lend his divine spirit to aid the transfiguration. Nor do I dwell much on the great cosmical emotion and deep pantheism of science to which Shelley has given its first and Swinburne its latest glory of song, but rather on its influence on the artistic spirit in preserving that close observation and the sense of limitation as well as of clearness of vision which are the characteristics of the real artist.

The great and golden rule of art as well as of life, wrote William Blake, is that the more distinct, sharp and defined the boundary line, the more perfect is the work of art; and the less keen and sharp the greater is the evidence of weak imitation, plagiarism and bungling. 'Great inventors in all ages knew this—Michael Angelo and Albert Dürer are known by this and by this alone'; and another time he wrote, with all the simple directness of nineteenth-century prose, 'to generalise is to be an idiot.'

And this love of definite conception, this clearness of vision, this artistic sense of limit, is the characteristic of all great work and poetry; of the vision of Homer as of the vision of Dante, of Keats and William Morris as of Chaucer and Theocritus. It lies at the base of all noble, realistic and romantic work as opposed to colourless and empty abstractions of our own eighteenth-century poets and of the classical dramatists of France, or of the vague spiritualities of the German sentimental school: opposed, too, to that spirit of transcendentalism which also was root and flower itself of the great Revolution, underlying the impassioned contemplation of Wordsworth and giving wings and fire to the eagle-like flight of Shelley, and which in the sphere of philosophy, though displaced by the materialism and positiveness of our day, bequeathed two great schools of thought, the school of Newman to Oxford, the school of Emerson to America. Yet is this spirit of transcendentalism alien to the spirit of art. For the artist can accept no sphere of life in exchange for life itself. For him there is no escape from the bondage of the earth: there is not even the desire of escape.

He is indeed the only true realist: symbolism, which is the essence of the transcendental spirit, is alien to him. The metaphysical mind of Asia will create for itself the monstrous, many-breasted idol of Ephesus, but to the Greek, pure artist, that work is most instinct with spiritual life which conforms most clearly to the perfect facts of physical life.

'The storm of revolution,' as André Chenier said, 'blows out the torch of poetry.' It is not for some little time that the real influence of such a wild cataclysm of things is felt: at first the desire for equality seems to have produced personalities of more giant and Titan stature than the world had ever known before. Men heard the lyre of Byron and the legions of Napoleon; it was a period of measureless passions and of measureless despair; ambition, discontent, were the chords of life and art; the age was an age of revolt: a phase through which the human spirit must pass but one in which it cannot rest. For the aim of culture is not rebellion but peace, the valley perilous where ignorant armies clash by night being no dwelling-place meet for her to whom the gods have assigned the fresh uplands and sunny heights and clear, untroubled air.

And soon that desire for perfection, which lay at the base of the Revolution, found in a young English poet its most complete and flawless realisation.

Phidias and the achievements of Greek art are foreshadowed in Homer: Dante prefigures for us the passion and colour and intensity of Italian painting: the modern love of landscape dates from Rousseau, and it is in Keats that one discerns the beginning of the artistic renaissance of England.

Byron was a rebel and Shelley a dreamer; but in the calmness and clearness of his vision, his perfect self-control, his unerring sense of beauty and his recognition of a separate realm for the imagination, Keats was the pure and serene artist, the forerunner of the pre-Raphaelite school, and so of the great romantic movement of which I am to speak.

Blake had indeed, before him, claimed for art a lofty, spiritual mission, and had striven to raise design to the ideal level of poetry and music, but the remoteness of his vision both in painting and poetry and the incompleteness of his technical powers had been adverse to any real influence. It is in Keats that the artistic spirit of this century first found its absolute incarnation.

And these pre-Raphaelites, what were they? If you ask nine-tenths of the British public what is the meaning of the word æsthetics, they will tell you it is the French for affectation or the German for a dado; and if you inquire about the pre-Raphaelites you will hear something about an eccentric lot of young men to whom a sort of divine crookedness and holy awkwardness in drawing were the chief objects of art. To know nothing about their great men is one of the necessary elements of English education.

As regards the pre-Raphaelites the story is simple enough. In the year 1847 a number of young men in London, poets and painters, passionate admirers of Keats all of them, formed the habit of meeting together for discussions on art, the result of such discussions being that the English Philistine public was roused suddenly from its ordinary apathy by hearing that there was in its midst a body of young men who had determined to revolutionise English painting and poetry. They called themselves the pre-Raphaelite Brotherhood.

In England, then as now, it was enough for a man to try and produce any serious beautiful work to lose all his rights as a citizen; and besides this, the pre-Raphaelite Brotherhood—among whom the names of Dante Rossetti, Holman Hunt and Millais will be familiar to you—had on their side three things that the English public never forgives: youth, power and enthusiasm.

Satire, always as sterile as it is shameful and as impotent as it is insolent, paid them that usual homage which mediocrity pays to genius—doing, here as always, infinite harm to the public, blinding them to what is beautiful, teaching them that irreverence which is the source of all vileness and narrowness of life, but harming the artist not at all, rather confirming him in the perfect rightness of his work and ambition. For to disagree with three-fourths of the British public on all points is one of the first elements of sanity, one of the deepest consolations in all moments of spiritual doubt.

As regards the ideas these young men brought to the regeneration of English art, we may see at the base of their artistic creations a desire for a deeper spiritual value to be given to art as well as a more decorative value.

Pre-Raphaelites they called themselves; not that they imitated the early Italian masters at all, but that in their work, as opposed to the facile abstractions of Raphael, they found a stronger realism of imagination, a more careful realism of technique, a vision at once more fervent and more vivid, an individuality more intimate and more intense.

For it is not enough that a work of art should conform to the æsthetic demands of its age: there must be also about it, if it is to affect us with any permanent delight, the impress of a distinct individuality, an individuality remote from that of ordinary men, and coming near to us only by virtue of a certain newness and wonder in the work, and through channels whose very strangeness makes us more ready to give them welcome.

La personalité, said one of the greatest of modern French critics, voilà ce qui nous sauvera.

But above all things was it a return to Nature—that formula which seems to suit so many and such diverse movements: they would draw and paint nothing but what they saw, they would try and imagine things as they really happened. Later there came to the old house by Blackfriars Bridge, where this young brotherhood used to meet and work, two young men from Oxford, Edward Burne-Jones and William Morris—the latter substituting for the simpler realism of the early days a more exquisite spirit of choice, a more faultless devotion to beauty, a more intense seeking for perfection: a master of all exquisite design and of all spiritual vision. It is of the school of Florence rather than of that of Venice that he is kinsman, feeling that the close imitation of Nature is a disturbing element in imaginative art. The visible aspect of modern life disturbs him not; rather is it for him to render eternal all that is beautiful in Greek, Italian, and Celtic legend. To Morris we owe poetry whose perfect precision and clearness of word and vision has not been excelled in the literature of our country, and by the revival of the decorative arts he has given to our individualised romantic movement the social idea and the social factor also.

But the revolution accomplished by this clique of young men, with Ruskin's faultless and fervent eloquence to help them, was not one of ideas merely but of execution, not one of conceptions but of creations.

For the great eras in the history of the development of all the arts have been eras not of increased feeling or enthusiasm in feeling for art, but of new technical improvements primarily and specially. The discovery of marble quarries in the purple ravines of Pentelicus and on the little low-lying hills of the island of Paros gave to the Greeks the opportunity for that intensified vitality of action, that more sensuous and simple humanism, to which the Egyptian sculptor working laboriously in the hard porphyry and rose-coloured granite of the desert could not attain. The splendour of the Venetian school began with the introduction of the new oil medium for painting. The progress in modern music has been due to the invention of new instruments entirely, and in no way to an increased consciousness on the part of the musician of any wider social aim. The critic may try and trace the deferred resolutions of Beethoven {253} to some sense of the incompleteness of the modern intellectual spirit, but the artist would have answered, as one of them did afterwards, 'Let them pick out the fifths and leave us at peace.'

And so it is in poetry also: all this love of curious French metres like the Ballade, the Villanelle, the Rondel; all this increased value laid on elaborate alliterations, and on curious words and refrains, such as you will find in Dante Rossetti and Swinburne, is merely the attempt to perfect flute and viol and trumpet through which the spirit of the age and the lips of the poet may blow the music of their many messages.

And so it has been with this romantic movement of ours: it is a reaction against the empty conventional workmanship, the lax execution of previous poetry and painting, showing itself in the work of such men as Rossetti and Burne-Jones by a far greater splendour of colour, a far more intricate wonder of design than English imaginative art has shown before. In Rossetti's poetry and the poetry of Morris, Swinburne and Tennyson a perfect precision and choice of language, a style flawless and fearless, a seeking for all sweet and precious melodies and a sustaining consciousness of the musical value of each word are opposed to that value which is merely intellectual. In this respect they are one with the romantic movement of France of which not the least characteristic note was struck by Théophile Gautier's advice to the young poet to read his dictionary every day, as being the only book worth a poet's reading.

While, then, the material of workmanship is being thus elaborated and discovered to have in itself incommunicable and eternal qualities of its own, qualities entirely satisfying to the poetic sense and not needing for their æsthetic effect any lofty intellectual vision, any deep criticism of life or even any passionate human emotion at all, the spirit and the method of the poet's working—what people call his inspiration—have not escaped the controlling influence of the artistic spirit. Not that the imagination has lost its wings, but we have accustomed ourselves to count their innumerable pulsations, to estimate their limitless strength, to govern their ungovernable freedom.

To the Greeks this problem of the conditions of poetic production, and the places occupied by either spontaneity or self-consciousness in any artistic work, had a peculiar fascination. We find it in the mysticism of Plato and in the rationalism of Aristotle. We find it later in the Italian Renaissance agitating the minds of such men as Leonardo da Vinci. Schiller tried to adjust the balance between form and feeling, and Goethe to estimate the position of self-consciousness in art. Wordsworth's definition of poetry as 'emotion remembered in tranquillity' may be taken as an analysis of one of the stages through which all imaginative work has to pass; and in Keats's longing to be 'able to compose without this fever' (I quote from one of his letters), his desire to substitute for poetic ardour 'a more thoughtful and quiet power,' we may discern the most important moment in the evolution of that artistic life. The question made an early and strange appearance in your literature too; and I need not remind you how deeply the young poets of the French romantic movement were excited and stirred by Edgar Allan Poe's analysis of the workings of his own imagination in the creating of that supreme imaginative work which we know by the name of The Raven.

In the last century, when the intellectual and didactic element had intruded to such an extent into the kingdom which belongs to poetry, it was against the claims of the understanding that an artist like Goethe had to protest. 'The more incomprehensible to the understanding a poem is the better for it,' he said once, asserting the complete supremacy of the imagination in poetry as of reason in prose. But in this century it is rather against the claims of the emotional faculties, the claims of mere sentiment and feeling, that the artist must react. The simple utterance of joy is not poetry any more than a mere personal cry of pain, and the real experiences of the artist are always those which do not find their direct expression but are gathered up and absorbed into some artistic form which seems, from such real experiences, to be the farthest removed and the most alien.

'The heart contains passion but the imagination alone contains poetry,' says Charles Baudelaire. This too was the lesson that Théophile Gautier, most subtle of all modern critics, most fascinating of all modern poets, was never tired of teaching—'Everybody is affected by a sunrise or a sunset.' The absolute distinction of the artist is not his capacity to feel nature so much as his power of rendering it. The entire subordination of all intellectual and emotional faculties to the vital and informing poetic principle is the surest sign of the strength of our Renaissance.

We have seen the artistic spirit working, first in the delightful and technical sphere of language, the sphere of expression as opposed to subject, then controlling the imagination of the poet in dealing with his subject. And now I would point out to you its operation in the choice of subject. The recognition of a separate realm for the artist, a consciousness of the absolute difference between the world of art and the world of real fact, between classic grace and absolute reality, forms not merely the essential element of any æsthetic charm but is the characteristic of all great imaginative work and of all great eras of artistic creation—of the age of Phidias as of the age of Michael Angelo, of the age of Sophocles as of the age of Goethe.

Art never harms itself by keeping aloof from the social problems of the day: rather, by so doing, it more completely realises for us that which we desire. For to most of us the real life is the life we do not lead, and thus, remaining more true to the essence of its own perfection, more jealous of its own unattainable beauty, is less likely to forget form in feeling or to accept the passion of creation as any substitute for the beauty of the created thing.

The artist is indeed the child of his own age, but the present will not be to him a whit more real than the past; for, like the philosopher of the Platonic vision, the poet is the spectator of all time and of all existence. For him no form is obsolete, no subject out of date; rather, whatever of life and passion the world has known, in desert of Judæa or in Arcadian valley, by the rivers of Troy or the rivers of Damascus, in the crowded and hideous streets of a modern city or by the pleasant ways of Camelot—all lies before him like an open scroll, all is still instinct with beautiful life. He will take of it what is salutary for his own spirit, no more; choosing some facts and rejecting others with the calm artistic control of one who is in possession of the secret of beauty.

There is indeed a poetical attitude to be adopted towards all things, but all things are not fit subjects for poetry. Into the secure and sacred house of Beauty the true artist will admit nothing that is harsh or disturbing, nothing that gives pain, nothing that is debatable, nothing about which men argue. He can steep himself, if he wishes, in the discussion of all the social problems of his day, poor-laws and local taxation, free trade and bimetallic currency, and the like; but when he writes on these subjects it will be, as Milton nobly expressed it, with his left hand, in prose and not in verse, in a pamphlet and not in a lyric. This exquisite spirit of artistic choice was not in Byron: Wordsworth had it not. In the work of both these men there is much that we have to reject, much that does not give us that sense of calm and perfect repose which should be the effect of all fine, imaginative work. But in Keats it seemed to have been incarnate, and in his lovely Ode on a Grecian Urn it found its most secure and faultless expression; in the pageant of The Earthly Paradise and the knights and ladies of Burne-Jones it is the one dominant note.

It is to no avail that the Muse of Poetry be called, even by such a clarion note as Whitman's, to migrate from Greece and Ionia and to placard REMOVED and TO LET on the rocks of the snowy Parnassus. Calliope's call is not yet closed, nor are the epics of Asia ended; the Sphinx is not yet silent, nor the fountain of Castaly dry. For art is very life itself and knows nothing of death; she is absolute truth and takes no care of fact; she sees (as I remember Mr. Swinburne insisting on at dinner) that Achilles is even now more actual and real than Wellington, not merely more noble and interesting as a type and figure but more positive and real.

Literature must rest always on a principle, and temporal considerations are no principle at all. For to the poet all times and places are one; the stuff he deals with is eternal and eternally the same: no theme is inept, no past or present preferable. The steam whistle will not affright him nor the flutes of Arcadia weary him: for him there is but one time, the artistic moment; but one law, the law of form; but one land, the land of Beauty—a land removed indeed from the real world and yet more sensuous because more enduring; calm, yet with that calm which dwells in the faces of the Greek statues, the calm which comes not from the rejection but from the absorption of passion, the calm which despair and sorrow cannot disturb but intensify only. And so it comes that he who seems to stand most remote from his age is he who mirrors it best, because he has stripped life of what is accidental and transitory, stripped it of that 'mist of familiarity which makes life obscure to us.'

Those strange, wild-eyed sibyls fixed eternally in the whirlwind of ecstasy, those mighty-limbed and Titan prophets, labouring with the secret of the earth and the burden of mystery, that guard and glorify the chapel of Pope Sixtus at Rome—do they not tell us more of the real spirit of the Italian Renaissance, of the dream of Savonarola and of the sin of Borgia, than all the brawling boors and cooking women of Dutch art can teach us of the real spirit of the history of Holland?

And so in our own day, also, the two most vital tendencies of the nineteenth century—the democratic and pantheistic tendency and the tendency to value life for the sake of art—found their most complete and perfect utterance in the poetry of Shelley and Keats who, to the blind eyes of their own time, seemed to be as wanderers in the wilderness, preachers of vague or unreal things. And I remember once, in talking to Mr. Burne-Jones about modern science, his saying to me, 'the more materialistic science becomes, the more angels shall I paint: their wings are my protest in favour of the immortality of the soul.'

But these are the intellectual speculations that underlie art. Where in

300

the arts themselves are we to find that breadth of human sympathy which is the condition of all noble work; where in the arts are we to look for what Mazzini would call the social ideas as opposed to the merely personal ideas? By virtue of what claim do I demand for the artist the love and loyalty of the men and women of the world? I think I can answer that.

Whatever spiritual message an artist brings to his aid is a matter for his own soul. He may bring judgment like Michael Angelo or peace like Angelico; he may come with mourning like the great Athenian or with mirth like the singer of Sicily; nor is it for us to do aught but accept his teaching, knowing that we cannot smite the bitter lips of Leopardi into laughter or burden with our discontent Goethe's serene calm. But for warrant of its truth such message must have the flame of eloquence in the lips that speak it, splendour and glory in the vision that is its witness, being justified by one thing only—the flawless beauty and perfect form of its expression: this indeed being the social idea, being the meaning of joy in art.

Not laughter where none should laugh, nor the calling of peace where there is no peace; not in painting the subject ever, but the pictorial charm only, the wonder of its colour, the satisfying beauty of its design.

You have most of you seen, probably, that great masterpiece of Rubens which hangs in the gallery of Brussels, that swift and wonderful pageant of horse and rider arrested in its most exquisite and fiery moment when the winds are caught in crimson banner and the air lit by the gleam of armour and the flash of plume. Well, that is joy in art, though that golden hillside be trodden by the wounded feet of Christ and it is for the death of the Son of Man that that gorgeous cavalcade is passing.

But this restless modern intellectual spirit of ours is not receptive enough of the sensuous element of art; and so the real influence of the arts is hidden from many of us: only a few, escaping from the tyranny of the soul, have learned the secret of those high hours when thought is not.

And this indeed is the reason of the influence which Eastern art is having on us in Europe, and of the fascination of all Japanese work. While the Western world has been laying on art the intolerable burden of its own intellectual doubts and the spiritual tragedy of its own sorrows, the East has always kept true to art's primary and pictorial conditions.

In judging of a beautiful statue the æsthetic faculty is absolutely and completely gratified by the splendid curves of those marble lips that are dumb to our complaint, the noble modelling of those limbs that are powerless to help us. In its primary aspect a painting has no more spiritual message or meaning than an exquisite fragment of Venetian glass or a blue tile from the wall of Damascus: it is a beautifully coloured surface, nothing more. The channels by which all noble imaginative work in painting should touch, and do touch the soul, are not those of the truths of life, nor metaphysical truths. But that pictorial charm which does not depend on any literary reminiscence for its effect on the one hand, nor is yet a mere result of communicable technical skill on the other, comes of a certain inventive and creative handling of colour. Nearly always in Dutch painting and often in the works of Giorgione or Titian, it is entirely independent of anything definitely poetical in the subject, a kind of form and choice in workmanship which is itself entirely satisfying, and is (as the Greeks would say) an end in itself.

And so in poetry too, the real poetical quality, the joy of poetry, comes never from the subject but from an inventive handling of rhythmical language, from what Keats called the 'sensuous life of verse.' The element of song in the singing accompanied by the profound joy of motion, is so sweet that, while the incomplete lives of ordinary men bring no healing power with them, the thorn-crown of the poet will blossom into roses for our pleasure; for our delight his despair will gild its own thorns, and his pain, like Adonis, be beautiful in its agony; and when the poet's heart breaks it will break in music.

And health in art—what is that? It has nothing to do with a sane criticism of life. There is more health in Baudelaire than there is in [Kingsley]. Health is the artist's recognition of the limitations of the form in which he works. It is the honour and the homage which he gives to the material he uses—whether it be language with its glories, or marble or pigment with their glories—knowing that the true brotherhood of the arts consists not in their borrowing one another's method, but in their producing, each of them by its own individual means, each of them by keeping its objective limits, the same unique artistic delight. The delight is like that given to us by music—for music is the art in which form and matter are always one, the art whose subject cannot be separated from the method of its expression, the art which most completely realises the artistic ideal, and is the condition to which all the other arts are constantly aspiring.

And criticism—what place is that to have in our culture? Well, I think that the first duty of an art critic is to hold his tongue at all times, and upon all subjects: C'est une grande avantage de n'avoir rien fait, mais il ne faut pas en abuser.

It is only through the mystery of creation that one can gain any knowledge of the quality of created things. You have listened to Patience for a hundred nights and you have heard me only for one. It will make, no doubt, that satire more piquant by knowing something about the subject of it, but you must not judge of æstheticism by the satire of Mr. Gilbert. As little should you judge of the strength and splendour of sun or sea by the dust that dances in the beam, or the bubble that breaks on the wave, as take your critic for any sane test of art. For the artists, like the Greek gods, are revealed only to one another, as Emerson says somewhere; their real value and place time only can show. In this respect also omnipotence is with the ages. The true critic addresses not the artist ever but the public only. His work lies with them. Art can never have any other claim but her own perfection: it is for the critic to create for art the social aim, too, by teaching the people the spirit in which they are to approach all artistic work, the love they are to give it, the lesson they are to draw from it.

All these appeals to art to set herself more in harmony with modern progress and civilisation, and to make herself the mouthpiece for the voice of humanity, these appeals to art 'to have a mission,' are appeals which should be made to the public. The art which has fulfilled the conditions of beauty has fulfilled all conditions: it is for the critic to teach the people how to find in the calm of such art the highest expression of their own most stormy passions. 'I have no reverence,' said Keats, 'for the public, nor for anything in existence but the Eternal Being, the memory of great men and the principle of Beauty.'

Such then is the principle which I believe to be guiding and underlying our English Renaissance, a Renaissance many-sided and wonderful, productive of strong ambitions and lofty personalities, yet for all its splendid achievements in poetry and in the decorative arts and in painting, for all the increased comeliness and grace of dress, and the furniture of houses and the like, not complete. For there can be no great sculpture without a beautiful national life, and the commercial spirit of England has killed that; no great drama without a noble national life, and the commercial spirit of England has killed that too.

It is not that the flawless serenity of marble cannot bear the burden of the modern intellectual spirit, or become instinct with the fire of romantic passion—the tomb of Duke Lorenzo and the chapel of the Medici show us that—but it is that, as Théophile Gautier used to say, the visible world is dead, le monde visible a disparu.

Nor is it again that the novel has killed the play, as some critics would persuade us—the romantic movement of France shows us that. The work of Balzac and of Hugo grew up side by side together; nay, more, were complementary to each other, though neither of them saw it. While all other forms of poetry may flourish in an ignoble age, the splendid individualism of the lyrist, fed by its own passion, and lit by its own power, may pass as a pillar of fire as well across the desert as across places that are pleasant. It is none the less glorious though no man follow it—nay, by the greater sublimity of its loneliness it may be quickened into loftier utterance and intensified into clearer song. From the mean squalor of the sordid life that limits him, the dreamer or the idyllist may soar on poesy's viewless wings, may traverse with fawn-skin and spear the moonlit heights of Cithæron though Faun and Bassarid dance there no more. Like Keats he may wander through the old-world forests of Latmos, or stand like Morris on the galley's deck with the Viking when king and galley have long since passed away. But the drama is the meeting-place of art and life; it deals, as Mazzini said, not merely with man, but with social man, with man in his relation to God and to Humanity. It is the product of a period of great national united energy; it is impossible without a noble public, and belongs to such ages as the age of Elizabeth in London and of Pericles at Athens; it is part of such lofty moral and spiritual ardour as came to Greek after the defeat of the Persian fleet, and to Englishman after the wreck of the Armada of Spain.

Shelley felt how incomplete our movement was in this respect, and has shown in one great tragedy by what terror and pity he would have purified our age; but in spite of The Cenci the drama is one of the artistic forms through which the genius of the England of this century seeks in vain to find outlet and expression. He has had no worthy imitators.

It is rather, perhaps, to you that we should turn to complete and perfect this great movement of ours, for there is something Hellenic in your air and world, something that has a quicker breath of the joy and power of Elizabeth's England about it than our ancient civilisation can give us. For you, at least, are young; 'no hungry generations tread you down,' and the past does not weary you with the intolerable burden of its memories nor mock you with the ruins of a beauty, the secret of whose creation you have lost. That very absence of tradition, which Mr. Ruskin thought would rob your rivers of their laughter and your flowers of their light, may be rather the source of your freedom and your strength.

To speak in literature with the perfect rectitude and insouciance of the movements of animals, and the unimpeachableness of the sentiment of trees in the woods and grass by the roadside, has been defined by one of your poets as a flawless triumph of art. It is a triumph which you above all nations may be destined to achieve. For the voices that have their dwelling in sea and mountain are not the chosen music of Liberty only; other messages are there in the wonder of wind-swept height and the majesty of silent deep—messages that, if you will but listen to them, may yield you the splendour of some new imagination, the marvel of some new beauty.

'I foresee,' said Goethe, 'the dawn of a new literature which all people may claim as their own, for all have contributed to its foundation.' If, then, this is so, and if the materials for a civilisation as great as that of Europe lie all around you, what profit, you will ask me, will all this study of our poets and painters be to you? I might answer that the intellect can be engaged without direct didactic object on an artistic and historical problem; that the demand of the intellect is merely to feel itself alive; that nothing which has ever interested men or women can cease to be a fit subject for culture.

I might remind you of what all Europe owes to the sorrow of a single Florentine in exile at Verona, or to the love of Petrarch by that little well in Southern France; nay, more, how even in this dull, materialistic age the simple expression of an old man's simple life, passed away from the clamour of great cities amid the lakes and misty hills of Cumberland, has opened out for England treasures of new joy compared with which the treasures of her luxury are as barren as the sea which she has made her highway, and as bitter as the fire which she would make her slave.

But I think it will bring you something besides this, something that is the knowledge of real strength in art: not that you should imitate the works of these men; but their artistic spirit, their artistic attitude, I think you should absorb that.

For in nations, as in individuals, if the passion for creation be not accompanied by the critical, the æsthetic faculty also, it will be sure to waste its strength aimlessly, failing perhaps in the artistic spirit of choice, or in the mistaking of feeling for form, or in the following of false ideals.

For the various spiritual forms of the imagination have a natural affinity with certain sensuous forms of art—and to discern the qualities of each art, to intensify as well its limitations as its powers of expression, is one of the aims that culture sets before us. It is not an increased moral sense, an increased moral supervision that your literature needs. Indeed, one should never talk of a moral or an immoral poem—poems are either well written or badly written, that is all. And, indeed, any element of morals or implied reference to a standard of good or evil in art is often a sign of a certain incompleteness of vision, often a note of discord in the harmony of an imaginative creation; for all good work aims at a purely artistic effect. 'We must be careful,' said Goethe, 'not to be always looking for culture merely in what is obviously moral. Everything that is great promotes civilisation as soon as we are aware of it.'

But, as in your cities so in your literature, it is a permanent canon and standard of taste, an increased sensibility to beauty (if I may say so) that is lacking. All noble work is not national merely, but universal. The political independence of a nation must not be confused with any intellectual isolation. The spiritual freedom, indeed, your own generous lives and liberal air will give you. From us you will learn the classical restraint of form.

For all great art is delicate art, roughness having very little to do with strength, and harshness very little to do with power. 'The artist,' as Mr. Swinburne says, 'must be perfectly articulate.'

This limitation is for the artist perfect freedom: it is at once the origin and the sign of his strength. So that all the supreme masters of style—Dante, Sophocles, Shakespeare—are the supreme masters of spiritual and intellectual vision also.

Love art for its own sake, and then all things that you need will be added to you.

This devotion to beauty and to the creation of beautiful things is the test of all great civilised nations. Philosophy may teach us to bear with equanimity the misfortunes of our neighbours, and science resolve the moral sense into a secretion of sugar, but art is what makes the life of each citizen a sacrament and not a speculation, art is what makes the life of the whole race immortal.

For beauty is the only thing that time cannot harm. Philosophies fall away like sand, and creeds follow one another like the withered leaves of autumn; but what is beautiful is a joy for all seasons and a possession for all eternity.

Wars and the clash of armies and the meeting of men in battle by trampled field or leagured city, and the rising of nations there must always be. But I think that art, by creating a common intellectual atmosphere between all countries, might—if it could not overshadow the world with the silver wings of peace—at least make men such brothers that they would not go out to slay one another for the whim or folly of some king or minister, as they do in Europe. Fraternity would come no more with the hands of Cain, nor Liberty betray freedom with the kiss of Anarchy; for national hatreds are always strongest where culture is lowest.

'How could I?' said Goethe, when reproached for not writing like Korner against the French. 'How could I, to whom barbarism and culture alone are of importance, hate a nation which is among the most cultivated of the earth, a nation to which I owe a great part of my own cultivation?'

Mighty empires, too, there must always be as long as personal ambition and the spirit of the age are one, but art at least is the only empire which a nation's enemies cannot take from her by conquest, but which is taken by submission only. The sovereignty of Greece and Rome is not yet passed away, though the gods of the one be dead and the eagles of the other tired.

And we in our Renaissance are seeking to create a sovereignty that will still be England's when her yellow leopards have grown weary of wars and the rose of her shield is crimsoned no more with the blood of battle; and you, too, absorbing into the generous heart of a great people this pervading artistic spirit, will create for yourselves such riches as you have never yet created, though your land be a network of railways and your cities the harbours for the galleys of the world.

I know, indeed, that the divine natural prescience of beauty which is the inalienable inheritance of Greek and Italian is not our inheritance. For such an informing and presiding spirit of art to shield us from all harsh and alien influences, we of the Northern races must turn rather to that strained self-consciousness of our age which, as it is the key-note of all our romantic art, must be the source of all or nearly all our culture. I mean that intellectual curiosity of the nineteenth century which is always looking for the secret of the life that still lingers round old and bygone forms of culture. It takes from each what is serviceable for the modern spirit—from Athens its wonder without its worship, from Venice its splendour without its sin. The same spirit is always analysing its own strength and its own weakness, counting what it owes to East and to West, to the olive-trees of Colonus and to the palm-trees of Lebanon, to Gethsemane and to the garden of Proserpine.

And yet the truths of art cannot be taught: they are revealed only, revealed to natures which have made themselves receptive of all beautiful impressions by the study and worship of all beautiful things. And hence the enormous importance given to the decorative arts in our English Renaissance; hence all that marvel of design that comes from the hand of Edward Burne-Jones, all that weaving of tapestry and staining of glass, that beautiful working in clay and metal and wood which we owe to William Morris, the greatest handicraftsman we have had in England since the fourteenth century.

So, in years to come there will be nothing in any man's house which has not given delight to its maker and does not give delight to its user. The children, like the children of Plato's perfect city, will grow up 'in a simple atmosphere of all fair things'—I quote from the passage in the Republic—'a simple atmosphere of all fair things, where beauty, which is the spirit of art, will come on eye and ear like a fresh breath of wind that brings health from a clear upland, and insensibly and gradually draw the child's soul into harmony with all knowledge and all wisdom, so that he will love what is beautiful and good, and hate what is evil and ugly (for they always go together) long before he knows the reason why; and then when reason comes will kiss her on the cheek as a friend.'

That is what Plato thought decorative art could do for a nation, feeling that the secret not of philosophy merely but of all gracious existence might be externally hidden from any one whose youth had been passed in uncomely and vulgar surroundings, and that the beauty of form and colour even, as he says, in the meanest vessels of the house, will find its way into the inmost places of the soul and lead the boy naturally to look for that divine harmony of spiritual life of which art was to him the material symbol and warrant.

Prelude indeed to all knowledge and all wisdom will this love of beautiful things be for us; yet there are times when wisdom becomes a burden and knowledge is one with sorrow: for as every body has its shadow so every soul has its scepticism. In such dread moments of discord and despair where should we, of this torn and troubled age, turn our steps if not to that secure house of beauty where there is always a little forgetfulness, always a great joy; to that città divina, as the old Italian heresy called it, the divine city where one can stand, though only for a brief moment, apart from the division and terror of the world and the choice of the world too?

This is that consolation des arts which is the keynote of Gautier's poetry, the secret of modern life foreshadowed—as indeed what in our century is not?—by Goethe. You remember what he said to the German people: 'Only have the courage,' he said, 'to give yourselves up to your impressions, allow yourselves to be delighted, moved, elevated, nay instructed, inspired for something great.' The courage to give yourselves up to your impressions: yes, that is the secret of the artistic life—for while art has been defined as an escape from the tyranny of the senses, it is an escape rather from the tyranny of the soul. But only to those who worship her above all things does she ever reveal her true treasure: else will she be as powerless to aid you as the mutilated Venus of the Louvre was before the romantic but sceptical nature of Heine.

And indeed I think it would be impossible to overrate the gain that might follow if we had about us only what gave pleasure to the maker of it and gives pleasure to its user, that being the simplest of all rules about decoration. One thing, at least, I think it would do for us: there is no surer test of a great country than how near it stands to its own poets; but between the singers of our day and the workers to whom they would sing there seems to be an ever-widening and dividing chasm, a chasm which slander and mockery cannot traverse, but which is spanned by the luminous wings of love.

And of such love I think that the abiding presence in our houses of noble imaginative work would be the surest seed and preparation. I do not mean merely as regards that direct literary expression of art by which, from the little red-and-black cruse of oil or wine, a Greek boy could learn of the lionlike splendour of Achilles, of the strength of Hector and the beauty of Paris and the wonder of Helen, long before he stood and listened in crowded market-place or in theatre of marble; or by which an Italian child of the fifteenth century could know of the chastity of Lucrece and the death of Camilla from carven doorway and from painted chest. For the good we get from art is not what we learn from it; it is what we become through it. Its real influence will be in giving the mind that enthusiasm which is the secret of Hellenism, accustoming it to demand from art all that art can do in rearranging the facts of common life for us—whether it be by giving the most spiritual interpretation of one's own moments of highest passion or the most sensuous expression of those thoughts that are the farthest removed from sense; in accustoming it to love the things of the imagination for their own sake, and to desire beauty and grace in all things. For he who does not love art in all things does not love it at all, and he who does not need art in all things does not need it at all.

I will not dwell here on what I am sure has delighted you all in our great Gothic cathedrals. I mean how the artist of that time, handicraftsman himself in stone or glass, found the best motives for his art, always ready for his hand and always beautiful, in the daily work of the artificers he saw around him—as in those lovely windows of Chartres—where the dyer dips in the vat and the potter sits at the wheel, and the weaver stands at the loom: real manufacturers these, workers with the hand, and entirely delightful to look at, not like the smug and vapid shopman of our time, who knows nothing of the web or vase he sells, except that he is charging you double its value and thinking you a fool for buying it. Nor can I but just note, in passing, the immense influence the decorative work of Greece and Italy had on its artists, the one teaching the sculptor that restraining influence of design which is the glory of the Parthenon, the other keeping painting always true to its primary, pictorial condition of noble colour which is the secret of the school of Venice; for I wish rather, in this lecture at least, to dwell on the effect that decorative art has on human life—on its social not its purely artistic effect.

There are two kinds of men in the world, two great creeds, two different forms of natures: men to whom the end of life is action, and men to whom the end of life is thought. As regards the latter, who seek for experience itself and not for the fruits of experience, who must burn always with one of the passions of this fiery-coloured world, who find life interesting not for its secret but for its situations, for its pulsations and not for its purpose; the passion for beauty engendered by the decorative arts will be to them more satisfying than any political or religious enthusiasm, any enthusiasm for humanity, any ecstasy or sorrow for love. For art comes to one professing primarily to give nothing but the highest quality to one's moments, and for those moments' sake. So far for those to whom the end of life is thought.

As regards the others, who hold that life is inseparable from labour, to them should this movement be specially dear: for, if our days are barren without industry, industry without art is barbarism.

Hewers of wood and drawers of water there must be always indeed among us. Our modern machinery has not much lightened the labour of man after all: but at least let the pitcher that stands by the well be beautiful and surely the labour of the day will be lightened: let the wood be made receptive of some lovely form, some gracious design, and there will come no longer discontent but joy to the toiler. For what is decoration but the worker's expression of joy in his work? And not joy merely—that is a great thing yet not enough—but that opportunity of expressing his own individuality which, as it is the essence of all life, is the source of all art. 'I have tried,' I remember William Morris saying to me once, 'I have tried to make each of my workers an artist, and when I say an artist I mean a man.' For the worker then, handicraftsman of whatever kind he is, art is no longer to be a purple robe woven by a slave and thrown over the whitened body of a leprous king to hide and to adorn the sin of his luxury, but rather the beautiful and noble expression of a life that has in it something beautiful and noble.

And so you must seek out your workman and give him, as far as possible, the right surroundings, for remember that the real test and virtue of a workman is not his earnestness nor his industry even, but his power of design merely; and that 'design is not the offspring of idle fancy: it is the studied result of accumulative observation and delightful habit.' All the teaching in the world is of no avail if you do not surround your workman with happy influences and with beautiful things. It is impossible for him to have right ideas about colour unless he sees the lovely colours of Nature unspoiled; impossible for him to supply beautiful incident and action unless he sees beautiful incident and action in the world about him.

For to cultivate sympathy you must be among living things and thinking about them, and to cultivate admiration you must be among beautiful things and looking at them. 'The steel of Toledo and the silk of Genoa did but give strength to oppression and lustre to pride,' as Mr. Ruskin says; let it be for you to create an art that is made by the hands of the people for the joy of the people, to please the hearts of the people, too; an art that will be your expression of your delight in life. There is nothing 'in common life too mean, in common things too trivial to be ennobled by your touch'; nothing in life that art cannot sanctify.

You have heard, I think, a few of you, of two flowers connected with the æsthetic movement in England, and said (I assure you, erroneously) to be the food of some æsthetic young men. Well, let me tell you that the reason we love the lily and the sunflower, in spite of what Mr. Gilbert may tell you, is not for any vegetable fashion at all. It is because these two lovely flowers are in England the two most perfect models of design, the most naturally adapted for decorative art—the gaudy leonine beauty of the one and the precious loveliness of the other giving to the artist the most entire and perfect joy. And so with you: let there be no flower in your meadows that does not wreathe its tendrils around your pillows, no little leaf in your Titan forests that does not lend its form to design, no curving spray of wild rose or brier that does not live for ever in carven arch or window or marble, no bird in your air that is not giving the iridescent wonder of its colour, the exquisite curves of its wings in flight, to make more precious the preciousness of simple adornment. For the voices that have their dwelling in sea and mountain are not the chosen music of liberty only. Other messages are there in the wonder of wind-swept heights and the majesty of silent deep—messages that, if you will listen to them, will give you the wonder of all new imagination, the treasure of all new beauty.

We spend our days, each one of us, in looking for the secret of life. Well, the secret of life is in art.

HOUSE DECORATION

A lecture delivered in America during Wilde's tour in 1882. It was announced as a lecture on 'The Practical Application of the Principles of the Æsthetic Theory to Exterior and Interior House Decoration, With Observations upon Dress and Personal Ornaments.' The earliest date on which it is known to have been given is May 11, 1882.

In my last lecture I gave you something of the history of Art in England. I sought to trace the influence of the French Revolution upon its development. I said something of the song of Keats and the school of the pre-Raphaelites. But I do not want to shelter the movement, which I have called the English Renaissance, under any palladium however noble, or any name however revered. The roots of it have, indeed, to be sought for in things that have long passed away, and not, as some suppose, in the fancy of a few young men—although I am not altogether sure that there is anything much better than the fancy of a few young men.

When I appeared before you on a previous occasion, I had seen nothing of American art save the Doric columns and Corinthian chimney-pots visible on your Broadway and Fifth Avenue. Since then, I have been through your country to some fifty or sixty different cities, I think. I find that what your people need is not so much high imaginative art but that which hallows the vessels of everyday use. I suppose that the poet will sing and the artist will paint regardless whether the world praises or blames. He has his own world and is independent of his fellow-men. But the handicraftsman is dependent on your pleasure and opinion. He needs your encouragement and he must have beautiful surroundings. Your people love art but do not sufficiently honour the handicraftsman. Of course, those millionaires who can pillage Europe for their pleasure need have no care to encourage such; but I speak for those whose desire for beautiful things is larger than their means. I find that one great trouble all over is that your workmen are not given to noble designs. You cannot be indifferent to this, because Art is not something which you can take or leave. It is a necessity of human life.

And what is the meaning of this beautiful decoration which we call art? In the first place, it means value to the workman and it means the pleasure which he must necessarily take in making a beautiful thing. The mark of all good art is not that the thing done is done exactly or finely, for machinery may do as much, but that it is worked out with the head and the workman's heart. I cannot impress the point too frequently that beautiful and rational designs are necessary in all work. I did not imagine, until I went into some of your simpler cities, that there was so much bad work done. I found, where I went, bad wall-papers horribly designed, and coloured carpets, and that old offender the horse-hair sofa, whose stolid look of indifference is always so depressing. I found meaningless chandeliers and machine-made furniture, generally of rosewood, which creaked dismally under the weight of the ubiquitous interviewer. I came across the small iron stove which they always persist in decorating with machine-made ornaments, and which is as great a bore as a wet day or any other particularly dreadful institution. When unusual extravagance was indulged in, it was garnished with two funeral urns.

It must always be remembered that what is well and carefully made by an honest workman, after a rational design, increases in beauty and value as the years go on. The old furniture brought over by the Pilgrims, two hundred years ago, which I saw in New England, is just as good and as beautiful today as it was when it first came here. Now, what you must do is to bring artists and handicraftsmen together. Handicraftsmen cannot live, certainly cannot thrive, without such companionship. Separate these two and you rob art of all spiritual motive.

Having done this, you must place your workman in the midst of beautiful surroundings. The artist is not dependent on the visible and the tangible. He has his visions and his dreams to feed on. But the workman must see lovely forms as he goes to his work in the morning and returns at eventide. And, in connection with this, I want to assure you that noble and beautiful designs are never the result of idle fancy or purposeless day-dreaming. They come only as the accumulation of habits of long and delightful observation. And yet such things may not be taught. Right ideas concerning them can

315

certainly be obtained only by those who have been accustomed to rooms that are beautiful and colours that are satisfying.

Perhaps one of the most difficult things for us to do is to choose a notable and joyous dress for men. There would be more joy in life if we were to accustom ourselves to use all the beautiful colours we can in fashioning our own clothes. The dress of the future, I think, will use drapery to a great extent and will abound with joyous colour. At present we have lost all nobility of dress and, in doing so, have almost annihilated the modern sculptor. And, in looking around at the figures which adorn our parks, one could almost wish that we had completely killed the noble art. To see the frockcoat of the drawing-room done in bronze, or the double waistcoat perpetuated in marble, adds a new horror to death. But indeed, in looking through the history of costume, seeking an answer to the questions we have propounded, there is little that is either beautiful or appropriate. One of the earliest forms is the Greek drapery which is so exquisite for young girls. And then, I think we may be pardoned a little enthusiasm over the dress of the time of Charles I., so beautiful indeed, that in spite of its invention being with the Cavaliers it was copied by the Puritans. And the dress for the children of that time must not be passed over. It was a very golden age of the little ones. I do not think that they have ever looked so lovely as they do in the pictures of that time. The dress of the last century in England is also peculiarly gracious and graceful. There is nothing bizarre or strange about it, but it is full of harmony and beauty. In these days, when we have suffered so dreadfully from the incursions of the modern milliner, we hear ladies boast that they do not wear a dress more than once. In the old days, when the dresses were decorated with beautiful designs and worked with exquisite embroidery, ladies rather took a pride in bringing out the garment and wearing it many times and handing it down to their daughters—a process that would, I think, be quite appreciated by a modern husband when called upon to settle his wife's bills.

And how shall men dress? Men say that they do not particularly care how they dress, and that it is little matter. I am bound to reply that I do not think that you do. In all my journeys through the country, the only well-dressed men that I saw—and in saying this I earnestly deprecate the polished indignation of your Fifth Avenue dandies—were the Western miners. Their wide-brimmed hats, which shaded their faces from the sun and protected them from the rain, and the cloak, which is by far the most beautiful piece of drapery ever invented, may well be dwelt on with admiration. Their high boots, too, were sensible and practical. They wore only what was comfortable, and therefore beautiful. As I looked at them I could not help thinking with regret of the time when these picturesque miners would have made their fortunes and would go East to assume again all the abominations of modern fashionable attire. Indeed, so concerned was I that I made some of them promise that when they again appeared in the more crowded scenes of Eastern civilisation they would still continue to wear their lovely costume. But I do not believe they will.

Now, what America wants today is a school of rational art. Bad art is a great deal worse than no art at all. You must show your workmen specimens of good work so that they come to know what is simple and true and beautiful. To that end I would have you have a museum attached to these schools—not one of those dreadful modern institutions where there is a stuffed and very dusty giraffe, and a case or two of fossils, but a place where there are gathered examples of art decoration from various periods and countries. Such a place is the South Kensington Museum in London whereon we build greater hopes for the future than on any other one thing. There I go every Saturday night, when the museum is open later than usual, to see the handicraftsman, the wood-worker, the glass-blower and the worker in metals. And it is here that the man of refinement and culture comes face to face with the workman who ministers to his joy. He comes to know more of the nobility of the workman, and the workman, feeling the appreciation, comes to know more of the nobility of his work.

You have too many white walls. More colour is wanted. You should have such men as Whistler among you to teach you the beauty and joy of colour. Take Mr. Whistler's 'Symphony in White,' which you no doubt have imagined to be something quite bizarre. It is nothing of the sort. Think of a cool grey sky flecked here and there with white clouds, a grey ocean and three wonderfully beautiful figures robed in white, leaning over the water and dropping white flowers from their fingers. Here is no extensive intellectual scheme to trouble you, and no metaphysics of which we have had quite enough in art. But if the simple and unaided colour strike the right keynote, the whole conception is made clear. I regard Mr. Whistler's famous Peacock Room as the finest thing in colour and art decoration which the world has known since Correggio painted that wonderful room in Italy where the little children are dancing on the walls. Mr. Whistler finished another room just before I came away—a breakfast room in blue and yellow. The ceiling was a light blue, the cabinet-work and the furniture were of a yellow wood, the curtains at the windows were white and worked in yellow, and when the table was set for breakfast with dainty blue china nothing can be conceived at once so simple and so joyous.

The fault which I have observed in most of your rooms is that there is apparent no definite scheme of colour. Everything is not attuned to a keynote as it should be. The apartments are crowded with pretty things which have no relation to one another. Again, your artists must decorate what is more simply useful. In your art schools I found no attempt to decorate such things as the vessels for water. I know of nothing uglier than the ordinary jug or pitcher. A museum could be filled with the different kinds of water vessels which are used in hot countries. Yet we continue to submit to the depressing jug with the handle all on one side. I do not see the wisdom of decorating dinner-plates with sunsets and soup-plates with moonlight scenes. I do not think it adds anything to the pleasure of the canvas-back duck to take it out of such glories. Besides, we do not want a soup-plate whose bottom seems to vanish in the distance. One feels neither safe nor comfortable under such conditions. In fact, I did not find in the art schools of the country that the difference was explained between decorative and imaginative art.

The conditions of art should be simple. A great deal more depends upon the heart than upon the head. Appreciation of art is not secured by any elaborate scheme of learning. Art requires a good healthy atmosphere. The motives for art are still around about us as they were round about the ancients. And the subjects are also easily found by the earnest sculptor and the painter. Nothing is more picturesque and graceful than a man at work.

318

The artist who goes to the children's playground, watches them at their sport and sees the boy stop to tie his shoe, will find the same themes that engaged the attention of the ancient Greeks, and such observation and the illustrations which follow will do much to correct that foolish impression that mental and physical beauty are always divorced.

To you, more than perhaps to any other country, has Nature been generous in furnishing material for art workers to work in. You have marble quarries where the stone is more beautiful in colour than any the Greeks ever had for their beautiful work, and yet day after day I am confronted with the great building of some stupid man who has used the beautiful material as if it were not precious almost beyond speech. Marble should not be used save by noble workmen. There is nothing which gave me a greater sense of barrenness in travelling through the country than the entire absence of wood carving on your houses. Wood carving is the simplest of the decorative arts. In Switzerland the little barefooted boy beautifies the porch of his father's house with examples of skill in this direction. Why should not American boys do a great deal more and better than Swiss boys?

There is nothing to my mind more coarse in conception and more vulgar in execution than modern jewellery. This is something that can easily be corrected. Something better should be made out of the beautiful gold which is stored up in your mountain hollows and strewn along your river beds. When I was at Leadville and reflected that all the shining silver that I saw coming from the mines would be made into ugly dollars, it made me sad. It should be made into something more permanent. The golden gates at Florence are as beautiful today as when Michael Angelo saw them.

We should see more of the workman than we do. We should not be content to have the salesman stand between us—the salesman who knows nothing of what he is selling save that he is charging a great deal too much for it. And watching the workman will teach that most important lesson—the nobility of all rational workmanship.

I said in my last lecture that art would create a new brotherhood among men by furnishing a universal language. I said that under its beneficent influences war might pass away. Thinking this, what place can I ascribe to art in our education? If children grow up among all fair and lovely things, they will grow to love beauty and detest ugliness before they know the reason why. If you go into a house where everything is coarse, you find things chipped and broken and unsightly. Nobody exercises any care. If everything is dainty and delicate, gentleness and refinement of manner are unconsciously acquired. When I was in San Francisco I used to visit the Chinese Quarter frequently. There I used to watch a great hulking Chinese workman at his task of digging, and used to see him every day drink his tea from a little cup as delicate in texture as the petal of a flower, whereas in all the grand hotels of the land, where thousands of dollars have been lavished on great gilt mirrors and gaudy columns, I have been given my coffee or my chocolate in cups an inch and a quarter thick. I think I have deserved something nicer.

The art systems of the past have been devised by philosophers who looked upon human beings as obstructions. They have tried to educate boys' minds before they had any. How much better it would be in these early years to teach children to use their hands in the rational service of mankind. I would have a workshop attached to every school, and one hour a day given up to the teaching of simple decorative arts. It would be a golden hour to the children. And you would soon raise up a race of handicraftsmen who would transform the face of your country. I have seen only one such school in the United States, and this was in Philadelphia and was founded by my friend Mr. Leyland. I stopped there yesterday and have brought some of the work here this afternoon to show you. Here are two discs of beaten brass: the designs on them are beautiful, the workmanship is simple, and the entire result is satisfactory. The work was done by a little boy twelve years old. This is a wooden bowl decorated by a little girl of thirteen. The design is lovely and the colouring delicate and pretty. Here you see a piece of beautiful wood carving accomplished by a little boy of nine. In such work as this, children learn sincerity in art. They learn to abhor the liar in art—the man who paints wood to look like iron, or iron to look like stone. It is a practical school of morals. No better way is there to learn to love Nature than to understand Art. It dignifies every flower of the field. And, the boy who sees the thing of beauty which a bird on the wing becomes when transferred to wood or canvas will probably not throw the customary stone. What we want is something spiritual added to life. Nothing is so ignoble that Art cannot sanctify it.

ART AND THE HANDICRAFTSMAN

The fragments of which this lecture is composed are taken entirely from the original manuscripts which have but recently been discovered. It is not certain that they all belong to the same lecture, nor that all were written at the same period. Some portions were written in Philadelphia in 1882.

People often talk as if there was an opposition between what is beautiful and what is useful. There is no opposition to beauty except ugliness: all things are either beautiful or ugly, and utility will be always on the side of the beautiful thing, because beautiful decoration is always on the side of the beautiful thing, because beautiful decoration is always an expression of the use you put a thing to and the value placed on it. No workman will beautifully decorate bad work, nor can you possibly get good handicraftsmen or workmen without having beautiful designs. You should be quite sure of that. If you have poor and worthless designs in any craft or trade you will get poor and worthless workmen only, but the minute you have noble and beautiful designs, then you get men of power and intellect and feeling to work for you. By having good designs you have workmen who work not merely with their hands but with their hearts and heads too; otherwise you will get merely the fool or the loafer to work for you.

That the beauty of life is a thing of no moment, I suppose few people would venture to assert. And yet most civilised people act as if it were of none, and in so doing are wronging both themselves and those that are to come after them. For that beauty which is meant by art is no mere accident of human life which people can take or leave, but a positive necessity of life if we are to live as nature meant us to, that is to say unless we are content to be less than men.

Do not think that the commercial spirit which is the basis of your life and cities here is opposed to art. Who built the beautiful cities of the world but commercial men and commercial men only? Genoa built by its traders, Florence by its bankers, and Venice, most lovely of all, by its noble and honest merchants.

I do not wish you, remember, 'to build a new Pisa,' nor to bring 'the life or the decorations of the thirteenth century back again.' 'The circumstances with which you must surround your workmen are those' of modern American life, 'because the designs you have now to ask for from your workmen are such as will make modern' American 'life beautiful.' The art we want is the art based on all the inventions of modern civilisation, and to suit all the needs of nineteenth century life.

Do you think, for instance, that we object to machinery? I tell you we reverence it; we reverence it when it does its proper work, when it relieves man from ignoble and soulless labour, not when it seeks to do that which is valuable only when wrought by the hands and hearts of men. Let us have no machine-made ornament at all; it is all bad and worthless and ugly. And let us not mistake the means of civilisation for the end of civilisation; steam-engine, telephone and the like, are all wonderful, but remember that their value depends entirely on the noble uses we make of them, on the noble spirit in which we employ them, not on the things themselves.

It is, no doubt, a great advantage to talk to a man at the Antipodes through a telephone; its advantage depends entirely on the value of what the two men have to say to one another. If one merely shrieks slander through a tube and the other whispers folly into a wire, do not think that anybody is very much benefited by the invention.

The train that whirls an ordinary Englishman through Italy at the rate of forty miles an hour and finally sends him home without any memory of that lovely country but that he was cheated by a courier at Rome, or that he got a bad dinner at Verona, does not do him or civilisation much good. But that swift legion of fiery-footed engines that bore to the burning ruins of Chicago the loving help and generous treasure of the world was as noble and as beautiful as any golden troop of angels that ever fed the hungry and clothed the naked in the antique times. As beautiful, yes; all machinery may be beautiful when it is undecorated even. Do not seek to decorate it. We cannot but think all good machinery is graceful, also, the line of strength and

322

the line of beauty being one.

Give then, as I said, to your workmen of today the bright and noble surroundings that you can yourself create. Stately and simple architecture for your cities, bright and simple dress for your men and women; those are the conditions of a real artistic movement. For the artist is not concerned primarily with any theory of life but with life itself, with the joy and loveliness that should come daily on eye and ear for a beautiful external world.

But the simplicity must not be barrenness nor the bright colour gaudy. For all beautiful colours are graduated colours, the colours that seem about to pass into one another's realm—colour without tone being like music without harmony, mere discord. Barren architecture, the vulgar and glaring advertisements that desecrate not merely your cities but every rock and river that I have seen yet in America—all this is not enough. A school of design we must have too in each city. It should be a stately and noble building, full of the best examples of the best art of the world. Furthermore, do not put your designers in a barren whitewashed room and bid them work in that depressing and colourless atmosphere as I have seen many of the American schools of design, but give them beautiful surroundings. Because you want to produce a permanent canon and standard of taste in your workman, he must have always by him and before him specimens of the best decorative art of the world, so that you can say to him: 'This is good work. Greek or Italian or Japanese wrought it so many years ago, but it is eternally young because eternally beautiful.' Work in this spirit and you will be sure to be right. Do not copy it, but work with the same love, the same reverence, the same freedom of imagination. You must teach him colour and design, how all beautiful colours are graduated colours and glaring colours the essence of vulgarity. Show him the quality of any beautiful work of nature like the rose, or any beautiful work of art like an Eastern carpet—being merely the exquisite graduation of colour, one tone answering another like the answering chords of a symphony. Teach him how the true designer is not he who makes the design and then colours it, but he who designs in colour, creates in colour, thinks in colour too. Show him how the most gorgeous stained glass windows of Europe are filled with white glass, and the most gorgeous Eastern tapestry with toned colours—the primary colours in both places being set in the white glass, and the tone colours like brilliant jewels set in dusky gold. And then as regards design, show him how the real designer will take first any given limited space, little disk of silver, it may be, like a Greek coin, or wide expanse of fretted ceiling or lordly wall as Tintoret chose at Venice (it does not matter which), and to this limited space—the first condition of decoration being the limitation of the size of the material used—he will give the effect of its being filled with beautiful decoration, filled with it as a golden cup will be filled with wine, so complete that you should not be able to take away anything from it or add anything to it. For from a good piece of design you can take away nothing, nor can you add anything to it, each little bit of design being as absolutely necessary and as vitally important to the whole effect as a note or chord of music is for a sonata of Beethoven.

But I said the effect of its being so filled, because this, again, is of the essence of good design. With a simple spray of leaves and a bird in flight a Japanese artist will give you the impression that he has completely covered with lovely design the reed fan or lacquer cabinet at which he is working, merely because he knows the exact spot in which to place them. All good design depends on the texture of the utensil used and the use you wish to put it to. One of the first things I saw in an American school of design was a young lady painting a romantic moonlight landscape on a large round dish, and another young lady covering a set of dinner plates with a series of sunsets of the most remarkable colours. Let your ladies paint moonlight landscapes and sunsets, but do not let them paint them on dinner plates or dishes. Let them take canvas or paper for such work, but not clay or china. They are merely painting the wrong subjects on the wrong material, that is all. They have not been taught that every material and texture has certain qualities of its own. The design suitable for one is quite wrong for the other, just as the design which you should work on a flat table-cover ought to be quite different from the design you would work on a curtain, for the one will always be straight, the other broken into folds; and the use too one puts the object to should guide one in the choice of design. One does not want to eat one's terrapins off a romantic moonlight nor one's clams off a harrowing sunset. Glory of sun and moon, let them be wrought for us by our landscape artist and be on the walls of the rooms we sit in to remind us of the undying beauty of the sunsets that fade and die, but do not let us eat our soup off them and send them down to the kitchen twice a day to be washed and scrubbed by the handmaid.

All these things are simple enough, yet nearly always forgotten. Your school of design here will teach your girls and your boys, your handicraftsmen of the future (for all your schools of art should be local schools, the schools of particular cities). We talk of the Italian school of painting, but there is no Italian school; there were the schools of each city. Every town in Italy, from Venice itself, queen of the sea, to the little hill fortress of Perugia, each had its own school of art, each different and all beautiful.

So do not mind what art Philadelphia or New York is having, but make by the hands of your own citizens beautiful art for the joy of your own citizens, for you have here the primary elements of a great artistic movement.

For, believe me, the conditions of art are much simpler than people imagine. For the noblest art one requires a clear healthy atmosphere, not polluted as the air of our English cities is by the smoke and grime and horridness which comes from open furnace and from factory chimney. You must have strong, sane, healthy physique among your men and women. Sickly or idle or melancholy people do not do much in art. And lastly, you require a sense of individualism about each man and woman, for this is the essence of art—a desire on the part of man to express himself in the noblest way possible. And this is the reason that the grandest art of the world always came from a republic, Athens, Venice, and Florence—there were no kings there and so their art was as noble and simple as sincere. But if you want to know what kind of art the folly of kings will impose on a country look at the decorative art of France under the grand monarch, under Louis the Fourteenth; the gaudy gilt furniture writhing under a sense of its own horror and ugliness, with a nymph smirking at every angle and a dragon mouthing on every claw. Unreal and monstrous art this, and fit only for such periwigged pomposities as the nobility of France at that time, but not at all fit for you or me. We do not want the rich to possess more beautiful things but the poor to create more beautiful things; for every man is poor who cannot create.

Nor shall the art which you and I need be merely a purple robe woven by a slave and thrown over the whitened body of some leprous king to adorn or to conceal the sin of his luxury, but rather shall it be the noble and beautiful expression of a people's noble and beautiful life. Art shall be again the most glorious of all the chords through which the spirit of a great nation finds its noblest utterance.

All around you, I said, lie the conditions for a great artistic movement for every great art. Let us think of one of them; a sculptor, for instance.

If a modern sculptor were to come and say, 'Very well, but where can one find subjects for sculpture out of men who wear frock-coats and chimney-pot hats?' I would tell him to go to the docks of a great city and watch the men loading or unloading the stately ships, working at wheel or windlass, hauling at rope or gangway. I have never watched a man do anything useful who has not been graceful at some moment of his labour; it is only the loafer and the idle saunterer who is as useless and uninteresting to the artist as he is to himself. I would ask the sculptor to go with me to any of your schools or universities, to the running ground and gymnasium, to watch the young men start for a race, hurling quoit or club, kneeling to tie their shoes before leaping, stepping from the boat or bending to the oar, and to carve them; and when he was weary of cities I would ask him to come to your fields and meadows to watch the reaper with his sickle and the cattle driver with lifted lasso. For if a man cannot find the noblest motives for his art in such simple daily things as a woman drawing water from the well or a man leaning with his scythe, he will not find them anywhere at all. Gods and goddesses the Greek carved because he loved them; saint and king the Goth because he believed in them. But you, you do not care much for Greek gods and goddesses, and you are perfectly and entirely right; and you do not think much of kings either, and you are quite right. But what you do love are your own men and women, your own flowers and fields, your own hills and mountains, and these are what your art should represent to you.

Ours has been the first movement which has brought the handicraftsman and the artist together, for remember that by separating the one from the other you do ruin to both; you rob the one of all spiritual motive and all imaginative joy, you isolate the other from all real technical perfection. The two greatest schools of art in the world, the sculptor at Athens and the school of painting at Venice, had their origin entirely in a long succession of simple and earnest handicraftsmen. It was the Greek potter who taught the sculptor that restraining influence of design which was the glory of the Parthenon; it was the Italian decorator of chests and household goods who kept Venetian painting always true to its primary pictorial condition of noble colour. For we should remember that all the arts are fine arts and all the arts decorative arts. The greatest triumph of Italian painting was the decoration of a pope's chapel in Rome and the wall of a room in Venice. Michael Angelo wrought the one, and Tintoret, the dyer's son, the other. And the little 'Dutch landscape, which you put over your sideboard today, and between the windows tomorrow, is' no less a glorious 'piece of work than the extents of field and forest with which Benozzo has made green and beautiful the once melancholy arcade of the Campo Santo at Pisa,' as Ruskin says.

Do not imitate the works of a nation, Greek or Japanese, Italian or English; but their artistic spirit of design and their artistic attitude today, their own world, you should absorb but imitate never, copy never. Unless you can make as beautiful a design in painted china or embroidered screen or beaten brass out of your American turkey as the Japanese does out of his grey silver-winged stork, you will never do anything. Let the Greek carve his lions and the Goth his dragons: buffalo and wild deer are the animals for you.

Golden rod and aster and rose and all the flowers that cover your valleys in the spring and your hills in the autumn: let them be the flowers for your art. Not merely has Nature given you the noblest motives for a new school of decoration, but to you above all other countries has she given the utensils to work in.

You have quarries of marble richer than Pantelicus, more varied than Paros, but do not build a great white square house of marble and think that it is beautiful, or that you are using marble nobly. If you build in marble you must either carve it into joyous decoration, like the lives of dancing children that adorn the marble castles of the Loire, or fill it with beautiful sculpture, frieze and pediment, as the Greeks did, or inlay it with other coloured marbles as they did in Venice. Otherwise you had better build in simple red brick as your Puritan fathers, with no pretence and with some beauty. Do not treat your marble as if it was ordinary stone and build a house of mere blocks of it. For it is indeed a precious stone, this marble of yours, and only workmen of nobility of invention and delicacy of hand should be allowed to touch it at all, carving it into noble statues or into beautiful decoration, or inlaying it with other coloured marbles: for the true colours of architecture are those of natural stone, and I would fain see them taken advantage of to the full. Every variety is here, from pale yellow to purple passing through orange, red and brown, entirely at your command; nearly every kind of green and grey also is attainable, and with these and with pure white what harmony might you not achieve. Of stained and variegated stone the quantity is unlimited, the kinds innumerable. Were brighter colours required, let glass, and gold protected by glass, be used in mosaic, a kind of work as durable as the solid stone and incapable of losing its lustre by time. And let the painter's work be reserved for the shadowed loggia and inner chamber.

This is the true and faithful way of building. Where this cannot be, the device of external colouring may indeed be employed without dishonour—but it must be with the warning reflection that a time will come when such aids will pass away and when the building will be judged in its lifelessness, dying the death of the dolphin. Better the less bright, more enduring fabric. The transparent alabasters of San Miniato and the mosaics of Saint Mark's are more warmly filled and more brightly touched by every return of morning and evening rays, while the hues of the Gothic cathedrals have died like the iris out of the cloud, and the temples, whose azure and purple once flamed above the Grecian promontory, stand in their faded whiteness like snows which the sunset has left cold.

* * * * *

I do not know anything so perfectly commonplace in design as most modern jewellery. How easy for you to change that and to produce goldsmiths' work that would be a joy to all of us. The gold is ready for you in unexhausted treasure, stored up in the mountain hollow or strewn on the river sand, and was not given to you merely for barren speculation. There should be some better record of it left in your history than the merchant's panic and the ruined home. We do not remember often enough how constantly the history of a great nation will live in and by its art. Only a few thin wreaths of beaten gold remain to tell us of the stately empire of Etruria; and, while from the streets of Florence the noble knight and haughty duke have long since passed away, the gates which the simple goldsmith Gheberti made for their pleasure still guard their lovely house of baptism, worthy still of the praise of Michael Angelo who called them worthy to be the Gates of Paradise.

Have then your school of design, search out your workmen and, when you find one who has delicacy of hand and that wonder of invention necessary for goldsmiths' work, do not leave him to toil in obscurity and dishonour and have a great glaring shop and two great glaring shop-boys in it (not to take your orders: they never do that; but to force you to buy something you do not want at all). When you want a thing wrought in gold, goblet or shield for the feast, necklace or wreath for the women, tell him what you like most in decoration, flower or wreath, bird in flight or hound in the chase, image of the woman you love or the friend you honour. Watch him as he beats out the gold into those thin plates delicate as the petals of a yellow rose, or draws it into the long wires like tangled sunbeams at dawn. Whoever that workman be help him, cherish him, and you will have such lovely work from his hand as will be a joy to you for all time.

This is the spirit of our movement in England, and this is the spirit in which we would wish you to work, making eternal by your art all that is noble in your men and women, stately in your lakes and mountains, beautiful in your own flowers and natural life. We want to see that you have nothing in your houses that has not been a joy to the man who made it, and is not a joy to those that use it. We want to see you create an art made by the hands of the people to please the hearts of the people too. Do you like this spirit or not? Do you think it simple and strong, noble in its aim, and beautiful in its result? I know you do.

Folly and slander have their own way for a little time, but for a little time only. You now know what we mean: you will be able to estimate what is said of us—its value and its motive.

There should be a law that no ordinary newspaper should be allowed to write about art. The harm they do by their foolish and random writing it would be impossible to overestimate—not to the artist but to the public, blinding them to all, but harming the artist not at all. Without them we would judge a man simply by his work; but at present the newspapers are trying hard to induce the public to judge a sculptor, for instance, never by his statues but by the way he treats his wife; a painter by the amount of his income and a poet by the colour of his necktie. I said there should be a law, but there is really no necessity for a new law: nothing could be easier than to bring the ordinary critic under the head of the criminal classes. But let us leave such an inartistic subject and return to beautiful and comely things, remembering that the art which would represent the spirit of modern newspapers would be exactly the art which you and I want to avoid—grotesque art, malice mocking you from every gateway, slander sneering at you from every corner.

Perhaps you may be surprised at my talking of labour and the workman. You have heard of me, I fear, through the medium of your somewhat imaginative newspapers as, if not a 'Japanese young man,' at least a young man to whom the rush and clamour and reality of the modern world were distasteful, and whose greatest difficulty in life was the difficulty of living up to the level of his blue china—a paradox from which England has not yet recovered.

Well, let me tell you how it first came to me at all to create an artistic movement in England, a movement to show the rich what beautiful things they might enjoy and the poor what beautiful things they might create.

One summer afternoon in Oxford—'that sweet city with her dreaming spires,' lovely as Venice in its splendour, noble in its learning as Rome, down the long High Street that winds from tower to tower, past silent cloister and stately gateway, till it reaches that long, grey seven-arched bridge which Saint Mary used to guard (used to, I say, because they are now pulling it down to build a tramway and a light cast-iron bridge in its place, desecrating the loveliest city in England)—well, we were coming down the street—a troop of young men, some of them like myself only nineteen, going to river or tennis-court or cricket-field—when Ruskin going up to lecture in cap and gown met us. He seemed troubled and prayed us to go back with him to his lecture, which a few of us did, and there he spoke to us not on art this time but on life, saying that it seemed to him to be wrong that all the best physique and strength of the young men in England should be spent aimlessly on cricket-ground or river, without any result at all except that if one rowed well one got a pewter-pot, and if one made a good score, a cane-handled bat. He thought, he said, that we should be working at something that would do good to other people, at something by which we might show that in all labour there was something noble. Well, we were a good deal moved, and said we would do anything he wished. So he went out round Oxford and found two villages, Upper and Lower Hinksey, and between them there lay a great swamp, so that the villagers could not pass from one to the other without many miles of a round. And when we came back in winter he asked us to help him to make a road across this morass for these village people to use. So out we went, day after day, and learned how to lay levels and to break stones, and to wheel barrows along a plank—a very difficult thing to do. And Ruskin worked with us in the mist and rain and mud of an Oxford winter, and our friends and our enemies came out and mocked us from the bank. We did not mind it much then, and we did not mind it afterwards at all, but worked away for two months at our road. And what became of the road? Well, like a bad lecture it ended abruptly—in the middle of the swamp. Ruskin going away to Venice, when we came back for the next term there was no leader, and the 'diggers,' as they called us, fell asunder. And I felt that if there was enough spirit amongst the young men to go out to such work as road-making for the sake of a noble ideal of life, I could from them create an artistic movement that might change, as it has changed, the face of England. So I sought them out—leader they would call me—but there was no leader: we were all searchers only and we were bound to each other by noble friendship and by noble art. There was none of us idle: poets most of us, so ambitious were we: painters some of us, or workers in metal or modellers, determined that we would try and create for ourselves beautiful work: for the handicraftsman beautiful work, for those who love us poems and pictures, for those who love us not epigrams and paradoxes and scorn.

Well, we have done something in England and we will do something more. Now, I do not want you, believe me, to ask your brilliant young men, your beautiful young girls, to go out and make a road on a swamp for any village in America, but I think you might each of you have some art to practise.

* * * * *

We must have, as Emerson said, a mechanical craft for our culture, a basis for our higher accomplishments in the work of our hands—the uselessness of most people's hands seems to me one of the most unpractical things. 'No separation from labour can be without some loss of power or truth to the seer,' says Emerson again. The heroism which would make on us the impression of Epaminondas must be that of a domestic conqueror. The hero of the future is he who shall bravely and gracefully subdue this Gorgon of fashion and of convention.

When you have chosen your own part, abide by it, and do not weakly try and reconcile yourself with the world. The heroic cannot be the common nor the common the heroic. Congratulate yourself if you have done something strange and extravagant and broken the monotony of a decorous age.

And lastly, let us remember that art is the one thing which Death cannot harm. The little house at Concord may be desolate, but the wisdom of New England's Plato is not silenced nor the brilliancy of that Attic genius dimmed: the lips of Longfellow are still musical for us though his dust be turning into the flowers which he loved: and as it is with the greater artists, poet and philosopher and songbird, so let it be with you.

LECTURE TO ART STUDENTS

Delivered to the Art students of the Royal Academy at their Club in Golden Square, Westminster, on June 30, 1883. The text is taken from the original manuscript.

In the lecture which it is my privilege to deliver before you to-night I do not desire to give you any abstract definition of beauty at all. For, we who are working in art cannot accept any theory of beauty in exchange for beauty itself, and, so far from desiring to isolate it in a formula appealing to the intellect, we, on the contrary, seek to materialise it in a form that gives joy to the soul through the senses. We want to create it, not to define it. The definition should follow the work: the work should not adapt itself to the definition.

Nothing, indeed, is more dangerous to the young artist than any conception of ideal beauty: he is constantly led by it either into weak prettiness or lifeless abstraction: whereas to touch the ideal at all you must not strip it of vitality. You must find it in life and re-create it in art.

While, then, on the one hand I do not desire to give you any philosophy of beauty—for, what I want to-night is to investigate how we can create art, not how we can talk of it—on the other hand, I do not wish to deal with anything like a history of English art.

To begin with, such an expression as English art is a meaningless expression. One might just as well talk of English mathematics. Art is the science of beauty, and Mathematics the science of truth: there is no national school of either. Indeed, a national school is a provincial school, merely. Nor is there any such thing as a school of art even. There are merely artists, that is all.

And as regards histories of art, they are quite valueless to you unless you are seeking the ostentatious oblivion of an art professorship. It is of no use to you to know the date of Perugino or the birthplace of Salvator Rosa: all that you should learn about art is to know a good picture when you see it, and a bad picture when you see it. As regards the date of the artist, all good work looks perfectly modern: a piece of Greek sculpture, a portrait of Velasquez— they are always modern, always of our time. And as regards the nationality of the artist, art is not national but universal. As regards archæology, then, avoid it altogether: archæology is merely the science of making excuses for bad art; it is the rock on which many a young artist founders and shipwrecks; it is the abyss from which no artist, old or young, ever returns. Or, if he does return, he is so covered with the dust of ages and the mildew of time, that he is quite unrecognisable as an artist, and has to conceal himself for the rest of his days under the cap of a professor, or as a mere illustrator of ancient history. How worthless archæology is in art you can estimate by the fact of its being so popular. Popularity is the crown of laurel which the world puts on bad art. Whatever is popular is wrong.

As I am not going to talk to you, then, about the philosophy of the beautiful, or the history of art, you will ask me what I am going to talk about. The subject of my lecture to-night is what makes an artist and what does the artist make; what are the relations of the artist to his surroundings, what is the education the artist should get, and what is the quality of a good work of art.

Now, as regards the relations of the artist to his surroundings, by which I mean the age and country in which he is born. All good art, as I said before, has nothing to do with any particular century; but this universality is the quality of the work of art; the conditions that produce that quality are different. And what, I think, you should do is to realise completely your age in order completely to abstract yourself from it; remembering that if you are an artist at all, you will be not the mouthpiece of a century, but the master of eternity; that all art rests on a principle, and that mere temporal considerations are no principle at all; and that those who advise you to make your art representative of the nineteenth century are advising you to produce an art which your children, when you have them, will think old-fashioned. But you will tell me this is an inartistic age, and we are an inartistic people, and the artist suffers much in this nineteenth century of ours.

Of course he does. I, of all men, am not going to deny that. But remember that there never has been an artistic age, or an artistic people, since the beginning of the world. The artist has always been, and will always be, an exquisite exception. There is no golden age of art; only artists who have produced what is more golden than gold.

What, you will say to me, the Greeks? were not they an artistic people?

Well, the Greeks certainly not, but, perhaps, you mean the Athenians, the citizens of one out of a thousand cities.

Do you think that they were an artistic people? Take them even at the time of their highest artistic development, the latter part of the fifth century before Christ, when they had the greatest poets and the greatest artists of the antique world, when the Parthenon rose in loveliness at the bidding of a Phidias, and the philosopher spake of wisdom in the shadow of the painted portico, and tragedy swept in the perfection of pageant and pathos across the marble of the stage. Were they an artistic people then? Not a bit of it. What is an artistic people but a people who love their artists and understand their art? The Athenians could do neither.

How did they treat Phidias? To Phidias we owe the great era, not merely in Greek, but in all art—I mean of the introduction of the use of the living model.

And what would you say if all the English bishops, backed by the English people, came down from Exeter Hall to the Royal Academy one day and took off Sir Frederick Leighton in a prison van to Newgate on the charge of having allowed you to make use of the living model in your designs for sacred pictures?

Would you not cry out against the barbarism and the Puritanism of such an idea? Would you not explain to them that the worst way to honour God is to dishonour man who is made in His image, and is the work of His hands; and, that if one wants to paint Christ one must take the most Christlike person one can find, and if one wants to paint the Madonna, the purest girl one knows?

Would you not rush off and burn down Newgate, if necessary, and say that such a thing was without parallel in history?

Without parallel? Well, that is exactly what the Athenians did.

In the room of the Parthenon marbles, in the British Museum, you will see a marble shield on the wall. On it there are two figures; one of a man whose face is half hidden, the other of a man with the godlike lineaments of Pericles. For having done this, for having introduced into a bas relief, taken from Greek sacred history, the image of the great statesman who was ruling Athens at the time, Phidias was flung into prison and there, in the common gaol of Athens, died, the supreme artist of the old world.

And do you think that this was an exceptional case? The sign of a Philistine age is the cry of immorality against art, and this cry was raised by the Athenian people against every great poet and thinker of their day—Æschylus, Euripides, Socrates. It was the same with Florence in the thirteenth century. Good handicrafts are due to guilds not to the people. The moment the guilds lost their power and the people rushed in, beauty and honesty of work died.

And so, never talk of an artistic people; there never has been such a thing.

But, perhaps, you will tell me that the external beauty of the world has almost entirely passed away from us, that the artist dwells no longer in the midst of the lovely surroundings which, in ages past, were the natural inheritance of every one, and that art is very difficult in this unlovely town of ours, where, as you go to your work in the morning, or return from it at eventide, you have to pass through street after street of the most foolish and stupid architecture that the world has ever seen; architecture, where every lovely Greek form is desecrated and defiled, and every lovely Gothic form defiled and desecrated, reducing three-fourths of the London houses to being, merely, like square boxes of the vilest proportions, as gaunt as they are grimy, and as poor as they are pretentious—the hall door always of the wrong colour, and the windows of the wrong size, and where, even when wearied of the houses you turn to contemplate the street itself, you have nothing to look at but chimney-pot hats, men with sandwich boards, vermilion letterboxes, and do that even at the risk of being run over by an emerald-green omnibus.

Is not art difficult, you will say to me, in such surroundings as these? Of course it is difficult, but then art was never easy; you yourselves would not wish it to be easy; and, besides, nothing is worth doing except what the world says is impossible.

Still, you do not care to be answered merely by a paradox. What are the relations of the artist to the external world, and what is the result of the loss of beautiful surroundings to you, is one of the most important questions of modern art; and there is no point on which Mr. Ruskin so insists as that the decadence of art has come from the decadence of beautiful things; and that when the artist can not feed his eye on beauty, beauty goes from his work.

I remember in one of his lectures, after describing the sordid aspect of a great English city, he draws for us a picture of what were the artistic surroundings long ago.

Think, he says, in words of perfect and picturesque imagery, whose beauty I can but feebly echo, think of what was the scene which presented itself, in his afternoon walk, to a designer of the Gothic school of Pisa—Nino Pisano or any of his men {317}:

On each side of a bright river he saw rise a line of brighter palaces, arched and pillared, and inlaid with deep red porphyry, and with serpentine; along the quays before their gates were riding troops of knights, noble in face and form, dazzling in crest and shield; horse and man one labyrinth of quaint colour and gleaming light—the purple, and silver, and scarlet fringes flowing over the strong limbs and clashing mail, like sea-waves over rocks at sunset. Opening on each side from the river were gardens, courts, and cloisters; long successions of white pillars among wreaths of vine; leaping of fountains through buds of pomegranate and orange: and still along the garden-paths, and under and through the crimson of the pomegranate shadows, moving slowly, groups of the fairest women that Italy ever saw—fairest, because purest and thoughtfullest; trained in all high knowledge, as in all courteous art—in dance, in song, in sweet wit, in lofty learning, in loftier courage, in loftiest love—able alike to cheer, to enchant, or save, the souls of men. Above all this scenery of perfect human life, rose dome and bell-tower, burning with white alabaster and gold: beyond dome and bell-tower the slopes of mighty hills, hoary with olive; far in the north, above a purple sea of peaks of solemn Apennine, the clear, sharp-cloven Carrara mountains sent up their steadfast flames of marble summit into amber sky; the great sea itself, scorching with expanse of light, stretching from their feet to the Gorgonian isles; and over all these, ever present, near or far—seen through the leaves of vine, or imaged with all its march of clouds in the Arno's stream, or set with its depth of blue close against the golden hair and burning cheek of lady and knight,—that untroubled and sacred sky, which was to all men, in those days of innocent faith, indeed the unquestioned abode of spirits, as the earth was of men; and which opened straight through its gates of cloud and veils of dew into the awfulness of the eternal world;—a heaven in which every cloud that passed was literally the chariot of an angel, and every ray of its Evening and Morning streamed from the throne of God.

What think you of that for a school of design?

And then look at the depressing, monotonous appearance of any modern city, the sombre dress of men and women, the meaningless and barren architecture, the colourless and dreadful surroundings. Without a beautiful national life, not sculpture merely, but all the arts will die.

Well, as regards the religious feeling of the close of the passage, I do not think I need speak about that. Religion springs from religious feeling, art from artistic feeling: you never get one from the other; unless you have the right root you will not get the right flower; and, if a man sees in a cloud the chariot of an angel, he will probably paint it very unlike a cloud.

But, as regards the general idea of the early part of that lovely bit of prose, is it really true that beautiful surroundings are necessary for the artist? I think not; I am sure not. Indeed, to me the most inartistic thing in this age of ours is not the indifference of the public to beautiful things, but the indifference of the artist to the things that are called ugly. For, to the real artist, nothing is beautiful or ugly in itself at all. With the facts of the object he has nothing to do, but with its appearance only, and appearance is a matter of light and shade, of masses, of position, and of value.

Appearance is, in fact, a matter of effect merely, and it is with the effects of nature that you have to deal, not with the real condition of the object. What you, as painters, have to paint is not things as they are but things as they seem to be, not things as they are but things as they are not.

No object is so ugly that, under certain conditions of light and shade, or proximity to other things, it will not look beautiful; no object is so beautiful that, under certain conditions, it will not look ugly. I believe that in every twenty-four hours what is beautiful looks ugly, and what is ugly looks beautiful, once.

And, the commonplace character of so much of our English painting seems to me due to the fact that so many of our young artists look merely at what we may call 'ready-made beauty,' whereas you exist as artists not to copy beauty but to create it in your art, to wait and watch for it in nature.

What would you say of a dramatist who would take nobody but virtuous people as characters in his play? Would you not say he was missing half of life? Well, of the young artist who paints nothing but beautiful things, I say he misses one half of the world.

Do not wait for life to be picturesque, but try and see life under picturesque conditions. These conditions you can create for yourself in your studio, for they are merely conditions of light. In nature, you must wait for them, watch for them, choose them; and, if you wait and watch, come they will.

In Gower Street at night you may see a letterbox that is picturesque; on the Thames Embankment you may see picturesque policemen. Even Venice is not always beautiful, nor France.

To paint what you see is a good rule in art, but to see what is worth painting is better. See life under pictorial conditions. It is better to live in a city of changeable weather than in a city of lovely surroundings.

Now, having seen what makes the artist, and what the artist makes, who is the artist? There is a man living amongst us who unites in himself all the qualities of the noblest art, whose work is a joy for all time, who is, himself, a master of all time. That man is Mr. Whistler.

But, you will say, modern dress, that is bad. If you cannot paint black cloth you could not have painted silken doublet. Ugly dress is better for art—facts of vision, not of the object.

What is a picture? Primarily, a picture is a beautifully coloured surface, merely, with no more spiritual message or meaning for you than an exquisite fragment of Venetian glass or a blue tile from the wall of Damascus. It is, primarily, a purely decorative thing, a delight to look at.

All archæological pictures that make you say 'How curious!' all sentimental pictures that make you say 'How sad!' all historical pictures that make you say 'How interesting!' all pictures that do not immediately give you such artistic joy as to make you say 'How beautiful!' are bad pictures.

* * * * *

We never know what an artist is going to do. Of course not. The artist is not a specialist. All such divisions as animal painters, landscape painters, painters of Scotch cattle in an English mist, painters of English cattle in a Scotch mist, racehorse painters, bull-terrier painters, all are shallow. If a man is an artist he can paint everything.

The object of art is to stir the most divine and remote of the chords which make music in our soul; and colour is, indeed, of itself a mystical presence on things, and tone a kind of sentinel.

Am I pleading, then, for mere technique? No. As long as there are any signs of technique at all, the picture is unfinished. What is finish? A picture is finished when all traces of work, and of the means employed to bring about the result, have disappeared.

In the case of handicraftsmen—the weaver, the potter, the smith—on their work are the traces of their hand. But it is not so with the painter; it is not so with the artist.

Art should have no sentiment about it but its beauty, no technique

340

except what you cannot observe. One should be able to say of a picture not that it is 'well painted,' but that it is 'not painted.'

What is the difference between absolutely decorative art and a painting? Decorative art emphasises its material: imaginative art annihilates it. Tapestry shows its threads as part of its beauty: a picture annihilates its canvas; it shows nothing of it. Porcelain emphasises its glaze: water-colours reject the paper.

A picture has no meaning but its beauty, no message but its joy. That is the first truth about art that you must never lose sight of. A picture is a purely decorative thing.

BIBLIOGRAPHY BY STUART MASON

NOTE

Part I. includes all the authorised editions published in England, and the two French editions of Salomé published in Paris. Authorised editions of some of the works were issued in the United States of America simultaneously with the English publication.

Part II. contains the only two 'Privately Printed' editions which are authorised.

Part III. is a chronological list of all contributions (so far as at present known) to magazines, periodicals, etc., the date given being that of the first publication only. Those marked with an asterisk (*) were published anonymously. Many of the poems have been included in anthologies of modern verse, but no attempt has been made to give particulars of such reprints in this Bibliography.

I.—AUTHORISED ENGLISH EDITIONS

NEWDIGATE PRIZE POEM. RAVENNA. Recited in the Theatre, Oxford, June 26, 1878. By OSCAR WILDE, Magdalen College. Oxford: Thos. Shrimpton and Son, 1878.

POEMS. London: David Bogue, 1881 (June 30).

Second and Third Editions, 1881.

Fourth and Fifth Editions [Revised], 1882.

220 copies (200 for sale) of the Fifth Edition, with a new title-page and cover designed by Charles Ricketts. London: Elkin Mathews and John Lane, 1892 (May 26).

THE HAPPY PRINCE AND OTHER TALES. ('The Happy Prince,' 'The Nightingale and the Rose,' 'The Selfish Giant,' 'The Devoted Friend,' 'The Remarkable Rocket.') Illustrated by Walter Crane and Jacomb Hood.

London: David Nutt, 1888 (May).

Also 75 copies (65 for sale) on Large Paper, with the plates in two states.

Second Edition, January 1889.

Third Edition, February 1902.

Fourth Impression, September 1905.

Fifth Impression, February 1907.

INTENTIONS. ('The Decay of Lying,' 'Pen, Pencil, and Poison,' 'The Critic as Artist,' 'The Truth of Masks.') London: James R. Osgood, McIlvaine and Co., 1891 (May). New Edition, 1894.

Edition for Continental circulation only. The English Library, No. 54. Leipzig: Heinemann and Balestier, 1891. Frequently reprinted.

THE PICTURE OF DORIAN GRAY. London: Ward, Lock and Co. [1891 (July 1).]

Also 250 copies on Large Paper. Dated 1891.

[Note.—July 1 is the official date of publication, but presentation copies signed by the author and dated May 1891 are known.]

New Edition [1894 (October 1).] London: Ward, Lock and Bowden.

Reprinted. Paris: Charles Carrington, 1901, 1905, 1908 (January).

Edition for Continental circulation only. Leipzig: Bernhard Tauchnitz, vol. 4049. 1908 (July).

LORD ARTHUR SAVILE'S CRIME AND OTHER STORIES. ('Lord Arthur Savile's Crime,' 'The Sphinx Without a Secret,' 'The Canterville Ghost,' 'The Model Millionaire.') London: James R. Osgood, McIlvaine and Co., 1891 (July).

A HOUSE OF POMEGRANATES. ('The Young King,' 'The Birthday of the Infanta,' 'The Fisherman and His Soul,' 'The Star Child.') With Designs and Decorations by Charles Ricketts and C. H. Shannon. London:

James R. Osgood, McIlvaine and Co., 1891 (November).

SALOMÉ. DRAME EN UN ACTE. Paris: Librairie de l'Art Indépendant. Londres: Elkin Mathews et John Lane, 1893 (February 22).

600 copies (500 for sale) and 25 on Large Paper.

New Edition. With sixteen Illustrations by Aubrey Beardsley. Paris: Edition à petit nombre imprimée pour les Souscripteurs. 1907.

500 copies.

[Note.—Several editions, containing only a portion of the text, have been issued for the performance of the Opera by Richard Strauss. London: Methuen and Co.; Berlin: Adolph Fürstner.]

LADY WINDERMERE'S FAN. A PLAY ABOUT A GOOD WOMAN. London: Elkin Mathews and John Lane, 1893 (November 8).

500 copies and 50 on Large Paper.

Acting Edition. London: Samuel French. (Text Incomplete.)

SALOME. A TRAGEDY IN ONE ACT. Translated from the French [by Lord Alfred Bruce Douglas.] Pictured by Aubrey Beardsley. London: Elkin Mathews and John Lane, 1894 (February 9).

500 copies and 100 on Large Paper.

With the two suppressed plates and extra title-page. Preface by Robert Ross. London: John Lane, 1907 (September 1906).

New Edition (without illustrations). London: John Lane, 1906 (June), 1908.

THE SPHINX. With Decorations by Charles Ricketts. London: Elkin Mathews and John Lane, 1894 (July).

200 copies and 25 on Large Paper.

A WOMAN OF NO IMPORTANCE. London: John Lane, 1894 (October 9).

500 copies and 50 on Large Paper.

THE SOUL OF MAN. London: Privately Printed, 1895.

[Reprinted from the Fortnightly Review (February 1891), by permission of the Proprietors, and published by A. L. Humphreys.]

New Edition. London: Arthur L. Humphreys, 1907.

Reprinted in Sebastian Melmoth. London: Arthur L. Humphreys, 1904, 1905.

THE BALLAD OF READING GAOL. By C.3.3. London: Leonard Smithers, 1898 (February 13).

800 copies and 30 on Japanese Vellum.

Second Edition, March 1898.

Third Edition, 1898. 99 copies only, signed by the author.

Fourth, Fifth and Sixth Editions, 1898.

Seventh Edition, 1899. {328a}

[Note.—The above are printed at the Chiswick Press on handmade paper. All reprints on ordinary paper are unauthorised.]

THE IMPORTANCE OF BEING EARNEST. A TRIVIAL COMEDY FOR SERIOUS PEOPLE. BY THE AUTHOR OF LADY WINDERMERE'S FAN. London: Leonard Smithers and Co., 1899 (February).

1000 copies. Also 100 copies on Large Paper, and 12 on Japanese Vellum.

Acting Edition. London: Samuel French. (Text Incomplete.)

AN IDEAL HUSBAND. BY THE AUTHOR OF LADY WINDERMERE'S FAN. London: Leonard Smithers and Co., 1889 (July).

1000 copies. Also 100 copies on Large Paper, and 12 on Japanese

Vellum.

DE PROFUNDIS. London: Methuen and Co., 1905 (February 23).

Also 200 copies on Large Paper, and 50 on Japanese Vellum.

Second Edition, March 1905.

Third Edition, March 1905.

Fourth Edition, April 1905.

Fifth Edition, September 1905.

Sixth Edition, March 1906.

Seventh Edition, January 1907.

Eighth Edition, April 1907.

Ninth Edition, July 1907.

Tenth Edition, October 1907.

Eleventh Edition, January 1908. {328b}

THE WORKS OF OSCAR WILDE. London: Methuen and Co., 1908 (February 13). In thirteen volumes. 1000 copies on Handmade Paper and 80 on Japanese Vellum.

THE DUCHESS OF PADUA. A PLAY.

SALOMÉ. A FLORENTINE TRAGEDY. VERA.

LADY WINDERMERE'S FAN. A PLAY ABOUT A GOOD WOMAN.

A WOMAN OF NO IMPORTANCE. A PLAY.

AN IDEAL HUSBAND. A PLAY.

THE IMPORTANCE OF BEING EARNEST. A TRIVIAL COMEDY FOR SERIOUS PEOPLE.

LORD ARTHUR SAVILE'S CRIME AND OTHER PROSE PIECES.

INTENTIONS AND THE SOUL OF MAN.

THE POEMS.

A HOUSE OF POMEGRANATES, THE HAPPY PRINCE AND OTHER TALES.

DE PROFUNDIS.

REVIEWS.

MISCELLANIES.

Uniform with the above. Paris: Charles Carrington, 1908 (April 16).

THE PICTURE OF DORIAN GRAY.

II.—EDITIONS PRIVATELY PRINTED FOR THE AUTHOR

VERA; OR, THE NIHILISTS. A DRAMA IN A PROLOGUE AND FOUR ACTS. [New York] 1882.

THE DUCHESS OF PADUA: A TRAGEDY OF THE XVI CENTURY WRITTEN IN PARIS IN THE XIX CENTURY. Privately Printed as Manuscript. [New York, 1883 (March 15).]

III.—MISCELLANEOUS CONTRIBUTIONS TO MAGAZINES, PERIODICALS, Etc.

1875

November. CHORUS OF CLOUD MAIDENS (Αριστοφανους Νεφελαι, 275-287 and 295-307). Dublin University Magazine, Vol. LXXXVI. No. 515, page 622.

1876

January. FROM SPRING DAYS TO WINTER. (FOR MUSIC.) Dublin University Magazine, Vol. LXXXVII. No. 517, page 47.

March. GRAFFITI D'ITALIA. I. SAN MINIATO. (JUNE 15.) Dublin University Magazine, Vol. LXXXVII. No. 519, page 297.

June.   THE DOLE OF THE KING'S DAUGHTER.   Dublin University Magazine, Vol. LXXXVII. No. 522, page 682.

Trinity Term.   ΔΗΞΙΘΥΜΟΝ ΕΡΩΤΟΣ ΑΝΘΟΣ.   (THE ROSE OF LOVE, AND WITH A ROSE'S THORNS.) Kottabos, Vol. II. No. 10, page 268.

September.   Αιλινον, αιλινον ειπε, το δ' ευ νικατω.   Dublin University Magazine, Vol. LXXXVIII. No. 525, page 291.

September.   THE TRUE KNOWLEDGE.   Irish Monthly, Vol. IV. No. 39, page 594.

September.   GRAFFITI D'ITALIA. (ARONA. LAGO MAGGIORE.) Month and Catholic Review, Vol. xxviii. No. 147, page 77.

Michaelmas Term.   ΘΡΗΝΩΙΔΙΑ.   Kottabos, Vol. II. No. 11, page 298.

1877

February.   LOTUS LEAVES.   Irish Monthly, Vol. v. No. 44, page 133.

Hilary Term.   A FRAGMENT FROM THE AGAMEMNON OF ÆSCHYLOS.   Kottabos, Vol. II. No. 12, page 320.

Hilary Term.   A NIGHT VISION.   Kottabos, Vol. II. No. 12, page 331.

June.   SALVE SATURNIA TELLUS.   Irish Monthly, Vol. V. No. 48, page 415.

June.   URBS SACRA ÆTERNA.   Illustrated Monitor, Vol. IV. No. 3, page 130.

July.   THE TOMB OF KEATS.   Irish Monthly, Vol. V. No. 49, page 476.

July.   SONNET WRITTEN DURING HOLY WEEK.   Illustrated Monitor, Vol. IV. No. 4, page 186.

July.   THE GROSVENOR GALLERY.   Dublin University Magazine, Vol. XC. No. 535, page 118.

Michaelmas Term. WASTED DAYS. (FROM A PICTURE PAINTED BY MISS V. T.) Kottabos, Vol. III. No. 2, page 56.

December. Ιλοντος Ατρυγετος. Irish Monthly, Vol. V. No. 54, page 746.

1878

April. MAGDALEN WALKS. Irish Monthly, Vol. VI. No. 58, page 211.

1879

Hilary Term. 'LA BELLE MARGUERITE.' BALLADE DU MOYEN AGE. Kottabos, Vol. III. No. 6, page 146.

April. THE CONQUEROR OF TIME. Time, Vol. I. No. 1, page 30.

May 5. GROSVENOR GALLERY (First Notice.) Saunders' Irish Daily News, Vol. CXC. No. 42,886, page 5.

June. EASTER DAY. Waifs and Strays, Vol. I. No. 1, page 2.

June 11. TO SARAH BERNHARDT. World, No. 258, page 18.

July. THE NEW HELEN. Time, Vol. I. No. 4, page 400.

July 16. QUEEN HENRIETTA MARIA. (Charles I,, act iii.) World, No. 263, page 18.

Michaelmas Term. AVE! MARIA. Kottabos, Vol. III. No. 8, page 206.

1880

January 14. PORTIA. World, No. 289, page 13.

March. IMPRESSION DE VOYAGE. Waifs and Strays, Vol. I. No. 3, page 77.

August 25. AVE IMPERATRIX! A POEM ON ENGLAND. World, No. 321, page 12.

November 10. LIBERTATIS SACRA FAMES. World, No. 332, page

15.

December. SEN ARTYSTY; OR, THE ARTIST'S DREAM. Translated from the Polish of Madame Helena Modjeska. Routledge's Christmas Annual: The Green Room, page 66.

1881

January. THE GRAVE OF KEATS. Burlington, Vol. I. No. 1, page 35.

March 2. IMPRESSION DE MATIN. World, No. 348, page 15.

1882

February 15. IMPRESSIONS: I. LE JARDIN. II. LA MER. Our Continent (Philadelphia), Vol. I. No. 1, page 9.

November 7. MRS. LANGTRY AS HESTER GRAZEBROOK. New York World, page 5.

L'ENVOI, An Introduction to Rose Leaf and Apple Leaf, by Rennell Rodd, page 11. Philadelphia: J. M. Stoddart and Co.

[Besides the ordinary edition a limited number of an édition de luxe was issued printed in brown ink on one side only of a thin transparent handmade parchment paper, the whole book being interleaved with green tissue.]

1883

November 14. TELEGRAM TO WHISTLER. World, No. 489, page 16.

1884

May 29. UNDER THE BALCONY. Shaksperean Show-Book, page 23.

(Set to Music by Lawrence Kellie as OH! BEAUTIFUL STAR. SERENADE. London: Robert Cocks and Co., 1892.)

October 14. MR. OSCAR WILDE ON WOMAN'S DRESS. Pall Mall Gazette, Vol. XL. No. 6114, page 6.

November 11. MORE RADICAL IDEAS UPON DRESS REFORM. (With two illustrations.) Pall Mall Gazette, Vol. XL. No. 6138, page 14.

1885

February 21. MR. WHISTLER'S TEN O'CLOCK. Pall Mall Gazette, Vol. XLI. No. 6224, page 1.

February 25. TENDERNESS IN TITE STREET. World, No. 556, page 14.

February 28. THE RELATION OF DRESS TO ART. A NOTE IN BLACK AND WHITE ON MR. WHISTLER'S LECTURE. Pall Mall Gazette, Vol. XLI. No. 6230, page 4.

March 7. *DINNERS AND DISHES. Pall Mall Gazette, Vol. XLI. No. 6236, page 5.

March 13. *A MODERN EPIC. Pall Mall Gazette, Vol. XLI. No. 6241, page 11.

March 14. SHAKESPEARE ON SCENERY. Dramatic Review, Vol. I. No. 7, page 99.

March 27. *A BEVY OF POETS. Pall Mall Gazette, Vol. XLI. No. 6253, page 5.

April 1. *PARNASSUS VERSUS PHILOLOGY. Pall Mall Gazette, Vol. XLI. No. 6257, page 6.

April 11. THE HARLOT'S HOUSE. Dramatic Review, Vol. I. No. 11, page 167.

May. SHAKESPEARE AND STAGE COSTUME. Nineteenth Century, Vol. XVII. No. 99, page 800.

May 9. HAMLET AT THE LYCEUM. Dramatic Review, Vol. I. No. 15, page 227.

May 15. *TWO NEW NOVELS. Pall Mall Gazette, Vol. XLI. No. 6293, page 4.

May 23. HENRY THE FOURTH AT OXFORD. Dramatic Review, Vol. I. No. 17, page 264.

May 27. *MODERN GREEK POETRY. Pall Mall Gazette, Vol. XLI. No. 6302, page 5.

May 30. OLIVIA AT THE LYCEUM. Dramatic Review, Vol. I. No. 18, page 278.

June. LE JARDIN DES TUILERIES. (With an illustration by L. Troubridge.) In a Good Cause, page 83. London: Wells Gardner, Darton and Co.

June 6. AS YOU LIKE IT AT COOMBE HOUSE. Dramatic Review, Vol. I. No. 19, page 296.

July. ROSES AND RUE. Midsummer Dreams, Summer Number of Society.

(No copy of this is known to exist.)

November 18. *A HANDBOOK TO MARRIAGE. Pall Mall Gazette, Vol. XLII. No. 6452, page 5.

1886

January 15. *HALF-HOURS WITH THE WORST AUTHORS. Pall Mall Gazette, Vol. XLIII. No. 6501, page 4.

January 23. SONNET. ON THE RECENT SALE BY AUCTION OF KEATS' LOVE LETTERS. Dramatic Review, Vol. II. No. 52, page 249.

February 1. *ONE OF MR. CONWAY'S REMAINDERS. Pall Mall Gazette, Vol. XLIII. No. 6515, page 5.

February 8. TO READ OR NOT TO READ. Pall Mall Gazette, Vol. XLIII. No. 6521, page 11.

February 20. TWELFTH NIGHT AT OXFORD. Dramatic Review, Vol. III. No. 56, page 34.

March 6. *THE LETTERS OF A GREAT WOMAN. Pall Mall

Gazette, Vol. XLIII. No. 6544, page 4.

April 12. *NEWS FROM PARNASSUS. Pall Mall Gazette, Vol. XLIII. No. 6575, page 5.

April 14. *SOME NOVELS. Pall Mall Gazette, Vol. XLIII. No. 6577, page 5.

April 17. *A LITERARY PILGRIM. Pall Mall Gazette, Vol. XLIII. No. 6580, page 5.

April 21. *BERANGER IN ENGLAND. Pall Mall Gazette, Vol. XLIII. No. 6583, page 5.

May 13. *THE POETRY OF THE PEOPLE. Pall Mall Gazette, Vol. XLIII. No. 6601, page 5.

May 15. THE CENCI. Dramatic Review, Vol. III. No. 68, page 151.

May 22. HELENA IN TROAS. Dramatic Review, Vol. III. No. 69, page 161.

July. KEATS' SONNET ON BLUE. (With facsimile of original Manuscript.) Century Guild Hobby Horse, Vol. I. No. 3, page 83.

August 4. *PLEASING AND PRATTLING. Pall Mall Gazette, Vol. XLIV. No. 6672, page 5.

September 13. *BALZAC IN ENGLISH. Pall Mall Gazette, Vol. XLIV. No. 6706, page 5.

September 16. *TWO NEW NOVELS. Pall Mall Gazette, Vol. XLIV. No. 6709, page 5.

September 20. *BEN JONSON. Pall Mall Gazette, Vol. XLIV. No. 6712, page 6.

September 27. *THE POETS' CORNER. Pall Mall Gazette, Vol. XLIV. No. 6718, page 5.

October 8. *A RIDE THROUGH MOROCCO. Pall Mall Gazette,

Vol. XLIV. No. 6728, page 5.

October 14. *THE CHILDREN OF THE POETS. Pall Mall Gazette, Vol. XLIV. No. 6733, page 5.

October 28. *NEW NOVELS. Pall Mall Gazette, Vol. XLIV. No. 6745, page 4.

November 3. *A POLITICIAN'S POETRY. Pall Mall Gazette, Vol. XLIV. No. 6750, page 4.

November 10. *MR. SYMONDS' HISTORY OF THE RENAISSANCE. Pall Mall Gazette, Vol. XLIV. No. 6756, page 5.

November 18. *A 'JOLLY' ART CRITIC. Pall Mall Gazette, Vol. XLIV. No. 6763, page 6.

November 24. NOTE ON WHISTLER. World, No. 647, page 14.

December 1. *A 'SENTIMENTAL JOURNEY' THROUGH LITERATURE. Pall Mall Gazette, Vol. XLIV. No. 6774, page 5.

December 11. *TWO BIOGRAPHIES OF SIR PHILIP SIDNEY. Pall Mall Gazette, Vol. XLIV. No. 6783, page 5.

1887

January 8. *COMMON SENSE IN ART. Pall Mall Gazette, Vol. XLV. No. 6806, page 5.

February 1. *MINER AND MINOR POETS. Pall Mall Gazette, Vol. XLV. No. 6826, page 5.

February 17. *A NEW CALENDAR. Pall Mall Gazette, Vol. XLV. No. 6840, page 5.

February 23. THE CANTERVILLE GHOST—I. Illustrated by F. H. Townsend. Court and Society Review, Vol. IV. No. 138, page 193.

March 2. THE CANTERVILLE GHOST—II. Illustrated by F. H. Townsend. Court and Society Review, Vol. IV. No. 139, page 207.

March 8. *THE POETS' CORNER. Pall Mall Gazette, Vol. XLV. No. 6856, page 5.

March 23. *THE AMERICAN INVASION. Court and Society Review, Vol. IV. No. 142, page 270.

March 28. *GREAT WRITERS BY LITTLE MEN. Pall Mall Gazette, Vol. XLV. No. 6873, page 5.

March 31. *A NEW BOOK ON DICKENS. Pall Mall Gazette, Vol. XLV. No. 6876, page 5.

April 12. *OUR BOOK SHELF. Pall Mall Gazette, Vol. XLV. No. 6885, page 5.

April 18. *A CHEAP EDITION OF A GREAT MAN. Pall Mall Gazette, Vol. XLV. No. 6890, page 5.

April 26. *MR. MORRIS'S ODYSSEY. Pall Mall Gazette, Vol. XLV. No. 6897, page 5.

May 2. *A BATCH OF NOVELS. Pall Mall Gazette, Vol. XLV. No. 6902, page 11.

May 7. *SOME NOVELS. Saturday Review, Vol. LXIII. No. 1645, page 663.

May 11. LORD ARTHUR SAVILE'S CRIME. A STORY OF CHEIROMANCY.—I. II. Illustrated by F. H. Townsend. Court and Society Review, Vol. IV. No. 149, page 447.

May 18. LORD ARTHUR SAVILE'S CRIME. A STORY OF CHEIROMANCY.—III. IV. Court and Society Review, Vol. IV. No. 150, page 471.

May 25. LORD ARTHUR SAVILE'S CRIME. A STORY OF CHEIROMANCY.—V. VI. Illustrated by F. H. Townsend. Court and Society Review, Vol. IV. No. 151, page 495.

May 25. LADY ALROY. World, No. 673, page 18.

May 30. *THE POETS' CORNER. Pall Mall Gazette, Vol. XLV. No. 6926, page 5.

June 11. *MR. PATER'S IMAGINARY PORTRAITS. Pall Mall Gazette, Vol. XLV. No. 6937, page 2.

June 22. THE MODEL MILLIONAIRE. World, No. 677, page 18.

August 8. *A GOOD HISTORICAL NOVEL. Pall Mall Gazette, Vol. XLVI. No. 6986, page 3.

August 20. *NEW NOVELS. Saturday Review, Vol. LXIV. No. 1660, page 264.

September 27. *TWO BIOGRAPHIES OF KEATS. Pall Mall Gazette, Vol. XLVI. No. 7029, page 3.

October 15. *SERMONS IN STONES AT BLOOMSBURY. Pall Mall Gazette, Vol. XLVI. No. 7045, page 5.

October 24. *A SCOTCHMAN ON SCOTTISH POETRY. Pall Mall Gazette, Vol. XLVI. No. 7052, page 3.

November. LITERARY AND OTHER NOTES. Woman's World, Vol. I. No. 1, page 36.

November 9. *MR. MAHAFFY'S NEW BOOK. Pall Mall Gazette, Vol. XLVI. No. 7066, page 3.

November 24. *MR. MORRIS'S COMPLETION OF THE ODYSSEY. Pall Mall Gazette, Vol. XLVI. No. 7079, page 3.

November 30. *SIR CHARLES BOWEN'S VIRGIL. Pall Mall Gazette, Vol. XLVI. No. 7084, page 3.

December. LITERARY AND OTHER NOTES. Woman's World, Vol. I. No. 2, page 81.

December 12. *THE UNITY OF THE ARTS. Pall Mall Gazette, Vol. XLVI. No. 7094, page 13.

December 13. UN AMANT DE NOS JOURS. Court and Society

Review, Vol. IV. No. 180, page 587.

December 16. *ARISTOTLE AT AFTERNOON TEA. Pall Mall Gazette, Vol. XLVI. No. 7098, page 3.

December 17. *EARLY CHRISTIAN ART IN IRELAND. Pall Mall Gazette, Vol. XLVI. No. 7099, page 3.

December 25. *ART AT WILLIS'S ROOMS. Sunday Times, No. 3376, page 7.

December 25. FANTAISIES DÉCORATIVES. I. LE PANNEAU. II. LES BALLONS. Illustrated by Bernard Partridge. Lady's Pictorial Christmas Number, pages 2, 3.

1888

January. LITERARY AND OTHER NOTES. Woman's World, Vol. I. No. 3, page 132.

January 20. *THE POETS' CORNER. Pall Mall Gazette, Vol. XLVII. No. 7128, page 3.

February. LITERARY AND OTHER NOTES. Woman's World, Vol. I. No. 4, page 180.

February 15. THE POETS' CORNER. Pall Mall Gazette, Vol. XLVII. No. 7150, page 3.

February 24. *VENUS OR VICTORY. Pall Mall Gazette, Vol. XLVII. No. 7158, page 2.

March. LITERARY AND OTHER NOTES. Woman's World, Vol. I. No. 5, page 229.

April. CANZONET. Art and Letters, Vol. II. No. 1, page 46.

April 6. *THE POETS' CORNER. Pall Mall Gazette, Vol. XLVII. No. 7193, page 3.

April 14. *M. CARO ON GEORGE SAND. Pall Mall Gazette, Vol.

XLVII. No. 7200, page 3.

October 24. *THE POETS' CORNER. Pall Mall Gazette, Vol. XLVIII. No. 7365, page 5.

November. A FASCINATING BOOK. A NOTE BY THE EDITOR. Woman's World, Vol. II. No. 13, page 53.

November 2. *MR. MORRIS ON TAPESTRY. Pall Mall Gazette, Vol. XLVIII. No. 7373, page 6.

November 9. *SCULPTURE AT THE 'ARTS AND CRAFTS.' Pall Mall Gazette, Vol. XLVIII. No. 7379, page 3.

November 16. *THE POETS' CORNER. Pall Mall Gazette, Vol. XLVIII. No. 7385, page 2.

November 16. *PRINTING AND PRINTERS. Pall Mall Gazette, Vol. XLVIII. No. 7385, page 5.

November 23. *THE BEAUTIES OF BOOKBINDING. Pall Mall Gazette, Vol. XLVIII. No. 7391, page 3.

November 30. *THE CLOSE OF THE 'ARTS AND CRAFTS.' Pall Mall Gazette, Vol. XLVIII. No. 7397, page 3.

December. A NOTE ON SOME MODERN POETS. Woman's World, Vol. II. No. 14, page 108.

December 8. ENGLISH POETESSES. Queen, Vol. LXXXIV. No. 2189, page 742.

December 11. *SIR EDWIN ARNOLD'S LAST VOLUME. Pall Mall Gazette, Vol. XLVIII. No. 7046, page 3.

December 14. *AUSTRALIAN POETS. Pall Mall Gazette, Vol. XLVIII. No. 7409, page 3.

December. THE YOUNG KING. Illustrated by Bernard Partridge. Lady's Pictorial Christmas Number, page 1.

1889

January. THE DECAY OF LYING: A DIALOGUE. Nineteenth Century, Vol. XXV. No. 143, page 35.

January. PEN, PENCIL, AND POISON: A STUDY. Fortnightly Review, Vol. XLV. No. 265, page 41.

January. LONDON MODELS. Illustrated by Harper Pennington. English Illustrated Magazine, Vol. VI. No. 64, page 313.

January. SOME LITERARY NOTES. Woman's World, Vol. II. No. 15, page 164.

January 3. *POETRY AND PRISON. Pall Mall Gazette, Vol. XLIX. No. 7425, page 3.

January 25. *THE GOSPEL ACCORDING TO WALT WHITMAN. Pall Mall Gazette, Vol. XLIX. No. 7444, page 3.

January 26. *THE NEW PRESIDENT. Pall Mall Gazette, Vol. XLIX. No. 7445, page 3.

February. SOME LITERARY NOTES. Woman's World, Vol. II. No. 16, page 221.

February. SYMPHONY IN YELLOW. Centennial Magazine (Sydney), Vol. II. No. 7, page 437.

February 12. *ONE OF THE BIBLES OF THE WORLD. Pall Mall Gazette, Vol. XLIX. No. 7459, page 3.

February 15. *POETICAL SOCIALISTS. Pall Mall Gazette, Vol. XLIX. No. 7462, page 3.

February 27. *MR. BRANDER MATTHEWS' ESSAYS. Pall Mall Gazette, Vol. XLIX. No. 7472, page 3.

March. SOME LITERARY NOTES. Woman's World, Vol. III. No. 17, page 277.

March 2. *MR. WILLIAM MORRIS'S LAST BOOK. Pall Mall Gazette, Vol. XLIX. No. 7475, page 3.

March 25. *ADAM LINDSAY GORDON. Pall Mall Gazette, Vol. XLIX. No. 7494, page 3.

March 30. *THE POETS' CORNER. Pall Mall Gazette, Vol. XLIX. No. 7499, page 3.

April. SOME LITERARY NOTES. Woman's World, Vol. II. No. 18, page 333.

April 13. MR. FROUDE'S BLUE-BOOK. Pall Mall Gazette, Vol. XLIX. No. 7511, page 3.

May. SOME LITERARY NOTES. Woman's World, Vol. ii. No. 19, page 389.

May 17. *OUIDA'S NEW NOVEL. Pall Mall Gazette, Vol. XLIX. No. 7539, page 3.

June. SOME LITERARY NOTES. Woman's World, Vol. II. No. 20, page 446.

June 5. *A THOUGHT-READER'S NOVEL. Pall Mall Gazette, Vol. XLIX. No. 7555, page 2.

June 24. *THE POETS' CORNER. Pall Mall Gazette, Vol. XLIX. No. 7571, page 3.

June 27. *MR. SWINBURNE'S LAST VOLUME. Pall Mall Gazette, Vol. XLIX. No. 7574, page 3.

July. THE PORTRAIT OF MR. W. H. Blackwood's Edinburgh Magazine, Vol. CXLVI. No. 885, page 1.

July 12. *THREE NEW POETS. Pall Mall Gazette, Vol. I. No. 7587, page 3.

December. IN THE FOREST. Illustrated by Bernard Partridge. Lady's Pictorial Christmas Number, page 9.

(Set to music by Edwin Tilden and published by Miles and Thompson, Boston, U.S.A., 1891.)

360

1890

January 9. REPLY TO MR. WHISTLER. Truth, Vol. XXVII. No. 680, page 51.

February 8. A CHINESE SAGE. Speaker, Vol. I. No. 6, page 144.

March 22. MR. PATER'S LAST VOLUME. Speaker, Vol. I. No. 12, page 319.

May 24. *PRIMAVERA. Pall Mall Gazette, Vol. LI. No. 7856, page 3.

June 20. THE PICTURE OF DORIAN GRAY. Lippincott's Monthly Magazine (July), Vol. XLVI. No. 271, page 3.

(Containing thirteen chapters only.)

June 26. MR. WILDE'S BAD CASE. St. James's Gazette, Vol. XX. No. 3135, page 4.

June 27. MR. OSCAR WILDE AGAIN. St. James's Gazette, Vol. XX. No. 3136, page 5.

June 28. MR. OSCAR WILDE'S DEFENCE. St. James's Gazette, Vol. XX. No. 3137, page 5.

June 30. MR. OSCAR WILDE'S DEFENCE. St. James's Gazette, Vol. XX. No. 3138, page 5.

July. THE TRUE FUNCTION AND VALUE OF CRITICISM; WITH SOME REMARKS ON THE IMPORTANCE OF DOING NOTHING: A DIALOGUE. Nineteenth Century, Vol. XXVIII. No. 161, page 123.

July 2. 'DORIAN GRAY.' Daily Chronicle and Clerkenwell News, No. 8830, page 5.

July 12. MR. WILDE'S REJOINDER. Scots Observer, Vol. IV. No. 86, page 201.

August 2. ART AND MORALITY. Scots Observer, Vol. IV. No. 89, page 279.

August 16. ART AND MORALITY. Scots Observer, Vol. IV. No. 91, page 332.

September. THE TRUE FUNCTION AND VALUE OF CRITICISM; WITH SOME REMARKS ON THE IMPORTANCE OF DOING NOTHING: A DIALOGUE (concluded). Nineteenth Century, Vol. XXVIII. No. 163, page 435.

1891

February. THE SOUL OF MAN UNDER SOCIALISM. Fortnightly Review, Vol. XLIX. No. 290, page 292.

March. A PREFACE TO 'DORIAN GRAY.' Fortnightly Review, Vol. XLIX. No. 291, page 480.

September 26. AN ANGLO-INDIAN'S COMPLAINT. Times, No. 33,440, page 10.

December 5. 'A HOUSE OF POMEGRANATES.' Speaker, Vol. IV. No. 101, page 682.

December 11. MR. OSCAR WILDE'S 'HOUSE OF POMEGRANATES.' Pall Mall Gazette, Vol. LIII. No. 8339, page 2.

1892

February 20. PUPPETS AND ACTORS. Daily Telegraph, No. 11,470, page 3.

February 27. MR. OSCAR WILDE EXPLAINS. St. James's Gazette, Vol. XXIV. No. 3654, page 4.

December 6. THE NEW REMORSE. Spirit Lamp, Vol. II. No. 4, page 97.

1893

February 17. THE HOUSE OF JUDGMENT. Spirit Lamp, Vol. III.

No. 2, page 52.

March 2. MR. OSCAR WILDE ON 'SALOMÉ.' Times, No. 33,888, page 4.

June 6. THE DISCIPLE. Spirit Lamp, Vol. IV. No. 2, page 49.

TO MY WIFE: WITH A COPY OF MY POEMS; AND WITH A COPY OF 'THE HOUSE OF POMEGRANATES.' Book-Song, An Anthology of Poems of Books and Bookmen from Modern Authors. Edited by Gleeson White, pages 156, 157. London: Elliot Stock.

[This was the first publication of these two poems. Anthologies containing reprints are not included in this list.]

1894

January 15. LETTER TO THE PRESIDENT OF THE THIRTEEN CLUB. Times, No. 34,161, page 7.

July. POEMS IN PROSE. ('The Artist,' 'The Doer of Good,' 'The Disciple,' 'The Master,' 'The House of Judgment.') Fortnightly Review, Vol. LIV. No. 331, page 22.

September 20. THE ETHICS OF JOURNALISM. Pall Mall Gazette, Vol. LIX. No. 9202, page 3.

September 25. THE ETHICS OF JOURNALISM. Pall Mall Gazette, Vol. LIX. No. 9206, page 3.

October 2. 'THE GREEN CARNATION.' Pall Mall Gazette, Vol. LIX. No. 9212, page 3.

December. PHRASES AND PHILOSOPHIES FOR THE USE OF THE YOUNG. Chameleon, Vol. I. No. 1, page 1.

1895

April 6. LETTER ON THE QUEENSBERRY CASE. Evening News, No. 4226, page 3.

1897

May 28. THE CASE OF WARDER MARTIN. SOME CRUELTIES OF PRISON LIFE. Daily Chronicle, No. 10,992, page 9.

1898

March 24. LETTER ON PRISON REFORM. Daily Chronicle, No. 11,249, page 5.

Footnotes.

{0a} See *Lord Arthur Savile's Crime and other Prose Pieces* in this edition, page 223.

{3} Reverently some well-meaning persons have placed a marble slab on the wall of the cemetery with a medallion-profile of Keats on it and some mediocre lines of poetry. The face is ugly, and rather hatchet-shaped, with thick sensual lips, and is utterly unlike the poet himself, who was very beautiful to look upon. 'His countenance,' says a lady who saw him at one of Hazlitt's lectures, 'lives in my mind as one of singular beauty and brightness; it had the expression as if he had been looking on some glorious sight.' And this is the idea which Severn's picture of him gives. Even Haydon's rough pen-and-ink sketch of him is better than this 'marble libel,' which I hope will soon be taken down. I think the best representation of the poet would be a coloured bust, like that of the young Rajah of Koolapoor at Florence, which is a lovely and lifelike work of art.

{19} It is perhaps not generally known that there is another and older peacock ceiling in the world besides the one Mr. Whistler has done at Kensington. I was surprised lately at Ravenna to come across a mosaic ceiling done in the keynote of a peacock's tail—blue, green, purple, and gold—and with four peacocks in the four spandrils. Mr. Whistler was unaware of the existence of this ceiling at the time he did his own.

{43} An Unequal Match, by Tom Taylor, at Wallack's Theatre, New York, November 6, 1882.

{74} 'Make' is of course a mere printer's error for 'mock,' and was subsequently corrected by Lord Houghton. The sonnet as given in The Garden of Florence reads 'orbs' for 'those.'

{158} September 1890. See Intentions, page 214.

{163} November 30, 1891.

{164} February 12, 1892.

{170} February 23, 1893.

{172} The verses called 'The Shamrock' were printed in the Sunday Sun, August 5, 1894, and the charge of plagiarism was made in the issue dated September 16, 1894.

{188} Cousin errs a good deal in this respect. To say, as he did, 'Give me the latitude and the longitude of a country, its rivers and its mountains, and I will deduce the race,' is surely a glaring exaggeration.

{190} The monarchical, aristocratical, and democratic elements of the Roman constitution are referred to.

{193a} Polybius, vi. 9. αυτη πολιτειων ανακυκλωσις, αυτη φυσεως οικνομια.

{193b} χωρις οργης η φθονου ποιουμενος την αποδειξιν.

{193c} The various stages are συστασις, αυξησις, ακμη, μεταβολη ες τουμπαλιν.

{197a} Polybius, xii. 24.

{197b} Polybius, i. 4, viii. 4, specially; and really passim.

{198a} He makes one exception.

{198b} Polybius, viii. 4.

{199} Polybius, xvi. 12.

{200a} Polybius, viii. 4: το παραδοξοτον των καθ ημας εργον ητυχη συνετελεσε; τουτο δ' εστι το παντα τα γνωριζομενα μερη της οικουμενης υπο μιαν αρχην και δυναστειαν αγαγειν, ο προτερον ουχ ευρισκεται γεγονος

{200b} Polybius resembled Gibbon in many respects. Like him he held that all religions were to the philosopher equally false, to the vulgar equally true, to the statesman equally useful.

{203} Cf. Polybius, xii. 25, ψιλως λεγομενον το γεγονος ψυχαγωγει μεν, ωφελει δ'ουδεν προστεθεισης δε της αιτιας εγκαρπος η της ιστοριας γιγνεται χρησις.

{205} Polybius, xxii. 22.

{207} I mean particularly as regards his sweeping denunciation of the complete moral decadence of Greek society during the Peloponnesian War which, from what remains to us of Athenian literature, we know must have been completely exaggerated. Or, rather, he is looking at men merely in their political dealings: and in politics the man who is personally honourable and refined will not scruple to do anything for his party.

{211} Polybius, xii. 25.

{253} As an instance of the inaccuracy of published reports of this lecture, it may be mentioned that all previous versions give this passage as The artist may trace the depressed revolution of Bunthorne simply to the lack of technical means!

{317} The Two Paths, Lect. III. p. 123 (1859 ed.).

{328a} Edition for Continental circulation only. Leipzig: Bernhard Tauchnitz, vol. 4056. 1908 (August).

{328b} Edition for Continental circulation only. Leipzig: Bernhard Tauchnitz, vol. 4056. 1908 (August).

POEMS, WITH THE BALLAD OF READING GAOL

NOTE

This collection of Wilde's Poems contains the volume of 1881 in its entirety, 'The Sphinx', 'The Ballad of Reading Gaol,' and 'Ravenna.' Of the Uncollected Poems published in the Uniform Edition of 1908, a few, including the Translations from the Greek and the Polish, are omitted. Two new poems, 'Désespoir' and 'Pan,' which I have recently discovered in manuscript, are now printed for the first time. Particulars as to the original publication of each poem will be found in 'A Bibliography of the Poems of Oscar Wilde,' by Stuart Mason, London 1907.

ROBERT ROSS.

HÉLAS!

To drift with every passion till my soul

Is a stringed lute on which all winds can play,

Is it for this that I have given away

Mine ancient wisdom, and austere control?

Methinks my life is a twice-written scroll

Scrawled over on some boyish holiday

With idle songs for pipe and virelay,

Which do but mar the secret of the whole.

Surely there was a time I might have trod

The sunlit heights, and from life's dissonance

Struck one clear chord to reach the ears of God:

Is that time dead? lo! with a little rod

I did but touch the honey of romance—

And must I lose a soul's inheritance?

ELEUTHERIA

SONNET TO LIBERTY

Not that I love thy children, whose dull eyes

See nothing save their own unlovely woe,

Whose minds know nothing, nothing care to know,—

But that the roar of thy Democracies,

Thy reigns of Terror, thy great Anarchies,

Mirror my wildest passions like the sea

And give my rage a brother—! Liberty!

For this sake only do thy dissonant cries

Delight my discreet soul, else might all kings

By bloody knout or treacherous cannonades

Rob nations of their rights inviolate

And I remain unmoved—and yet, and yet,

These Christs that die upon the barricades,

God knows it I am with them, in some things.

AVE IMPERATRIX

Set in this stormy Northern sea,

  Queen of these restless fields of tide,

England! what shall men say of thee,

Before whose feet the worlds divide?

The earth, a brittle globe of glass,

   Lies in the hollow of thy hand,

And through its heart of crystal pass,

   Like shadows through a twilight land,

The spears of crimson-suited war,

   The long white-crested waves of fight,

And all the deadly fires which are

   The torches of the lords of Night.

The yellow leopards, strained and lean,

   The treacherous Russian knows so well,

With gaping blackened jaws are seen

   Leap through the hail of screaming shell.

The strong sea-lion of England's wars

   Hath left his sapphire cave of sea,

To battle with the storm that mars

   The stars of England's chivalry.

The brazen-throated clarion blows

Across the Pathan's reedy fen,

And the high steeps of Indian snows

Shake to the tread of armèd men.

And many an Afghan chief, who lies

Beneath his cool pomegranate-trees,

Clutches his sword in fierce surmise

When on the mountain-side he sees

The fleet-foot Marri scout, who comes

To tell how he hath heard afar

The measured roll of English drums

Beat at the gates of Kandahar.

For southern wind and east wind meet

Where, girt and crowned by sword and fire,

England with bare and bloody feet

Climbs the steep road of wide empire.

O lonely Himalayan height,

Grey pillar of the Indian sky,

Where saw'st thou last in clanging flight

Our wingèd dogs of Victory?

376

The almond-groves of Samarcand,

   Bokhara, where red lilies blow,

And Oxus, by whose yellow sand

   The grave white-turbaned merchants go:

And on from thence to Ispahan,

   The gilded garden of the sun,

Whence the long dusty caravan

   Brings cedar wood and vermilion;

And that dread city of Cabool

   Set at the mountain's scarpèd feet,

Whose marble tanks are ever full

   With water for the noonday heat:

Where through the narrow straight Bazaar

   A little maid Circassian

Is led, a present from the Czar

   Unto some old and bearded khan,—

Here have our wild war-eagles flown,

   And flapped wide wings in fiery fight;

But the sad dove, that sits alone
  In England—she hath no delight.

In vain the laughing girl will lean
  To greet her love with love-lit eyes:
Down in some treacherous black ravine,
  Clutching his flag, the dead boy lies.

And many a moon and sun will see
  The lingering wistful children wait
To climb upon their father's knee;
  And in each house made desolate

Pale women who have lost their lord
  Will kiss the relics of the slain—
Some tarnished epaulette—some sword—
  Poor toys to soothe such anguished pain.

For not in quiet English fields
  Are these, our brothers, lain to rest,
Where we might deck their broken shields
  With all the flowers the dead love best.

For some are by the Delhi walls,

And many in the Afghan land,

And many where the Ganges falls

Through seven mouths of shifting sand.

And some in Russian waters lie,

And others in the seas which are

The portals to the East, or by

The wind-swept heights of Trafalgar.

O wandering graves! O restless sleep!

O silence of the sunless day!

O still ravine! O stormy deep!

Give up your prey! Give up your prey!

And thou whose wounds are never healed,

Whose weary race is never won,

O Cromwell's England! must thou yield

For every inch of ground a son?

Go! crown with thorns thy gold-crowned head,

Change thy glad song to song of pain;

Wind and wild wave have got thy dead,

And will not yield them back again.

Wave and wild wind and foreign shore

    Possess the flower of English land—

Lips that thy lips shall kiss no more,

    Hands that shall never clasp thy hand.

What profit now that we have bound

    The whole round world with nets of gold,

If hidden in our heart is found

    The care that groweth never old?

What profit that our galleys ride,

    Pine-forest-like, on every main?

Ruin and wreck are at our side,

    Grim warders of the House of Pain.

Where are the brave, the strong, the fleet?

    Where is our English chivalry?

Wild grasses are their burial-sheet,

    And sobbing waves their threnody.

O loved ones lying far away,

    What word of love can dead lips send!

O wasted dust! O senseless clay!

  Is this the end! is this the end!

Peace, peace! we wrong the noble dead

  To vex their solemn slumber so;

Though childless, and with thorn-crowned head,

  Up the steep road must England go,

Yet when this fiery web is spun,

  Her watchmen shall descry from far

The young Republic like a sun

  Rise from these crimson seas of war.

TO MILTON

Milton! I think thy spirit hath passed away

From these white cliffs and high-embattled towers;

  This gorgeous fiery-coloured world of ours

Seems fallen into ashes dull and grey,

And the age changed unto a mimic play

  Wherein we waste our else too-crowded hours:

  For all our pomp and pageantry and powers

We are but fit to delve the common clay,

Seeing this little isle on which we stand,

  This England, this sea-lion of the sea,

By ignorant demagogues is held in fee,

Who love her not: Dear God! is this the land

Which bare a triple empire in her hand

When Cromwell spake the word Democracy!

LOUIS NAPOLEON

Eagle of Austerlitz! where were thy wings

When far away upon a barbarous strand,

In fight unequal, by an obscure hand,

Fell the last scion of thy brood of Kings!

Poor boy! thou shalt not flaunt thy cloak of red,

Or ride in state through Paris in the van

Of thy returning legions, but instead

Thy mother France, free and republican,

Shall on thy dead and crownless forehead place

The better laurels of a soldier's crown,

That not dishonoured should thy soul go down

To tell the mighty Sire of thy race

That France hath kissed the mouth of Liberty,

And found it sweeter than his honied bees,

And that the giant wave Democracy

Breaks on the shores where Kings lay couched at ease.

SONNET ON THE MASSACRE OF THE CHRISTIANS IN BULGARIA

Christ, dost Thou live indeed? or are Thy bones

Still straitened in their rock-hewn sepulchre?

And was Thy Rising only dreamed by her

Whose love of Thee for all her sin atones?

For here the air is horrid with men's groans,

The priests who call upon Thy name are slain,

Dost Thou not hear the bitter wail of pain

From those whose children lie upon the stones?

Come down, O Son of God! incestuous gloom

Curtains the land, and through the starless night

Over Thy Cross a Crescent moon I see!

If Thou in very truth didst burst the tomb

Come down, O Son of Man! and show Thy might

Lest Mahomet be crowned instead of Thee!

QUANTUM MUTATA

There was a time in Europe long ago

   When no man died for freedom anywhere,

   But England's lion leaping from its lair

Laid hands on the oppressor! it was so

While England could a great Republic show.

   Witness the men of Piedmont, chiefest care

   Of Cromwell, when with impotent despair

The Pontiff in his painted portico

Trembled before our stern ambassadors.

   How comes it then that from such high estate

   We have thus fallen, save that Luxury

With barren merchandise piles up the gate

Where noble thoughts and deeds should enter by:

   Else might we still be Milton's heritors.

LIBERTATIS SACRA FAMES

Albeit nurtured in democracy,

   And liking best that state republican

   Where every man is Kinglike and no man

Is crowned above his fellows, yet I see,

Spite of this modern fret for Liberty,

   Better the rule of One, whom all obey,

   Than to let clamorous demagogues betray

Our freedom with the kiss of anarchy.

Wherefore I love them not whose hands profane

   Plant the red flag upon the piled-up street

   For no right cause, beneath whose ignorant reign

Arts, Culture, Reverence, Honour, all things fade,

Save Treason and the dagger of her trade,

Or Murder with his silent bloody feet.

THEORETIKOS

This mighty empire hath but feet of clay:

Of all its ancient chivalry and might

Our little island is forsaken quite:

Some enemy hath stolen its crown of bay,

And from its hills that voice hath passed away

Which spake of Freedom: O come out of it,

Come out of it, my Soul, thou art not fit

For this vile traffic-house, where day by day

Wisdom and reverence are sold at mart,

And the rude people rage with ignorant cries

Against an heritage of centuries.

It mars my calm: wherefore in dreams of Art

And loftiest culture I would stand apart,

Neither for God, nor for his enemies.

THE GARDEN OF EROS

It is full summer now, the heart of June;

    Not yet the sunburnt reapers are astir

Upon the upland meadow where too soon

    Rich autumn time, the season's usurer,

Will lend his hoarded gold to all the trees,

And see his treasure scattered by the wild and spendthrift breeze.

Too soon indeed! yet here the daffodil,

    That love-child of the Spring, has lingered on

To vex the rose with jealousy, and still

    The harebell spreads her azure pavilion,

And like a strayed and wandering reveller

Abandoned of its brothers, whom long since June's messenger

The missel-thrush has frighted from the glade,

    One pale narcissus loiters fearfully

Close to a shadowy nook, where half afraid

    Of their own loveliness some violets lie

That will not look the gold sun in the face

For fear of too much splendour,—ah! methinks it is a place

Which should be trodden by Persephone

   When wearied of the flowerless fields of Dis!

Or danced on by the lads of Arcady!

   The hidden secret of eternal bliss

Known to the Grecian here a man might find,

Ah! you and I may find it now if Love and Sleep be kind.

There are the flowers which mourning Herakles

   Strewed on the tomb of Hylas, columbine,

Its white doves all a-flutter where the breeze

   Kissed them too harshly, the small celandine,

That yellow-kirtled chorister of eve,

And lilac lady's-smock,—but let them bloom alone, and leave

Yon spirèd hollyhock red-crocketed

   To sway its silent chimes, else must the bee,

Its little bellringer, go seek instead

   Some other pleasaunce; the anemone

That weeps at daybreak, like a silly girl

Before her love, and hardly lets the butterflies unfurl

Their painted wings beside it,—bid it pine

In pale virginity; the winter snow

Will suit it better than those lips of thine

Whose fires would but scorch it, rather go

And pluck that amorous flower which blooms alone,

Fed by the pander wind with dust of kisses not its own.

The trumpet-mouths of red convolvulus

So dear to maidens, creamy meadow-sweet

Whiter than Juno's throat and odorous

As all Arabia, hyacinths the feet

Of Huntress Dian would be loth to mar

For any dappled fawn,—pluck these, and those fond flowers which are

Fairer than what Queen Venus trod upon

Beneath the pines of Ida, eucharis,

That morning star which does not dread the sun,

And budding marjoram which but to kiss

Would sweeten Cytheræa's lips and make

Adonis jealous,—these for thy head,—and for thy girdle take

Yon curving spray of purple clematis

Whose gorgeous dye outflames the Tyrian King,

And foxgloves with their nodding chalices,

But that one narciss which the startled Spring

Let from her kirtle fall when first she heard

In her own woods the wild tempestuous song of summer's bird,

Ah! leave it for a subtle memory

 Of those sweet tremulous days of rain and sun,

When April laughed between her tears to see

 The early primrose with shy footsteps run

From the gnarled oak-tree roots till all the wold,

 Spite of its brown and trampled leaves, grew bright with shimmering gold.

Nay, pluck it too, it is not half so sweet

 As thou thyself, my soul's idolatry!

And when thou art a-wearied at thy feet

 Shall oxlips weave their brightest tapestry,

For thee the woodbine shall forget its pride

And veil its tangled whorls, and thou shalt walk on daisies pied.

And I will cut a reed by yonder spring

 And make the wood-gods jealous, and old Pan

Wonder what young intruder dares to sing

 In these still haunts, where never foot of man

Should tread at evening, lest he chance to spy

The marble limbs of Artemis and all her company.

And I will tell thee why the jacinth wears

   Such dread embroidery of dolorous moan,

And why the hapless nightingale forbears

   To sing her song at noon, but weeps alone

When the fleet swallow sleeps, and rich men feast,

And why the laurel trembles when she sees the lightening east.

And I will sing how sad Proserpina

   Unto a grave and gloomy Lord was wed,

And lure the silver-breasted Helena

   Back from the lotus meadows of the dead,

So shalt thou see that awful loveliness

For which two mighty Hosts met fearfully in war's abyss!

And then I'll pipe to thee that Grecian tale

   How Cynthia loves the lad Endymion,

And hidden in a grey and misty veil

   Hies to the cliffs of Latmos once the Sun

Leaps from his ocean bed in fruitless chase

Of those pale flying feet which fade away in his embrace.

And if my flute can breathe sweet melody,

We may behold Her face who long ago

Dwelt among men by the Ægean sea,

   And whose sad house with pillaged portico

And friezeless wall and columns toppled down

Looms o'er the ruins of that fair and violet cinctured town.

Spirit of Beauty! tarry still awhile,

   They are not dead, thine ancient votaries;

Some few there are to whom thy radiant smile

   Is better than a thousand victories,

Though all the nobly slain of Waterloo

Rise up in wrath against them! tarry still, there are a few

Who for thy sake would give their manlihood

   And consecrate their being; I at least

Have done so, made thy lips my daily food,

   And in thy temples found a goodlier feast

Than this starved age can give me, spite of all

Its new-found creeds so sceptical and so dogmatical.

Here not Cephissos, not Ilissos flows,

   The woods of white Colonos are not here,

On our bleak hills the olive never blows,

No simple priest conducts his lowing steer

Up the steep marble way, nor through the town

Do laughing maidens bear to thee the crocus-flowered gown.

Yet tarry! for the boy who loved thee best,

   Whose very name should be a memory

To make thee linger, sleeps in silent rest

   Beneath the Roman walls, and melody

Still mourns her sweetest lyre; none can play

The lute of Adonais: with his lips Song passed away.

Nay, when Keats died the Muses still had left

   One silver voice to sing his threnody,

But ah! too soon of it we were bereft

   When on that riven night and stormy sea

Panthea claimed her singer as her own,

And slew the mouth that praised her; since which time we walk alone,

Save for that fiery heart, that morning star

   Of re-arisen England, whose clear eye

Saw from our tottering throne and waste of war

   The grand Greek limbs of young Democracy

Rise mightily like Hesperus and bring

The great Republic! him at least thy love hath taught to sing,

And he hath been with thee at Thessaly,

   And seen white Atalanta fleet of foot

In passionless and fierce virginity

   Hunting the tuskèd boar, his honied lute

Hath pierced the cavern of the hollow hill,

And Venus laughs to know one knee will bow before her still.

And he hath kissed the lips of Proserpine,

   And sung the Galilæan's requiem,

That wounded forehead dashed with blood and wine

   He hath discrowned, the Ancient Gods in him

Have found their last, most ardent worshipper,

And the new Sign grows grey and dim before its conqueror.

Spirit of Beauty! tarry with us still,

   It is not quenched the torch of poesy,

The star that shook above the Eastern hill

   Holds unassailed its argent armoury

From all the gathering gloom and fretful fight—

O tarry with us still! for through the long and common night,

Morris, our sweet and simple Chaucer's child,

Dear heritor of Spenser's tuneful reed,

With soft and sylvan pipe has oft beguiled

The weary soul of man in troublous need,

And from the far and flowerless fields of ice

Has brought fair flowers to make an earthly paradise.

We know them all, Gudrun the strong men's bride,

Aslaug and Olafson we know them all,

How giant Grettir fought and Sigurd died,

And what enchantment held the king in thrall

When lonely Brynhild wrestled with the powers

That war against all passion, ah! how oft through summer hours,

Long listless summer hours when the noon

Being enamoured of a damask rose

Forgets to journey westward, till the moon

The pale usurper of its tribute grows

From a thin sickle to a silver shield

And chides its loitering car—how oft, in some cool grassy field

Far from the cricket-ground and noisy eight,

At Bagley, where the rustling bluebells come

Almost before the blackbird finds a mate

And overstay the swallow, and the hum

Of many murmuring bees flits through the leaves,

Have I lain poring on the dreamy tales his fancy weaves,

And through their unreal woes and mimic pain

  Wept for myself, and so was purified,

And in their simple mirth grew glad again;

  For as I sailed upon that pictured tide

The strength and splendour of the storm was mine

Without the storm's red ruin, for the singer is divine;

The little laugh of water falling down

  Is not so musical, the clammy gold

Close hoarded in the tiny waxen town

  Has less of sweetness in it, and the old

Half-withered reeds that waved in Arcady

Touched by his lips break forth again to fresher harmony.

Spirit of Beauty, tarry yet awhile!

  Although the cheating merchants of the mart

With iron roads profane our lovely isle,

  And break on whirling wheels the limbs of Art,

Ay! though the crowded factories beget

The blindworm Ignorance that slays the soul, O tarry yet!

For One at least there is,—He bears his name

    From Dante and the seraph Gabriel,—

Whose double laurels burn with deathless flame

    To light thine altar; He too loves thee well,

Who saw old Merlin lured in Vivien's snare,

And the white feet of angels coming down the golden stair,

Loves thee so well, that all the World for him

    A gorgeous-coloured vestiture must wear,

And Sorrow take a purple diadem,

    Or else be no more Sorrow, and Despair

Gild its own thorns, and Pain, like Adon, be

Even in anguish beautiful;—such is the empery

Which Painters hold, and such the heritage

    This gentle solemn Spirit doth possess,

Being a better mirror of his age

    In all his pity, love, and weariness,

Than those who can but copy common things,

And leave the Soul unpainted with its mighty questionings.

But they are few, and all romance has flown,

And men can prophesy about the sun,

And lecture on his arrows—how, alone,

   Through a waste void the soulless atoms run,

How from each tree its weeping nymph has fled,

And that no more 'mid English reeds a Naiad shows her head.

Methinks these new Actæons boast too soon

   That they have spied on beauty; what if we

Have analysed the rainbow, robbed the moon

   Of her most ancient, chastest mystery,

Shall I, the last Endymion, lose all hope

Because rude eyes peer at my mistress through a telescope!

What profit if this scientific age

   Burst through our gates with all its retinue

Of modern miracles! Can it assuage

   One lover's breaking heart? what can it do

To make one life more beautiful, one day

More godlike in its period? but now the Age of Clay

Returns in horrid cycle, and the earth

   Hath borne again a noisy progeny

Of ignorant Titans, whose ungodly birth

Hurls them against the august hierarchy

Which sat upon Olympus; to the Dust

They have appealed, and to that barren arbiter they must

Repair for judgment; let them, if they can,

From Natural Warfare and insensate Chance,

Create the new Ideal rule for man!

Methinks that was not my inheritance;

For I was nurtured otherwise, my soul

Passes from higher heights of life to a more supreme goal.

Lo! while we spake the earth did turn away

Her visage from the God, and Hecate's boat

Rose silver-laden, till the jealous day

Blew all its torches out: I did not note

The waning hours, to young Endymions

Time's palsied fingers count in vain his rosary of suns!

Mark how the yellow iris wearily

Leans back its throat, as though it would be kissed

By its false chamberer, the dragon-fly,

Who, like a blue vein on a girl's white wrist,

Sleeps on that snowy primrose of the night,

Which 'gins to flush with crimson shame, and die beneath the light.

Come let us go, against the pallid shield

   Of the wan sky the almond blossoms gleam,

The corncrake nested in the unmown field

   Answers its mate, across the misty stream

On fitful wing the startled curlews fly,

And in his sedgy bed the lark, for joy that Day is nigh,

Scatters the pearlèd dew from off the grass,

   In tremulous ecstasy to greet the sun,

Who soon in gilded panoply will pass

   Forth from yon orange-curtained pavilion

Hung in the burning east: see, the red rim

O'ertops the expectant hills! it is the God! for love of him

Already the shrill lark is out of sight,

   Flooding with waves of song this silent dell,—

Ah! there is something more in that bird's flight

   Than could be tested in a crucible!—

But the air freshens, let us go, why soon

The woodmen will be here; how we have lived this night of June!

ROSA MYSTICA

REQUIESCAT

Tread lightly, she is near

   Under the snow,

Speak gently, she can hear

   The daisies grow.

All her bright golden hair

   Tarnished with rust,

She that was young and fair

   Fallen to dust.

Lily-like, white as snow,

   She hardly knew

She was a woman, so

   Sweetly she grew.

Coffin-board, heavy stone,

   Lie on her breast,

I vex my heart alone,

She is at rest.

Peace, Peace, she cannot hear

Lyre or sonnet,

All my life's buried here,

Heap earth upon it.

Avignon.

SONNET ON APPROACHING ITALY

I reached the Alps: the soul within me burned,

Italia, my Italia, at thy name:

And when from out the mountain's heart I came

And saw the land for which my life had yearned,

I laughed as one who some great prize had earned:

And musing on the marvel of thy fame

I watched the day, till marked with wounds of flame

The turquoise sky to burnished gold was turned.

The pine-trees waved as waves a woman's hair,

And in the orchards every twining spray

Was breaking into flakes of blossoming foam:

But when I knew that far away at Rome

In evil bonds a second Peter lay,

I wept to see the land so very fair.

Turin.

SAN MINIATO

See, I have climbed the mountain side

Up to this holy house of God,

Where once that Angel-Painter trod

Who saw the heavens opened wide,

And throned upon the crescent moon

The Virginal white Queen of Grace,—

Mary! could I but see thy face

Death could not come at all too soon.

O crowned by God with thorns and pain!

Mother of Christ! O mystic wife!

My heart is weary of this life

And over-sad to sing again.

O crowned by God with love and flame!

O crowned by Christ the Holy One!

O listen ere the searching sun

Show to the world my sin and shame.

AVE MARIA GRATIA PLENA

Was this His coming! I had hoped to see

    A scene of wondrous glory, as was told

    Of some great God who in a rain of gold

Broke open bars and fell on Danae:

Or a dread vision as when Semele

    Sickening for love and unappeased desire

    Prayed to see God's clear body, and the fire

Caught her brown limbs and slew her utterly:

With such glad dreams I sought this holy place,

    And now with wondering eyes and heart I stand

    Before this supreme mystery of Love:

Some kneeling girl with passionless pale face,

    An angel with a lily in his hand,

    And over both the white wings of a Dove.

FLORENCE.

ITALIA

Italia! thou art fallen, though with sheen

    Of battle-spears thy clamorous armies stride

    From the north Alps to the Sicilian tide!

Ay! fallen, though the nations hail thee Queen

Because rich gold in every town is seen,

　　And on thy sapphire-lake in tossing pride

　　Of wind-filled vans thy myriad galleys ride

Beneath one flag of red and white and green.

O Fair and Strong! O Strong and Fair in vain!

　　Look southward where Rome's desecrated town

　　Lies mourning for her God-anointed King!

Look heaven-ward! shall God allow this thing?

　　Nay! but some flame-girt Raphael shall come down,

　　And smite the Spoiler with the sword of pain.

VENICE.

SONNET WRITTEN IN HOLY WEEK AT GENOA

I wandered through Scoglietto's far retreat,

　　The oranges on each o'erhanging spray

　　Burned as bright lamps of gold to shame the day;

Some startled bird with fluttering wings and fleet

Made snow of all the blossoms; at my feet

　　Like silver moons the pale narcissi lay:

　　And the curved waves that streaked the great green bay

Laughed i' the sun, and life seemed very sweet.

Outside the young boy-priest passed singing clear,

404

'Jesus the son of Mary has been slain,

O come and fill His sepulchre with flowers.'

Ah, God! Ah, God! those dear Hellenic hours

Had drowned all memory of Thy bitter pain,

The Cross, the Crown, the Soldiers and the Spear.

ROME UNVISITED

I.

The corn has turned from grey to red,

Since first my spirit wandered forth

From the drear cities of the north,

And to Italia's mountains fled.

And here I set my face towards home,

For all my pilgrimage is done,

Although, methinks, yon blood-red sun

Marshals the way to Holy Rome.

O Blessed Lady, who dost hold

Upon the seven hills thy reign!

O Mother without blot or stain,

Crowned with bright crowns of triple gold!

O Roma, Roma, at thy feet

  I lay this barren gift of song!

  For, ah! the way is steep and long

That leads unto thy sacred street.

II.

And yet what joy it were for me

  To turn my feet unto the south,

  And journeying towards the Tiber mouth

To kneel again at Fiesole!

And wandering through the tangled pines

  That break the gold of Arno's stream,

  To see the purple mist and gleam

Of morning on the Apennines

By many a vineyard-hidden home,

  Orchard and olive-garden grey,

  Till from the drear Campagna's way

The seven hills bear up the dome!

III.

A pilgrim from the northern seas—

   What joy for me to seek alone

   The wondrous temple and the throne

Of him who holds the awful keys!

When, bright with purple and with gold

   Come priest and holy cardinal,

   And borne above the heads of all

The gentle Shepherd of the Fold.

O joy to see before I die

   The only God-anointed king,

   And hear the silver trumpets ring

A triumph as he passes by!

Or at the brazen-pillared shrine

   Holds high the mystic sacrifice,

   And shows his God to human eyes

Beneath the veil of bread and wine.

IV.

For lo, what changes time can bring!

The cycles of revolving years

May free my heart from all its fears,

And teach my lips a song to sing.

Before yon field of trembling gold

Is garnered into dusty sheaves,

Or ere the autumn's scarlet leaves

Flutter as birds adown the wold,

I may have run the glorious race,

And caught the torch while yet aflame,

And called upon the holy name

Of Him who now doth hide His face.

ARONA.

URBS SACRA ÆTERNA

Rome! what a scroll of History thine has been;

In the first days thy sword republican

Ruled the whole world for many an age's span:

Then of the peoples wert thou royal Queen,

Till in thy streets the bearded Goth was seen;

And now upon thy walls the breezes fan

(Ah, city crowned by God, discrowned by man!)

The hated flag of red and white and green.

When was thy glory! when in search for power

Thine eagles flew to greet the double sun,

And the wild nations shuddered at thy rod?

Nay, but thy glory tarried for this hour,

When pilgrims kneel before the Holy One,

The prisoned shepherd of the Church of God.

MONTRE MARIO.

SONNET ON HEARING THE DIES IRÆ SUNG IN THE SISTINE CHAPEL

Nay, Lord, not thus! white lilies in the spring,

Sad olive-groves, or silver-breasted dove,

Teach me more clearly of Thy life and love

Than terrors of red flame and thundering.

The hillside vines dear memories of Thee bring:

A bird at evening flying to its nest

Tells me of One who had no place of rest:

I think it is of Thee the sparrows sing.

Come rather on some autumn afternoon,

When red and brown are burnished on the leaves,

And the fields echo to the gleaner's song,

Come when the splendid fulness of the moon

Looks down upon the rows of golden sheaves,

And reap Thy harvest: we have waited long.

EASTER DAY

The silver trumpets rang across the Dome:

The people knelt upon the ground with awe:

And borne upon the necks of men I saw,

Like some great God, the Holy Lord of Rome.

Priest-like, he wore a robe more white than foam,

And, king-like, swathed himself in royal red,

Three crowns of gold rose high upon his head:

In splendour and in light the Pope passed home.

My heart stole back across wide wastes of years

To One who wandered by a lonely sea,

And sought in vain for any place of rest:

'Foxes have holes, and every bird its nest.

I, only I, must wander wearily,

And bruise my feet, and drink wine salt with tears.'

E TENEBRIS

Come down, O Christ, and help me! reach Thy hand,

For I am drowning in a stormier sea

Than Simon on Thy lake of Galilee:

The wine of life is spilt upon the sand,

My heart is as some famine-murdered land

    Whence all good things have perished utterly,

    And well I know my soul in Hell must lie

If I this night before God's throne should stand.

'He sleeps perchance, or rideth to the chase,

    Like Baal, when his prophets howled that name

    From morn to noon on Carmel's smitten height.'

Nay, peace, I shall behold, before the night,

    The feet of brass, the robe more white than flame,

    The wounded hands, the weary human face.

VITA NUOVA

I stood by the unvintageable sea

    Till the wet waves drenched face and hair with spray;

    The long red fires of the dying day

Burned in the west; the wind piped drearily;

And to the land the clamorous gulls did flee:

    'Alas!' I cried, 'my life is full of pain,

    And who can garner fruit or golden grain

From these waste fields which travail ceaselessly!'

My nets gaped wide with many a break and flaw,

    Nathless I threw them as my final cast

    Into the sea, and waited for the end.

When lo! a sudden glory! and I saw

From the black waters of my tortured past

The argent splendour of white limbs ascend!

MADONNA MIA

A lily-girl, not made for this world's pain,

    With brown, soft hair close braided by her ears,

    And longing eyes half veiled by slumberous tears

Like bluest water seen through mists of rain:

Pale cheeks whereon no love hath left its stain,

    Red underlip drawn in for fear of love,

    And white throat, whiter than the silvered dove,

Through whose wan marble creeps one purple vein.

Yet, though my lips shall praise her without cease,

    Even to kiss her feet I am not bold,

    Being o'ershadowed by the wings of awe,

Like Dante, when he stood with Beatrice

    Beneath the flaming Lion's breast, and saw

    The seventh Crystal, and the Stair of Gold.

THE NEW HELEN

Where hast thou been since round the walls of Troy

    The sons of God fought in that great emprise?

      Why dost thou walk our common earth again?

    Hast thou forgotten that impassioned boy,

412

His purple galley and his Tyrian men

And treacherous Aphrodite's mocking eyes?

For surely it was thou, who, like a star

Hung in the silver silence of the night,

Didst lure the Old World's chivalry and might

Into the clamorous crimson waves of war!

Or didst thou rule the fire-laden moon?

In amorous Sidon was thy temple built

Over the light and laughter of the sea

Where, behind lattice scarlet-wrought and gilt,

Some brown-limbed girl did weave thee tapestry,

All through the waste and wearied hours of noon;

Till her wan cheek with flame of passion burned,

And she rose up the sea-washed lips to kiss

Of some glad Cyprian sailor, safe returned

From Calpé and the cliffs of Herakles!

No! thou art Helen, and none other one!

It was for thee that young Sarpedôn died,

And Memnôn's manhood was untimely spent;

It was for thee gold-crested Hector tried

With Thetis' child that evil race to run,

In the last year of thy beleaguerment;

Ay! even now the glory of thy fame

Burns in those fields of trampled asphodel,

Where the high lords whom Ilion knew so well

Clash ghostly shields, and call upon thy name.

Where hast thou been? in that enchanted land

Whose slumbering vales forlorn Calypso knew,

Where never mower rose at break of day

But all unswathed the trammelling grasses grew,

And the sad shepherd saw the tall corn stand

Till summer's red had changed to withered grey?

Didst thou lie there by some Lethæan stream

Deep brooding on thine ancient memory,

The crash of broken spears, the fiery gleam

From shivered helm, the Grecian battle-cry?

Nay, thou wert hidden in that hollow hill

With one who is forgotten utterly,

That discrowned Queen men call the Erycine;

Hidden away that never mightst thou see

The face of Her, before whose mouldering shrine

To-day at Rome the silent nations kneel;

Who gat from Love no joyous gladdening,

But only Love's intolerable pain,

Only a sword to pierce her heart in twain,

Only the bitterness of child-bearing.

The lotus-leaves which heal the wounds of Death

Lie in thy hand; O, be thou kind to me,

While yet I know the summer of my days;

For hardly can my tremulous lips draw breath

To fill the silver trumpet with thy praise,

So bowed am I before thy mystery;

So bowed and broken on Love's terrible wheel,

That I have lost all hope and heart to sing,

Yet care I not what ruin time may bring

If in thy temple thou wilt let me kneel.

Alas, alas, thou wilt not tarry here,

But, like that bird, the servant of the sun,

Who flies before the north wind and the night,

So wilt thou fly our evil land and drear,

Back to the tower of thine old delight,

And the red lips of young Euphorion;

Nor shall I ever see thy face again,

But in this poisonous garden-close must stay,

Crowning my brows with the thorn-crown of pain,

Till all my loveless life shall pass away.

O Helen! Helen! Helen! yet a while,

Yet for a little while, O, tarry here,

Till the dawn cometh and the shadows flee!

For in the gladsome sunlight of thy smile

Of heaven or hell I have no thought or fear,

Seeing I know no other god but thee:

No other god save him, before whose feet

In nets of gold the tired planets move,

The incarnate spirit of spiritual love

Who in thy body holds his joyous seat.

Thou wert not born as common women are!

But, girt with silver splendour of the foam,

Didst from the depths of sapphire seas arise!

And at thy coming some immortal star,

Bearded with flame, blazed in the Eastern skies,

And waked the shepherds on thine island-home.

Thou shalt not die: no asps of Egypt creep

Close at thy heels to taint the delicate air;

No sullen-blooming poppies stain thy hair,

Those scarlet heralds of eternal sleep.

Lily of love, pure and inviolate!

  Tower of ivory! red rose of fire!

    Thou hast come down our darkness to illume:

For we, close-caught in the wide nets of Fate,

  Wearied with waiting for the World's Desire,

    Aimlessly wandered in the House of gloom,

Aimlessly sought some slumberous anodyne

  For wasted lives, for lingering wretchedness,

Till we beheld thy re-arisen shrine,

  And the white glory of thy loveliness.

THE BURDEN OF ITYS

This English Thames is holier far than Rome,

   Those harebells like a sudden flush of sea

Breaking across the woodland, with the foam

   Of meadow-sweet and white anemone

To fleck their blue waves,—God is likelier there

Than hidden in that crystal-hearted star the pale monks bear!

Those violet-gleaming butterflies that take

   Yon creamy lily for their pavilion

Are monsignores, and where the rushes shake

   A lazy pike lies basking in the sun,

His eyes half shut,—he is some mitred old

Bishop in partibus! look at those gaudy scales all green and gold.

The wind the restless prisoner of the trees

   Does well for Palæstrina, one would say

The mighty master's hands were on the keys

   Of the Maria organ, which they play

When early on some sapphire Easter morn

In a high litter red as blood or sin the Pope is borne

From his dark House out to the Balcony

    Above the bronze gates and the crowded square,

Whose very fountains seem for ecstasy

    To toss their silver lances in the air,

And stretching out weak hands to East and West

In vain sends peace to peaceless lands, to restless nations rest.

Is not yon lingering orange after-glow

    That stays to vex the moon more fair than all

Rome's lordliest pageants! strange, a year ago

    I knelt before some crimson Cardinal

Who bare the Host across the Esquiline,

And now—those common poppies in the wheat seem twice as fine.

The blue-green beanfields yonder, tremulous

    With the last shower, sweeter perfume bring

Through this cool evening than the odorous

    Flame-jewelled censers the young deacons swing,

When the grey priest unlocks the curtained shrine,

And makes God's body from the common fruit of corn and vine.

Poor Fra Giovanni bawling at the mass

Were out of tune now, for a small brown bird

Sings overhead, and through the long cool grass

    I see that throbbing throat which once I heard

On starlit hills of flower-starred Arcady,

Once where the white and crescent sand of Salamis meets sea.

Sweet is the swallow twittering on the eaves

    At daybreak, when the mower whets his scythe,

And stock-doves murmur, and the milkmaid leaves

    Her little lonely bed, and carols blithe

To see the heavy-lowing cattle wait

Stretching their huge and dripping mouths across the farmyard gate.

And sweet the hops upon the Kentish leas,

    And sweet the wind that lifts the new-mown hay,

And sweet the fretful swarms of grumbling bees

    That round and round the linden blossoms play;

And sweet the heifer breathing in the stall,

And the green bursting figs that hang upon the red-brick wall,

And sweet to hear the cuckoo mock the spring

    While the last violet loiters by the well,

And sweet to hear the shepherd Daphnis sing

The song of Linus through a sunny dell

Of warm Arcadia where the corn is gold

And the slight lithe-limbed reapers dance about the wattled fold.

And sweet with young Lycoris to recline

  In some Illyrian valley far away,

Where canopied on herbs amaracine

  We too might waste the summer-trancèd day

Matching our reeds in sportive rivalry,

While far beneath us frets the troubled purple of the sea.

But sweeter far if silver-sandalled foot

  Of some long-hidden God should ever tread

The Nuneham meadows, if with reeded flute

  Pressed to his lips some Faun might raise his head

By the green water-flags, ah! sweet indeed

To see the heavenly herdsman call his white-fleeced flock to feed.

Then sing to me thou tuneful chorister,

  Though what thou sing'st be thine own requiem!

Tell me thy tale thou hapless chronicler

  Of thine own tragedies! do not contemn

These unfamiliar haunts, this English field,

For many a lovely coronal our northern isle can yield

Which Grecian meadows know not, many a rose

   Which all day long in vales Æolian

A lad might seek in vain for over-grows

   Our hedges like a wanton courtesan

Unthrifty of its beauty; lilies too

Ilissos never mirrored star our streams, and cockles blue

Dot the green wheat which, though they are the signs

   For swallows going south, would never spread

Their azure tents between the Attic vines;

   Even that little weed of ragged red,

Which bids the robin pipe, in Arcady

Would be a trespasser, and many an unsung elegy

Sleeps in the reeds that fringe our winding Thames

   Which to awake were sweeter ravishment

Than ever Syrinx wept for; diadems

   Of brown bee-studded orchids which were meant

For Cytheræa's brows are hidden here

Unknown to Cytheræa, and by yonder pasturing steer

There is a tiny yellow daffodil,

The butterfly can see it from afar,

Although one summer evening's dew could fill

    Its little cup twice over ere the star

Had called the lazy shepherd to his fold

And be no prodigal; each leaf is flecked with spotted gold

As if Jove's gorgeous leman Danae

    Hot from his gilded arms had stooped to kiss

The trembling petals, or young Mercury

    Low-flying to the dusky ford of Dis

Had with one feather of his pinions

Just brushed them! the slight stem which bears the burden of its suns

Is hardly thicker than the gossamer,

    Or poor Arachne's silver tapestry,—

Men say it bloomed upon the sepulchre

    Of One I sometime worshipped, but to me

It seems to bring diviner memories

Of faun-loved Heliconian glades and blue nymph-haunted seas,

Of an untrodden vale at Tempe where

    On the clear river's marge Narcissus lies,

The tangle of the forest in his hair,

The silence of the woodland in his eyes,

Wooing that drifting imagery which is

No sooner kissed than broken; memories of Salmacis

Who is not boy nor girl and yet is both,

   Fed by two fires and unsatisfied

Through their excess, each passion being loth

   For love's own sake to leave the other's side

Yet killing love by staying; memories

Of Oreads peeping through the leaves of silent moonlit trees,

Of lonely Ariadne on the wharf

   At Naxos, when she saw the treacherous crew

Far out at sea, and waved her crimson scarf

   And called false Theseus back again nor knew

That Dionysos on an amber pard

Was close behind her; memories of what Mæonia's bard

With sightless eyes beheld, the wall of Troy,

   Queen Helen lying in the ivory room,

And at her side an amorous red-lipped boy

   Trimming with dainty hand his helmet's plume,

And far away the moil, the shout, the groan,

424

As Hector shielded off the spear and Ajax hurled the stone;

Of wingèd Perseus with his flawless sword

   Cleaving the snaky tresses of the witch,

And all those tales imperishably stored

   In little Grecian urns, freightage more rich

Than any gaudy galleon of Spain

Bare from the Indies ever! these at least bring back again,

For well I know they are not dead at all,

   The ancient Gods of Grecian poesy:

They are asleep, and when they hear thee call

   Will wake and think 't is very Thessaly,

This Thames the Daulian waters, this cool glade

The yellow-irised mead where once young Itys laughed and played.

If it was thou dear jasmine-cradled bird

   Who from the leafy stillness of thy throne

Sang to the wondrous boy, until he heard

   The horn of Atalanta faintly blown

Across the Cumnor hills, and wandering

Through Bagley wood at evening found the Attic poets' spring,—

Ah! tiny sober-suited advocate

That pleadest for the moon against the day!

If thou didst make the shepherd seek his mate

  On that sweet questing, when Proserpina

Forgot it was not Sicily and leant

Across the mossy Sandford stile in ravished wonderment,—

Light-winged and bright-eyed miracle of the wood!

  If ever thou didst soothe with melody

One of that little clan, that brotherhood

  Which loved the morning-star of Tuscany

More than the perfect sun of Raphael

And is immortal, sing to me! for I too love thee well.

Sing on! sing on! let the dull world grow young,

  Let elemental things take form again,

And the old shapes of Beauty walk among

  The simple garths and open crofts, as when

The son of Leto bare the willow rod,

And the soft sheep and shaggy goats followed the boyish God.

Sing on! sing on! and Bacchus will be here

  Astride upon his gorgeous Indian throne,

And over whimpering tigers shake the spear

With yellow ivy crowned and gummy cone,

While at his side the wanton Bassarid

Will throw the lion by the mane and catch the mountain kid!

Sing on! and I will wear the leopard skin,

   And steal the moonèd wings of Ashtaroth,

Upon whose icy chariot we could win

   Cithæron in an hour ere the froth

Has over-brimmed the wine-vat or the Faun

Ceased from the treading! ay, before the flickering lamp of dawn

Has scared the hooting owlet to its nest,

   And warned the bat to close its filmy vans,

Some Mænad girl with vine-leaves on her breast

   Will filch their beech-nuts from the sleeping Pans

So softly that the little nested thrush

Will never wake, and then with shrilly laugh and leap will rush

Down the green valley where the fallen dew

   Lies thick beneath the elm and count her store,

Till the brown Satyrs in a jolly crew

   Trample the loosestrife down along the shore,

And where their hornèd master sits in state

Bring strawberries and bloomy plums upon a wicker crate!

Sing on! and soon with passion-wearied face
   Through the cool leaves Apollo's lad will come,
The Tyrian prince his bristled boar will chase
   Adown the chestnut-copses all a-bloom,
And ivory-limbed, grey-eyed, with look of pride,
After yon velvet-coated deer the virgin maid will ride.

Sing on! and I the dying boy will see
   Stain with his purple blood the waxen bell
That overweighs the jacinth, and to me
   The wretched Cyprian her woe will tell,
And I will kiss her mouth and streaming eyes,
And lead her to the myrtle-hidden grove where Adon lies!

Cry out aloud on Itys! memory
   That foster-brother of remorse and pain
Drops poison in mine ear,—O to be free,
   To burn one's old ships! and to launch again
Into the white-plumed battle of the waves
And fight old Proteus for the spoil of coral-flowered caves!

O for Medea with her poppied spell!

O for the secret of the Colchian shrine!

O for one leaf of that pale asphodel

  Which binds the tired brows of Proserpine,

And sheds such wondrous dews at eve that she

Dreams of the fields of Enna, by the far Sicilian sea,

Where oft the golden-girdled bee she chased

  From lily to lily on the level mead,

Ere yet her sombre Lord had bid her taste

  The deadly fruit of that pomegranate seed,

Ere the black steeds had harried her away

Down to the faint and flowerless land, the sick and sunless day.

O for one midnight and as paramour

  The Venus of the little Melian farm!

O that some antique statue for one hour

  Might wake to passion, and that I could charm

The Dawn at Florence from its dumb despair,

Mix with those mighty limbs and make that giant breast my lair!

Sing on! sing on! I would be drunk with life,

  Drunk with the trampled vintage of my youth,

I would forget the wearying wasted strife,

The riven veil, the Gorgon eyes of Truth,

The prayerless vigil and the cry for prayer,

The barren gifts, the lifted arms, the dull insensate air!

Sing on! sing on! O feathered Niobe,

   Thou canst make sorrow beautiful, and steal

From joy its sweetest music, not as we

   Who by dead voiceless silence strive to heal

Our too untented wounds, and do but keep

Pain barricadoed in our hearts, and murder pillowed sleep.

Sing louder yet, why must I still behold

   The wan white face of that deserted Christ,

Whose bleeding hands my hands did once enfold,

   Whose smitten lips my lips so oft have kissed,

And now in mute and marble misery

Sits in his lone dishonoured House and weeps, perchance for me?

O Memory cast down thy wreathèd shell!

   Break thy hoarse lute O sad Melpomene!

O Sorrow, Sorrow keep thy cloistered cell

   Nor dim with tears this limpid Castaly!

Cease, Philomel, thou dost the forest wrong

430

To vex its sylvan quiet with such wild impassioned song!

Cease, cease, or if 't is anguish to be dumb
　　Take from the pastoral thrush her simpler air,
Whose jocund carelessness doth more become
　　This English woodland than thy keen despair,
Ah! cease and let the north wind bear thy lay
Back to the rocky hills of Thrace, the stormy Daulian bay.

A moment more, the startled leaves had stirred,
　　Endymion would have passed across the mead
Moonstruck with love, and this still Thames had heard
　　Pan plash and paddle groping for some reed
To lure from her blue cave that Naiad maid
Who for such piping listens half in joy and half afraid.

A moment more, the waking dove had cooed,
　　The silver daughter of the silver sea
With the fond gyves of clinging hands had wooed
　　Her wanton from the chase, and Dryope
Had thrust aside the branches of her oak
To see the lusty gold-haired lad rein in his snorting yoke.

A moment more, the trees had stooped to kiss

Pale Daphne just awakening from the swoon

Of tremulous laurels, lonely Salmacis

  Had bared his barren beauty to the moon,

And through the vale with sad voluptuous smile

Antinous had wandered, the red lotus of the Nile

Down leaning from his black and clustering hair,

  To shade those slumberous eyelids' caverned bliss,

Or else on yonder grassy slope with bare

  High-tuniced limbs unravished Artemis

Had bade her hounds give tongue, and roused the deer

From his green ambuscade with shrill halloo and pricking spear.

Lie still, lie still, O passionate heart, lie still!

  O Melancholy, fold thy raven wing!

O sobbing Dryad, from thy hollow hill

  Come not with such despondent answering!

No more thou wingèd Marsyas complain,

Apollo loveth not to hear such troubled songs of pain!

It was a dream, the glade is tenantless,

  No soft Ionian laughter moves the air,

The Thames creeps on in sluggish leadenness,

And from the copse left desolate and bare

Fled is young Bacchus with his revelry,

Yet still from Nuneham wood there comes that thrilling melody

So sad, that one might think a human heart

   Brake in each separate note, a quality

Which music sometimes has, being the Art

   Which is most nigh to tears and memory;

Poor mourning Philomel, what dost thou fear?

Thy sister doth not haunt these fields, Pandion is not here,

Here is no cruel Lord with murderous blade,

   No woven web of bloody heraldries,

But mossy dells for roving comrades made,

   Warm valleys where the tired student lies

With half-shut book, and many a winding walk

Where rustic lovers stray at eve in happy simple talk.

The harmless rabbit gambols with its young

   Across the trampled towing-path, where late

A troop of laughing boys in jostling throng

   Cheered with their noisy cries the racing eight;

The gossamer, with ravelled silver threads,

Works at its little loom, and from the dusky red-eaved sheds

Of the lone Farm a flickering light shines out
   Where the swinked shepherd drives his bleating flock
Back to their wattled sheep-cotes, a faint shout
   Comes from some Oxford boat at Sandford lock,
And starts the moor-hen from the sedgy rill,
And the dim lengthening shadows flit like swallows up the hill.

The heron passes homeward to the mere,
   The blue mist creeps among the shivering trees,
Gold world by world the silent stars appear,
   And like a blossom blown before the breeze
A white moon drifts across the shimmering sky,
Mute arbitress of all thy sad, thy rapturous threnody.

She does not heed thee, wherefore should she heed,
   She knows Endymion is not far away;
'Tis I, 'tis I, whose soul is as the reed
   Which has no message of its own to play,
So pipes another's bidding, it is I,
Drifting with every wind on the wide sea of misery.

Ah! the brown bird has ceased: one exquisite trill

434

About the sombre woodland seems to cling

Dying in music, else the air is still,

So still that one might hear the bat's small wing

Wander and wheel above the pines, or tell

Each tiny dew-drop dripping from the bluebell's brimming cell.

And far away across the lengthening wold,

Across the willowy flats and thickets brown,

Magdalen's tall tower tipped with tremulous gold

Marks the long High Street of the little town,

And warns me to return; I must not wait,

Hark! 't is the curfew booming from the bell at Christ Church gate.

WIND FLOWERS

IMPRESSION DU MATIN

The Thames nocturne of blue and gold
   Changed to a Harmony in grey:
   A barge with ochre-coloured hay
Dropt from the wharf: and chill and cold

The yellow fog came creeping down
   The bridges, till the houses' walls
   Seemed changed to shadows and St. Paul's
Loomed like a bubble o'er the town.

Then suddenly arose the clang
   Of waking life; the streets were stirred
   With country waggons: and a bird
Flew to the glistening roofs and sang.

But one pale woman all alone,
   The daylight kissing her wan hair,
   Loitered beneath the gas lamps' flare,
With lips of flame and heart of stone.

MAGDALEN WALKS

The little white clouds are racing over the sky,

    And the fields are strewn with the gold of the flower of March,

    The daffodil breaks under foot, and the tasselled larch

Sways and swings as the thrush goes hurrying by.

A delicate odour is borne on the wings of the morning breeze,

    The odour of deep wet grass, and of brown new-furrowed earth,

    The birds are singing for joy of the Spring's glad birth,

Hopping from branch to branch on the rocking trees.

And all the woods are alive with the murmur and sound of Spring,

    And the rose-bud breaks into pink on the climbing briar,

    And the crocus-bed is a quivering moon of fire

Girdled round with the belt of an amethyst ring.

And the plane to the pine-tree is whispering some tale of love

    Till it rustles with laughter and tosses its mantle of green,

    And the gloom of the wych-elm's hollow is lit with the iris sheen

Of the burnished rainbow throat and the silver breast of a dove.

See! the lark starts up from his bed in the meadow there,

    Breaking the gossamer threads and the nets of dew,

437

And flashing adown the river, a flame of blue!

The kingfisher flies like an arrow, and wounds the air.

ATHANASIA

To that gaunt House of Art which lacks for naught

   Of all the great things men have saved from Time,

The withered body of a girl was brought

   Dead ere the world's glad youth had touched its prime,

And seen by lonely Arabs lying hid

In the dim womb of some black pyramid.

But when they had unloosed the linen band

   Which swathed the Egyptian's body,—lo! was found

Closed in the wasted hollow of her hand

   A little seed, which sown in English ground

Did wondrous snow of starry blossoms bear

And spread rich odours through our spring-tide air.

With such strange arts this flower did allure

   That all forgotten was the asphodel,

And the brown bee, the lily's paramour,

   Forsook the cup where he was wont to dwell,

For not a thing of earth it seemed to be,

But stolen from some heavenly Arcady.

438

In vain the sad narcissus, wan and white

  At its own beauty, hung across the stream,

The purple dragon-fly had no delight

  With its gold dust to make his wings a-gleam,

Ah! no delight the jasmine-bloom to kiss,

Or brush the rain-pearls from the eucharis.

For love of it the passionate nightingale

  Forgot the hills of Thrace, the cruel king,

And the pale dove no longer cared to sail

  Through the wet woods at time of blossoming,

But round this flower of Egypt sought to float,

With silvered wing and amethystine throat.

While the hot sun blazed in his tower of blue

  A cooling wind crept from the land of snows,

And the warm south with tender tears of dew

  Drenched its white leaves when Hesperos up-rose

Amid those sea-green meadows of the sky

On which the scarlet bars of sunset lie.

But when o'er wastes of lily-haunted field

The tired birds had stayed their amorous tune,

And broad and glittering like an argent shield

High in the sapphire heavens hung the moon,

Did no strange dream or evil memory make

Each tremulous petal of its blossoms shake?

Ah no! to this bright flower a thousand years

Seemed but the lingering of a summer's day,

It never knew the tide of cankering fears

Which turn a boy's gold hair to withered grey,

The dread desire of death it never knew,

Or how all folk that they were born must rue.

For we to death with pipe and dancing go,

Nor would we pass the ivory gate again,

As some sad river wearied of its flow

Through the dull plains, the haunts of common men,

Leaps lover-like into the terrible sea!

And counts it gain to die so gloriously.

We mar our lordly strength in barren strife

With the world's legions led by clamorous care,

It never feels decay but gathers life

From the pure sunlight and the supreme air,

We live beneath Time's wasting sovereignty,

It is the child of all eternity.

SERENADE

(FOR MUSIC)

The western wind is blowing fair

   Across the dark Ægean sea,

And at the secret marble stair

   My Tyrian galley waits for thee.

Come down! the purple sail is spread,

   The watchman sleeps within the town,

O leave thy lily-flowered bed,

   O Lady mine come down, come down!

She will not come, I know her well,

   Of lover's vows she hath no care,

And little good a man can tell

   Of one so cruel and so fair.

True love is but a woman's toy,

   They never know the lover's pain,

And I who loved as loves a boy

   Must love in vain, must love in vain.

O noble pilot, tell me true,

   Is that the sheen of golden hair?

Or is it but the tangled dew

   That binds the passion-flowers there?

Good sailor come and tell me now

   Is that my Lady's lily hand?

Or is it but the gleaming prow,

   Or is it but the silver sand?

No! no! 'tis not the tangled dew,

   'Tis not the silver-fretted sand,

It is my own dear Lady true

   With golden hair and lily hand!

O noble pilot, steer for Troy,

   Good sailor, ply the labouring oar,

This is the Queen of life and joy

   Whom we must bear from Grecian shore!

The waning sky grows faint and blue,

   It wants an hour still of day,

Aboard! aboard! my gallant crew,

   O Lady mine, away! away!

O noble pilot, steer for Troy,

    Good sailor, ply the labouring oar,

O loved as only loves a boy!

    O loved for ever evermore!

ENDYMION

(FOR MUSIC)

The apple trees are hung with gold,

    And birds are loud in Arcady,

The sheep lie bleating in the fold,

The wild goat runs across the wold,

But yesterday his love he told,

    I know he will come back to me.

O rising moon! O Lady moon!

    Be you my lover's sentinel,

    You cannot choose but know him well,

For he is shod with purple shoon,

You cannot choose but know my love,

    For he a shepherd's crook doth bear,

And he is soft as any dove,

    And brown and curly is his hair.

The turtle now has ceased to call

Upon her crimson-footed groom,

The grey wolf prowls about the stall,

The lily's singing seneschal

Sleeps in the lily-bell, and all

   The violet hills are lost in gloom.

O risen moon! O holy moon!

   Stand on the top of Helice,

   And if my own true love you see,

Ah! if you see the purple shoon,

The hazel crook, the lad's brown hair,

   The goat-skin wrapped about his arm,

Tell him that I am waiting where

   The rushlight glimmers in the Farm.

The falling dew is cold and chill,

   And no bird sings in Arcady,

The little fauns have left the hill,

Even the tired daffodil

Has closed its gilded doors, and still

   My lover comes not back to me.

False moon! False moon! O waning moon!

   Where is my own true lover gone,

   Where are the lips vermilion,

The shepherd's crook, the purple shoon?

Why spread that silver pavilion,

   Why wear that veil of drifting mist?

Ah! thou hast young Endymion,

   Thou hast the lips that should be kissed!

LA BELLA DONNA DELLA MIA MENTE

My limbs are wasted with a flame,

   My feet are sore with travelling,

For, calling on my Lady's name,

   My lips have now forgot to sing.

O Linnet in the wild-rose brake

   Strain for my Love thy melody,

O Lark sing louder for love's sake,

   My gentle Lady passeth by.

She is too fair for any man

   To see or hold his heart's delight,

Fairer than Queen or courtesan

   Or moonlit water in the night.

Her hair is bound with myrtle leaves,

   (Green leaves upon her golden hair!)

Green grasses through the yellow sheaves

    Of autumn corn are not more fair.

Her little lips, more made to kiss

    Than to cry bitterly for pain,

Are tremulous as brook-water is,

    Or roses after evening rain.

Her neck is like white melilote

    Flushing for pleasure of the sun,

The throbbing of the linnet's throat

    Is not so sweet to look upon.

As a pomegranate, cut in twain,

    White-seeded, is her crimson mouth,

Her cheeks are as the fading stain

    Where the peach reddens to the south.

O twining hands! O delicate

    White body made for love and pain!

O House of love! O desolate

    Pale flower beaten by the rain!

446

CHANSON

A ring of gold and a milk-white dove

  Are goodly gifts for thee,

And a hempen rope for your own love

  To hang upon a tree.

For you a House of Ivory,

  (Roses are white in the rose-bower)!

A narrow bed for me to lie,

  (White, O white, is the hemlock flower)!

Myrtle and jessamine for you,

  (O the red rose is fair to see)!

For me the cypress and the rue,

  (Finest of all is rosemary)!

For you three lovers of your hand,

  (Green grass where a man lies dead)!

For me three paces on the sand,

  (Plant lilies at my head)!

CHARMIDES

I.

He was a Grecian lad, who coming home

   With pulpy figs and wine from Sicily

Stood at his galley's prow, and let the foam

   Blow through his crisp brown curls unconsciously,

And holding wave and wind in boy's despite

Peered from his dripping seat across the wet and stormy night.

Till with the dawn he saw a burnished spear

   Like a thin thread of gold against the sky,

And hoisted sail, and strained the creaking gear,

   And bade the pilot head her lustily

Against the nor'west gale, and all day long

Held on his way, and marked the rowers' time with measured song.

And when the faint Corinthian hills were red

   Dropped anchor in a little sandy bay,

And with fresh boughs of olive crowned his head,

   And brushed from cheek and throat the hoary spray,

And washed his limbs with oil, and from the hold

Brought out his linen tunic and his sandals brazen-soled,

And a rich robe stained with the fishers' juice
  Which of some swarthy trader he had bought
Upon the sunny quay at Syracuse,
  And was with Tyrian broideries inwrought,
And by the questioning merchants made his way
Up through the soft and silver woods, and when the labouring day

Had spun its tangled web of crimson cloud,
  Clomb the high hill, and with swift silent feet
Crept to the fane unnoticed by the crowd
  Of busy priests, and from some dark retreat
Watched the young swains his frolic playmates bring
The firstling of their little flock, and the shy shepherd fling

The crackling salt upon the flame, or hang
  His studded crook against the temple wall
To Her who keeps away the ravenous fang
  Of the base wolf from homestead and from stall;
And then the clear-voiced maidens 'gan to sing,
And to the altar each man brought some goodly offering,

A beechen cup brimming with milky foam,

A fair cloth wrought with cunning imagery

Of hounds in chase, a waxen honey-comb

   Dripping with oozy gold which scarce the bee

Had ceased from building, a black skin of oil

Meet for the wrestlers, a great boar the fierce and white-tusked spoil

Stolen from Artemis that jealous maid

   To please Athena, and the dappled hide

Of a tall stag who in some mountain glade

   Had met the shaft; and then the herald cried,

And from the pillared precinct one by one

Went the glad Greeks well pleased that they their simple vows had done.

And the old priest put out the waning fires

   Save that one lamp whose restless ruby glowed

For ever in the cell, and the shrill lyres

   Came fainter on the wind, as down the road

In joyous dance these country folk did pass,

And with stout hands the warder closed the gates of polished brass.

Long time he lay and hardly dared to breathe,

   And heard the cadenced drip of spilt-out wine,

And the rose-petals falling from the wreath

450

As the night breezes wandered through the shrine,

And seemed to be in some entrancèd swoon

Till through the open roof above the full and brimming moon

Flooded with sheeny waves the marble floor,

　　When from his nook up leapt the venturous lad,

And flinging wide the cedar-carven door

　　Beheld an awful image saffron-clad

And armed for battle! the gaunt Griffin glared

From the huge helm, and the long lance of wreck and ruin flared

Like a red rod of flame, stony and steeled

　　The Gorgon's head its leaden eyeballs rolled,

And writhed its snaky horrors through the shield,

　　And gaped aghast with bloodless lips and cold

In passion impotent, while with blind gaze

The blinking owl between the feet hooted in shrill amaze.

The lonely fisher as he trimmed his lamp

　　Far out at sea off Sunium, or cast

The net for tunnies, heard a brazen tramp

　　Of horses smite the waves, and a wild blast

Divide the folded curtains of the night,

451

And knelt upon the little poop, and prayed in holy fright.

And guilty lovers in their venery

   Forgat a little while their stolen sweets,

Deeming they heard dread Dian's bitter cry;

   And the grim watchmen on their lofty seats

Ran to their shields in haste precipitate,

Or strained black-bearded throats across the dusky parapet.

For round the temple rolled the clang of arms,

   And the twelve Gods leapt up in marble fear,

And the air quaked with dissonant alarums

   Till huge Poseidon shook his mighty spear,

And on the frieze the prancing horses neighed,

And the low tread of hurrying feet rang from the cavalcade.

Ready for death with parted lips he stood,

   And well content at such a price to see

That calm wide brow, that terrible maidenhood,

   The marvel of that pitiless chastity,

Ah! well content indeed, for never wight

Since Troy's young shepherd prince had seen so wonderful a sight.

Ready for death he stood, but lo! the air

Grew silent, and the horses ceased to neigh,

And off his brow he tossed the clustering hair,

And from his limbs he throw the cloak away;

For whom would not such love make desperate?

And nigher came, and touched her throat, and with hands violate

Undid the cuirass, and the crocus gown,

And bared the breasts of polished ivory,

Till from the waist the peplos falling down

Left visible the secret mystery

Which to no lover will Athena show,

The grand cool flanks, the crescent thighs, the bossy hills of snow.

Those who have never known a lover's sin

Let them not read my ditty, it will be

To their dull ears so musicless and thin

That they will have no joy of it, but ye

To whose wan cheeks now creeps the lingering smile,

Ye who have learned who Eros is,—O listen yet awhile.

A little space he let his greedy eyes

Rest on the burnished image, till mere sight

Half swooned for surfeit of such luxuries,

And then his lips in hungering delight

Fed on her lips, and round the towered neck

He flung his arms, nor cared at all his passion's will to check.

Never I ween did lover hold such tryst,

   For all night long he murmured honeyed word,

And saw her sweet unravished limbs, and kissed

   Her pale and argent body undisturbed,

And paddled with the polished throat, and pressed

His hot and beating heart upon her chill and icy breast.

It was as if Numidian javelins

   Pierced through and through his wild and whirling brain,

And his nerves thrilled like throbbing violins

   In exquisite pulsation, and the pain

Was such sweet anguish that he never drew

His lips from hers till overhead the lark of warning flew.

They who have never seen the daylight peer

   Into a darkened room, and drawn the curtain,

And with dull eyes and wearied from some dear

   And worshipped body risen, they for certain

Will never know of what I try to sing,

How long the last kiss was, how fond and late his lingering.

The moon was girdled with a crystal rim,

  The sign which shipmen say is ominous

Of wrath in heaven, the wan stars were dim,

  And the low lightening east was tremulous

With the faint fluttering wings of flying dawn,

Ere from the silent sombre shrine his lover had withdrawn.

Down the steep rock with hurried feet and fast

  Clomb the brave lad, and reached the cave of Pan,

And heard the goat-foot snoring as he passed,

  And leapt upon a grassy knoll and ran

Like a young fawn unto an olive wood

Which in a shady valley by the well-built city stood;

And sought a little stream, which well he knew,

  For oftentimes with boyish careless shout

The green and crested grebe he would pursue,

  Or snare in woven net the silver trout,

And down amid the startled reeds he lay

Panting in breathless sweet affright, and waited for the day.

On the green bank he lay, and let one hand

Dip in the cool dark eddies listlessly,

And soon the breath of morning came and fanned

His hot flushed cheeks, or lifted wantonly

The tangled curls from off his forehead, while

He on the running water gazed with strange and secret smile.

And soon the shepherd in rough woollen cloak

With his long crook undid the wattled cotes,

And from the stack a thin blue wreath of smoke

Curled through the air across the ripening oats,

And on the hill the yellow house-dog bayed

As through the crisp and rustling fern the heavy cattle strayed.

And when the light-foot mower went afield

Across the meadows laced with threaded dew,

And the sheep bleated on the misty weald,

And from its nest the waking corncrake flew,

Some woodmen saw him lying by the stream

And marvelled much that any lad so beautiful could seem,

Nor deemed him born of mortals, and one said,

'It is young Hylas, that false runaway

Who with a Naiad now would make his bed

Forgetting Herakles,' but others, 'Nay,

It is Narcissus, his own paramour,

Those are the fond and crimson lips no woman can allure.'

And when they nearer came a third one cried,

   'It is young Dionysos who has hid

His spear and fawnskin by the river side

   Weary of hunting with the Bassarid,

And wise indeed were we away to fly:

They live not long who on the gods immortal come to spy.'

So turned they back, and feared to look behind,

   And told the timid swain how they had seen

Amid the reeds some woodland god reclined,

   And no man dared to cross the open green,

And on that day no olive-tree was slain,

Nor rushes cut, but all deserted was the fair domain,

Save when the neat-herd's lad, his empty pail

   Well slung upon his back, with leap and bound

Raced on the other side, and stopped to hail,

   Hoping that he some comrade new had found,

And gat no answer, and then half afraid

Passed on his simple way, or down the still and silent glade

A little girl ran laughing from the farm,

    Not thinking of love's secret mysteries,

And when she saw the white and gleaming arm

    And all his manlihood, with longing eyes

Whose passion mocked her sweet virginity

Watched him awhile, and then stole back sadly and wearily.

Far off he heard the city's hum and noise,

    And now and then the shriller laughter where

The passionate purity of brown-limbed boys

    Wrestled or raced in the clear healthful air,

And now and then a little tinkling bell

As the shorn wether led the sheep down to the mossy well.

Through the grey willows danced the fretful gnat,

    The grasshopper chirped idly from the tree,

In sleek and oily coat the water-rat

    Breasting the little ripples manfully

Made for the wild-duck's nest, from bough to bough

Hopped the shy finch, and the huge tortoise crept across the slough.

On the faint wind floated the silky seeds

As the bright scythe swept through the waving grass,

   The ouzel-cock splashed circles in the reeds

     And flecked with silver whorls the forest's glass,

   Which scarce had caught again its imagery

Ere from its bed the dusky tench leapt at the dragon-fly.

But little care had he for any thing

    Though up and down the beech the squirrel played,

And from the copse the linnet 'gan to sing

    To its brown mate its sweetest serenade;

Ah! little care indeed, for he had seen

The breasts of Pallas and the naked wonder of the Queen.

But when the herdsman called his straggling goats

    With whistling pipe across the rocky road,

And the shard-beetle with its trumpet-notes

    Boomed through the darkening woods, and seemed to bode

Of coming storm, and the belated crane

Passed homeward like a shadow, and the dull big drops of rain

Fell on the pattering fig-leaves, up he rose,

    And from the gloomy forest went his way

Past sombre homestead and wet orchard-close,

And came at last unto a little quay,

And called his mates aboard, and took his seat

On the high poop, and pushed from land, and loosed the dripping sheet,

And steered across the bay, and when nine suns

   Passed down the long and laddered way of gold,

And nine pale moons had breathed their orisons

   To the chaste stars their confessors, or told

Their dearest secret to the downy moth

That will not fly at noonday, through the foam and surging froth

Came a great owl with yellow sulphurous eyes

   And lit upon the ship, whose timbers creaked

As though the lading of three argosies

   Were in the hold, and flapped its wings and shrieked,

And darkness straightway stole across the deep,

Sheathed was Orion's sword, dread Mars himself fled down the steep,

And the moon hid behind a tawny mask

   Of drifting cloud, and from the ocean's marge

Rose the red plume, the huge and hornèd casque,

   The seven-cubit spear, the brazen targe!

And clad in bright and burnished panoply

Athena strode across the stretch of sick and shivering sea!

To the dull sailors' sight her loosened looks

   Seemed like the jagged storm-rack, and her feet

Only the spume that floats on hidden rocks,

   And, marking how the rising waters beat

Against the rolling ship, the pilot cried

To the young helmsman at the stern to luff to windward side

But he, the overbold adulterer,

   A dear profaner of great mysteries,

An ardent amorous idolater,

   When he beheld those grand relentless eyes

Laughed loud for joy, and crying out 'I come'

Leapt from the lofty poop into the chill and churning foam.

Then fell from the high heaven one bright star,

   One dancer left the circling galaxy,

And back to Athens on her clattering car

   In all the pride of venged divinity

Pale Pallas swept with shrill and steely clank,

And a few gurgling bubbles rose where her boy lover sank.

And the mast shuddered as the gaunt owl flew

With mocking hoots after the wrathful Queen,

And the old pilot bade the trembling crew

Hoist the big sail, and told how he had seen

Close to the stern a dim and giant form,

And like a dipping swallow the stout ship dashed through the storm.

And no man dared to speak of Charmides

Deeming that he some evil thing had wrought,

And when they reached the strait Symplegades

They beached their galley on the shore, and sought

The toll-gate of the city hastily,

And in the market showed their brown and pictured pottery.

II.

But some good Triton-god had ruth, and bare

The boy's drowned body back to Grecian land,

And mermaids combed his dank and dripping hair

And smoothed his brow, and loosed his clenching hand;

Some brought sweet spices from far Araby,

And others bade the halcyon sing her softest lullaby.

And when he neared his old Athenian home,

A mighty billow rose up suddenly

Upon whose oily back the clotted foam

    Lay diapered in some strange fantasy,

And clasping him unto its glassy breast

Swept landward, like a white-maned steed upon a venturous quest!

Now where Colonos leans unto the sea

    There lies a long and level stretch of lawn;

The rabbit knows it, and the mountain bee

    For it deserts Hymettus, and the Faun

Is not afraid, for never through the day

Comes a cry ruder than the shout of shepherd lads at play.

But often from the thorny labyrinth

    And tangled branches of the circling wood

The stealthy hunter sees young Hyacinth

    Hurling the polished disk, and draws his hood

Over his guilty gaze, and creeps away,

Nor dares to wind his horn, or—else at the first break of day

The Dryads come and throw the leathern ball

    Along the reedy shore, and circumvent

Some goat-eared Pan to be their seneschal

    For fear of bold Poseidon's ravishment,

And loose their girdles, with shy timorous eyes,

Lest from the surf his azure arms and purple beard should rise.

On this side and on that a rocky cave,

   Hung with the yellow-belled laburnum, stands

Smooth is the beach, save where some ebbing wave

   Leaves its faint outline etched upon the sands,

As though it feared to be too soon forgot

By the green rush, its playfellow,—and yet, it is a spot

So small, that the inconstant butterfly

   Could steal the hoarded money from each flower

Ere it was noon, and still not satisfy

   Its over-greedy love,—within an hour

A sailor boy, were he but rude enow

To land and pluck a garland for his galley's painted prow,

Would almost leave the little meadow bare,

   For it knows nothing of great pageantry,

Only a few narcissi here and there

   Stand separate in sweet austerity,

Dotting the unmown grass with silver stars,

And here and there a daffodil waves tiny scimitars.

Hither the billow brought him, and was glad

   Of such dear servitude, and where the land

Was virgin of all waters laid the lad

   Upon the golden margent of the strand,

And like a lingering lover oft returned

To kiss those pallid limbs which once with intense fire burned,

Ere the wet seas had quenched that holocaust,

   That self-fed flame, that passionate lustihead,

Ere grisly death with chill and nipping frost

   Had withered up those lilies white and red

Which, while the boy would through the forest range,

Answered each other in a sweet antiphonal counter-change.

And when at dawn the wood-nymphs, hand-in-hand,

   Threaded the bosky dell, their satyr spied

The boy's pale body stretched upon the sand,

   And feared Poseidon's treachery, and cried,

And like bright sunbeams flitting through a glade

Each startled Dryad sought some safe and leafy ambuscade.

Save one white girl, who deemed it would not be

So dread a thing to feel a sea-god's arms

Crushing her breasts in amorous tyranny,

    And longed to listen to those subtle charms

Insidious lovers weave when they would win

Some fencèd fortress, and stole back again, nor thought it sin

To yield her treasure unto one so fair,

    And lay beside him, thirsty with love's drouth,

Called him soft names, played with his tangled hair,

    And with hot lips made havoc of his mouth

Afraid he might not wake, and then afraid

Lest he might wake too soon, fled back, and then, fond renegade,

Returned to fresh assault, and all day long

    Sat at his side, and laughed at her new toy,

And held his hand, and sang her sweetest song,

    Then frowned to see how froward was the boy

Who would not with her maidenhood entwine,

Nor knew that three days since his eyes had looked on Proserpine;

Nor knew what sacrilege his lips had done,

    But said, 'He will awake, I know him well,

He will awake at evening when the sun

Hangs his red shield on Corinth's citadel;

This sleep is but a cruel treachery

To make me love him more, and in some cavern of the sea

Deeper than ever falls the fisher's line

   Already a huge Triton blows his horn,

And weaves a garland from the crystalline

   And drifting ocean-tendrils to adorn

The emerald pillars of our bridal bed,

For sphered in foaming silver, and with coral crownèd head,

We two will sit upon a throne of pearl,

   And a blue wave will be our canopy,

And at our feet the water-snakes will curl

   In all their amethystine panoply

Of diamonded mail, and we will mark

The mullets swimming by the mast of some storm-foundered bark,

Vermilion-finned with eyes of bossy gold

   Like flakes of crimson light, and the great deep

His glassy-portaled chamber will unfold,

   And we will see the painted dolphins sleep

Cradled by murmuring halcyons on the rocks

Where Proteus in quaint suit of green pastures his monstrous flocks.

And tremulous opal-hued anemones
  Will wave their purple fringes where we tread
Upon the mirrored floor, and argosies
  Of fishes flecked with tawny scales will thread
The drifting cordage of the shattered wreck,
And honey-coloured amber beads our twining limbs will deck.'

But when that baffled Lord of War the Sun
  With gaudy pennon flying passed away
Into his brazen House, and one by one
  The little yellow stars began to stray
Across the field of heaven, ah! then indeed
She feared his lips upon her lips would never care to feed,

And cried, 'Awake, already the pale moon
  Washes the trees with silver, and the wave
Creeps grey and chilly up this sandy dune,
  The croaking frogs are out, and from the cave
The nightjar shrieks, the fluttering bats repass,
And the brown stoat with hollow flanks creeps through the dusky grass.

Nay, though thou art a god, be not so coy,

For in yon stream there is a little reed

That often whispers how a lovely boy

   Lay with her once upon a grassy mead,

Who when his cruel pleasure he had done

Spread wings of rustling gold and soared aloft into the sun.

Be not so coy, the laurel trembles still

   With great Apollo's kisses, and the fir

Whose clustering sisters fringe the seaward hill

   Hath many a tale of that bold ravisher

Whom men call Boreas, and I have seen

The mocking eyes of Hermes through the poplar's silvery sheen.

Even the jealous Naiads call me fair,

   And every morn a young and ruddy swain

Woos me with apples and with locks of hair,

   And seeks to soothe my virginal disdain

By all the gifts the gentle wood-nymphs love;

But yesterday he brought to me an iris-plumaged dove

With little crimson feet, which with its store

   Of seven spotted eggs the cruel lad

Had stolen from the lofty sycamore

At daybreak, when her amorous comrade had

Flown off in search of berried juniper

Which most they love; the fretful wasp, that earliest vintager

Of the blue grapes, hath not persistency

   So constant as this simple shepherd-boy

For my poor lips, his joyous purity

   And laughing sunny eyes might well decoy

A Dryad from her oath to Artemis;

For very beautiful is he, his mouth was made to kiss;

His argent forehead, like a rising moon

   Over the dusky hills of meeting brows,

Is crescent shaped, the hot and Tyrian noon

   Leads from the myrtle-grove no goodlier spouse

For Cytheræa, the first silky down

Fringes his blushing cheeks, and his young limbs are strong and brown;

And he is rich, and fat and fleecy herds

   Of bleating sheep upon his meadows lie,

And many an earthen bowl of yellow curds

   Is in his homestead for the thievish fly

To swim and drown in, the pink clover mead

Keeps its sweet store for him, and he can pipe on oaten reed.

And yet I love him not; it was for thee

   I kept my love; I knew that thou would'st come

To rid me of this pallid chastity,

   Thou fairest flower of the flowerless foam

Of all the wide Ægean, brightest star

Of ocean's azure heavens where the mirrored planets are!

I knew that thou would'st come, for when at first

   The dry wood burgeoned, and the sap of spring

Swelled in my green and tender bark or burst

   To myriad multitudinous blossoming

Which mocked the midnight with its mimic moons

That did not dread the dawn, and first the thrushes' rapturous tunes

Startled the squirrel from its granary,

   And cuckoo flowers fringed the narrow lane,

Through my young leaves a sensuous ecstasy

   Crept like new wine, and every mossy vein

Throbbed with the fitful pulse of amorous blood,

And the wild winds of passion shook my slim stem's maidenhood.

The trooping fawns at evening came and laid

Their cool black noses on my lowest boughs,

And on my topmost branch the blackbird made

  A little nest of grasses for his spouse,

And now and then a twittering wren would light

On a thin twig which hardly bare the weight of such delight.

I was the Attic shepherd's trysting place,

  Beneath my shadow Amaryllis lay,

And round my trunk would laughing Daphnis chase

  The timorous girl, till tired out with play

She felt his hot breath stir her tangled hair,

And turned, and looked, and fled no more from such delightful snare.

Then come away unto my ambuscade

  Where clustering woodbine weaves a canopy

For amorous pleasaunce, and the rustling shade

  Of Paphian myrtles seems to sanctify

The dearest rites of love; there in the cool

And green recesses of its farthest depth there is pool,

The ouzel's haunt, the wild bee's pasturage,

  For round its rim great creamy lilies float

Through their flat leaves in verdant anchorage,

Each cup a white-sailed golden-laden boat

Steered by a dragon-fly,—be not afraid

To leave this wan and wave-kissed shore, surely the place was made

For lovers such as we; the Cyprian Queen,

   One arm around her boyish paramour,

Strays often there at eve, and I have seen

   The moon strip off her misty vestiture

For young Endymion's eyes; be not afraid,

The panther feet of Dian never tread that secret glade.

Nay if thou will'st, back to the beating brine,

   Back to the boisterous billow let us go,

And walk all day beneath the hyaline

   Huge vault of Neptune's watery portico,

And watch the purple monsters of the deep

Sport in ungainly play, and from his lair keen Xiphias leap.

For if my mistress find me lying here

   She will not ruth or gentle pity show,

But lay her boar-spear down, and with austere

   Relentless fingers string the cornel bow,

And draw the feathered notch against her breast,

And loose the archèd cord; aye, even now upon the quest

I hear her hurrying feet,—awake, awake,

   Thou laggard in love's battle! once at least

Let me drink deep of passion's wine, and slake

   My parchèd being with the nectarous feast

Which even gods affect! O come, Love, come,

Still we have time to reach the cavern of thine azure home.'

Scarce had she spoken when the shuddering trees

   Shook, and the leaves divided, and the air

Grew conscious of a god, and the grey seas

   Crawled backward, and a long and dismal blare

Blew from some tasselled horn, a sleuth-hound bayed,

And like a flame a barbèd reed flew whizzing down the glade.

And where the little flowers of her breast

   Just brake into their milky blossoming,

This murderous paramour, this unbidden guest,

   Pierced and struck deep in horrid chambering,

And ploughed a bloody furrow with its dart,

And dug a long red road, and cleft with wingèd death her heart.

Sobbing her life out with a bitter cry

On the boy's body fell the Dryad maid,

Sobbing for incomplete virginity,

   And raptures unenjoyed, and pleasures dead,

And all the pain of things unsatisfied,

And the bright drops of crimson youth crept down her throbbing side.

Ah! pitiful it was to hear her moan,

   And very pitiful to see her die

Ere she had yielded up her sweets, or known

   The joy of passion, that dread mystery

Which not to know is not to live at all,

And yet to know is to be held in death's most deadly thrall.

But as it hapt the Queen of Cythere,

   Who with Adonis all night long had lain

Within some shepherd's hut in Arcady,

   On team of silver doves and gilded wain

Was journeying Paphos-ward, high up afar

From mortal ken between the mountains and the morning star,

And when low down she spied the hapless pair,

   And heard the Oread's faint despairing cry,

Whose cadence seemed to play upon the air

As though it were a viol, hastily

She bade her pigeons fold each straining plume,

And dropt to earth, and reached the strand, and saw their dolorous doom.

For as a gardener turning back his head

   To catch the last notes of the linnet, mows

With careless scythe too near some flower bed,

   And cuts the thorny pillar of the rose,

And with the flower's loosened loneliness

Strews the brown mould; or as some shepherd lad in wantonness

Driving his little flock along the mead

   Treads down two daffodils, which side by aide

Have lured the lady-bird with yellow brede

   And made the gaudy moth forget its pride,

Treads down their brimming golden chalices

Under light feet which were not made for such rude ravages;

Or as a schoolboy tired of his book

   Flings himself down upon the reedy grass

And plucks two water-lilies from the brook,

   And for a time forgets the hour glass,

Then wearies of their sweets, and goes his way,

And lets the hot sun kill them, even go these lovers lay.

And Venus cried, 'It is dread Artemis

  Whose bitter hand hath wrought this cruelty,

Or else that mightier maid whose care it is

  To guard her strong and stainless majesty

Upon the hill Athenian,—alas!

That they who loved so well unloved into Death's house should pass.'

So with soft hands she laid the boy and girl

  In the great golden waggon tenderly

(Her white throat whiter than a moony pearl

  Just threaded with a blue vein's tapestry

Had not yet ceased to throb, and still her breast

Swayed like a wind-stirred lily in ambiguous unrest)

And then each pigeon spread its milky van,

  The bright car soared into the dawning sky,

And like a cloud the aerial caravan

  Passed over the Ægean silently,

Till the faint air was troubled with the song

From the wan mouths that call on bleeding Thammuz all night long.

But when the doves had reached their wonted goal

Where the wide stair of orbèd marble dips

Its snows into the sea, her fluttering soul

  Just shook the trembling petals of her lips

And passed into the void, and Venus knew

That one fair maid the less would walk amid her retinue,

And bade her servants carve a cedar chest

  With all the wonder of this history,

Within whose scented womb their limbs should rest

  Where olive-trees make tender the blue sky

On the low hills of Paphos, and the Faun

Pipes in the noonday, and the nightingale sings on till dawn.

Nor failed they to obey her hest, and ere

  The morning bee had stung the daffodil

With tiny fretful spear, or from its lair

  The waking stag had leapt across the rill

And roused the ouzel, or the lizard crept

Athwart the sunny rock, beneath the grass their bodies slept.

And when day brake, within that silver shrine

  Fed by the flames of cressets tremulous,

Queen Venus knelt and prayed to Proserpine

That she whose beauty made Death amorous

Should beg a guerdon from her pallid Lord,

And let Desire pass across dread Charon's icy ford.

III

In melancholy moonless Acheron,

   Farm for the goodly earth and joyous day

Where no spring ever buds, nor ripening sun

   Weighs down the apple trees, nor flowery May

Chequers with chestnut blooms the grassy floor,

Where thrushes never sing, and piping linnets mate no more,

There by a dim and dark Lethæan well

   Young Charmides was lying; wearily

He plucked the blossoms from the asphodel,

   And with its little rifled treasury

Strewed the dull waters of the dusky stream,

And watched the white stars founder, and the land was like a dream,

When as he gazed into the watery glass

   And through his brown hair's curly tangles scanned

His own wan face, a shadow seemed to pass

   Across the mirror, and a little hand

Stole into his, and warm lips timidly

Brushed his pale cheeks, and breathed their secret forth into a sigh.

Then turned he round his weary eyes and saw,

   And ever nigher still their faces came,

And nigher ever did their young mouths draw

   Until they seemed one perfect rose of flame,

And longing arms around her neck he cast,

And felt her throbbing bosom, and his breath came hot and fast,

And all his hoarded sweets were hers to kiss,

   And all her maidenhood was his to slay,

And limb to limb in long and rapturous bliss

   Their passion waxed and waned,—O why essay

To pipe again of love, too venturous reed!

Enough, enough that Eros laughed upon that flowerless mead.

Too venturous poesy, O why essay

   To pipe again of passion! fold thy wings

O'er daring Icarus and bid thy lay

   Sleep hidden in the lyre's silent strings

Till thou hast found the old Castalian rill,

   Or from the Lesbian waters plucked drowned Sappho's golden quid!

480

Enough, enough that he whose life had been

   A fiery pulse of sin, a splendid shame,

Could in the loveless land of Hades glean

   One scorching harvest from those fields of flame

Where passion walks with naked unshod feet

And is not wounded,—ah! enough that once their lips could meet

In that wild throb when all existences

   Seemed narrowed to one single ecstasy

Which dies through its own sweetness and the stress

   Of too much pleasure, ere Persephone

Had bade them serve her by the ebon throne

Of the pale God who in the fields of Enna loosed her zone.

FLOWERS OF GOLD

IMPRESSIONS

I
LES SILHOUETTES

The sea is flecked with bars of grey,
The dull dead wind is out of tune,
And like a withered leaf the moon
Is blown across the stormy bay.

Etched clear upon the pallid sand
Lies the black boat: a sailor boy
Clambers aboard in careless joy
With laughing face and gleaming hand.

And overhead the curlews cry,
Where through the dusky upland grass
The young brown-throated reapers pass,
Like silhouettes against the sky.

II
LA FUITE DE LA LUNE

To outer senses there is peace,

A dreamy peace on either hand

Deep silence in the shadowy land,

Deep silence where the shadows cease.

Save for a cry that echoes shrill

From some lone bird disconsolate;

A corncrake calling to its mate;

The answer from the misty hill.

And suddenly the moon withdraws

Her sickle from the lightening skies,

And to her sombre cavern flies,

Wrapped in a veil of yellow gauze.

THE GRAVE OF KEATS

Rid of the world's injustice, and his pain,

He rests at last beneath God's veil of blue:

Taken from life when life and love were new

The youngest of the martyrs here is lain,

Fair as Sebastian, and as early slain.

No cypress shades his grave, no funeral yew,

But gentle violets weeping with the dew

Weave on his bones an ever-blossoming chain.

O proudest heart that broke for misery!

O sweetest lips since those of Mitylene!

O poet-painter of our English Land!

Thy name was writ in water—it shall stand:

And tears like mine will keep thy memory green,

As Isabella did her Basil-tree.

Rome.

THEOCRITUS:A VILLANELLE

O singer of Persephone!

In the dim meadows desolate

Dost thou remember Sicily?

Still through the ivy flits the bee

Where Amaryllis lies in state;

O Singer of Persephone!

Simætha calls on Hecate

And hears the wild dogs at the gate;

Dost thou remember Sicily?

Still by the light and laughing sea

Poor Polypheme bemoans his fate;

O Singer of Persephone!

And still in boyish rivalry

   Young Daphnis challenges his mate;

Dost thou remember Sicily?

Slim Lacon keeps a goat for thee,

   For thee the jocund shepherds wait;

O Singer of Persephone!

Dost thou remember Sicily?

IN THE GOLD ROOM: A HARMONY

Her ivory hands on the ivory keys

   Strayed in a fitful fantasy,

Like the silver gleam when the poplar trees

   Rustle their pale-leaves listlessly,

Or the drifting foam of a restless sea

When the waves show their teeth in the flying breeze.

Her gold hair fell on the wall of gold

   Like the delicate gossamer tangles spun

On the burnished disk of the marigold,

   Or the sunflower turning to meet the sun

When the gloom of the dark blue night is done,

And the spear of the lily is aureoled.

And her sweet red lips on these lips of mine

Burned like the ruby fire set

In the swinging lamp of a crimson shrine,

Or the bleeding wounds of the pomegranate,

Or the heart of the lotus drenched and wet

With the spilt-out blood of the rose-red wine.

BALLADE DE MARGUERITE

(NORMANDE)

I am weary of lying within the chase

When the knights are meeting in market-place.

Nay, go not thou to the red-roofed town

Lest the hoofs of the war-horse tread thee down.

But I would not go where the Squires ride,

I would only walk by my Lady's side.

Alack! and alack! thou art overbold,

A Forester's son may not eat off gold.

486

Will she love me the less that my Father is seen

Each Martinmas day in a doublet green?

Perchance she is sewing at tapestrie,

Spindle and loom are not meet for thee.

Ah, if she is working the arras bright

I might ravel the threads by the fire-light.

Perchance she is hunting of the deer,

How could you follow o'er hill and mere?

Ah, if she is riding with the court,

I might run beside her and wind the morte.

Perchance she is kneeling in St. Denys,

(On her soul may our Lady have gramercy!)

Ah, if she is praying in lone chapelle,

I might swing the censer and ring the bell.

Come in, my son, for you look sae pale,

The father shall fill thee a stoup of ale.

But who are these knights in bright array?
Is it a pageant the rich folks play?

'T is the King of England from over sea,
Who has come unto visit our fair countrie.

But why does the curfew toll sae low?
And why do the mourners walk a-row?

O 't is Hugh of Amiens my sister's son
Who is lying stark, for his day is done.

Nay, nay, for I see white lilies clear,
It is no strong man who lies on the bier.

O 't is old Dame Jeannette that kept the hall,
I knew she would die at the autumn fall.

Dame Jeannette had not that gold-brown hair,
Old Jeannette was not a maiden fair.

O 't is none of our kith and none of our kin,

(Her soul may our Lady assoil from sin!)

But I hear the boy's voice chaunting sweet,
'Elle est morte, la Marguerite.'

Come in, my son, and lie on the bed,
And let the dead folk bury their dead.

O mother, you know I loved her true:
O mother, hath one grave room for two?

THE DOLE OF THE KING'S DAUGHTER

(BRETON)

Seven stars in the still water,
 And seven in the sky;
Seven sins on the King's daughter,
 Deep in her soul to lie.

Red roses are at her feet,
 (Roses are red in her red-gold hair)
And O where her bosom and girdle meet
 Red roses are hidden there.

Fair is the knight who lieth slain

Amid the rush and reed,

See the lean fishes that are fain

Upon dead men to feed.

Sweet is the page that lieth there,

(Cloth of gold is goodly prey,)

See the black ravens in the air,

Black, O black as the night are they.

What do they there so stark and dead?

(There is blood upon her hand)

Why are the lilies flecked with red?

(There is blood on the river sand.)

There are two that ride from the south and east,

And two from the north and west,

For the black raven a goodly feast,

For the King's daughter rest.

There is one man who loves her true,

(Red, O red, is the stain of gore!)

He hath duggen a grave by the darksome yew,

(One grave will do for four.)

490

No moon in the still heaven,

   In the black water none,

The sins on her soul are seven,

   The sin upon his is one.

AMOR INTELLECTUALIS

Oft have we trod the vales of Castaly

   And heard sweet notes of sylvan music blown

   From antique reeds to common folk unknown:

And often launched our bark upon that sea

Which the nine Muses hold in empery,

   And ploughed free furrows through the wave and foam,

   Nor spread reluctant sail for more safe home

Till we had freighted well our argosy.

Of which despoilèd treasures these remain,

   Sordello's passion, and the honeyed line

Of young Endymion, lordly Tamburlaine

   Driving his pampered jades, and more than these,

The seven-fold vision of the Florentine,

   And grave-browed Milton's solemn harmonies.

SANTA DECCA

The Gods are dead: no longer do we bring

To grey-eyed Pallas crowns of olive-leaves!

Demeter's child no more hath tithe of sheaves,

And in the noon the careless shepherds sing,

For Pan is dead, and all the wantoning

By secret glade and devious haunt is o'er:

Young Hylas seeks the water-springs no more;

Great Pan is dead, and Mary's son is King.

And yet—perchance in this sea-trancèd isle,

Chewing the bitter fruit of memory,

Some God lies hidden in the asphodel.

Ah Love! if such there be, then it were well

For us to fly his anger: nay, but see,

The leaves are stirring: let us watch awhile.

CORFU.

A VISION

Two crownèd Kings, and One that stood alone

With no green weight of laurels round his head,

But with sad eyes as one uncomforted,

And wearied with man's never-ceasing moan

For sins no bleating victim can atone,

And sweet long lips with tears and kisses fed.

492

Girt was he in a garment black and red,

And at his feet I marked a broken stone

  Which sent up lilies, dove-like, to his knees.

Now at their sight, my heart being lit with flame,

I cried to Beatricé, 'Who are these?'

And she made answer, knowing well each name,

  'Æschylos first, the second Sophokles,

  And last (wide stream of tears!) Euripides.'

IMPRESSION DE VOYAGE

The sea was sapphire coloured, and the sky

  Burned like a heated opal through the air;

  We hoisted sail; the wind was blowing fair

For the blue lands that to the eastward lie.

From the steep prow I marked with quickening eye

  Zakynthos, every olive grove and creek,

  Ithaca's cliff, Lycaon's snowy peak,

And all the flower-strewn hills of Arcady.

  The flapping of the sail against the mast,

  The ripple of the water on the side,

The ripple of girls' laughter at the stern,

The only sounds:—when 'gan the West to burn,

  And a red sun upon the seas to ride,

  I stood upon the soil of Greece at last!

Katakolo.

THE GRAVE OF SHELLEY

Like burnt-out torches by a sick man's bed
   Gaunt cypress-trees stand round the sun-bleached stone;
   Here doth the little night-owl make her throne,
And the slight lizard show his jewelled head.
And, where the chaliced poppies flame to red,
   In the still chamber of yon pyramid
   Surely some Old-World Sphinx lurks darkly hid,
Grim warder of this pleasaunce of the dead.

Ah! sweet indeed to rest within the womb
   Of Earth, great mother of eternal sleep,
But sweeter far for thee a restless tomb
   In the blue cavern of an echoing deep,
Or where the tall ships founder in the gloom
   Against the rocks of some wave-shattered steep.

Rome.

BY THE ARNO

The oleander on the wall

494

Grows crimson in the dawning light,

Though the grey shadows of the night

Lie yet on Florence like a pall.

The dew is bright upon the hill,

And bright the blossoms overhead,

But ah! the grasshoppers have fled,

The little Attic song is still.

Only the leaves are gently stirred

By the soft breathing of the gale,

And in the almond-scented vale

The lonely nightingale is heard.

The day will make thee silent soon,

O nightingale sing on for love!

While yet upon the shadowy grove

Splinter the arrows of the moon.

Before across the silent lawn

In sea-green vest the morning steals,

And to love's frightened eyes reveals

The long white fingers of the dawn

Fast climbing up the eastern sky

To grasp and slay the shuddering night,

All careless of my heart's delight,

Or if the nightingale should die.

IMPRESSIONS DE THÉÂTRE

FABIEN DEI FRANCHI

To my Friend Henry Irving

The silent room, the heavy creeping shade,

    The dead that travel fast, the opening door,

    The murdered brother rising through the floor,

The ghost's white fingers on thy shoulders laid,

And then the lonely duel in the glade,

    The broken swords, the stifled scream, the gore,

    Thy grand revengeful eyes when all is o'er,—

These things are well enough,—but thou wert made

    For more august creation! frenzied Lear

    Should at thy bidding wander on the heath

    With the shrill fool to mock him, Romeo

For thee should lure his love, and desperate fear

Pluck Richard's recreant dagger from its sheath—

Thou trumpet set for Shakespeare's lips to blow!

PHÈDRE

To Sarah Bernhardt

How vain and dull this common world must seem

    To such a One as thou, who should'st have talked

At Florence with Mirandola, or walked

Through the cool olives of the Academe:

Thou should'st have gathered reeds from a green stream

    For Goat-foot Pan's shrill piping, and have played

    With the white girls in that Phæacian glade

Where grave Odysseus wakened from his dream.

Ah! surely once some urn of Attic clay

    Held thy wan dust, and thou hast come again

    Back to this common world so dull and vain,

For thou wert weary of the sunless day,

    The heavy fields of scentless asphodel,

    The loveless lips with which men kiss in Hell.

SONNETS WRITTEN AT THE LYCEUM THEATRE

I. PORTIA

To Ellen Terry

I marvel not Bassanio was so bold

    To peril all he had upon the lead,

498

Or that proud Aragon bent low his head

Or that Morocco's fiery heart grew cold:

For in that gorgeous dress of beaten gold

  Which is more golden than the golden sun

  No woman Veronesé looked upon

Was half so fair as thou whom I behold.

Yet fairer when with wisdom as your shield

  The sober-suited lawyer's gown you donned,

And would not let the laws of Venice yield

  Antonio's heart to that accursèd Jew—

  O Portia! take my heart: it is thy due:

I think I will not quarrel with the Bond.

II. QUEEN HENRIETTA MARIA

To Ellen Terry

In the lone tent, waiting for victory,

  She stands with eyes marred by the mists of pain,

  Like some wan lily overdrenched with rain:

The clamorous clang of arms, the ensanguined sky,

War's ruin, and the wreck of chivalry

  To her proud soul no common fear can bring:

  Bravely she tarrieth for her Lord the King,

Her soul a-flame with passionate ecstasy.

O Hair of Gold! O Crimson Lips! O Face

    Made for the luring and the love of man!

    With thee I do forget the toil and stress,

The loveless road that knows no resting place,

    Time's straitened pulse, the soul's dread weariness,

    My freedom, and my life republican!

III. CAMMA

To Ellen Terry

As one who poring on a Grecian urn

    Scans the fair shapes some Attic hand hath made,

    God with slim goddess, goodly man with maid,

And for their beauty's sake is loth to turn

And face the obvious day, must I not yearn

    For many a secret moon of indolent bliss,

    When in midmost shrine of Artemis

I see thee standing, antique-limbed, and stern?

And yet—methinks I'd rather see thee play

    That serpent of old Nile, whose witchery

Made Emperors drunken,—come, great Egypt, shake

    Our stage with all thy mimic pageants! Nay,

I am grown sick of unreal passions, make

The world thine Actium, me thine Anthony!

PANTHEA

Nay, let us walk from fire unto fire,

   From passionate pain to deadlier delight,—

I am too young to live without desire,

   Too young art thou to waste this summer night

Asking those idle questions which of old

Man sought of seer and oracle, and no reply was told.

For, sweet, to feel is better than to know,

   And wisdom is a childless heritage,

One pulse of passion—youth's first fiery glow,—

   Are worth the hoarded proverbs of the sage:

Vex not thy soul with dead philosophy,

Have we not lips to kiss with, hearts to love and eyes to see!

Dost thou not hear the murmuring nightingale,

   Like water bubbling from a silver jar,

So soft she sings the envious moon is pale,

   That high in heaven she is hung so far

She cannot hear that love-enraptured tune,—

   Mark how she wreathes each horn with mist, yon late and labouring moon.

White lilies, in whose cups the gold bees dream,

   The fallen snow of petals where the breeze

Scatters the chestnut blossom, or the gleam

   Of boyish limbs in water,—are not these

Enough for thee, dost thou desire more?

Alas! the Gods will give nought else from their eternal store.

For our high Gods have sick and wearied grown

   Of all our endless sins, our vain endeavour

For wasted days of youth to make atone

   By pain or prayer or priest, and never, never,

Hearken they now to either good or ill,

But send their rain upon the just and the unjust at will.

They sit at ease, our Gods they sit at ease,

   Strewing with leaves of rose their scented wine,

They sleep, they sleep, beneath the rocking trees

   Where asphodel and yellow lotus twine,

Mourning the old glad days before they knew

What evil things the heart of man could dream, and dreaming do.

And far beneath the brazen floor they see

Like swarming flies the crowd of little men,

The bustle of small lives, then wearily

   Back to their lotus-haunts they turn again

Kissing each others' mouths, and mix more deep

The poppy-seeded draught which brings soft purple-lidded sleep.

There all day long the golden-vestured sun,

   Their torch-bearer, stands with his torch ablaze,

And, when the gaudy web of noon is spun

   By its twelve maidens, through the crimson haze

Fresh from Endymion's arms comes forth the moon,

And the immortal Gods in toils of mortal passions swoon.

There walks Queen Juno through some dewy mead,

   Her grand white feet flecked with the saffron dust

Of wind-stirred lilies, while young Ganymede

   Leaps in the hot and amber-foaming must,

His curls all tossed, as when the eagle bare

The frightened boy from Ida through the blue Ionian air.

There in the green heart of some garden close

   Queen Venus with the shepherd at her side,

Her warm soft body like the briar rose

Which would be white yet blushes at its pride,

Laughs low for love, till jealous Salmacis

Peers through the myrtle-leaves and sighs for pain of lonely bliss.

There never does that dreary north-wind blow

   Which leaves our English forests bleak and bare,

Nor ever falls the swift white-feathered snow,

    Nor ever doth the red-toothed lightning dare

To wake them in the silver-fretted night

When we lie weeping for some sweet sad sin, some dead delight.

Alas! they know the far Lethæan spring,

   The violet-hidden waters well they know,

Where one whose feet with tired wandering

    Are faint and broken may take heart and go,

And from those dark depths cool and crystalline

Drink, and draw balm, and sleep for sleepless souls, and anodyne.

But we oppress our natures, God or Fate

   Is our enemy, we starve and feed

On vain repentance—O we are born too late!

    What balm for us in bruisèd poppy seed

Who crowd into one finite pulse of time

The joy of infinite love and the fierce pain of infinite crime.

O we are wearied of this sense of guilt,

   Wearied of pleasure's paramour despair,

Wearied of every temple we have built,

   Wearied of every right, unanswered prayer,

For man is weak; God sleeps: and heaven is high:

One fiery-coloured moment: one great love; and lo! we die.

Ah! but no ferry-man with labouring pole

   Nears his black shallop to the flowerless strand,

No little coin of bronze can bring the soul

   Over Death's river to the sunless land,

Victim and wine and vow are all in vain,

The tomb is sealed; the soldiers watch; the dead rise not again.

We are resolved into the supreme air,

   We are made one with what we touch and see,

With our heart's blood each crimson sun is fair,

   With our young lives each spring-impassioned tree

Flames into green, the wildest beasts that range

The moor our kinsmen are, all life is one, and all is change.

With beat of systole and of diastole

One grand great life throbs through earth's giant heart,

And mighty waves of single Being roll

    From nerveless germ to man, for we are part

Of every rock and bird and beast and hill,

One with the things that prey on us, and one with what we kill.

From lower cells of waking life we pass

    To full perfection; thus the world grows old:

We who are godlike now were once a mass

    Of quivering purple flecked with bars of gold,

Unsentient or of joy or misery,

And tossed in terrible tangles of some wild and wind-swept sea.

This hot hard flame with which our bodies burn

    Will make some meadow blaze with daffodil,

Ay! and those argent breasts of thine will turn

    To water-lilies; the brown fields men till

Will be more fruitful for our love to-night,

Nothing is lost in nature, all things live in Death's despite.

The boy's first kiss, the hyacinth's first bell,

    The man's last passion, and the last red spear

That from the lily leaps, the asphodel

Which will not let its blossoms blow for fear

Of too much beauty, and the timid shame

Of the young bridegroom at his lover's eyes,—these with the same

One sacrament are consecrate, the earth

   Not we alone hath passions hymeneal,

The yellow buttercups that shake for mirth

   At daybreak know a pleasure not less real

Than we do, when in some fresh-blossoming wood,

We draw the spring into our hearts, and feel that life is good.

So when men bury us beneath the yew

   Thy crimson-stainèd mouth a rose will be,

And thy soft eyes lush bluebells dimmed with dew,

   And when the white narcissus wantonly

Kisses the wind its playmate some faint joy

Will thrill our dust, and we will be again fond maid and boy.

And thus without life's conscious torturing pain

   In some sweet flower we will feel the sun,

And from the linnet's throat will sing again,

   And as two gorgeous-mailèd snakes will run

Over our graves, or as two tigers creep

Through the hot jungle where the yellow-eyed huge lions sleep

And give them battle! How my heart leaps up
  To think of that grand living after death
In beast and bird and flower, when this cup,
  Being filled too full of spirit, bursts for breath,
And with the pale leaves of some autumn day
The soul earth's earliest conqueror becomes earth's last great prey.

O think of it! We shall inform ourselves
  Into all sensuous life, the goat-foot Faun,
The Centaur, or the merry bright-eyed Elves
  That leave their dancing rings to spite the dawn
Upon the meadows, shall not be more near
Than you and I to nature's mysteries, for we shall hear

The thrush's heart beat, and the daisies grow,
  And the wan snowdrop sighing for the sun
On sunless days in winter, we shall know
  By whom the silver gossamer is spun,
Who paints the diapered fritillaries,
On what wide wings from shivering pine to pine the eagle flies.

Ay! had we never loved at all, who knows

If yonder daffodil had lured the bee

Into its gilded womb, or any rose

    Had hung with crimson lamps its little tree!

Methinks no leaf would ever bud in spring,

But for the lovers' lips that kiss, the poets' lips that sing.

Is the light vanished from our golden sun,

    Or is this dædal-fashioned earth less fair,

That we are nature's heritors, and one

    With every pulse of life that beats the air?

Rather new suns across the sky shall pass,

New splendour come unto the flower, new glory to the grass.

And we two lovers shall not sit afar,

    Critics of nature, but the joyous sea

Shall be our raiment, and the bearded star

    Shoot arrows at our pleasure! We shall be

Part of the mighty universal whole,

And through all æons mix and mingle with the Kosmic Soul!

We shall be notes in that great Symphony

    Whose cadence circles through the rhythmic spheres,

And all the live World's throbbing heart shall be

One with our heart; the stealthy creeping years

Have lost their terrors now, we shall not die,

The Universe itself shall be our Immortality.

THE FOURTH MOVEMENT

IMPRESSION: LE RÉVEILLON

The sky is laced with fitful red,
The circling mists and shadows flee,
The dawn is rising from the sea,
Like a white lady from her bed.

And jagged brazen arrows fall
Athwart the feathers of the night,
And a long wave of yellow light
Breaks silently on tower and hall,

And spreading wide across the wold
Wakes into flight some fluttering bird,
And all the chestnut tops are stirred,
And all the branches streaked with gold.

AT VERONA

How steep the stairs within Kings' houses are
For exile-wearied feet as mine to tread,

And O how salt and bitter is the bread

Which falls from this Hound's table,—better far

That I had died in the red ways of war,

   Or that the gate of Florence bare my head,

   Than to live thus, by all things comraded

Which seek the essence of my soul to mar.

'Curse God and die: what better hope than this?

   He hath forgotten thee in all the bliss

   Of his gold city, and eternal day'—

Nay peace: behind my prison's blinded bars

   I do possess what none can take away

   My love, and all the glory of the stars.

APOLOGIA

Is it thy will that I should wax and wane,

   Barter my cloth of gold for hodden grey,

And at thy pleasure weave that web of pain

   Whose brightest threads are each a wasted day?

Is it thy will—Love that I love so well—

   That my Soul's House should be a tortured spot

Wherein, like evil paramours, must dwell

   The quenchless flame, the worm that dieth not?

Nay, if it be thy will I shall endure,

    And sell ambition at the common mart,

And let dull failure be my vesture,

    And sorrow dig its grave within my heart.

Perchance it may be better so—at least

    I have not made my heart a heart of stone,

Nor starved my boyhood of its goodly feast,

    Nor walked where Beauty is a thing unknown.

Many a man hath done so; sought to fence

    In straitened bonds the soul that should be free,

Trodden the dusty road of common sense,

    While all the forest sang of liberty,

Not marking how the spotted hawk in flight

    Passed on wide pinion through the lofty air,

To where some steep untrodden mountain height

    Caught the last tresses of the Sun God's hair.

Or how the little flower he trod upon,

    The daisy, that white-feathered shield of gold,

Followed with wistful eyes the wandering sun

    Content if once its leaves were aureoled.

But surely it is something to have been

    The best belovèd for a little while,

To have walked hand in hand with Love, and seen

    His purple wings flit once across thy smile.

Ay! though the gorgèd asp of passion feed

    On my boy's heart, yet have I burst the bars,

Stood face to face with Beauty, known indeed

    The Love which moves the Sun and all the stars!

QUIA MULTUM AMAVI

Dear Heart, I think the young impassioned priest

    When first he takes from out the hidden shrine

His God imprisoned in the Eucharist,

    And eats the bread, and drinks the dreadful wine,

Feels not such awful wonder as I felt

    When first my smitten eyes beat full on thee,

And all night long before thy feet I knelt

    Till thou wert wearied of Idolatry.

515

Ah! hadst thou liked me less and loved me more,

 Through all those summer days of joy and rain,

I had not now been sorrow's heritor,

 Or stood a lackey in the House of Pain.

Yet, though remorse, youth's white-faced seneschal,

 Tread on my heels with all his retinue,

I am most glad I loved thee—think of all

 The suns that go to make one speedwell blue!

SILENTIUM AMORIS

As often-times the too resplendent sun

 Hurries the pallid and reluctant moon

Back to her sombre cave, ere she hath won

 A single ballad from the nightingale,

 So doth thy Beauty make my lips to fail,

And all my sweetest singing out of tune.

And as at dawn across the level mead

 On wings impetuous some wind will come,

And with its too harsh kisses break the reed

 Which was its only instrument of song,

 So my too stormy passions work me wrong,

And for excess of Love my Love is dumb.

But surely unto Thee mine eyes did show

   Why I am silent, and my lute unstrung;

Else it were better we should part, and go,

   Thou to some lips of sweeter melody,

   And I to nurse the barren memory

Of unkissed kisses, and songs never sung.

HER VOICE

The wild bee reels from bough to bough

   With his furry coat and his gauzy wing,

Now in a lily-cup, and now

   Setting a jacinth bell a-swing,

     In his wandering;

Sit closer love: it was here I trow

     I made that vow,

Swore that two lives should be like one

   As long as the sea-gull loved the sea,

As long as the sunflower sought the sun,—

   It shall be, I said, for eternity

     'Twixt you and me!

Dear friend, those times are over and done;

Love's web is spun.

Look upward where the poplar trees
  Sway and sway in the summer air,
Here in the valley never a breeze
  Scatters the thistledown, but there
    Great winds blow fair
From the mighty murmuring mystical seas,
    And the wave-lashed leas.

Look upward where the white gull screams,
  What does it see that we do not see?
Is that a star? or the lamp that gleams
  On some outward voyaging argosy,—
    Ah! can it be
We have lived our lives in a land of dreams!
    How sad it seems.

Sweet, there is nothing left to say
  But this, that love is never lost,
Keen winter stabs the breasts of May
  Whose crimson roses burst his frost,
    Ships tempest-tossed

Will find a harbour in some bay,

    And so we may.

And there is nothing left to do

  But to kiss once again, and part,

Nay, there is nothing we should rue,

  I have my beauty,—you your Art,

    Nay, do not start,

One world was not enough for two

    Like me and you.

MY VOICE

Within this restless, hurried, modern world

  We took our hearts' full pleasure—You and I,

And now the white sails of our ship are furled,

  And spent the lading of our argosy.

Wherefore my cheeks before their time are wan,

  For very weeping is my gladness fled,

Sorrow has paled my young mouth's vermilion,

  And Ruin draws the curtains of my bed.

But all this crowded life has been to thee

  No more than lyre, or lute, or subtle spell

519

Of viols, or the music of the sea

    That sleeps, a mimic echo, in the shell.

TÆDIUM VITÆ

To stab my youth with desperate knives, to wear

This paltry age's gaudy livery,

To let each base hand filch my treasury,

To mesh my soul within a woman's hair,

And be mere Fortune's lackeyed groom,—I swear

I love it not! these things are less to me

Than the thin foam that frets upon the sea,

Less than the thistledown of summer air

Which hath no seed: better to stand aloof

Far from these slanderous fools who mock my life

Knowing me not, better the lowliest roof

Fit for the meanest hind to sojourn in,

Than to go back to that hoarse cave of strife

Where my white soul first kissed the mouth of sin.

HUMANITAD

It is full winter now: the trees are bare,
  Save where the cattle huddle from the cold
Beneath the pine, for it doth never wear
  The autumn's gaudy livery whose gold
Her jealous brother pilfers, but is true
To the green doublet; bitter is the wind, as though it blew

From Saturn's cave; a few thin wisps of hay
  Lie on the sharp black hedges, where the wain
Dragged the sweet pillage of a summer's day
  From the low meadows up the narrow lane;
Upon the half-thawed snow the bleating sheep
Press close against the hurdles, and the shivering house-dogs creep

From the shut stable to the frozen stream
  And back again disconsolate, and miss
The bawling shepherds and the noisy team;
  And overhead in circling listlessness
The cawing rooks whirl round the frosted stack,
Or crowd the dripping boughs; and in the fen the ice-pools crack

Where the gaunt bittern stalks among the reeds

And flaps his wings, and stretches back his neck,

And hoots to see the moon; across the meads

   Limps the poor frightened hare, a little speck;

And a stray seamew with its fretful cry

Flits like a sudden drift of snow against the dull grey sky.

Full winter: and the lusty goodman brings

   His load of faggots from the chilly byre,

And stamps his feet upon the hearth, and flings

   The sappy billets on the waning fire,

And laughs to see the sudden lightening scare

His children at their play, and yet,—the spring is in the air;

Already the slim crocus stirs the snow,

   And soon yon blanchèd fields will bloom again

With nodding cowslips for some lad to mow,

   For with the first warm kisses of the rain

The winter's icy sorrow breaks to tears,

And the brown thrushes mate, and with bright eyes the rabbit peers

From the dark warren where the fir-cones lie,

   And treads one snowdrop under foot, and runs

Over the mossy knoll, and blackbirds fly

Across our path at evening, and the suns

Stay longer with us; ah! how good to see

Grass-girdled spring in all her joy of laughing greenery

Dance through the hedges till the early rose,

  (That sweet repentance of the thorny briar!)

Burst from its sheathèd emerald and disclose

  The little quivering disk of golden fire

Which the bees know so well, for with it come

Pale boy's-love, sops-in-wine, and daffadillies all in bloom.

Then up and down the field the sower goes,

  While close behind the laughing younker scares

With shrilly whoop the black and thievish crows,

  And then the chestnut-tree its glory wears,

And on the grass the creamy blossom falls

In odorous excess, and faint half-whispered madrigals

Steal from the bluebells' nodding carillons

  Each breezy morn, and then white jessamine,

That star of its own heaven, snap-dragons

  With lolling crimson tongues, and eglantine

In dusty velvets clad usurp the bed

And woodland empery, and when the lingering rose hath shed

Red leaf by leaf its folded panoply,
   And pansies closed their purple-lidded eyes,
Chrysanthemums from gilded argosy
   Unload their gaudy scentless merchandise,
And violets getting overbold withdraw
From their shy nooks, and scarlet berries dot the leafless haw.

O happy field! and O thrice happy tree!
   Soon will your queen in daisy-flowered smock
And crown of flower-de-luce trip down the lea,
   Soon will the lazy shepherds drive their flock
Back to the pasture by the pool, and soon
Through the green leaves will float the hum of murmuring bees at noon.

Soon will the glade be bright with bellamour,
   The flower which wantons love, and those sweet nuns
Vale-lilies in their snowy vestiture
   Will tell their beaded pearls, and carnations
With mitred dusky leaves will scent the wind,
And straggling traveller's-joy each hedge with yellow stars will bind.

Dear bride of Nature and most bounteous spring,

That canst give increase to the sweet-breath'd kine,

And to the kid its little horns, and bring

   The soft and silky blossoms to the vine,

Where is that old nepenthe which of yore

Man got from poppy root and glossy-berried mandragore!

There was a time when any common bird

   Could make me sing in unison, a time

When all the strings of boyish life were stirred

   To quick response or more melodious rhyme

By every forest idyll;—do I change?

Or rather doth some evil thing through thy fair pleasaunce range?

Nay, nay, thou art the same: 'tis I who seek

   To vex with sighs thy simple solitude,

And because fruitless tears bedew my cheek

   Would have thee weep with me in brotherhood;

Fool! shall each wronged and restless spirit dare

To taint such wine with the salt poison of own despair!

Thou art the same: 'tis I whose wretched soul

   Takes discontent to be its paramour,

And gives its kingdom to the rude control

Of what should be its servitor,—for sure

Wisdom is somewhere, though the stormy sea

Contain it not, and the huge deep answer ''Tis not in me.'

To burn with one clear flame, to stand erect

   In natural honour, not to bend the knee

In profitless prostrations whose effect

   Is by itself condemned, what alchemy

Can teach me this? what herb Medea brewed

Will bring the unexultant peace of essence not subdued?

The minor chord which ends the harmony,

   And for its answering brother waits in vain

Sobbing for incompleted melody,

   Dies a swan's death; but I the heir of pain,

A silent Memnon with blank lidless eyes,

Wait for the light and music of those suns which never rise.

The quenched-out torch, the lonely cypress-gloom,

   The little dust stored in the narrow urn,

The gentle XAIPE of the Attic tomb,—

   Were not these better far than to return

To my old fitful restless malady,

Or spend my days within the voiceless cave of misery?

Nay! for perchance that poppy-crownèd god

   Is like the watcher by a sick man's bed

Who talks of sleep but gives it not; his rod

   Hath lost its virtue, and, when all is said,

Death is too rude, too obvious a key

To solve one single secret in a life's philosophy.

And Love! that noble madness, whose august

   And inextinguishable might can slay

The soul with honeyed drugs,—alas! I must

   From such sweet ruin play the runaway,

Although too constant memory never can

Forget the archèd splendour of those brows Olympian

Which for a little season made my youth

   So soft a swoon of exquisite indolence

That all the chiding of more prudent Truth

   Seemed the thin voice of jealousy,—O hence

Thou huntress deadlier than Artemis!

Go seek some other quarry! for of thy too perilous bliss.

My lips have drunk enough,—no more, no more,—

Though Love himself should turn his gilded prow

Back to the troubled waters of this shore

   Where I am wrecked and stranded, even now

The chariot wheels of passion sweep too near,

Hence! Hence! I pass unto a life more barren, more austere.

More barren—ay, those arms will never lean

   Down through the trellised vines and draw my soul

In sweet reluctance through the tangled green;

   Some other head must wear that aureole,

For I am hers who loves not any man

Whose white and stainless bosom bears the sign Gorgonian.

Let Venus go and chuck her dainty page,

   And kiss his mouth, and toss his curly hair,

With net and spear and hunting equipage

   Let young Adonis to his tryst repair,

But me her fond and subtle-fashioned spell

Delights no more, though I could win her dearest citadel.

Ay, though I were that laughing shepherd boy

   Who from Mount Ida saw the little cloud

Pass over Tenedos and lofty Troy

528

And knew the coming of the Queen, and bowed

In wonder at her feet, not for the sake

Of a new Helen would I bid her hand the apple take.

Then rise supreme Athena argent-limbed!

  And, if my lips be musicless, inspire

At least my life: was not thy glory hymned

  By One who gave to thee his sword and lyre

Like Æschylos at well-fought Marathon,

And died to show that Milton's England still could bear a son!

And yet I cannot tread the Portico

  And live without desire, fear and pain,

Or nurture that wise calm which long ago

  The grave Athenian master taught to men,

Self-poised, self-centred, and self-comforted,

To watch the world's vain phantasies go by with unbowed head.

Alas! that serene brow, those eloquent lips,

  Those eyes that mirrored all eternity,

Rest in their own Colonos, an eclipse

  Hath come on Wisdom, and Mnemosyne

Is childless; in the night which she had made

For lofty secure flight Athena's owl itself hath strayed.

Nor much with Science do I care to climb,

   Although by strange and subtle witchery

She drew the moon from heaven: the Muse Time

   Unrolls her gorgeous-coloured tapestry

To no less eager eyes; often indeed

In the great epic of Polymnia's scroll I love to read

How Asia sent her myriad hosts to war

   Against a little town, and panoplied

In gilded mail with jewelled scimitar,

   White-shielded, purple-crested, rode the Mede

Between the waving poplars and the sea

Which men call Artemisium, till he saw Thermopylæ

Its steep ravine spanned by a narrow wall,

   And on the nearer side a little brood

Of careless lions holding festival!

   And stood amazèd at such hardihood,

And pitched his tent upon the reedy shore,

And stayed two days to wonder, and then crept at midnight o'er

Some unfrequented height, and coming down

The autumn forests treacherously slew

What Sparta held most dear and was the crown

   Of far Eurotas, and passed on, nor knew

How God had staked an evil net for him

In the small bay at Salamis,—and yet, the page grows dim,

Its cadenced Greek delights me not, I feel

   With such a goodly time too out of tune

To love it much: for like the Dial's wheel

   That from its blinded darkness strikes the noon

Yet never sees the sun, so do my eyes

Restlessly follow that which from my cheated vision flies.

O for one grand unselfish simple life

   To teach us what is Wisdom! speak ye hills

Of lone Helvellyn, for this note of strife

   Shunned your untroubled crags and crystal rills,

Where is that Spirit which living blamelessly

Yet dared to kiss the smitten mouth of his own century!

Speak ye Rydalian laurels! where is he

   Whose gentle head ye sheltered, that pure soul

Whose gracious days of uncrowned majesty

Through lowliest conduct touched the lofty goal

Where love and duty mingle! Him at least

The most high Laws were glad of, he had sat at Wisdom's feast;

But we are Learning's changelings, know by rote

   The clarion watchword of each Grecian school

And follow none, the flawless sword which smote

   The pagan Hydra is an effete tool

Which we ourselves have blunted, what man now

Shall scale the august ancient heights and to old Reverence bow?

One such indeed I saw, but, Ichabod!

   Gone is that last dear son of Italy,

Who being man died for the sake of God,

   And whose unrisen bones sleep peacefully,

O guard him, guard him well, my Giotto's tower,

Thou marble lily of the lily town! let not the lour

Of the rude tempest vex his slumber, or

   The Arno with its tawny troubled gold

O'er-leap its marge, no mightier conqueror

   Clomb the high Capitol in the days of old

When Rome was indeed Rome, for Liberty

Walked like a bride beside him, at which sight pale Mystery

Fled shrieking to her farthest sombrest cell

  With an old man who grabbled rusty keys,

Fled shuddering, for that immemorial knell

  With which oblivion buries dynasties

Swept like a wounded eagle on the blast,

As to the holy heart of Rome the great triumvir passed.

He knew the holiest heart and heights of Rome,

  He drave the base wolf from the lion's lair,

And now lies dead by that empyreal dome

  Which overtops Valdarno hung in air

By Brunelleschi—O Melpomene

Breathe through thy melancholy pipe thy sweetest threnody!

Breathe through the tragic stops such melodies

  That Joy's self may grow jealous, and the Nine

Forget awhile their discreet emperies,

  Mourning for him who on Rome's lordliest shrine

Lit for men's lives the light of Marathon,

And bare to sun-forgotten fields the fire of the sun!

O guard him, guard him well, my Giotto's tower!

Let some young Florentine each eventide

Bring coronals of that enchanted flower

Which the dim woods of Vallombrosa hide,

And deck the marble tomb wherein he lies

Whose soul is as some mighty orb unseen of mortal eyes;

Some mighty orb whose cycled wanderings,

Being tempest-driven to the farthest rim

Where Chaos meets Creation and the wings

Of the eternal chanting Cherubim

Are pavilioned on Nothing, passed away

Into a moonless void,—and yet, though he is dust and clay,

He is not dead, the immemorial Fates

Forbid it, and the closing shears refrain.

Lift up your heads ye everlasting gates!

Ye argent clarions, sound a loftier strain

For the vile thing he hated lurks within

Its sombre house, alone with God and memories of sin.

Still what avails it that she sought her cave

That murderous mother of red harlotries?

At Munich on the marble architrave

 The Grecian boys die smiling, but the seas

Which wash Ægina fret in loneliness

Not mirroring their beauty; so our lives grow colourless

For lack of our ideals, if one star

 Flame torch-like in the heavens the unjust

Swift daylight kills it, and no trump of war

 Can wake to passionate voice the silent dust

Which was Mazzini once! rich Niobe

For all her stony sorrows hath her sons; but Italy,

What Easter Day shall make her children rise,

 Who were not Gods yet suffered? what sure feet

Shall find their grave-clothes folded? what clear eyes

 Shall see them bodily? O it were meet

To roll the stone from off the sepulchre

And kiss the bleeding roses of their wounds, in love of her,

Our Italy! our mother visible!

 Most blessed among nations and most sad,

For whose dear sake the young Calabrian fell

 That day at Aspromonte and was glad

That in an age when God was bought and sold

One man could die for Liberty! but we, burnt out and cold,

See Honour smitten on the cheek and gyves

   Bind the sweet feet of Mercy: Poverty

Creeps through our sunless lanes and with sharp knives

   Cuts the warm throats of children stealthily,

And no word said:—O we are wretched men

Unworthy of our great inheritance! where is the pen

Of austere Milton? where the mighty sword

   Which slew its master righteously? the years

Have lost their ancient leader, and no word

   Breaks from the voiceless tripod on our ears:

While as a ruined mother in some spasm

Bears a base child and loathes it, so our best enthusiasm

Genders unlawful children, Anarchy

   Freedom's own Judas, the vile prodigal

Licence who steals the gold of Liberty

   And yet has nothing, Ignorance the real

One Fraticide since Cain, Envy the asp

That stings itself to anguish, Avarice whose palsied grasp

Is in its extent stiffened, moneyed Greed

　For whose dull appetite men waste away

Amid the whirr of wheels and are the seed

　Of things which slay their sower, these each day

Sees rife in England, and the gentle feet

Of Beauty tread no more the stones of each unlovely street.

What even Cromwell spared is desecrated

　By weed and worm, left to the stormy play

Of wind and beating snow, or renovated

　By more destructful hands: Time's worst decay

Will wreathe its ruins with some loveliness,

But these new Vandals can but make a rain-proof barrenness.

Where is that Art which bade the Angels sing

　Through Lincoln's lofty choir, till the air

Seems from such marble harmonies to ring

　With sweeter song than common lips can dare

To draw from actual reed? ah! where is now

The cunning hand which made the flowering hawthorn branches bow

For Southwell's arch, and carved the House of One

Who loved the lilies of the field with all

Our dearest English flowers? the same sun

Rises for us: the seasons natural

Weave the same tapestry of green and grey:

The unchanged hills are with us: but that Spirit hath passed away.

And yet perchance it may be better so,

For Tyranny is an incestuous Queen,

Murder her brother is her bedfellow,

And the Plague chambers with her: in obscene

And bloody paths her treacherous feet are set;

Better the empty desert and a soul inviolate!

For gentle brotherhood, the harmony

Of living in the healthful air, the swift

Clean beauty of strong limbs when men are free

And women chaste, these are the things which lift

Our souls up more than even Agnolo's

Gaunt blinded Sibyl poring o'er the scroll of human woes,

Or Titian's little maiden on the stair

White as her own sweet lily and as tall,

Or Mona Lisa smiling through her hair,—

Ah! somehow life is bigger after all

Than any painted angel, could we see

The God that is within us! The old Greek serenity

Which curbs the passion of that level line

Of marble youths, who with untroubled eyes

And chastened limbs ride round Athena's shrine

And mirror her divine economies,

And balanced symmetry of what in man

Would else wage ceaseless warfare,—this at least within the span

Between our mother's kisses and the grave

Might so inform our lives, that we could win

Such mighty empires that from her cave

Temptation would grow hoarse, and pallid Sin

Would walk ashamed of his adulteries,

And Passion creep from out the House of Lust with startled eyes.

To make the body and the spirit one

With all right things, till no thing live in vain

From morn to noon, but in sweet unison

With every pulse of flesh and throb of brain

The soul in flawless essence high enthroned,

Against all outer vain attack invincibly bastioned,

Mark with serene impartiality
　　The strife of things, and yet be comforted,
Knowing that by the chain causality
　　All separate existences are wed
Into one supreme whole, whose utterance
Is joy, or holier praise! ah! surely this were governance

Of Life in most august omnipresence,
　　Through which the rational intellect would find
In passion its expression, and mere sense,
　　Ignoble else, lend fire to the mind,
And being joined with it in harmony
More mystical than that which binds the stars planetary,

Strike from their several tones one octave chord
　　Whose cadence being measureless would fly
Through all the circling spheres, then to its Lord
　　Return refreshed with its new empery
And more exultant power,—this indeed
Could we but reach it were to find the last, the perfect creed.

Ah! it was easy when the world was young

To keep one's life free and inviolate,

From our sad lips another song is rung,

   By our own hands our heads are desecrate,

Wanderers in drear exile, and dispossessed

Of what should be our own, we can but feed on wild unrest.

Somehow the grace, the bloom of things has flown,

   And of all men we are most wretched who

Must live each other's lives and not our own

   For very pity's sake and then undo

All that we lived for—it was otherwise

When soul and body seemed to blend in mystic symphonies.

But we have left those gentle haunts to pass

   With weary feet to the new Calvary,

Where we behold, as one who in a glass

   Sees his own face, self-slain Humanity,

And in the dumb reproach of that sad gaze

Learn what an awful phantom the red hand of man can raise.

O smitten mouth! O forehead crowned with thorn!

   O chalice of all common miseries!

Thou for our sakes that loved thee not hast borne

An agony of endless centuries,

And we were vain and ignorant nor knew

That when we stabbed thy heart it was our own real hearts we slew.

Being ourselves the sowers and the seeds,

   The night that covers and the lights that fade,

The spear that pierces and the side that bleeds,

   The lips betraying and the life betrayed;

The deep hath calm: the moon hath rest: but we

Lords of the natural world are yet our own dread enemy.

Is this the end of all that primal force

   Which, in its changes being still the same,

From eyeless Chaos cleft its upward course,

   Through ravenous seas and whirling rocks and flame,

Till the suns met in heaven and began

Their cycles, and the morning stars sang, and the Word was Man!

Nay, nay, we are but crucified, and though

   The bloody sweat falls from our brows like rain

Loosen the nails—we shall come down I know,

   Staunch the red wounds—we shall be whole again,

No need have we of hyssop-laden rod,

That which is purely human, that is godlike, that is God.

FLOWER OF LOVE

ΓΛΥΚΥΠΙΚΡΟΣ ΕΡΩΣ

Sweet, I blame you not, for mine the fault
    was, had I not been made of common clay
I had climbed the higher heights unclimbed
    yet, seen the fuller air, the larger day.

From the wildness of my wasted passion I had
    struck a better, clearer song,
Lit some lighter light of freer freedom, battled
    with some Hydra-headed wrong.

Had my lips been smitten into music by the
    kisses that but made them bleed,
You had walked with Bice and the angels on
    that verdant and enamelled mead.

I had trod the road which Dante treading saw
    the suns of seven circles shine,
Ay! perchance had seen the heavens opening,

as they opened to the Florentine.

And the mighty nations would have crowned
   me, who am crownless now and without name,
And some orient dawn had found me kneeling
   on the threshold of the House of Fame.

I had sat within that marble circle where the
   oldest bard is as the young,
And the pipe is ever dropping honey, and the
   lyre's strings are ever strung.

Keats had lifted up his hymeneal curls from out
   the poppy-seeded wine,
With ambrosial mouth had kissed my forehead,
   clasped the hand of noble love in mine.

And at springtide, when the apple-blossoms brush
   the burnished bosom of the dove,
Two young lovers lying in an orchard would
   have read the story of our love.

Would have read the legend of my passion,

known the bitter secret of my heart,

Kissed as we have kissed, but never parted as

we two are fated now to part.

For the crimson flower of our life is eaten by

the cankerworm of truth,

And no hand can gather up the fallen withered

petals of the rose of youth.

Yet I am not sorry that I loved you—ah! what

else had I a boy to do,—

For the hungry teeth of time devour, and the

silent-footed years pursue.

Rudderless, we drift athwart a tempest, and

when once the storm of youth is past,

Without lyre, without lute or chorus, Death

the silent pilot comes at last.

And within the grave there is no pleasure, for

the blindworm battens on the root,

And Desire shudders into ashes, and the tree of

Passion bears no fruit.

Ah! what else had I to do but love you, God's

    own mother was less dear to me,

And less dear the Cytheræan rising like an

    argent lily from the sea.

I have made my choice, have lived my poems,

    and, though youth is gone in wasted days,

I have found the lover's crown of myrtle better

    than the poet's crown of bays.

UNCOLLECTED POEMS

FROM SPRING DAYS TO WINTER

(FOR MUSIC)

In the glad springtime when leaves were green,
  O merrily the throstle sings!
I sought, amid the tangled sheen,
Love whom mine eyes had never seen,
  O the glad dove has golden wings!

Between the blossoms red and white,
  O merrily the throstle sings!
My love first came into my sight,
O perfect vision of delight,
  O the glad dove has golden wings!

The yellow apples glowed like fire,
  O merrily the throstle sings!
O Love too great for lip or lyre,
Blown rose of love and of desire,
  O the glad dove has golden wings!

But now with snow the tree is grey,

Ah, sadly now the throstle sings!

My love is dead: ah! well-a-day,

See at her silent feet I lay

A dove with broken wings!

Ah, Love! ah, Love! that thou wert slain—

Fond Dove, fond Dove return again!

TRISTITÆ

Αἴλινον, αἴλινον εἰπέ, τὸ δ' εὖ νικάτω

O well for him who lives at ease

With garnered gold in wide domain,

Nor heeds the splashing of the rain,

The crashing down of forest trees.

O well for him who ne'er hath known

The travail of the hungry years,

A father grey with grief and tears,

A mother weeping all alone.

But well for him whose foot hath trod

The weary road of toil and strife,

Yet from the sorrows of his life.

Builds ladders to be nearer God.

THE TRUE KNOWLEDGE

. . . ἀναγκαίως δ' ἔχει
Βίον θερίζειν ὥστε κάρπιμον στάχυν,
καὶ τὸν γὲν εἶναι τὸν δὲ γῄ.

Thou knowest all; I seek in vain
    What lands to till or sow with seed—
    The land is black with briar and weed,
Nor cares for falling tears or rain.

Thou knowest all; I sit and wait
    With blinded eyes and hands that fail,
    Till the last lifting of the veil
And the first opening of the gate.

Thou knowest all; I cannot see.
    I trust I shall not live in vain,
    I know that we shall meet again
In some divine eternity.

IMPRESSIONS

I. LE JARDIN

The lily's withered chalice falls

    Around its rod of dusty gold,

    And from the beech-trees on the wold

The last wood-pigeon coos and calls.

The gaudy leonine sunflower

    Hangs black and barren on its stalk,

    And down the windy garden walk

The dead leaves scatter,—hour by hour.

Pale privet-petals white as milk

    Are blown into a snowy mass:

    The roses lie upon the grass

Like little shreds of crimson silk.

II. LA MER

A white mist drifts across the shrouds,

    A wild moon in this wintry sky

    Gleams like an angry lion's eye

Out of a mane of tawny clouds.

The muffled steersman at the wheel

Is but a shadow in the gloom;—

And in the throbbing engine-room

Leap the long rods of polished steel.

The shattered storm has left its trace

Upon this huge and heaving dome,

For the thin threads of yellow foam

Float on the waves like ravelled lace.

UNDER THE BALCONY

O beautiful star with the crimson mouth!

O moon with the brows of gold!

Rise up, rise up, from the odorous south!

And light for my love her way,

Lest her little feet should stray

On the windy hill and the wold!

O beautiful star with the crimson mouth!

O moon with the brows of gold!

O ship that shakes on the desolate sea!

O ship with the wet, white sail!

Put in, put in, to the port to me!

For my love and I would go

To the land where the daffodils blow

In the heart of a violet dale!

O ship that shakes on the desolate sea!

O ship with the wet, white sail!

O rapturous bird with the low, sweet note!

O bird that sits on the spray!

Sing on, sing on, from your soft brown throat!

And my love in her little bed

Will listen, and lift her head

From the pillow, and come my way!

O rapturous bird with the low, sweet note!

O bird that sits on the spray!

O blossom that hangs in the tremulous air!

O blossom with lips of snow!

Come down, come down, for my love to wear!

You will die on her head in a crown,

You will die in a fold of her gown,

To her little light heart you will go!

O blossom that hangs in the tremulous air!

O blossom with lips of snow!

THE HARLOT'S HOUSE

We caught the tread of dancing feet,

We loitered down the moonlit street,

And stopped beneath the harlot's house.

Inside, above the din and fray,

We heard the loud musicians play

The 'Treues Liebes Herz' of Strauss.

Like strange mechanical grotesques,

Making fantastic arabesques,

The shadows raced across the blind.

We watched the ghostly dancers spin

To sound of horn and violin,

Like black leaves wheeling in the wind.

Like wire-pulled automatons,

Slim silhouetted skeletons

Went sidling through the slow quadrille,

Then took each other by the hand,

And danced a stately saraband;

Their laughter echoed thin and shrill.

Sometimes a clockwork puppet pressed

A phantom lover to her breast,

Sometimes they seemed to try to sing.

Sometimes a horrible marionette

Came out, and smoked its cigarette

Upon the steps like a live thing.

Then, turning to my love, I said,

'The dead are dancing with the dead,

The dust is whirling with the dust.'

But she—she heard the violin,

And left my side, and entered in:

Love passed into the house of lust.

Then suddenly the tune went false,

The dancers wearied of the waltz,

The shadows ceased to wheel and whirl.

And down the long and silent street,

The dawn, with silver-sandalled feet,

Crept like a frightened girl.

554

LE JARDIN DES TUILERIES

This winter air is keen and cold,
   And keen and cold this winter sun,
   But round my chair the children run
Like little things of dancing gold.

Sometimes about the painted kiosk
   The mimic soldiers strut and stride,
   Sometimes the blue-eyed brigands hide
In the bleak tangles of the bosk.

And sometimes, while the old nurse cons
   Her book, they steal across the square,
   And launch their paper navies where
Huge Triton writhes in greenish bronze.

And now in mimic flight they flee,
   And now they rush, a boisterous band—
   And, tiny hand on tiny hand,
Climb up the black and leafless tree.

Ah! cruel tree! if I were you,
   And children climbed me, for their sake

Though it be winter I would break

Into spring blossoms white and blue!

ON THE SALE BY AUCTION OF KEATS' LOVE LETTERS

These are the letters which Endymion wrote

   To one he loved in secret, and apart.

   And now the brawlers of the auction mart

Bargain and bid for each poor blotted note,

Ay! for each separate pulse of passion quote

   The merchant's price. I think they love not art

   Who break the crystal of a poet's heart

That small and sickly eyes may glare and gloat.

Is it not said that many years ago,

   In a far Eastern town, some soldiers ran

   With torches through the midnight, and began

To wrangle for mean raiment, and to throw

   Dice for the garments of a wretched man,

Not knowing the God's wonder, or His woe?

THE NEW REMORSE

The sin was mine; I did not understand.

   So now is music prisoned in her cave,

   Save where some ebbing desultory wave

Frets with its restless whirls this meagre strand.

And in the withered hollow of this land

    Hath Summer dug herself so deep a grave,

    That hardly can the leaden willow crave

One silver blossom from keen Winter's hand.

But who is this who cometh by the shore?

(Nay, love, look up and wonder!) Who is this

    Who cometh in dyed garments from the South?

It is thy new-found Lord, and he shall kiss

    The yet unravished roses of thy mouth,

And I shall weep and worship, as before.

FANTAISIES DÉCORATIVES

I. LE PANNEAU

Under the rose-tree's dancing shade

    There stands a little ivory girl,

    Pulling the leaves of pink and pearl

With pale green nails of polished jade.

The red leaves fall upon the mould,

    The white leaves flutter, one by one,

    Down to a blue bowl where the sun,

Like a great dragon, writhes in gold.

The white leaves float upon the air,
   The red leaves flutter idly down,
   Some fall upon her yellow gown,
And some upon her raven hair.

She takes an amber lute and sings,
   And as she sings a silver crane
   Begins his scarlet neck to strain,
And flap his burnished metal wings.

She takes a lute of amber bright,
   And from the thicket where he lies
   Her lover, with his almond eyes,
Watches her movements in delight.

And now she gives a cry of fear,
   And tiny tears begin to start:
   A thorn has wounded with its dart
The pink-veined sea-shell of her ear.

And now she laughs a merry note:

There has fallen a petal of the rose

   Just where the yellow satin shows

The blue-veined flower of her throat.

With pale green nails of polished jade,

   Pulling the leaves of pink and pearl,

   There stands a little ivory girl

Under the rose-tree's dancing shade.

II. LES BALLONS

Against these turbid turquoise skies

   The light and luminous balloons

   Dip and drift like satin moons,

Drift like silken butterflies;

Reel with every windy gust,

   Rise and reel like dancing girls,

   Float like strange transparent pearls,

Fall and float like silver dust.

Now to the low leaves they cling,

   Each with coy fantastic pose,

   Each a petal of a rose

Straining at a gossamer string.

Then to the tall trees they climb,

Like thin globes of amethyst,

Wandering opals keeping tryst

With the rubies of the lime.

CANZONET

I have no store

Of gryphon-guarded gold;

Now, as before,

Bare is the shepherd's fold.

Rubies nor pearls

Have I to gem thy throat;

Yet woodland girls

Have loved the shepherd's note.

Then pluck a reed

And bid me sing to thee,

For I would feed

Thine ears with melody,

Who art more fair

Than fairest fleur-de-lys,

More sweet and rare

Than sweetest ambergris.

What dost thou fear?

Young Hyacinth is slain,

  Pan is not here,

And will not come again.

  No hornèd Faun

Treads down the yellow leas,

  No God at dawn

Steals through the olive trees.

  Hylas is dead,

Nor will he e'er divine

  Those little red

Rose-petalled lips of thine.

  On the high hill

No ivory dryads play,

  Silver and still

Sinks the sad autumn day.

SYMPHONY IN YELLOW

An omnibus across the bridge

  Crawls like a yellow butterfly,

  And, here and there, a passer-by

Shows like a little restless midge.

Big barges full of yellow hay

    Are moored against the shadowy wharf,

    And, like a yellow silken scarf,

The thick fog hangs along the quay.

The yellow leaves begin to fade

    And flutter from the Temple elms,

    And at my feet the pale green Thames

Lies like a rod of rippled jade.

IN THE FOREST

Out of the mid-wood's twilight

    Into the meadow's dawn,

Ivory limbed and brown-eyed,

    Flashes my Faun!

He skips through the copses singing,

    And his shadow dances along,

And I know not which I should follow,

    Shadow or song!

O Hunter, snare me his shadow!

    O Nightingale, catch me his strain!

Else moonstruck with music and madness

    I track him in vain!

TO MY WIFE: WITH A COPY OF MY POEMS

I can write no stately proem

    As a prelude to my lay;

From a poet to a poem

    I would dare to say.

For if of these fallen petals

    One to you seem fair,

Love will waft it till it settles

    On your hair.

And when wind and winter harden

    All the loveless land,

It will whisper of the garden,

    You will understand.

WITH A COPY OF 'A HOUSE OF POMEGRANATES'

Go, little book,

To him who, on a lute with horns of pearl,

Sang of the white feet of the Golden Girl:

And bid him look

Into thy pages: it may hap that he

May find that golden maidens dance through thee.

ROSES AND RUE

(To L. L.)

Could we dig up this long-buried treasure,

    Were it worth the pleasure,

We never could learn love's song,

    We are parted too long.

Could the passionate past that is fled

    Call back its dead,

Could we live it all over again,

    Were it worth the pain!

I remember we used to meet

    By an ivied seat,

And you warbled each pretty word

    With the air of a bird;

And your voice had a quaver in it,

    Just like a linnet,

And shook, as the blackbird's throat
With its last big note;

And your eyes, they were green and grey
Like an April day,
But lit into amethyst
When I stooped and kissed;

And your mouth, it would never smile
For a long, long while,
Then it rippled all over with laughter
Five minutes after.

You were always afraid of a shower,
Just like a flower:
I remember you started and ran
When the rain began.

I remember I never could catch you,
For no one could match you,
You had wonderful, luminous, fleet,
Little wings to your feet.

I remember your hair—did I tie it?

For it always ran riot—

Like a tangled sunbeam of gold:

These things are old.

I remember so well the room,

And the lilac bloom

That beat at the dripping pane

In the warm June rain;

And the colour of your gown,

It was amber-brown,

And two yellow satin bows

From your shoulders rose.

And the handkerchief of French lace

Which you held to your face—

Had a small tear left a stain?

Or was it the rain?

On your hand as it waved adieu

There were veins of blue;

In your voice as it said good-bye

Was a petulant cry,

566

'You have only wasted your life.'

   (Ah, that was the knife!)

When I rushed through the garden gate

   It was all too late.

Could we live it over again,

   Were it worth the pain,

Could the passionate past that is fled

   Call back its dead!

Well, if my heart must break,

   Dear love, for your sake,

It will break in music, I know,

   Poets' hearts break so.

But strange that I was not told

   That the brain can hold

In a tiny ivory cell

   God's heaven and hell.

DÉSESPOIR

The seasons send their ruin as they go,

For in the spring the narciss shows its head

Nor withers till the rose has flamed to red,

And in the autumn purple violets blow,

And the slim crocus stirs the winter snow;

Wherefore yon leafless trees will bloom again

And this grey land grow green with summer rain

And send up cowslips for some boy to mow.

But what of life whose bitter hungry sea

Flows at our heels, and gloom of sunless night

Covers the days which never more return?

Ambition, love and all the thoughts that burn

We lose too soon, and only find delight

In withered husks of some dead memory.

PAN: DOUBLE VILLANELLE

I

O goat-foot God of Arcady!

This modern world is grey and old,

And what remains to us of thee?

No more the shepherd lads in glee

Throw apples at thy wattled fold,

O goat-foot God of Arcady!

Nor through the laurels can one see

Thy soft brown limbs, thy beard of gold,

And what remains to us of thee?

And dull and dead our Thames would be,

For here the winds are chill and cold,

O goat-foot God of Arcady!

Then keep the tomb of Helice,

Thine olive-woods, thy vine-clad wold,

And what remains to us of thee?

Though many an unsung elegy

Sleeps in the reeds our rivers hold,

O goat-foot God of Arcady!

Ah, what remains to us of thee?

II

Ah, leave the hills of Arcady,

Thy satyrs and their wanton play,

This modern world hath need of thee.

No nymph or Faun indeed have we,

For Faun and nymph are old and grey,

Ah, leave the hills of Arcady!

This is the land where liberty

Lit grave-browed Milton on his way,

This modern world hath need of thee!

A land of ancient chivalry

Where gentle Sidney saw the day,

Ah, leave the hills of Arcady!

This fierce sea-lion of the sea,

This England lacks some stronger lay,

This modern world hath need of thee!

Then blow some trumpet loud and free,

And give thine oaten pipe away,

Ah, leave the hills of Arcady!

This modern world hath need of thee!

THE SPHINX

TO

MARCEL SCHWOB

IN FRIENDSHIP

AND

IN ADMIRATION

THE SPHINX

In a dim corner of my room for longer than my fancy thinks
A beautiful and silent Sphinx has watched me through the shifting gloom.

Inviolate and immobile she does not rise she does not stir
For silver moons are naught to her and naught to her the suns that reel.

Red follows grey across the air, the waves of moonlight ebb and flow
But with the Dawn she does not go and in the night-time she is there.

Dawn follows Dawn and Nights grow old and all the while this curious cat
Lies couching on the Chinese mat with eyes of satin rimmed with gold.

Upon the mat she lies and leers and on the tawny throat of her
Flutters the soft and silky fur or ripples to her pointed ears.

Come forth, my lovely seneschal! so somnolent, so statuesque!

Come forth you exquisite grotesque! half woman and half animal!

Come forth my lovely languorous Sphinx! and put your head upon my knee!

And let me stroke your throat and see your body spotted like the Lynx!

And let me touch those curving claws of yellow ivory and grasp

The tail that like a monstrous Asp coils round your heavy velvet paws!

A thousand weary centuries are thine while I have hardly seen

Some twenty summers cast their green for Autumn's gaudy liveries.

But you can read the Hieroglyphs on the great sandstone obelisks,

And you have talked with Basilisks, and you have looked on Hippogriffs.

O tell me, were you standing by when Isis to Osiris knelt?

And did you watch the Egyptian melt her union for Antony

And drink the jewel-drunken wine and bend her head in mimic awe

To see the huge proconsul draw the salted tunny from the brine?

And did you mark the Cyprian kiss white Adon on his catafalque?

And did you follow Amenalk, the God of Heliopolis?

And did you talk with Thoth, and did you hear the moon-horned Io weep?

And know the painted kings who sleep beneath the wedge-shaped Pyramid?

Lift up your large black satin eyes which are like cushions where one sinks!

Fawn at my feet, fantastic Sphinx! and sing me all your memories!

Sing to me of the Jewish maid who wandered with the Holy Child,

And how you led them through the wild, and how they slept beneath your shade.

Sing to me of that odorous green eve when crouching by the marge

You heard from Adrian's gilded barge the laughter of Antinous

And lapped the stream and fed your drouth and watched with hot and hungry stare

The ivory body of that rare young slave with his pomegranate mouth!

Sing to me of the Labyrinth in which the twi-formed bull was stalled!

Sing to me of the night you crawled across the temple's granite plinth

When through the purple corridors the screaming scarlet Ibis flew

In terror, and a horrid dew dripped from the moaning Mandragores,

And the great torpid crocodile within the tank shed slimy tears,

And tare the jewels from his ears and staggered back into the Nile,

And the priests cursed you with shrill psalms as in your claws you seized their snake

And crept away with it to slake your passion by the shuddering palms.

Who were your lovers? who were they who wrestled for you in the dust?

Which was the vessel of your Lust? What Leman had you, every day?

Did giant Lizards come and crouch before you on the reedy banks?

Did Gryphons with great metal flanks leap on you in your trampled couch?

Did monstrous hippopotami come sidling toward you in the mist?

Did gilt-scaled dragons writhe and twist with passion as you passed them by?

And from the brick-built Lycian tomb what horrible Chimera came

With fearful heads and fearful flame to breed new wonders from your womb?

Or had you shameful secret quests and did you harry to your home

Some Nereid coiled in amber foam with curious rock crystal breasts?

Or did you treading through the froth call to the brown Sidonian

For tidings of Leviathan, Leviathan or Behemoth?

Or did you when the sun was set climb up the cactus-covered slope

To meet your swarthy Ethiop whose body was of polished jet?

Or did you while the earthen skiffs dropped down the grey Nilotic flats

At twilight and the flickering bats flew round the temple's triple glyphs

Steal to the border of the bar and swim across the silent lake

And slink into the vault and make the Pyramid your lúpanar

Till from each black sarcophagus rose up the painted swathèd dead?

Or did you lure unto your bed the ivory-horned Tragelaphos?

Or did you love the god of flies who plagued the Hebrews and was splashed

With wine unto the waist? or Pasht, who had green beryls for her eyes?

Or that young god, the Tyrian, who was more amorous than the dove

Of Ashtaroth? or did you love the god of the Assyrian

Whose wings, like strange transparent talc, rose high above his hawk-faced head,

Painted with silver and with red and ribbed with rods of Oreichalch?

Or did huge Apis from his car leap down and lay before your feet

Big blossoms of the honey-sweet and honey-coloured nenuphar?

How subtle-secret is your smile! Did you love none then? Nay, I know

Great Ammon was your bedfellow! He lay with you beside the Nile!

The river-horses in the slime trumpeted when they saw him come

Odorous with Syrian galbanum and smeared with spikenard and with thyme.

He came along the river bank like some tall galley argent-sailed,

He strode across the waters, mailed in beauty, and the waters sank.

He strode across the desert sand: he reached the valley where you lay:

He waited till the dawn of day: then touched your black breasts with his hand.

You kissed his mouth with mouths of flame: you made the hornèd god your own:

You stood behind him on his throne: you called him by his secret name.

576

You whispered monstrous oracles into the caverns of his ears:

With blood of goats and blood of steers you taught him monstrous miracles.

White Ammon was your bedfellow! Your chamber was the steaming Nile!

And with your curved archaic smile you watched his passion come and go.

With Syrian oils his brows were bright: and wide-spread as a tent at noon

His marble limbs made pale the moon and lent the day a larger light.

His long hair was nine cubits' span and coloured like that yellow gem

Which hidden in their garment's hem the merchants bring from Kurdistan.

His face was as the must that lies upon a vat of new-made wine:

The seas could not insapphirine the perfect azure of his eyes.

His thick soft throat was white as milk and threaded with thin veins of blue:

And curious pearls like frozen dew were broidered on his flowing silk.

On pearl and porphyry pedestalled he was too bright to look upon:

For on his ivory breast there shone the wondrous ocean-emerald,

That mystic moonlit jewel which some diver of the Colchian caves
Had found beneath the blackening waves and carried to the Colchian witch.

Before his gilded galiot ran naked vine-wreathed corybants,
And lines of swaying elephants knelt down to draw his chariot,

And lines of swarthy Nubians bare up his litter as he rode
Down the great granite-paven road between the nodding peacock-fans.

The merchants brought him steatite from Sidon in their painted ships:
The meanest cup that touched his lips was fashioned from a chrysolite.

The merchants brought him cedar chests of rich apparel bound with cords:
His train was borne by Memphian lords: young kings were glad to be his guests.

Ten hundred shaven priests did bow to Ammon's altar day and night,
Ten hundred lamps did wave their light through Ammon's carven house—and now

Foul snake and speckled adder with their young ones crawl from stone to stone

For ruined is the house and prone the great rose-marble monolith!

Wild ass or trotting jackal comes and couches in the mouldering gates:

Wild satyrs call unto their mates across the fallen fluted drums.

And on the summit of the pile the blue-faced ape of Horus sits

And gibbers while the fig-tree splits the pillars of the peristyle

The god is scattered here and there: deep hidden in the windy sand

I saw his giant granite hand still clenched in impotent despair.

And many a wandering caravan of stately negroes silken-shawled,

Crossing the desert, halts appalled before the neck that none can span.

And many a bearded Bedouin draws back his yellow-striped burnous

To gaze upon the Titan thews of him who was thy paladin.

Go, seek his fragments on the moor and wash them in the evening dew,

And from their pieces make anew thy mutilated paramour!

Go, seek them where they lie alone and from their broken pieces make

Thy bruisèd bedfellow! And wake mad passions in the senseless stone!

Charm his dull ear with Syrian hymns! he loved your body! oh, be kind,

Pour spikenard on his hair, and wind soft rolls of linen round his limbs!

Wind round his head the figured coins! stain with red fruits those pallid lips!

Weave purple for his shrunken hips! and purple for his barren loins!

Away to Egypt! Have no fear. Only one God has ever died.

Only one God has let His side be wounded by a soldier's spear.

But these, thy lovers, are not dead. Still by the hundred-cubit gate

Dog-faced Anubis sits in state with lotus-lilies for thy head.

Still from his chair of porphyry gaunt Memnon strains his lidless eyes

Across the empty land, and cries each yellow morning unto thee.

And Nilus with his broken horn lies in his black and oozy bed

And till thy coming will not spread his waters on the withering corn.

Your lovers are not dead, I know. They will rise up and hear your voice

And clash their cymbals and rejoice and run to kiss your mouth! And so,

580

Set wings upon your argosies! Set horses to your ebon car!

Back to your Nile! Or if you are grown sick of dead divinities

Follow some roving lion's spoor across the copper-coloured plain,

Reach out and hale him by the mane and bid him be your paramour!

Couch by his side upon the grass and set your white teeth in his throat

And when you hear his dying note lash your long flanks of polished brass

And take a tiger for your mate, whose amber sides are flecked with black,

And ride upon his gilded back in triumph through the Theban gate,

And toy with him in amorous jests, and when he turns, and snarls, and gnaws,

O smite him with your jasper claws! and bruise him with your agate breasts!

Why are you tarrying? Get hence! I weary of your sullen ways,

I weary of your steadfast gaze, your somnolent magnificence.

Your horrible and heavy breath makes the light flicker in the lamp,

And on my brow I feel the damp and dreadful dews of night and death.

Your eyes are like fantastic moons that shiver in some stagnant lake,

Your tongue is like a scarlet snake that dances to fantastic tunes,

Your pulse makes poisonous melodies, and your black throat is like the hole

Left by some torch or burning coal on Saracenic tapestries.

Away! The sulphur-coloured stars are hurrying through the Western gate!

Away! Or it may be too late to climb their silent silver cars!

See, the dawn shivers round the grey gilt-dialled towers, and the rain

Streams down each diamonded pane and blurs with tears the wannish day.

What snake-tressed fury fresh from Hell, with uncouth gestures and unclean,

Stole from the poppy-drowsy queen and led you to a student's cell?

What songless tongueless ghost of sin crept through the curtains of the night,

And saw my taper burning bright, and knocked, and bade you enter in?

Are there not others more accursed, whiter with leprosies than I?

Are Abana and Pharphar dry that you come here to slake your thirst?

Get hence, you loathsome mystery! Hideous animal, get hence!
You wake in me each bestial sense, you make me what I would not be.

You make my creed a barren sham, you wake foul dreams of sensual life,
And Atys with his blood-stained knife were better than the thing I am.

False Sphinx! False Sphinx! By reedy Styx old Charon, leaning on his oar,
Waits for my coin. Go thou before, and leave me to my crucifix,

Whose pallid burden, sick with pain, watches the world with wearied eyes,
And weeps for every soul that dies, and weeps for every soul in vain.

THE BALLAD OF READING GAOL

IN MEMORIAM

C. T. W.

SOMETIME TROOPER OF THE ROYAL HORSE GUARDS

OBIIT H.M. PRISON, READING, BERKSHIRE

JULY 7, 1896

THE BALLAD OF READING GAOL

I

He did not wear his scarlet coat,
  For blood and wine are red,
And blood and wine were on his hands
  When they found him with the dead,
The poor dead woman whom he loved,
  And murdered in her bed.

He walked amongst the Trial Men
  In a suit of shabby grey;
A cricket cap was on his head,
  And his step seemed light and gay;
But I never saw a man who looked

So wistfully at the day.

I never saw a man who looked
  With such a wistful eye
Upon that little tent of blue
  Which prisoners call the sky,
And at every drifting cloud that went
  With sails of silver by.

I walked, with other souls in pain,
  Within another ring,
And was wondering if the man had done
  A great or little thing,
When a voice behind me whispered low,
  'That fellow's got to swing.'

Dear Christ! the very prison walls
  Suddenly seemed to reel,
And the sky above my head became
  Like a casque of scorching steel;
And, though I was a soul in pain,
  My pain I could not feel.

I only knew what hunted thought

Quickened his step, and why

He looked upon the garish day

   With such a wistful eye;

The man had killed the thing he loved,

   And so he had to die.

Yet each man kills the thing he loves,

   By each let this be heard,

Some do it with a bitter look,

   Some with a flattering word,

The coward does it with a kiss,

   The brave man with a sword!

Some kill their love when they are young,

   And some when they are old;

Some strangle with the hands of Lust,

   Some with the hands of Gold:

The kindest use a knife, because

   The dead so soon grow cold.

Some love too little, some too long,

   Some sell, and others buy;

Some do the deed with many tears,

And some without a sigh:

For each man kills the thing he loves,

    Yet each man does not die.

He does not die a death of shame

    On a day of dark disgrace,

Nor have a noose about his neck,

    Nor a cloth upon his face,

Nor drop feet foremost through the floor

    Into an empty space.

He does not sit with silent men

    Who watch him night and day;

Who watch him when he tries to weep,

    And when he tries to pray;

Who watch him lest himself should rob

    The prison of its prey.

He does not wake at dawn to see

    Dread figures throng his room,

The shivering Chaplain robed in white,

    The Sheriff stern with gloom,

And the Governor all in shiny black,

With the yellow face of Doom.

He does not rise in piteous haste
  To put on convict-clothes,
While some coarse-mouthed Doctor gloats, and notes
  Each new and nerve-twitched pose,
Fingering a watch whose little ticks
  Are like horrible hammer-blows.

He does not know that sickening thirst
  That sands one's throat, before
The hangman with his gardener's gloves
  Slips through the padded door,
And binds one with three leathern thongs,
  That the throat may thirst no more.

He does not bend his head to hear
  The Burial Office read,
Nor, while the terror of his soul
  Tells him he is not dead,
Cross his own coffin, as he moves
  Into the hideous shed.

He does not stare upon the air

Through a little roof of glass:

He does not pray with lips of clay

   For his agony to pass;

Nor feel upon his shuddering cheek

   The kiss of Caiaphas.

II

Six weeks our guardsman walked the yard,

   In the suit of shabby grey:

His cricket cap was on his head,

   And his step seemed light and gay,

But I never saw a man who looked

   So wistfully at the day.

I never saw a man who looked

   With such a wistful eye

Upon that little tent of blue

   Which prisoners call the sky,

And at every wandering cloud that trailed

   Its ravelled fleeces by.

He did not wring his hands, as do

   Those witless men who dare

To try to rear the changeling Hope

   In the cave of black Despair:

He only looked upon the sun,

   And drank the morning air.

He did not wring his hands nor weep,

   Nor did he peek or pine,

But he drank the air as though it held

   Some healthful anodyne;

With open mouth he drank the sun

   As though it had been wine!

And I and all the souls in pain,

   Who tramped the other ring,

Forgot if we ourselves had done

   A great or little thing,

And watched with gaze of dull amaze

   The man who had to swing.

And strange it was to see him pass

   With a step so light and gay,

And strange it was to see him look

   So wistfully at the day,

And strange it was to think that he

    Had such a debt to pay.

For oak and elm have pleasant leaves

    That in the springtime shoot:

But grim to see is the gallows-tree,

    With its adder-bitten root,

And, green or dry, a man must die

    Before it bears its fruit!

The loftiest place is that seat of grace

    For which all worldlings try:

But who would stand in hempen band

    Upon a scaffold high,

And through a murderer's collar take

    His last look at the sky?

It is sweet to dance to violins

    When Love and Life are fair:

To dance to flutes, to dance to lutes

    Is delicate and rare:

But it is not sweet with nimble feet

    To dance upon the air!

So with curious eyes and sick surmise

   We watched him day by day,

And wondered if each one of us

   Would end the self-same way,

For none can tell to what red Hell

   His sightless soul may stray.

At last the dead man walked no more

   Amongst the Trial Men,

And I knew that he was standing up

   In the black dock's dreadful pen,

And that never would I see his face

   In God's sweet world again.

Like two doomed ships that pass in storm

   We had crossed each other's way:

But we made no sign, we said no word,

   We had no word to say;

For we did not meet in the holy night,

   But in the shameful day.

A prison wall was round us both,

Two outcast men we were:

The world had thrust us from its heart,

And God from out His care:

And the iron gin that waits for Sin

Had caught us in its snare.

III

In Debtors' Yard the stones are hard,

And the dripping wall is high,

So it was there he took the air

Beneath the leaden sky,

And by each side a Warder walked,

For fear the man might die.

Or else he sat with those who watched

His anguish night and day;

Who watched him when he rose to weep,

And when he crouched to pray;

Who watched him lest himself should rob

Their scaffold of its prey.

The Governor was strong upon

The Regulations Act:

The Doctor said that Death was but

   A scientific fact:

And twice a day the Chaplain called,

   And left a little tract.

And twice a day he smoked his pipe,

   And drank his quart of beer:

His soul was resolute, and held

   No hiding-place for fear;

He often said that he was glad

   The hangman's hands were near.

But why he said so strange a thing

   No Warder dared to ask:

For he to whom a watcher's doom

   Is given as his task,

Must set a lock upon his lips,

   And make his face a mask.

Or else he might be moved, and try

   To comfort or console:

And what should Human Pity do

   Pent up in Murderers' Hole?

What word of grace in such a place

   Could help a brother's soul?

With slouch and swing around the ring

   We trod the Fools' Parade!

We did not care: we knew we were

   The Devil's Own Brigade:

And shaven head and feet of lead

   Make a merry masquerade.

We tore the tarry rope to shreds

   With blunt and bleeding nails;

We rubbed the doors, and scrubbed the floors,

   And cleaned the shining rails:

And, rank by rank, we soaped the plank,

   And clattered with the pails.

We sewed the sacks, we broke the stones,

   We turned the dusty drill:

We banged the tins, and bawled the hymns,

   And sweated on the mill:

But in the heart of every man

   Terror was lying still.

So still it lay that every day

   Crawled like a weed-clogged wave:

And we forgot the bitter lot

   That waits for fool and knave,

Till once, as we tramped in from work,

   We passed an open grave.

With yawning mouth the yellow hole

   Gaped for a living thing;

The very mud cried out for blood

   To the thirsty asphalte ring:

And we knew that ere one dawn grew fair

   Some prisoner had to swing.

Right in we went, with soul intent

   On Death and Dread and Doom:

The hangman, with his little bag,

   Went shuffling through the gloom:

And each man trembled as he crept

   Into his numbered tomb.

That night the empty corridors

Were full of forms of Fear,

And up and down the iron town

   Stole feet we could not hear,

And through the bars that hide the stars

   White faces seemed to peer.

He lay as one who lies and dreams

   In a pleasant meadow-land,

The watchers watched him as he slept,

   And could not understand

How one could sleep so sweet a sleep

   With a hangman close at hand.

But there is no sleep when men must weep

   Who never yet have wept:

So we—the fool, the fraud, the knave—

   That endless vigil kept,

And through each brain on hands of pain

   Another's terror crept.

Alas! it is a fearful thing

   To feel another's guilt!

For, right within, the sword of Sin

Pierced to its poisoned hilt,

And as molten lead were the tears we shed

For the blood we had not spilt.

The Warders with their shoes of felt

Crept by each padlocked door,

And peeped and saw, with eyes of awe,

Grey figures on the floor,

And wondered why men knelt to pray

Who never prayed before.

All through the night we knelt and prayed,

Mad mourners of a corse!

The troubled plumes of midnight were

The plumes upon a hearse:

And bitter wine upon a sponge

Was the savour of Remorse.

The grey cock crew, the red cock crew,

But never came the day:

And crooked shapes of Terror crouched,

In the corners where we lay:

And each evil sprite that walks by night

    Before us seemed to play.

They glided past, they glided fast,

    Like travellers through a mist:

They mocked the moon in a rigadoon

    Of delicate turn and twist,

And with formal pace and loathsome grace

    The phantoms kept their tryst.

With mop and mow, we saw them go,

    Slim shadows hand in hand:

About, about, in ghostly rout

    They trod a saraband:

And the damned grotesques made arabesques,

    Like the wind upon the sand!

With the pirouettes of marionettes,

    They tripped on pointed tread:

But with flutes of Fear they filled the ear,

    As their grisly masque they led,

And loud they sang, and long they sang,

    For they sang to wake the dead.

'Oho!' they cried, 'The world is wide,
    But fettered limbs go lame!
And once, or twice, to throw the dice
    Is a gentlemanly game,
But he does not win who plays with Sin
    In the secret House of Shame.'

No things of air these antics were,
    That frolicked with such glee:
To men whose lives were held in gyves,
    And whose feet might not go free,
Ah! wounds of Christ! they were living things,
    Most terrible to see.

Around, around, they waltzed and wound;
    Some wheeled in smirking pairs;
With the mincing step of a demirep
    Some sidled up the stairs:
And with subtle sneer, and fawning leer,
    Each helped us at our prayers.

The morning wind began to moan,

But still the night went on:

Through its giant loom the web of gloom

   Crept till each thread was spun:

And, as we prayed, we grew afraid

   Of the Justice of the Sun.

The moaning wind went wandering round

   The weeping prison-wall:

Till like a wheel of turning steel

   We felt the minutes crawl:

O moaning wind! what had we done

   To have such a seneschal?

At last I saw the shadowed bars,

   Like a lattice wrought in lead,

Move right across the whitewashed wall

   That faced my three-plank bed,

And I knew that somewhere in the world

   God's dreadful dawn was red.

At six o'clock we cleaned our cells,

   At seven all was still,

But the sough and swing of a mighty wing

The prison seemed to fill,

For the Lord of Death with icy breath

Had entered in to kill.

He did not pass in purple pomp,

Nor ride a moon-white steed.

Three yards of cord and a sliding board

Are all the gallows' need:

So with rope of shame the Herald came

To do the secret deed.

We were as men who through a fen

Of filthy darkness grope:

We did not dare to breathe a prayer,

Or to give our anguish scope:

Something was dead in each of us,

And what was dead was Hope.

For Man's grim Justice goes its way,

And will not swerve aside:

It slays the weak, it slays the strong,

It has a deadly stride:

With iron heel it slays the strong,

The monstrous parricide!

We waited for the stroke of eight:
　　Each tongue was thick with thirst:
For the stroke of eight is the stroke of Fate
　　That makes a man accursed,
And Fate will use a running noose
　　For the best man and the worst.

We had no other thing to do,
　　Save to wait for the sign to come:
So, like things of stone in a valley lone,
　　Quiet we sat and dumb:
But each man's heart beat thick and quick,
　　Like a madman on a drum!

With sudden shock the prison-clock
　　Smote on the shivering air,
And from all the gaol rose up a wail
　　Of impotent despair,
Like the sound that frightened marshes hear
　　From some leper in his lair.

And as one sees most fearful things

In the crystal of a dream,
We saw the greasy hempen rope
    Hooked to the blackened beam,
And heard the prayer the hangman's snare
    Strangled into a scream.

And all the woe that moved him so
    That he gave that bitter cry,
And the wild regrets, and the bloody sweats,
    None knew so well as I:
For he who lives more lives than one
    More deaths than one must die.

IV

There is no chapel on the day
    On which they hang a man:
The Chaplain's heart is far too sick,
    Or his face is far too wan,
Or there is that written in his eyes
    Which none should look upon.

So they kept us close till nigh on noon,
    And then they rang the bell,

And the Warders with their jingling keys

    Opened each listening cell,

And down the iron stair we tramped,

    Each from his separate Hell.

Out into God's sweet air we went,

    But not in wonted way,

For this man's face was white with fear,

    And that man's face was grey,

And I never saw sad men who looked

    So wistfully at the day.

I never saw sad men who looked

    With such a wistful eye

Upon that little tent of blue

    We prisoners called the sky,

And at every careless cloud that passed

    In happy freedom by.

But there were those amongst us all

    Who walked with downcast head,

And knew that, had each got his due,

    They should have died instead:

He had but killed a thing that lived,

    Whilst they had killed the dead.

For he who sins a second time

    Wakes a dead soul to pain,

And draws it from its spotted shroud,

    And makes it bleed again,

And makes it bleed great gouts of blood,

    And makes it bleed in vain!

Like ape or clown, in monstrous garb

    With crooked arrows starred,

Silently we went round and round

    The slippery asphalte yard;

Silently we went round and round,

    And no man spoke a word.

Silently we went round and round,

    And through each hollow mind

The Memory of dreadful things

    Rushed like a dreadful wind,

And Horror stalked before each man,

    And Terror crept behind.

The Warders strutted up and down,
  And kept their herd of brutes,
Their uniforms were spick and span,
  And they wore their Sunday suits,
But we knew the work they had been at,
  By the quicklime on their boots.

For where a grave had opened wide,
  There was no grave at all:
Only a stretch of mud and sand
  By the hideous prison-wall,
And a little heap of burning lime,
  That the man should have his pall.

For he has a pall, this wretched man,
  Such as few men can claim:
Deep down below a prison-yard,
  Naked for greater shame,
He lies, with fetters on each foot,
  Wrapt in a sheet of flame!

And all the while the burning lime

Eats flesh and bone away,

It eats the brittle bone by night,

And the soft flesh by day,

It eats the flesh and bone by turns,

But it eats the heart alway.

For three long years they will not sow

Or root or seedling there:

For three long years the unblessed spot

Will sterile be and bare,

And look upon the wondering sky

With unreproachful stare.

They think a murderer's heart would taint

Each simple seed they sow.

It is not true! God's kindly earth

Is kindlier than men know,

And the red rose would but blow more red,

The white rose whiter blow.

Out of his mouth a red, red rose!

Out of his heart a white!

For who can say by what strange way,

Christ brings His will to light,

Since the barren staff the pilgrim bore

Bloomed in the great Pope's sight?

But neither milk-white rose nor red

May bloom in prison-air;

The shard, the pebble, and the flint,

Are what they give us there:

For flowers have been known to heal

A common man's despair.

So never will wine-red rose or white,

Petal by petal, fall

On that stretch of mud and sand that lies

By the hideous prison-wall,

To tell the men who tramp the yard

That God's Son died for all.

Yet though the hideous prison-wall

Still hems him round and round,

And a spirit may not walk by night

That is with fetters bound,

And a spirit may but weep that lies

In such unholy ground,

He is at peace—this wretched man—
   At peace, or will be soon:
There is no thing to make him mad,
   Nor does Terror walk at noon,
For the lampless Earth in which he lies
   Has neither Sun nor Moon.

They hanged him as a beast is hanged:
   They did not even toll
A requiem that might have brought
   Rest to his startled soul,
But hurriedly they took him out,
   And hid him in a hole.

They stripped him of his canvas clothes,
   And gave him to the flies:
They mocked the swollen purple throat,
   And the stark and staring eyes:
And with laughter loud they heaped the shroud
   In which their convict lies.

The Chaplain would not kneel to pray

By his dishonoured grave:

Nor mark it with that blessed Cross

    That Christ for sinners gave,

Because the man was one of those

    Whom Christ came down to save.

Yet all is well; he has but passed

    To Life's appointed bourne:

And alien tears will fill for him

    Pity's long-broken urn,

For his mourners will be outcast men,

    And outcasts always mourn

V

I know not whether Laws be right,

    Or whether Laws be wrong;

All that we know who lie in gaol

    Is that the wall is strong;

And that each day is like a year,

    A year whose days are long.

But this I know, that every Law

    That men have made for Man,

Since first Man took his brother's life,

   And the sad world began,

But straws the wheat and saves the chaff

   With a most evil fan.

This too I know—and wise it were

   If each could know the same—

That every prison that men build

   Is built with bricks of shame,

And bound with bars lest Christ should see

   How men their brothers maim.

With bars they blur the gracious moon,

   And blind the goodly sun:

And they do well to hide their Hell,

   For in it things are done

That Son of God nor son of Man

   Ever should look upon!

The vilest deeds like poison weeds,

   Bloom well in prison-air;

It is only what is good in Man

   That wastes and withers there:

Pale Anguish keeps the heavy gate,

    And the Warder is Despair.

For they starve the little frightened child

    Till it weeps both night and day:

And they scourge the weak, and flog the fool,

    And gibe the old and grey,

And some grow mad, and all grow bad,

    And none a word may say.

Each narrow cell in which we dwell

    Is a foul and dark latrine,

And the fetid breath of living Death

    Chokes up each grated screen,

And all, but Lust, is turned to dust

    In Humanity's machine.

The brackish water that we drink

    Creeps with a loathsome slime,

And the bitter bread they weigh in scales

    Is full of chalk and lime,

And Sleep will not lie down, but walks

    Wild-eyed, and cries to Time.

But though lean Hunger and green Thirst

　Like asp with adder fight,

We have little care of prison fare,

　For what chills and kills outright

Is that every stone one lifts by day

　Becomes one's heart by night.

With midnight always in one's heart,

　And twilight in one's cell,

We turn the crank, or tear the rope,

　Each in his separate Hell,

And the silence is more awful far

　Than the sound of a brazen bell.

And never a human voice comes near

　To speak a gentle word:

And the eye that watches through the door

　Is pitiless and hard:

And by all forgot, we rot and rot,

　With soul and body marred.

And thus we rust Life's iron chain

Degraded and alone:

And some men curse, and some men weep,

And some men make no moan:

But God's eternal Laws are kind

And break the heart of stone.

And every human heart that breaks,

In prison-cell or yard,

Is as that broken box that gave

Its treasure to the Lord,

And filled the unclean leper's house

With the scent of costliest nard.

Ah! happy they whose hearts can break

And peace of pardon win!

How else may man make straight his plan

And cleanse his soul from Sin?

How else but through a broken heart

May Lord Christ enter in?

And he of the swollen purple throat,

And the stark and staring eyes,

Waits for the holy hands that took

The Thief to Paradise;

And a broken and a contrite heart

The Lord will not despise.

The man in red who reads the Law

Gave him three weeks of life,

Three little weeks in which to heal

His soul of his soul's strife,

And cleanse from every blot of blood

The hand that held the knife.

And with tears of blood he cleansed the hand,

The hand that held the steel:

For only blood can wipe out blood,

And only tears can heal:

And the crimson stain that was of Cain

Became Christ's snow-white seal.

VI

In Reading gaol by Reading town

There is a pit of shame,

And in it lies a wretched man

Eaten by teeth of flame,

In a burning winding-sheet he lies,

And his grave has got no name.

And there, till Christ call forth the dead,

In silence let him lie:

No need to waste the foolish tear,

Or heave the windy sigh:

The man had killed the thing he loved,

And so he had to die.

And all men kill the thing they love,

By all let this be heard,

Some do it with a bitter look,

Some with a flattering word,

The coward does it with a kiss,

The brave man with a sword!

RAVENNA

Newdigate Prize Poem

Recited in the Sheldonian Theatre

Oxford

June 26th, 1878

TO MY FRIEND

GEORGE FLEMING

AUTHOR OF

'THE NILE NOVEL' AND 'MIRAGE'

Ravenna, March 1877

Oxford, March 1878

RAVENNA

I.

A year ago I breathed the Italian air,—

And yet, methinks this northern Spring is fair,—

These fields made golden with the flower of March,

The throstle singing on the feathered larch,

The cawing rooks, the wood-doves fluttering by,

The little clouds that race across the sky;

And fair the violet's gentle drooping head,

The primrose, pale for love uncomforted,

The rose that burgeons on the climbing briar,

The crocus-bed, (that seems a moon of fire

Round-girdled with a purple marriage-ring);

And all the flowers of our English Spring,

Fond snowdrops, and the bright-starred daffodil.

Up starts the lark beside the murmuring mill,

And breaks the gossamer-threads of early dew;

And down the river, like a flame of blue,

Keen as an arrow flies the water-king,

While the brown linnets in the greenwood sing.

A year ago!—it seems a little time

Since last I saw that lordly southern clime,

Where flower and fruit to purple radiance blow,

And like bright lamps the fabled apples glow.

Full Spring it was—and by rich flowering vines,

Dark olive-groves and noble forest-pines,

I rode at will; the moist glad air was sweet,

The white road rang beneath my horse's feet,

And musing on Ravenna's ancient name,

I watched the day till, marked with wounds of flame,

The turquoise sky to burnished gold was turned.

O how my heart with boyish passion burned,

When far away across the sedge and mere

I saw that Holy City rising clear,

Crowned with her crown of towers!—On and on

I galloped, racing with the setting sun,

And ere the crimson after-glow was passed,

I stood within Ravenna's walls at last!

II.

How strangely still! no sound of life or joy

Startles the air; no laughing shepherd-boy

Pipes on his reed, nor ever through the day

Comes the glad sound of children at their play:

O sad, and sweet, and silent! surely here

A man might dwell apart from troublous fear,

Watching the tide of seasons as they flow

From amorous Spring to Winter's rain and snow,

And have no thought of sorrow;—here, indeed,

Are Lethe's waters, and that fatal weed

Which makes a man forget his fatherland.

Ay! amid lotus-meadows dost thou stand,

Like Proserpine, with poppy-laden head,

Guarding the holy ashes of the dead.

For though thy brood of warrior sons hath ceased,

Thy noble dead are with thee!—they at least

Are faithful to thine honour:—guard them well,

O childless city! for a mighty spell,

To wake men's hearts to dreams of things sublime,

Are the lone tombs where rest the Great of Time.

III.

Yon lonely pillar, rising on the plain,

Marks where the bravest knight of France was slain,—

The Prince of chivalry, the Lord of war,

Gaston de Foix: for some untimely star

Led him against thy city, and he fell,

As falls some forest-lion fighting well.

Taken from life while life and love were new,

He lies beneath God's seamless veil of blue;

Tall lance-like reeds wave sadly o'er his head,

And oleanders bloom to deeper red,

Where his bright youth flowed crimson on the ground.

Look farther north unto that broken mound,—

There, prisoned now within a lordly tomb

Raised by a daughter's hand, in lonely gloom,

Huge-limbed Theodoric, the Gothic king,

Sleeps after all his weary conquering.

Time hath not spared his ruin,—wind and rain

Have broken down his stronghold; and again

We see that Death is mighty lord of all,

And king and clown to ashen dust must fall

Mighty indeed their glory! yet to me

Barbaric king, or knight of chivalry,

Or the great queen herself, were poor and vain,

Beside the grave where Dante rests from pain.

His gilded shrine lies open to the air;

And cunning sculptor's hands have carven there

The calm white brow, as calm as earliest morn,

The eyes that flashed with passionate love and scorn,

The lips that sang of Heaven and of Hell,

The almond-face which Giotto drew so well,

The weary face of Dante;—to this day,

Here in his place of resting, far away

622

From Arno's yellow waters, rushing down

Through the wide bridges of that fairy town,

Where the tall tower of Giotto seems to rise

A marble lily under sapphire skies!

Alas! my Dante! thou hast known the pain

Of meaner lives,—the exile's galling chain,

How steep the stairs within kings' houses are,

And all the petty miseries which mar

Man's nobler nature with the sense of wrong.

Yet this dull world is grateful for thy song;

Our nations do thee homage,—even she,

That cruel queen of vine-clad Tuscany,

Who bound with crown of thorns thy living brow,

Hath decked thine empty tomb with laurels now,

And begs in vain the ashes of her son.

O mightiest exile! all thy grief is done:

Thy soul walks now beside thy Beatrice;

Ravenna guards thine ashes: sleep in peace.

IV.

How lone this palace is; how grey the walls!

No minstrel now wakes echoes in these halls.

The broken chain lies rusting on the door,

And noisome weeds have split the marble floor:

Here lurks the snake, and here the lizards run

By the stone lions blinking in the sun.

Byron dwelt here in love and revelry

For two long years—a second Anthony,

Who of the world another Actium made!

Yet suffered not his royal soul to fade,

Or lyre to break, or lance to grow less keen,

'Neath any wiles of an Egyptian queen.

For from the East there came a mighty cry,

And Greece stood up to fight for Liberty,

And called him from Ravenna: never knight

Rode forth more nobly to wild scenes of fight!

None fell more bravely on ensanguined field,

Borne like a Spartan back upon his shield!

O Hellas! Hellas! in thine hour of pride,

Thy day of might, remember him who died

To wrest from off thy limbs the trammelling chain:

O Salamis! O lone Platæan plain!

O tossing waves of wild Euboean sea!

O wind-swept heights of lone Thermopylæ!

624

He loved you well—ay, not alone in word,

Who freely gave to thee his lyre and sword,

Like Æschylos at well-fought Marathon:

  And England, too, shall glory in her son,

Her warrior-poet, first in song and fight.

No longer now shall Slander's venomed spite

Crawl like a snake across his perfect name,

Or mar the lordly scutcheon of his fame.

  For as the olive-garland of the race,

Which lights with joy each eager runner's face,

As the red cross which saveth men in war,

As a flame-bearded beacon seen from far

By mariners upon a storm-tossed sea,—

Such was his love for Greece and Liberty!

  Byron, thy crowns are ever fresh and green:

Red leaves of rose from Sapphic Mitylene

Shall bind thy brows; the myrtle blooms for thee,

In hidden glades by lonely Castaly;

The laurels wait thy coming: all are thine,

And round thy head one perfect wreath will twine.

V.

The pine-tops rocked before the evening breeze

With the hoarse murmur of the wintry seas,

And the tall stems were streaked with amber bright;—

I wandered through the wood in wild delight,

Some startled bird, with fluttering wings and fleet,

Made snow of all the blossoms; at my feet,

Like silver crowns, the pale narcissi lay,

And small birds sang on every twining spray.

O waving trees, O forest liberty!

Within your haunts at least a man is free,

And half forgets the weary world of strife:

The blood flows hotter, and a sense of life

Wakes i' the quickening veins, while once again

The woods are filled with gods we fancied slain.

Long time I watched, and surely hoped to see

Some goat-foot Pan make merry minstrelsy

Amid the reeds! some startled Dryad-maid

In girlish flight! or lurking in the glade,

The soft brown limbs, the wanton treacherous face

Of woodland god! Queen Dian in the chase,

White-limbed and terrible, with look of pride,

And leash of boar-hounds leaping at her side!

Or Hylas mirrored in the perfect stream.

   O idle heart! O fond Hellenic dream!

Ere long, with melancholy rise and swell,

The evening chimes, the convent's vesper bell,

Struck on mine ears amid the amorous flowers.

Alas! alas! these sweet and honied hours

Had whelmed my heart like some encroaching sea,

And drowned all thoughts of black Gethsemane.

VI.

   O lone Ravenna! many a tale is told

Of thy great glories in the days of old:

Two thousand years have passed since thou didst see

Cæsar ride forth to royal victory.

Mighty thy name when Rome's lean eagles flew

From Britain's isles to far Euphrates blue;

And of the peoples thou wast noble queen,

Till in thy streets the Goth and Hun were seen.

Discrowned by man, deserted by the sea,

627

Thou sleepest, rocked in lonely misery!

No longer now upon thy swelling tide,

Pine-forest-like, thy myriad galleys ride!

For where the brass-beaked ships were wont to float,

The weary shepherd pipes his mournful note;

And the white sheep are free to come and go

Where Adria's purple waters used to flow.

O fair! O sad! O Queen uncomforted!

In ruined loveliness thou liest dead,

Alone of all thy sisters; for at last

Italia's royal warrior hath passed

Rome's lordliest entrance, and hath worn his crown

In the high temples of the Eternal Town!

The Palatine hath welcomed back her king,

And with his name the seven mountains ring!

And Naples hath outlived her dream of pain,

And mocks her tyrant! Venice lives again,

New risen from the waters! and the cry

Of Light and Truth, of Love and Liberty,

Is heard in lordly Genoa, and where

The marble spires of Milan wound the air,

Rings from the Alps to the Sicilian shore,

And Dante's dream is now a dream no more.

But thou, Ravenna, better loved than all,

Thy ruined palaces are but a pall

That hides thy fallen greatness! and thy name

Burns like a grey and flickering candle-flame

Beneath the noonday splendour of the sun

Of new Italia! for the night is done,

The night of dark oppression, and the day

Hath dawned in passionate splendour: far away

The Austrian hounds are hunted from the land,

Beyond those ice-crowned citadels which stand

Girdling the plain of royal Lombardy,

From the far West unto the Eastern sea.

I know, indeed, that sons of thine have died

In Lissa's waters, by the mountain-side

Of Aspromonte, on Novara's plain,—

Nor have thy children died for thee in vain:

And yet, methinks, thou hast not drunk this wine

From grapes new-crushed of Liberty divine,

Thou hast not followed that immortal Star

Which leads the people forth to deeds of war.

Weary of life, thou liest in silent sleep,

As one who marks the lengthening shadows creep,

Careless of all the hurrying hours that run,

Mourning some day of glory, for the sun

Of Freedom hath not shewn to thee his face,

And thou hast caught no flambeau in the race.

    Yet wake not from thy slumbers,—rest thee well,

Amidst thy fields of amber asphodel,

Thy lily-sprinkled meadows,—rest thee there,

To mock all human greatness: who would dare

To vent the paltry sorrows of his life

Before thy ruins, or to praise the strife

Of kings' ambition, and the barren pride

Of warring nations! wert not thou the Bride

Of the wild Lord of Adria's stormy sea!

The Queen of double Empires! and to thee

Were not the nations given as thy prey!

And now—thy gates lie open night and day,

The grass grows green on every tower and hall,

The ghastly fig hath cleft thy bastioned wall;

And where thy mailèd warriors stood at rest

The midnight owl hath made her secret nest.

O fallen! fallen! from thy high estate,

O city trammelled in the toils of Fate,

Doth nought remain of all thy glorious days,

But a dull shield, a crown of withered bays!

Yet who beneath this night of wars and fears,

From tranquil tower can watch the coming years;

Who can foretell what joys the day shall bring,

Or why before the dawn the linnets sing?

Thou, even thou, mayst wake, as wakes the rose

To crimson splendour from its grave of snows;

As the rich corn-fields rise to red and gold

From these brown lands, now stiff with Winter's cold;

As from the storm-rack comes a perfect star!

O much-loved city! I have wandered far

From the wave-circled islands of my home;

Have seen the gloomy mystery of the Dome

Rise slowly from the drear Campagna's way,

Clothed in the royal purple of the day:

I from the city of the violet crown

Have watched the sun by Corinth's hill go down,

And marked the 'myriad laughter' of the sea

From starlit hills of flower-starred Arcady;

Yet back to thee returns my perfect love,

As to its forest-nest the evening dove.

   O poet's city! one who scarce has seen

Some twenty summers cast their doublets green

For Autumn's livery, would seek in vain

To wake his lyre to sing a louder strain,

Or tell thy days of glory;—poor indeed

Is the low murmur of the shepherd's reed,

Where the loud clarion's blast should shake the sky,

And flame across the heavens! and to try

Such lofty themes were folly: yet I know

That never felt my heart a nobler glow

Than when I woke the silence of thy street

With clamorous trampling of my horse's feet,

And saw the city which now I try to sing,

After long days of weary travelling.

VII.

   Adieu, Ravenna! but a year ago,

I stood and watched the crimson sunset glow

From the lone chapel on thy marshy plain:

The sky was as a shield that caught the stain

Of blood and battle from the dying sun,

And in the west the circling clouds had spun

A royal robe, which some great God might wear,

While into ocean-seas of purple air

Sank the gold galley of the Lord of Light.

  Yet here the gentle stillness of the night

Brings back the swelling tide of memory,

And wakes again my passionate love for thee:

Now is the Spring of Love, yet soon will come

On meadow and tree the Summer's lordly bloom;

And soon the grass with brighter flowers will blow,

And send up lilies for some boy to mow.

Then before long the Summer's conqueror,

Rich Autumn-time, the season's usurer,

Will lend his hoarded gold to all the trees,

And see it scattered by the spendthrift breeze;

And after that the Winter cold and drear.

So runs the perfect cycle of the year.

And so from youth to manhood do we go,

And fall to weary days and locks of snow.

Love only knows no winter; never dies:

Nor cares for frowning storms or leaden skies

And mine for thee shall never pass away,

Though my weak lips may falter in my lay.

Adieu! Adieu! yon silent evening star,

The night's ambassador, doth gleam afar,

And bid the shepherd bring his flocks to fold.

Perchance before our inland seas of gold

Are garnered by the reapers into sheaves,

Perchance before I see the Autumn leaves,

I may behold thy city; and lay down

Low at thy feet the poet's laurel crown.

Adieu! Adieu! yon silver lamp, the moon,

Which turns our midnight into perfect noon,

Doth surely light thy towers, guarding well

Where Dante sleeps, where Byron loved to dwell.

About Author

Oscar Fingal O'Flahertie Wills Wilde (16 October 1854 – 30 November 1900) was an Irish poet and playwright. After writing in different forms throughout the 1880s, the early 1890s saw him become one of the most popular playwrights in London. He is best remembered for his epigrams and plays, his novel The Picture of Dorian Gray, and the circumstances of his criminal conviction for "gross indecency", imprisonment, and early death at age 46.

Wilde's parents were successful Anglo-Irish intellectuals in Dublin. A young Wilde learned to speak fluent French and German. At university, Wilde read Greats; he demonstrated himself to be an exceptional classicist, first at Trinity College Dublin, then at Oxford. He became associated with the emerging philosophy of aestheticism, led by two of his tutors, Walter Pater and John Ruskin. After university, Wilde moved to London into fashionable cultural and social circles.

As a spokesman for aestheticism, he tried his hand at various literary activities: he published a book of poems, lectured in the United States and Canada on the new "English Renaissance in Art" and interior decoration, and then returned to London where he worked prolifically as a journalist. Known for his biting wit, flamboyant dress and glittering conversational skill, Wilde became one of the best-known personalities of his day. At the turn of the 1890s, he refined his ideas about the supremacy of art in a series of dialogues and essays, and incorporated themes of decadence, duplicity, and beauty into what would be his only novel, The Picture of Dorian Gray (1890). The opportunity to construct aesthetic details precisely, and combine them with larger social themes, drew Wilde to write drama. He wrote Salome (1891) in French while in Paris but it was refused a licence for England due to an absolute prohibition on the portrayal of Biblical subjects on the English stage. Unperturbed, Wilde produced four society comedies in the early 1890s, which made him one of the most successful playwrights of late-Victorian London.

At the height of his fame and success, while The Importance of Being Earnest (1895) was still being performed in London, Wilde had the Marquess of Queensberry prosecuted for criminal libel. The Marquess was the father of Wilde's lover, Lord Alfred Douglas. The libel trial unearthed evidence that caused Wilde to drop his charges and led to his own arrest and trial for gross indecency with men. After two more trials he was convicted and sentenced to two years' hard labour, the maximum penalty, and was jailed from 1895 to 1897. During his last year in prison, he wrote De Profundis (published posthumously in 1905), a long letter which discusses his spiritual journey through his trials, forming a dark counterpoint to his earlier philosophy of pleasure. On his release, he left immediately for France, never to return to Ireland or Britain. There he wrote his last work, The Ballad of Reading Gaol (1898), a long poem commemorating the harsh rhythms of prison life.

Early life

Oscar Wilde was born at 21 Westland Row, Dublin (now home of the Oscar Wilde Centre, Trinity College), the second of three children born to Anglo-Irish Sir William Wilde and Jane Wilde, two years behind his brother William ("Willie"). Wilde's mother had distant Italian ancestry,and under the pseudonym "Speranza" (the Italian word for 'hope'), wrote poetry for the revolutionary Young Irelanders in 1848; she was a lifelong Irish nationalist. She read the Young Irelanders' poetry to Oscar and Willie, inculcating a love of these poets in her sons. Lady Wilde's interest in the neo-classical revival showed in the paintings and busts of ancient Greece and Rome in her home.

William Wilde was Ireland's leading oto-ophthalmologic (ear and eye) surgeon and was knighted in 1864 for his services as medical adviser and assistant commissioner to the censuses of Ireland. He also wrote books about Irish archaeology and peasant folklore. A renowned philanthropist, his dispensary for the care of the city's poor at the rear of Trinity College, Dublin, was the forerunner of the Dublin Eye and Ear Hospital, now located at Adelaide Road. On his father's side Wilde was descended from a Dutchman, Colonel de Wilde, who went to Ireland with King William of Orange's invading army in 1690, and numerous Anglo-Irish ancestors. On his mother's side, Wilde's ancestors included a bricklayer from County Durham, who emigrated to Ireland sometime in the 1770s.

Wilde was baptised as an infant in St. Mark's Church, Dublin, the local Church of Ireland (Anglican) church. When the church was closed, the records were moved to the nearby St. Ann's Church, Dawson Street. Davis Coakley mentions a second baptism by a Catholic priest, Father Prideaux Fox, who befriended Oscar's mother circa 1859. According to Fox's testimony in Donahoe's Magazine in 1905, Jane Wilde would visit his chapel in Glencree, County Wicklow, for Mass and would take her sons with her. She asked Father Fox in this period to baptise her sons.

Fox described it in this way:

> "I am not sure if she ever became a Catholic herself but it was not long before she asked me to instruct two of her children, one of them being the future erratic genius, Oscar Wilde. After a few weeks I baptized these two children, Lady Wilde herself being present on the occasion.

In addition to his children with his wife, Sir William Wilde was the father of three children born out of wedlock before his marriage: Henry Wilson, born in 1838 to one woman, and Emily and Mary Wilde, born in 1847 and 1849, respectively, to a second woman. Sir William acknowledged paternity of his illegitimate or "natural" children and provided for their education, arranging for them to be reared by his relatives rather than with his legitimate children in his family household with his wife.

In 1855, the family moved to No. 1 Merrion Square, where Wilde's sister, Isola, was born in 1857. The Wildes' new home was larger. With both his parents' success and delight in social life, the house soon became the site of a "unique medical and cultural milieu". Guests at their salon included Sheridan Le Fanu, Charles Lever, George Petrie, Isaac Butt, William Rowan Hamilton and Samuel Ferguson.

Until he was nine, Oscar Wilde was educated at home, where a French nursemaid and a German governess taught him their languages. He attended Portora Royal School in Enniskillen, County Fermanagh, from 1864 to 1871. Until his early twenties, Wilde summered at the villa, Moytura House, which his father had built in Cong, County Mayo. There the young Wilde and his brother Willie played with George Moore.

Isola died at age nine of meningitis. Wilde's poem "Requiescat" is written to her memory.

"Tread lightly, she is near

Under the snow

Speak gently, she can hear

the daisies grow"

University education: 1870s

Trinity College, Dublin

Wilde left Portora with a royal scholarship to read classics at Trinity College, Dublin, from 1871 to 1874, sharing rooms with his older brother Willie Wilde. Trinity, one of the leading classical schools, placed him with scholars such as R. Y. Tyrell, Arthur Palmer, Edward Dowden and his tutor, Professor J. P. Mahaffy, who inspired his interest in Greek literature. As a student Wilde worked with Mahaffy on the latter's book Social Life in Greece. Wilde, despite later reservations, called Mahaffy "my first and best teacher" and "the scholar who showed me how to love Greek things".For his part, Mahaffy boasted of having created Wilde; later, he said Wilde was "the only blot on my tutorship".

The University Philosophical Society also provided an education, as members discussed intellectual and artistic subjects such as Dante Gabriel Rossetti and Algernon Charles Swinburne weekly. Wilde quickly became an established member – the members' suggestion book for 1874 contains two pages of banter (sportingly) mocking Wilde's emergent aestheticism. He presented a paper titled "Aesthetic Morality". At Trinity, Wilde established himself as an outstanding student: he came first in his class in his first year, won a scholarship by competitive examination in his second and, in his finals, won the Berkeley Gold Medal in Greek, the University's highest academic award. He was encouraged to compete for a demyship to Magdalen College, Oxford – which he won easily, having already studied Greek for over nine years.

Magdalen College, Oxford

At Magdalen, he read Greats from 1874 to 1878, and from there he applied to join the Oxford Union, but failed to be elected.

Attracted by its dress, secrecy, and ritual, Wilde petitioned the Apollo Masonic Lodge at Oxford, and was soon raised to the "Sublime Degree of Master Mason". During a resurgent interest in Freemasonry in his third year, he commented he "would be awfully sorry to give it up if I secede from the Protestant Heresy". Wilde's active involvement in Freemasonry lasted only for the time he spent at Oxford; he allowed his membership of the Apollo University Lodge to lapse after failing to pay subscriptions.

Catholicism deeply appealed to him, especially its rich liturgy, and he discussed converting to it with clergy several times. In 1877, Wilde was left speechless after an audience with Pope Pius IX in Rome. He eagerly read the books of Cardinal Newman, a noted Anglican priest who had converted to Catholicism and risen in the church hierarchy. He became more serious in 1878, when he met the Reverend Sebastian Bowden, a priest in the Brompton Oratory who had received some high-profile converts. Neither his father, who threatened to cut off his funds, nor Mahaffy thought much of the plan; but mostly Wilde, the supreme individualist, balked at the last minute from pledging himself to any formal creed. On the appointed day of his baptism, Wilde sent Father Bowden a bunch of altar lilies instead. Wilde did retain a lifelong interest in Catholic theology and liturgy.

While at Magdalen College, Wilde became particularly well known for his role in the aesthetic and decadent movements. He wore his hair long, openly scorned "manly" sports though he occasionally boxed, and he decorated his rooms with peacock feathers, lilies, sunflowers, blue china and other objets d'art. He once remarked to friends, whom he entertained lavishly, "I find it harder and harder every day to live up to my blue china." The line quickly became famous, accepted as a slogan by aesthetes but used against them by critics who sensed in it a terrible vacuousness. Some elements disdained the aesthetes, but their languishing attitudes and showy costumes became a recognised pose. Wilde was once physically attacked by a group of four fellow students, and dealt with them single-handedly, surprising critics. By his third year Wilde had truly begun to develop himself and his myth, and considered his learning to be more expansive than what was within the prescribed texts. This attitude resulted in his being rusticated for one term, after he had returned late to a college term from a trip to Greece with Mahaffy.

Wilde did not meet Walter Pater until his third year, but had been enthralled by his Studies in the History of the Renaissance, published during Wilde's final year in Trinity. Pater argued that man's sensibility to beauty should be refined above all else, and that each moment should be felt to its fullest extent. Years later, in De Profundis, Wilde described Pater's Studies... as "that book that has had such a strange influence over my life". He learned tracts of the book by heart, and carried it with him on travels in later years. Pater gave Wilde his sense of almost flippant devotion to art, though he gained a purpose for it through the lectures and writings of critic John Ruskin. Ruskin despaired at the self-validating aestheticism of Pater, arguing that the importance of art lies in its potential for the betterment of society. Ruskin admired beauty, but believed it must be allied with, and applied to, moral good. When Wilde eagerly attended Ruskin's lecture series The Aesthetic and Mathematic Schools of Art in Florence, he learned about aesthetics as the non-mathematical elements of painting. Despite being given to neither early rising nor manual labour, Wilde volunteered for Ruskin's project to convert a swampy country lane into a smart road neatly edged with flowers.

Wilde won the 1878 Newdigate Prize for his poem "Ravenna", which reflected on his visit there the year before, and he duly read it at Encaenia. In November 1878, he graduated with a double first in his B.A. of Classical Moderations and Literae Humaniores (Greats). Wilde wrote to a friend, "The dons are 'astonied' beyond words – the Bad Boy doing so well in the end!"

Apprenticeship of an aesthete: 1880s

Debut in society

After graduation from Oxford, Wilde returned to Dublin, where he met again Florence Balcombe, a childhood sweetheart. She became engaged to Bram Stoker and they married in 1878. Wilde was disappointed but stoic:

he wrote to her, remembering "the two sweet years – the sweetest years of all my youth" during which they had been close. He also stated his intention to "return to England, probably for good." This he did in 1878, only briefly visiting Ireland twice after that.

Unsure of his next step, Wilde wrote to various acquaintances enquiring about Classics positions at Oxford or Cambridge. The Rise of Historical Criticism was his submission for the Chancellor's Essay prize of 1879, which, though no longer a student, he was still eligible to enter. Its subject, "Historical Criticism among the Ancients" seemed ready-made for Wilde – with both his skill in composition and ancient learning – but he struggled to find his voice with the long, flat, scholarly style. Unusually, no prize was awarded that year.

With the last of his inheritance from the sale of his father's houses, he set himself up as a bachelor in London. The 1881 British Census listed Wilde as a boarder at 1 (now 44) Tite Street, Chelsea, where Frank Miles, a society painter, was the head of the household. Wilde spent the next six years in London and Paris, and in the United States, where he travelled to deliver lectures.

He had been publishing lyrics and poems in magazines since entering Trinity College, especially in Kottabos and the Dublin University Magazine. In mid-1881, at 27 years old, he published Poems, which collected, revised and expanded his poems.

The book was generally well received, and sold out its first print run of 750 copies. Punch was less enthusiastic, saying "The poet is Wilde, but his poetry's tame". By a tight vote, the Oxford Union condemned the book for alleged plagiarism. The librarian, who had requested the book for the library, returned the presentation copy to Wilde with a note of apology.Biographer Richard Ellmann argues that Wilde's poem "Hélas!" was a sincere, though flamboyant, attempt to explain the dichotomies the poet saw in himself; one line reads: "To drift with every passion till my soul

Is a stringed lute on which all winds can play".

The book had further printings in 1882. It was bound in a rich, enamel parchment cover (embossed with gilt blossom) and printed on hand-made Dutch paper; over the next few years, Wilde presented many copies to the dignitaries and writers who received him during his lecture tours.

America: 1882

Aestheticism was sufficiently in vogue to be caricatured by Gilbert and Sullivan in Patience (1881). Richard D'Oyly Carte, an English impresario, invited Wilde to make a lecture tour of North America, simultaneously priming the pump for the US tour of Patience and selling this most charming aesthete to the American public. Wilde journeyed on the SS Arizona, arriving 2 January 1882, and disembarking the following day. Originally planned to last four months, it continued for almost a year due to the commercial success. Wilde sought to transpose the beauty he saw in art into daily life. This was a practical as well as philosophical project: in Oxford he had surrounded himself with blue china and lilies, and now one of his lectures was on interior design.

When asked to explain reports that he had paraded down Piccadilly in London carrying a lily, long hair flowing, Wilde replied, "It's not whether I did it or not that's important, but whether people believed I did it". Wilde believed that the artist should hold forth higher ideals, and that pleasure and beauty would replace utilitarian ethics.

Wilde and aestheticism were both mercilessly caricatured and criticised in the press; the Springfield Republican, for instance, commented on Wilde's behaviour during his visit to Boston to lecture on aestheticism, suggesting that Wilde's conduct was more a bid for notoriety rather than devotion to beauty and the aesthetic. T. W. Higginson, a cleric and abolitionist, wrote in "Unmanly Manhood" of his general concern that Wilde, "whose only distinction is that he has written a thin volume of very mediocre verse", would improperly influence the behaviour of men and women.

According to biographer Michèle Mendelssohn, Wilde was the subject of anti-Irish caricature and was portrayed as a monkey, a blackface performer and a Christy's Minstrel throughout his career. "Harper's Weekly put a sunflower-worshipping monkey dressed as Wilde on the front of the January 1882 issue. The magazine didn't let its reputation for quality impede its expression of what are now considered odious ethnic and racial ideologies. The drawing stimulated other American maligners and, in England, had a full-page reprint in the Lady's Pictorial. ... When the National Republican discussed Wilde, it was to explain 'a few items as to the animal's pedigree.' And on 22 January 1882 the Washington Post illustrated the Wild Man of Borneo alongside Oscar Wilde of England and asked 'How far is it from this to this?' "Though his press reception was hostile, Wilde was well received in diverse settings across America; he drank whiskey with miners in Leadville, Colorado, and was fêted at the most fashionable salons in many cities he visited.

London life and marriage

His earnings, plus expected income from The Duchess of Padua, allowed him to move to Paris between February and mid-May 1883. While there he met Robert Sherard, whom he entertained constantly. "We are dining on the Duchess tonight", Wilde would declare before taking him to an expensive restaurant. In August he briefly returned to New York for the production of Vera, his first play, after it was turned down in London. He reportedly entertained the other passengers with "Ave Imperatrix!, A Poem on England", about the rise and fall of empires. E. C. Stedman, in Victorian Poets, describes this "lyric to England" as "manly verse – a poetic and eloquent invocation". The play was initially well received by the audience, but when the critics wrote lukewarm reviews, attendance fell sharply and the play closed a week after it had opened.

Wilde had to return to England, where he continued to lecture on topics including Personal Impressions of America, The Value of Art in Modern Life, and Dress.

In London, he had been introduced in 1881 to Constance Lloyd, daughter of Horace Lloyd, a wealthy Queen's Counsel, and his wife. She happened to be visiting Dublin in 1884, when Wilde was lecturing at the Gaiety Theatre. He proposed to her, and they married on 29 May 1884 at the Anglican St James's Church, Paddington, in London. Although Constance had an annual allowance of £250, which was generous for a young woman (equivalent to about £25,600 in current value), the Wildes had relatively luxurious tastes. They had preached to others for so long on the subject of design that people expected their home to set new standards. No. 16, Tite Street was duly renovated in seven months at considerable expense. The couple had two sons together, Cyril (1885) and Vyvyan (1886). Wilde became the sole literary signatory of George Bernard Shaw's petition for a pardon of the anarchists arrested (and later executed) after the Haymarket massacre in Chicago in 1886.

Robert Ross had read Wilde's poems before they met at Oxford in 1886. He seemed unrestrained by the Victorian prohibition against homosexuality, and became estranged from his family. By Richard Ellmann's account, he was a precocious seventeen-year-old who "so young and yet so knowing, was determined to seduce Wilde". According to Daniel Mendelsohn, Wilde, who had long alluded to Greek love, was "initiated into homosexual sex" by Ross, while his "marriage had begun to unravel after his wife's second pregnancy, which left him physically repelled".

Prose writing: 1886–91

Journalism and editorship: 1886–89

Criticism over artistic matters in The Pall Mall Gazette provoked a letter in self-defence, and soon Wilde was a contributor to that and other journals during 1885–87. He enjoyed reviewing and journalism; the form suited his style. He could organise and share his views on art, literature and life, yet in a format less tedious than lecturing. Buoyed up, his reviews were largely chatty and positive. Wilde, like his parents before him, also supported the cause of Irish nationalism. When Charles Stewart Parnell was falsely accused of inciting murder, Wilde wrote a series of astute columns defending him in the Daily Chronicle.

His flair, having previously been put mainly into socialising, suited journalism and rapidly attracted notice. With his youth nearly over, and a family to support, in mid-1887 Wilde became the editor of The Lady's World magazine, his name prominently appearing on the cover. He promptly renamed it as The Woman's World and raised its tone, adding serious articles on parenting, culture, and politics, while keeping discussions of fashion and arts. Two pieces of fiction were usually included, one to be read to children, the other for the ladies themselves. Wilde worked hard to solicit good contributions from his wide artistic acquaintance, including those of Lady Wilde and his wife Constance, while his own "Literary and Other Notes" were themselves popular and amusing.

The initial vigour and excitement which he brought to the job began to fade as administration, commuting and office life became tedious. At the same time as Wilde's interest flagged, the publishers became concerned anew about circulation: sales, at the relatively high price of one shilling, remained low. Increasingly sending instructions to the magazine by letter, Wilde began a new period of creative work and his own column appeared less regularly.In October 1889, Wilde had finally found his voice in prose and, at the end of the second volume, Wilde left The Woman's World. The magazine outlasted him by one issue.

If Wilde's period at the helm of the magazine was a mixed success from an organizational point of view, it played a pivotal role in his development as a writer and facilitated his ascent to fame. Whilst Wilde the journalist supplied articles under the guidance of his editors, Wilde the editor was forced to learn to manipulate the literary marketplace on his own terms.

During the late 1880s, Wilde was a close friend of the artist James NcNeill Whistler and they dined together on many occasions. At one of these dinners, Whistler said a bon mot that Wilde found particularly witty, Wilde exclaimed that he wished that he had said it, and Whistler retorted "You will, Oscar, you will".Herbert Vivian—a mutual friend of Wilde and Whistler—attended the dinner and recorded it in his article The Reminiscences of a Short Life which appeared in The Sun in 1889. The article alleged that Wilde had a habit of passing off other people's witticisms as his own—especially Whistler's. Wilde considered Vivian's article to be a scurrilous betrayal, and it directly caused the broken friendship between Wilde and Whistler. The Reminiscences also caused great acrimony between Wilde and Vivian, Wilde accusing Vivian of "the inaccuracy of an eavesdropper with the method of a blackmailer" and banishing Vivian from his circle.

Shorter fiction

Wilde published The Happy Prince and Other Tales in 1888, and had been regularly writing fairy stories for magazines. In 1891 he published two more collections, Lord Arthur Savile's Crime and Other Stories, and in September A House of Pomegranates was dedicated "To Constance Mary Wilde". "The Portrait of Mr. W. H.", which Wilde had begun in 1887, was first published in Blackwood's Edinburgh Magazine in July 1889.It is a short story, which reports a conversation, in which the theory that Shakespeare's sonnets were written out of the poet's love of the boy actor "Willie Hughes", is advanced, retracted, and then propounded again. The only evidence for this is two supposed puns within the sonnets themselves.

The anonymous narrator is at first sceptical, then believing, finally flirtatious with the reader: he concludes that "there is really a great deal to be said of the Willie Hughes theory of Shakespeare's sonnets." By the end fact and fiction have melded together.Arthur Ransome wrote that Wilde "read something of himself into Shakespeare's sonnets" and became fascinated with the "Willie Hughes theory" despite the lack of biographical evidence for the historical William Hughes' existence. Instead of writing a short but serious essay on the question, Wilde tossed the theory amongst the three characters of the story, allowing it to unfold as background to the plot. The story thus is an early masterpiece of Wilde's combining many elements that interested him: conversation, literature and the idea that to shed oneself of an idea one must first convince another of its truth.Ransome concludes that Wilde succeeds precisely because the literary criticism is unveiled with such a deft touch.

Though containing nothing but "special pleading", it would not, he says "be possible to build an airier castle in Spain than this of the imaginary William Hughes" we continue listening nonetheless to be charmed by the telling. "You must believe in Willie Hughes," Wilde told an acquaintance, "I almost do, myself."

Essays and dialogues

Wilde, having tired of journalism, had been busy setting out his aesthetic ideas more fully in a series of longer prose pieces which were published in the

648

major literary-intellectual journals of the day. In January 1889, The Decay of Lying: A Dialogue appeared in The Nineteenth Century, and Pen, Pencil and Poison, a satirical biography of Thomas Griffiths Wainewright, in The Fortnightly Review, edited by Wilde's friend Frank Harris. Two of Wilde's four writings on aesthetics are dialogues: though Wilde had evolved professionally from lecturer to writer, he retained an oral tradition of sorts. Having always excelled as a wit and raconteur, he often composed by assembling phrases, bons mots and witticisms into a longer, cohesive work.

Wilde was concerned about the effect of moralising on art; he believed in art's redemptive, developmental powers: "Art is individualism, and individualism is a disturbing and disintegrating force. There lies its immense value. For what it seeks is to disturb monotony of type, slavery of custom, tyranny of habit, and the reduction of man to the level of a machine." In his only political text, The Soul of Man Under Socialism, he argued political conditions should establish this primacy – private property should be abolished, and cooperation should be substituted for competition. At the same time, he stressed that the government most amenable to artists was no government at all. Wilde envisioned a society where mechanisation has freed human effort from the burden of necessity, effort which can instead be expended on artistic creation. George Orwell summarised, "In effect, the world will be populated by artists, each striving after perfection in the way that seems best to him."

This point of view did not align him with the Fabians, intellectual socialists who advocated using state apparatus to change social conditions, nor did it endear him to the monied classes whom he had previously entertained. Hesketh Pearson, introducing a collection of Wilde's essays in 1950, remarked how The Soul of Man Under Socialism had been an inspirational text for revolutionaries in Tsarist Russia but laments that in the Stalinist era "it is doubtful whether there are any uninspected places in which it could now be hidden".

Wilde considered including this pamphlet and The Portrait of Mr. W.H., his essay-story on Shakespeare's sonnets, in a new anthology in 1891, but eventually decided to limit it to purely aesthetic subjects. Intentions packaged revisions of four essays: The Decay of Lying, Pen, Pencil and Poison, The Truth of Masks (first published 1885), and The Critic as Artist in two parts. For Pearson the biographer, the essays and dialogues exhibit every aspect of Wilde's genius and character: wit, romancer, talker, lecturer, humanist and scholar and concludes that "no other productions of his have as varied an appeal". 1891 turned out to be Wilde's annus mirabilis; apart from his three collections he also produced his only novel.

The Picture of Dorian Gray

The first version of The Picture of Dorian Gray was published as the lead story in the July 1890 edition of Lippincott's Monthly Magazine, along with five others. The story begins with a man painting a picture of Gray. When Gray, who has a "face like ivory and rose leaves", sees his finished portrait, he breaks down. Distraught that his beauty will fade while the portrait stays beautiful, he inadvertently makes a Faustian bargain in which only the painted image grows old while he stays beautiful and young. For Wilde, the purpose of art would be to guide life as if beauty alone were its object. As Gray's portrait allows him to escape the corporeal ravages of his hedonism, Wilde sought to juxtapose the beauty he saw in art with daily life.

Reviewers immediately criticised the novel's decadence and homosexual allusions; The Daily Chronicle for example, called it "unclean", "poisonous", and "heavy with the mephitic odours of moral and spiritual putrefaction". Which he clarified his stance on ethics and aesthetics in art – "If a work of art is rich and vital and complete, those who have artistic instincts will see its beauty and those to whom ethics appeal more strongly will see its moral lesson." He nevertheless revised it extensively for book publication in 1891: six new chapters were added, some overtly decadent passages and homo-eroticism excised, and a preface was included consisting of twenty two epigrams, such as "Books are well written, or badly written. That is all."

Contemporary reviewers and modern critics have postulated numerous possible sources of the story, a search Jershua McCormack argues is futile because Wilde "has tapped a root of Western folklore so deep and ubiquitous that the story has escaped its origins and returned to the oral tradition." Wilde claimed the plot was "an idea that is as old as the history of literature but to which I have given a new form".Modern critic Robin McKie considered the novel to be technically mediocre, saying that the conceit of the plot had guaranteed its fame, but the device is never pushed to its full.On the other hand, Robert McCrum of The Guardian deemed it the 27th best novel ever written in English, calling it "an arresting, and slightly camp, exercise in late-Victorian gothic."

Theatrical career: 1892–95

Salomé

The 1891 census records the Wildes' residence at 16 Tite Street, where he lived with his wife Constance and two sons. Wilde though, not content with being better known than ever in London, returned to Paris in October 1891, this time as a respected writer. He was received at the salons littéraires, including the famous mardis of Stéphane Mallarmé, a renowned symbolist poet of the time. Wilde's two plays during the 1880s, Vera; or, The Nihilists and The Duchess of Padua, had not met with much success. He had continued his interest in the theatre and now, after finding his voice in prose, his thoughts turned again to the dramatic form as the biblical iconography of Salome filled his mind. One evening, after discussing depictions of Salome throughout history, he returned to his hotel and noticed a blank copybook lying on the desk, and it occurred to him to write in it what he had been saying. The result was a new play, Salomé, written rapidly and in French.

A tragedy, it tells the story of Salome, the stepdaughter of the tetrarch Herod Antipas, who, to her stepfather's dismay but mother's delight, requests the head of Jokanaan (John the Baptist) on a silver platter as a reward for dancing the Dance of the Seven Veils. When Wilde returned to London just before Christmas the Paris Echo referred to him as "le great event" of the season. Rehearsals of the play, starring Sarah Bernhardt, began but the play was refused a licence by the Lord Chamberlain, since it depicted biblical characters. Salome was published jointly in Paris and London in 1893, but was not performed until 1896 in Paris, during Wilde's later incarceration.

Comedies of society

Wilde, who had first set out to irritate Victorian society with his dress and talking points, then outrage it with Dorian Gray, his novel of vice hidden beneath art, finally found a way to critique society on its own terms. Lady Windermere's Fan was first performed on 20 February 1892 at St James's Theatre, packed with the cream of society. On the surface a witty comedy, there is subtle subversion underneath: "it concludes with collusive concealment rather than collective disclosure". The audience, like Lady Windermere, are forced to soften harsh social codes in favour of a more nuanced view. The play was enormously popular, touring the country for months, but largely trashed by conservative critics. It was followed by A Woman of No Importance in 1893, another Victorian comedy, revolving around the spectre of illegitimate births, mistaken identities and late revelations. Wilde was commissioned to write two more plays and An Ideal Husband, written in 1894, followed in January 1895.

Peter Raby said these essentially English plays were well-pitched, "Wilde, with one eye on the dramatic genius of Ibsen, and the other on the commercial competition in London's West End, targeted his audience with adroit precision".

Queensberry family

In mid-1891 Lionel Johnson introduced Wilde to Lord Alfred Douglas, Johnson's cousin and an undergraduate at Oxford at the time. Known to his family and friends as "Bosie", he was a handsome and spoilt young man. An intimate friendship sprang up between Wilde and Douglas and by 1893 Wilde was infatuated with Douglas and they consorted together regularly in a tempestuous affair. If Wilde was relatively indiscreet, even flamboyant, in the way he acted, Douglas was reckless in public. Wilde, who was earning up to £100 a week from his plays (his salary at The Woman's World had been £6), indulged Douglas's every whim: material, artistic or sexual.

Douglas soon initiated Wilde into the Victorian underground of gay prostitution and Wilde was introduced to a series of young working-class male prostitutes from 1892 onwards by Alfred Taylor. These infrequent rendezvous usually took the same form: Wilde would meet the boy, offer him gifts, dine him privately and then take him to a hotel room. Unlike Wilde's idealised relations with Ross, John Gray, and Douglas, all of whom remained part of his aesthetic circle, these consorts were uneducated and knew nothing of literature. Soon his public and private lives had become sharply divided; in De Profundis he wrote to Douglas that "It was like feasting with panthers; the danger was half the excitement... I did not know that when they were to strike at me it was to be at another's piping and at another's pay."

Douglas and some Oxford friends founded a journal, The Chameleon, to which Wilde "sent a page of paradoxes originally destined for the Saturday Review". "Phrases and Philosophies for the Use of the Young" was to come under attack six months later at Wilde's trial, where he was forced to defend the magazine to which he had sent his work.In any case, it became unique: The Chameleon was not published again.

Lord Alfred's father, the Marquess of Queensberry, was known for his outspoken atheism, brutish manner and creation of the modern rules of boxing. Queensberry, who feuded regularly with his son, confronted Wilde and Lord Alfred about the nature of their relationship several times, but Wilde was able to mollify him. In June 1894, he called on Wilde at 16 Tite Street, without an appointment, and clarified his stance: "I do not say that you are it, but you look it, and pose at it, which is just as bad. And if I catch you and my son again in any public restaurant I will thrash you" to which Wilde responded: "I don't know what the Queensberry rules are, but the Oscar Wilde rule is to shoot on sight".His account in De Profundis was less triumphant: "It was when, in my library at Tite Street, waving his small hands in the air in epileptic fury, your father... stood uttering every foul word his foul mind could think of, and screaming the loathsome threats he afterwards with such cunning carried out". Queensberry only described the scene once, saying Wilde had "shown him the white feather", meaning he had acted in a cowardly way. Though trying to remain calm, Wilde saw that he was becoming ensnared in a brutal family quarrel. He did not wish to bear Queensberry's insults, but he knew to confront him could lead to disaster were his liaisons disclosed publicly.

The Importance of Being Earnest

Wilde's final play again returns to the theme of switched identities: the play's two protagonists engage in "bunburying" (the maintenance of alternative personas in the town and country) which allows them to escape Victorian social mores.Earnest is even lighter in tone than Wilde's earlier comedies. While their characters often rise to serious themes in moments of crisis, Earnest lacks the by-now stock Wildean characters: there is no "woman with a past", the principals are neither villainous nor cunning, simply idle cultivés, and the idealistic young women are not that innocent. Mostly set in drawing rooms and almost completely lacking in action or violence, Earnest lacks the self-conscious decadence found in The Picture of Dorian Gray and Salome.

The play, now considered Wilde's masterpiece, was rapidly written in Wilde's artistic maturity in late 1894. It was first performed on 14 February 1895, at St James's Theatre in London, Wilde's second collaboration with George Alexander, the actor-manager. Both author and producer assiduously revised, prepared and rehearsed every line, scene and setting in the months before the premiere, creating a carefully constructed representation of late-Victorian society, yet simultaneously mocking it. During rehearsal Alexander requested that Wilde shorten the play from four acts to three, which the author did. Premieres at St James's seemed like "brilliant parties", and the opening of The Importance of Being Earnest was no exception. Allan Aynesworth (who played Algernon) recalled to Hesketh Pearson, "In my fifty-three years of acting, I never remember a greater triumph than [that] first night."Earnest's immediate reception as Wilde's best work to date finally crystallised his fame into a solid artistic reputation. The Importance of Being Earnest remains his most popular play.

Wilde's professional success was mirrored by an escalation in his feud with Queensberry. Queensberry had planned to insult Wilde publicly by throwing a bouquet of rotting vegetables onto the stage; Wilde was tipped off and had Queensberry barred from entering the theatre.Fifteen weeks later Wilde was in prison.

Trials

654

Wilde v. Queensberry

On 18 February 1895, the Marquess left his calling card at Wilde's club, the Albemarle, inscribed: "For Oscar Wilde, posing somdomite" Wilde, encouraged by Douglas and against the advice of his friends, initiated a private prosecution against Queensberry for libel, since the note amounted to a public accusation that Wilde had committed the crime of sodomy.

Queensberry was arrested for criminal libel; a charge carrying a possible sentence of up to two years in prison. Under the 1843 Libel Act, Queensberry could avoid conviction for libel only by demonstrating that his accusation was in fact true, and furthermore that there was some "public benefit" to having made the accusation openly. Queensberry's lawyers thus hired private detectives to find evidence of Wilde's homosexual liaisons.

Wilde's friends had advised him against the prosecution at a Saturday Review meeting at the Café Royal on 24 March 1895; Frank Harris warned him that "they are going to prove sodomy against you" and advised him to flee to France. Wilde and Douglas walked out in a huff, Wilde saying "it is at such moments as these that one sees who are one's true friends". The scene was witnessed by George Bernard Shaw who recalled it to Arthur Ransome a day or so before Ransome's trial for libelling Douglas in 1913. To Ransome it confirmed what he had said in his 1912 book on Wilde; that Douglas's rivalry for Wilde with Robbie Ross and his arguments with his father had resulted in Wilde's public disaster; as Wilde wrote in De Profundis. Douglas lost his case. Shaw included an account of the argument between Harris, Douglas and Wilde in the preface to his play The Dark Lady of the Sonnets.

The libel trial became a cause célèbre as salacious details of Wilde's private life with Taylor and Douglas began to appear in the press. A team of private detectives had directed Queensberry's lawyers, led by Edward Carson QC, to the world of the Victorian underground. Wilde's association with blackmailers and male prostitutes, cross-dressers and homosexual brothels was recorded, and various persons involved were interviewed, some being coerced to appear as witnesses since they too were accomplices to the crimes of which Wilde was accused.

The trial opened on 3 April 1895 before Justice Richard Henn Collins amid scenes of near hysteria both in the press and the public galleries. The extent of the evidence massed against Wilde forced him to declare meekly, "I am the prosecutor in this case"Wilde's lawyer, Sir Edward George Clarke, opened the case by pre-emptively asking Wilde about two suggestive letters Wilde had written to Douglas, which the defence had in its possession. He characterised the first as a "prose sonnet" and admitted that the "poetical language" might seem strange to the court but claimed its intent was innocent. Wilde stated that the letters had been obtained by blackmailers who had attempted to extort money from him, but he had refused, suggesting they should take the £60 (equal to £6,800 today) offered, "unusual for a prose piece of that length". He claimed to regard the letters as works of art rather than something of which to be ashamed.

Carson, a fellow Dubliner who had attended Trinity College, Dublin at the same time as Wilde, cross-examined Wilde on how he perceived the moral content of his works. Wilde replied with characteristic wit and flippancy, claiming that works of art are not capable of being moral or immoral but only well or poorly made, and that only "brutes and illiterates", whose views on art "are incalculably stupid", would make such judgements about art. Carson, a leading barrister, diverged from the normal practice of asking closed questions. Carson pressed Wilde on each topic from every angle, squeezing out nuances of meaning from Wilde's answers, removing them from their aesthetic context and portraying Wilde as evasive and decadent. While Wilde won the most laughs from the court, Carson scored the most legal points. To undermine Wilde's credibility, and to justify Queensberry's description of Wilde as a "posing somdomite", Carson drew from the witness an admission of his capacity for "posing", by demonstrating that he had lied about his age on oath. Playing on this, he returned to the topic throughout his cross-examination. Carson also tried to justify Queensberry's characterisation by quoting from Wilde's novel, The Picture of Dorian Gray, referring in particular to a scene in the second chapter, in which Lord Henry Wotton explains his decadent philosophy to Dorian, an "innocent young man", in Carson's words.

Carson then moved to the factual evidence and questioned Wilde about his friendships with younger, lower-class men. Wilde admitted being on a first-name basis and lavishing gifts upon them, but insisted that nothing untoward had occurred and that the men were merely good friends of his. Carson repeatedly pointed out the unusual nature of these relationships and insinuated that the men were prostitutes. Wilde replied that he did not believe in social barriers, and simply enjoyed the society of young men. Then Carson asked Wilde directly whether he had ever kissed a certain servant boy, Wilde responded, "Oh, dear no. He was a particularly plain boy – unfortunately ugly – I pitied him for it." Carson pressed him on the answer, repeatedly asking why the boy's ugliness was relevant. Wilde hesitated, then for the first time became flustered: "You sting me and insult me and try to unnerve me; and at times one says things flippantly when one ought to speak more seriously."

In his opening speech for the defence, Carson announced that he had located several male prostitutes who were to testify that they had had sex with Wilde. On the advice of his lawyers, Wilde dropped the prosecution. Queensberry was found not guilty, as the court declared that his accusation that Wilde was "posing as a Somdomite " was justified, "true in substance and in fact".Under the Libel Act 1843, Queensberry's acquittal rendered Wilde legally liable for the considerable expenses Queensberry had incurred in his defence, which left Wilde bankrupt.

Regina v. Wilde

After Wilde left the court, a warrant for his arrest was applied for on charges of sodomy and gross indecency. Robbie Ross found Wilde at the Cadogan Hotel, Pont Street, Knightsbridge, with Reginald Turner; both men advised Wilde to go at once to Dover and try to get a boat to France; his mother advised him to stay and fight. Wilde, lapsing into inaction, could only say, "The train has gone. It's too late."On 6 April 1895, Wilde was arrested for "gross indecency" under Section 11 of the Criminal Law Amendment Act 1885, a term meaning homosexual acts not amounting to buggery (an offence under a separate statute). At Wilde's instruction, Ross and Wilde's butler forced their way into the bedroom and library of 16 Tite Street, packing some personal effects, manuscripts, and letters. Wilde was then imprisoned on remand at Holloway, where he received daily visits from Douglas.

Events moved quickly and his prosecution opened on 26 April 1895, before Mr Justice Charles. Wilde pleaded not guilty. He had already begged Douglas to leave London for Paris, but Douglas complained bitterly, even wanting to give evidence; he was pressed to go and soon fled to the Hotel du Monde. Fearing persecution, Ross and many others also left the United Kingdom during this time. Under cross examination Wilde was at first hesitant, then spoke eloquently:

Charles Gill (prosecuting): What is "the love that dare not speak its name"?

Wilde: "The love that dare not speak its name" in this century is such a great affection of an elder for a younger man as there was between David and Jonathan, such as Plato made the very basis of his philosophy, and such as you find in the sonnets of Michelangelo and Shakespeare. It is that deep spiritual affection that is as pure as it is perfect. It dictates and pervades great works of art, like those of Shakespeare and Michelangelo, and those two letters of mine, such as they are. It is in this century misunderstood, so much misunderstood that it may be described as "the love that dare not speak its name", and on that account of it I am placed where I am now. It is beautiful, it is fine, it is the noblest form of affection. There is nothing unnatural about it. It is intellectual, and it repeatedly exists between an older and a younger man, when the older man has intellect, and the younger man has all the joy, hope and glamour of life before him. That it should be so, the world does not understand. The world mocks at it, and sometimes puts one in the pillory for it.

This response was counter-productive in a legal sense as it only served to reinforce the charges of homosexual behaviour.

The trial ended with the jury unable to reach a verdict. Wilde's counsel, Sir Edward Clarke, was finally able to get a magistrate to allow Wilde and his friends to post bail. The Reverend Stewart Headlam put up most of the £5,000 surety required by the court, having disagreed with Wilde's treatment by the press and the courts. Wilde was freed from Holloway and, shunning attention, went into hiding at the house of Ernest and Ada Leverson, two of his firm friends. Edward Carson approached Frank Lockwood QC, the Solicitor General and asked "Can we not let up on the fellow now?"Lockwood answered that he would like to do so, but feared that the case had become too politicised to be dropped.

The final trial was presided over by Mr Justice Wills. On 25 May 1895 Wilde and Alfred Taylor were convicted of gross indecency and sentenced to two years' hard labour. The judge described the sentence, the maximum allowed, as "totally inadequate for a case such as this", and that the case was "the worst case I have ever tried". Wilde's response "And I? May I say nothing, my Lord?" was drowned out in cries of "Shame" in the courtroom.

Imprisonment

When first I was put into prison some people advised me to try and forget who I was. It was ruinous advice. It is only by realising what I am that I have found comfort of any kind. Now I am advised by others to try on my release to forget that I have ever been in a prison at all. I know that would be equally fatal. It would mean that I would always be haunted by an intolerable sense of disgrace, and that those things that are meant for me as much as for anybody else – the beauty of the sun and moon, the pageant of the seasons, the music of daybreak and the silence of great nights, the rain falling through the leaves, or the dew creeping over the grass and making it silver – would all be tainted for me, and lose their healing power, and their power of communicating joy. To regret one's own experiences is to arrest one's own development. To deny one's own experiences is to put a lie into the lips of one's own life. It is no less than a denial of the soul.

De Profundis

Wilde was incarcerated from 25 May 1895 to 18 May 1897.

He first entered Newgate Prison in London for processing, then was moved to Pentonville Prison, where the "hard labour" to which he had been sentenced consisted of many hours of walking a treadmill and picking oakum (separating the fibres in scraps of old navy ropes), and where prisoners were allowed to read only the Bible and The Pilgrim's Progress.

A few months later he was moved to Wandsworth Prison in London. Inmates there also followed the regimen of "hard labour, hard fare and a hard bed", which wore harshly on Wilde's delicate health. In November he collapsed during chapel from illness and hunger. His right ear drum was ruptured in the fall, an injury that later contributed to his death. He spent two months in the infirmary.

Richard B. Haldane, the Liberal MP and reformer, visited Wilde and had him transferred in November to Reading Gaol, 30 miles (48 km) west of London on 23 November 1895. The transfer itself was the lowest point of his incarceration, as a crowd jeered and spat at him on the railway platform. He spent the remainder of his sentence there, addressed and identified only as "C33" – the occupant of the third cell on the third floor of C ward.

About five months after Wilde arrived at Reading Gaol, Charles Thomas Wooldridge, a trooper in the Royal Horse Guards, was brought to Reading to await his trial for murdering his wife on 29 March 1896; on 17 June Wooldridge was sentenced to death and returned to Reading for his execution, which took place on Tuesday, 7 July 1896 – the first hanging at Reading in 18 years. From Wooldridge's hanging, Wilde later wrote The Ballad of Reading Gaol.

Wilde was not, at first, even allowed paper and pen but Haldane eventually succeeded in allowing access to books and writing materials. Wilde requested, among others: the Bible in French; Italian and German grammars; some Ancient Greek texts, Dante's Divine Comedy, Joris-Karl Huysmans's new French novel about Christian redemption En route, and essays by St Augustine, Cardinal Newman and Walter Pater.

Between January and March 1897 Wilde wrote a 50,000-word letter to Douglas. He was not allowed to send it, but was permitted to take it with him when released from prison. In reflective mode, Wilde coldly examines his career to date, how he had been a colourful agent provocateur in Victorian society, his art, like his paradoxes, seeking to subvert as well as sparkle. His own estimation of himself was: one who "stood in symbolic relations to the art and culture of my age". It was from these heights that his life with Douglas began, and Wilde examines that particularly closely, repudiating him for what Wilde finally sees as his arrogance and vanity: he had not forgotten Douglas' remark, when he was ill, "When you are not on your pedestal you are not interesting." Wilde blamed himself, though, for the ethical degradation of character that he allowed Douglas to bring about in him and took responsibility for his own fall, "I am here for having tried to put your father in prison." The first half concludes with Wilde forgiving Douglas, for his own sake as much as Douglas's. The second half of the letter traces Wilde's spiritual journey of redemption and fulfilment through his prison reading. He realised that his ordeal had filled his soul with the fruit of experience, however bitter it tasted at the time.

> ... I wanted to eat of the fruit of all the trees in the garden of the world ... And so, indeed, I went out, and so I lived. My only mistake was that I confined myself so exclusively to the trees of what seemed to me the sun-lit side of the garden, and shunned the other side for its shadow and its gloom.

Wilde was released from prison on 19 May 1897 and sailed that evening for Dieppe, France. He never returned to the UK.

On his release, he gave the manuscript to Ross, who may or may not have carried out Wilde's instructions to send a copy to Douglas (who later denied having received it). The letter was partially published in 1905 as De Profundis; its complete and correct publication first occurred in 1962 in The Letters of Oscar Wilde.

Decline: 1897–1900

Exile

Though Wilde's health had suffered greatly from the harshness and diet of prison, he had a feeling of spiritual renewal. He immediately wrote to the Society of Jesus requesting a six-month Catholic retreat; when the request was denied, Wilde wept. "I intend to be received into the Catholic Church before long", Wilde told a journalist who asked about his religious intentions.

He spent his last three years impoverished and in exile. He took the name "Sebastian Melmoth", after Saint Sebastian and the titular character of Melmoth the Wanderer (a Gothic novel by Charles Maturin, Wilde's great-uncle). Wilde wrote two long letters to the editor of the Daily Chronicle, describing the brutal conditions of English prisons and advocating penal reform. His discussion of the dismissal of Warder Martin for giving biscuits to an anaemic child prisoner repeated the themes of the corruption and degeneration of punishment that he had earlier outlined in The Soul of Man under Socialism.

Wilde spent mid-1897 with Robert Ross in the seaside village of Berneval-le-Grand in northern France, where he wrote The Ballad of Reading Gaol, narrating the execution of Charles Thomas Wooldridge, who murdered his wife in a rage at her infidelity. It moves from an objective story-telling to symbolic identification with the prisoners. No attempt is made to assess the justice of the laws which convicted them but rather the poem highlights the brutalisation of the punishment that all convicts share. Wilde juxtaposes the executed man and himself with the line "Yet each man kills the thing he loves". He adopted the proletarian ballad form and the author was credited as "C33", Wilde's cell number in Reading Gaol. He suggested that it be published in Reynolds' Magazine, "because it circulates widely among the criminal classes – to which I now belong – for once I will be read by my peers – a new experience for me". It was an immediate roaring commercial success, going through seven editions in less than two years, only after which "[Oscar" was added to the title page, though many in literary circles had known Wilde to be the author. It brought him a small amount of money.

Although Douglas had been the cause of his misfortunes, he and Wilde were reunited in August 1897 at Rouen. This meeting was disapproved of by the friends and families of both men. Constance Wilde was already refusing to meet Wilde or allow him to see their sons, though she sent him money – three pounds a week. During the latter part of 1897, Wilde and Douglas lived together near Naples for a few months until they were separated by their families under the threat of cutting off all funds.

662

Wilde's final address was at the dingy Hôtel d'Alsace (now known as L'Hôtel), on rue des Beaux-Arts in Saint-Germain-des-Prés, Paris. "This poverty really breaks one's heart: it is so sale , so utterly depressing, so hopeless. Pray do what you can" he wrote to his publisher.He corrected and published An Ideal Husband and The Importance of Being Earnest, the proofs of which, according to Ellmann, show a man "very much in command of himself and of the play" but he refused to write anything else: "I can write, but have lost the joy of writing".

He wandered the boulevards alone and spent what little money he had on alcohol. A series of embarrassing chance encounters with hostile English visitors, or Frenchmen he had known in better days, drowned his spirit. Soon Wilde was sufficiently confined to his hotel to joke, on one of his final trips outside, "My wallpaper and I are fighting a duel to the death. One of us has got to go". On 12 October 1900 he sent a telegram to Ross: "Terribly weak. Please come". His moods fluctuated; Max Beerbohm relates how their mutual friend Reginald 'Reggie' Turner had found Wilde very depressed after a nightmare. "I dreamt that I had died, and was supping with the dead!" "I am sure", Turner replied, "that you must have been the life and soul of the party."Turner was one of the few of the old circle who remained with Wilde to the end and was at his bedside when he died.

Death

By 25 November 1900 Wilde had developed meningitis, then called "cerebral meningitis". Robbie Ross arrived on 29 November, sent for a priest, and Wilde was conditionally baptised into the Catholic Church by Fr Cuthbert Dunne, a Passionist priest from Dublin,Wilde having been baptised in the Church of Ireland and having moreover a recollection of Catholic baptism as a child, a fact later attested to by the minister of the sacrament, Fr Lawrence Fox.Fr Dunne recorded the baptism,

> As the voiture rolled through the dark streets that wintry night, the sad story of Oscar Wilde was in part repeated to me... Robert Ross knelt by the bedside, assisting me as best he could while I administered conditional baptism, and afterwards answering the responses while I

gave Extreme Unction to the prostrate man and recited the prayers for the dying. As the man was in a semi-comatose condition, I did not venture to administer the Holy Viaticum; still I must add that he could be roused and was roused from this state in my presence. When roused, he gave signs of being inwardly conscious... Indeed I was fully satisfied that he understood me when told that I was about to receive him into the Catholic Church and gave him the Last Sacraments... And when I repeated close to his ear the Holy Names, the Acts of Contrition, Faith, Hope and Charity, with acts of humble resignation to the Will of God, he tried all through to say the words after me.

Wilde died of meningitis on 30 November 1900.Different opinions are given as to the cause of the disease: Richard Ellmann claimed it was syphilitic; Merlin Holland, Wilde's grandson, thought this to be a misconception, noting that Wilde's meningitis followed a surgical intervention, perhaps a mastoidectomy; Wilde's physicians, Dr Paul Cleiss and A'Court Tucker, reported that the condition stemmed from an old suppuration of the right ear (from the prison injury, see above) treated for several years (une ancienne suppuration de l'oreille droite d'ailleurs en traitement depuis plusieurs années) and made no allusion to syphilis.

Burial

Wilde was initially buried in the Cimetière de Bagneux outside Paris; in 1909 his remains were disinterred and transferred to Père Lachaise Cemetery, inside the city. His tomb there was designed by Sir Jacob Epstein. It was commissioned by Robert Ross, who asked for a small compartment to be made for his own ashes, which were duly transferred in 1950. The modernist angel depicted as a relief on the tomb was originally complete with male genitalia, which were initially censored by French Authorities with a golden leaf. The genitals have since been vandalised; their current whereabouts are unknown. In 2000, Leon Johnson, a multimedia artist, installed a silver prosthesis to replace them.In 2011, the tomb was cleaned of the many lipstick marks left there by admirers and a glass barrier was installed to prevent further marks or damage.

The epitaph is a verse from The Ballad of Reading Gaol,

And alien tears will fill for him

Pity's long-broken urn,

For his mourners will be outcast men,

And outcasts always mourn.

Posthumous pardon

In 2017, Wilde was among an estimated 50,000 men who were pardoned for homosexual acts that were no longer considered offences under the Policing and Crime Act 2017. The Act is known informally as the Alan Turing law.

Honours

In 2014 Wilde was one of the inaugural honorees in the Rainbow Honor Walk, a walk of fame in San Francisco's Castro neighbourhood noting LGBTQ people who have "made significant contributions in their fields."

Biographies

Wilde's life has been the subject of numerous biographies since his death. The earliest were memoirs by those who knew him: often they are personal or impressionistic accounts which can be good character sketches, but are sometimes factually unreliable. Frank Harris, his friend and editor, wrote a biography, Oscar Wilde: His Life and Confessions (1916); though prone to exaggeration and sometimes factually inaccurate, it offers a good literary portrait of Wilde. Lord Alfred Douglas wrote two books about his relationship with Wilde. Oscar Wilde and Myself (1914), largely ghost-written by T. W. H. Crosland, vindictively reacted to Douglas's discovery that De Profundis was addressed to him and defensively tried to distance him from Wilde's scandalous reputation. Both authors later regretted their work. Later, in Oscar Wilde: A Summing Up (1939) and his Autobiography he was more sympathetic to Wilde. Of Wilde's other close friends, Robert Sherard; Robert Ross, his literary executor; and Charles Ricketts variously published biographies, reminiscences or correspondence. The first more or less objective biography of Wilde came about when Hesketh Pearson wrote Oscar Wilde: His Life and Wit (1946). In 1954 Wilde's son Vyvyan Holland published his memoir Son of Oscar Wilde, which recounts the difficulties Wilde's wife and children faced after his imprisonment. It was revised and updated by Merlin Holland in 1989.

Oscar Wilde, a critical study by Arthur Ransome was published in 1912. The book only briefly mentioned Wilde's life, but subsequently Ransome (and The Times Book Club) were sued for libel by Lord Alfred Douglas. In April 1913 Douglas lost the libel action after a reading of De Profundis refuted his claims.

Richard Ellmann wrote his 1987 biography Oscar Wilde, for which he posthumously won a National (USA) Book Critics Circle Award in 1988and a Pulitzer Prize in 1989. The book was the basis for the 1997 film Wilde, directed by Brian Gilbert and starring Stephen Fry as the title character.

Neil McKenna's 2003 biography, The Secret Life of Oscar Wilde, offers an exploration of Wilde's sexuality. Often speculative in nature, it was widely criticised for its pure conjecture and lack of scholarly rigour. Thomas Wright's Oscar's Books (2008) explores Wilde's reading from his childhood in Dublin to his death in Paris. After tracking down many books that once belonged to Wilde's Tite Street library (dispersed at the time of his trials), Wright was the first to examine Wilde's marginalia.

> Later on, I think everyone will recognise his achievements; his plays and essays will endure. Of course, you may think with others that his personality and conversation were far more wonderful than anything he wrote, so that his written works give only a pale reflection of his power. Perhaps that is so, and of course, it will be impossible to reproduce what is gone forever.

Robert Ross, 23 December 1900

In 2018, Matthew Sturgis' "Oscar: A Life," was published in London. The book incorporates rediscovered letters and other documents and is the most extensively researched biography of Wilde to appear since 1988.

Parisian literati, also produced several biographies and monographs on him. André Gide wrote In Memoriam, Oscar Wilde and Wilde also features in his journals. Thomas Louis, who had earlier translated books on Wilde into French, produced his own L'esprit d'Oscar Wilde in 1920. Modern books include Philippe Jullian's Oscar Wilde, and L'affaire Oscar Wilde, ou, Du danger de laisser la justice mettre le nez dans nos draps (The Oscar Wilde Affair, or, On the Danger of Allowing Justice to put its Nose in our Sheets) by Odon Vallet, a French religious historian. (Source: Wikipedia)

NOTABLE WORKS

ESSAYS

"The Decay of Lying" First published in Nineteenth Century (1889), republished in Intentions (1891).

"Pen, Pencil and Poison" First published in the Fortnightly Review (1889), republished in Intentions (1891).

"The Soul of Man under Socialism" First published in the Fortnightly Review (1891), republished in The Soul of Man (1895), privately printed.

Intentions (1891) Wilde revised his dialogues on aesthetic subjects for publication in this volume, which comprises:

- "The Critic as Artist"
- "The Decay of Lying"
- "Pen, Pencil and Poison"
- "The Truth of Masks"

"Phrases and Philosophies for the Use of the Young" first published in the Oxford student magazine The Chameleon, December 1894)

"A Few Maxims For The Instruction Of The Over-Educated" First published, anonymously, in the 1894 November 17 issue of Saturday Review.

FICTION

Novel

The Picture of Dorian Gray (1890/1891). The first version of "The Picture of Dorian Gray" was published, in a form highly edited by the magazine, as the lead story in the July 1890 edition of Lippincott's Monthly Magazine. Wilde published the longer and revised version in book form in 1891, with an added preface.

Stories

"The Portrait of Mr. W. H." (1889)

The Happy Prince and Other Tales (1888, a collection of fairy tales) consisting of:

- "The Happy Prince"

- "The Nightingale and the Rose"

- "The Selfish Giant"

- "The Devoted Friend"

- "The Remarkable Rocket"

A House of Pomegranates (1891, fairy tales)

Lord Arthur Savile's Crime and Other Stories (1891) Including "The Canterville Ghost" first published in periodical form in 1887.

Complete Short Fiction. Penguin Classics, 2003. Edited with an Introduction and Notes by Ian Small. Contains all works listed above plus Poems in Prose (1894) and one very short 'Elder-tree' (fragment).

POEMS

Ravenna (1878) Winner of the Newdigate Prize.

Poems (1881) Wilde's collection of poetry and first publication.

The Sphinx (1894)

Poems in Prose (1894)

The Ballad of Reading Gaol (1898)

PLAYS

Vera; or, The Nihilists (1880)

The Duchess of Padua (1883)

Lady Windermere's Fan (1892)

A Woman of No Importance (1893)

Salomé (French version) (1893, first performed in Paris 1896)

Salomé: A Tragedy in One Act: Translated from the French of Oscar Wilde by Lord Alfred Douglas, illustrated by Aubrey Beardsley (1894)

An Ideal Husband (1895) (text)

The Importance of Being Earnest (1895) (text)

La Sainte Courtisane and A Florentine Tragedy Fragmentary. First published 1908 in Methuen's Collected Works

(Dates are dates of first performance, which approximate better to the probable date of composition than dates of publication.)

The Importance of Being Earnest and Other Plays. Penguin Classics, 2000. Edited with an Introduction, Commentaries and Notes by Richard Allen Cave. Contains all from above save the first two. Salome is in English.

As an appendix there is one excised scene from The Importance of Being Earnest.

POSTHUMOUS (PREVIOUSLY UNPUBLISHED)

De Profundis (Written 1895-97, in Reading Gaol). Expurgated edition published 1905; suppressed portions 1913, expanded version in The Letters of Oscar Wilde (1962).

The Rise of Historical Criticism (Written while at college) First published in 1905 (Sherwood Press, Hartford, CT) privately printed. Reprinted in Miscellanies, the last volume of the First Collected Edition (1908).

The First Collected Edition (Methuen & Co., 14 volumes) appeared in 1908 and contained many previously unpublished works.

The Second Collected Edition (Methuen & Co., 12 volumes) appeared in installments between 1909–11 and contained several other unpublished works.

The Letters of Oscar Wilde (Written 1868-1900) Published in 1962. Republished as The Complete Letters of Oscar Wilde (2000), with letters discovered since 1962, and new annotations by Merlin Holland.

The Women of Homer (Written 1876, while at college). First published in Oscar Wilde: The Women of Homer (2008) by The Oscar Wilde Society.

The Philosophy of Dress First published in The New-York Tribune (1885), published for the first time in book form in Oscar Wilde On Dress (2013).

MISATTRIBUTED

Teleny, or The Reverse of the Medal (Paris, 1893) has been attributed to Wilde, but its authorship is unclear. One theory is that it was a combined effort by several of Wilde's friends, which he may have edited.

Constance On September 14, 2011, Wilde's grandson Merlin Holland contested Wilde's claimed authorship of this play entitled Constance, scheduled to open that week in the King's Head Theatre. It was not, in fact, "Oscar Wilde's final play," as its producers were claiming. Holland said Wilde did sketch out the play's scenario in 1894, but "never wrote a word" of it, and that "it is dishonest to foist this on the public." The Artistic Director Adam Spreadbury-Maher of the King's Head Theatre and producer of Constance pointed out that Wilde's son, Vyvyan Holland, wrote in 1954, "a significant amount of the dialogue (of Constance) bears the authentic stamp of my father's hand". There is further proof that the developed scenario that Constance was reconstituted from was written by Wilde between 1897 and his death in 1900, rather than the 1894 George Alexander scenario which Merlin Holland quotes.